FAITH
OF THEIR
FATHERS

**SAMUEL M.
SARGEANT**

Published by Neem Tree Press Limited, 2024

1 3 5 7 9 10 8 6 4 2

Neem Tree Press Limited
95A Ridgmount Gardens, London, WC1E 7AZ
United Kingdom
info@neemtreepress.com
www.neemtreepress.com

A catalogue record for this book is available from the British Library

ISBN 978-1-915584-05-2 Paperback
ISBN 978-1-915584-06-9 Ebook UK
ISBN 978-1-911107-22-4 Ebook US

Printed and bound in Great Britain.

FAITH
OF THEIR
FATHERS

SAMUEL M.
SARGEANT

NEEM TREE
PRESS

Mun þu mik, Man ek þik

Remember me, I will remember you

For Leila.

Dramatis Personae

Icelanders

Afli Einarsson, son of Einar Geirleifsson, pagan prisoner of Olaf Tryggvason

Arinbjorn Thorleiksson, farmer, son of Thorleikr Haraldsson, foster-son of Skjalti Olafsson

Bera Thrandssdottir, granddaughter of Yngvildr, witch, wise woman

Conall, thrall, owned by Njall Bjarnisson

Corcc, thrall, owned by Thorgeir Thorkelsson

Einar Geirleifsson, pagan prisoner of Olaf Tryggvason

Failend, thrall, owned by Njall Bjarnisson

Fergus, thrall, owned by Njall Bjarnisson

Freya Hoskuldsdottir, housewife, married to Njall Bjarnisson

Gellir Hundisson, chieftain to Njall Bjarnisson

Gizurr the White, Christian convert, chieftain

Gudrid Eiriksdottir, housewife, married to Thorgeir Thorkelsson

Gunnlaugr Egilsson, farmer, trapper

Hallr Thorsteinsson, Christian convert, chieftain

Hjalti Skeggjason, Christian convert, son-in-law of Gizurr the White

Hrapn Illugisson Freeman, friend of Arinbjorn Thorleiksson

Kormac Vekellsson, Christian convert

Mael, thrall of Hallr Thorsteinsson

Njall Bjarnisson, farmer, married to Freya Hoskuldsdottir

Runolfr Olsson, chieftain, prosecutor

Saemund, housecarl of Gellir Hundisson

Sigvaldi Magnusson, foster-brother and friend of Arinbjorn Thorleiksson

Skjalti Olafsson, farmer, foster-father of Arinbjorn Thorleiksson

Skuli Thorsteinsson, skald, poet

Thorleikr Haraldsson, farmer, father of Arinbjorn Thorleiksson

Thorgeir Thorkelsson, lawspeaker, chieftain from Ljósavatn,
married to Gudrid Eiriksdottir
Teitr Gunnolfsson, trader, captain of the *Morgin-Skin*, chieftain
Tongu-Oddr, lover of Njall Bjarnisson

Norwegians

Olaf Tryggvason, King of Norway
Thangbrander, missionary priest
Thormothr, missionary priest
Thorer Klakka, captain of the *Ormrinn Langi*
Tyra Haraldsdatter, wife of Olaf Tryggvason, sister of King
Sweyn of Denmark

Other

Burislav, King of Wendland, former betrothed of Tyra
Gunnar Steinsson, captain, housecarl of Jarl Sigurd
Sigurd Hlodvirsson, Jarl of Orkney
Sweyn Forkbeard, King of Denmark, brother of Tyra
Haraldsdatter

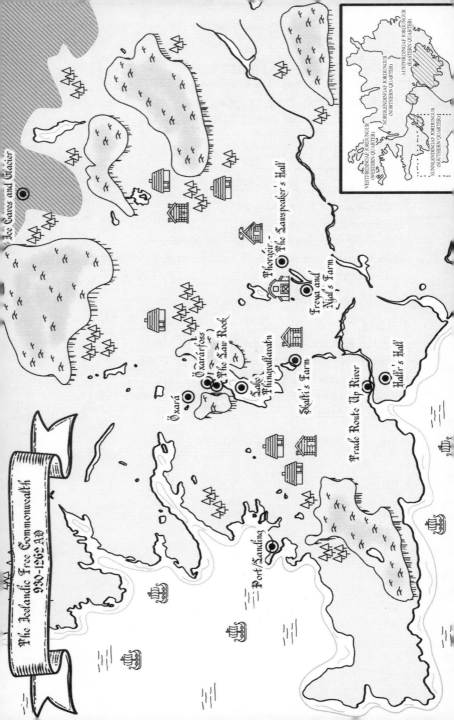

The Icelandic Free Commonwealth
930–1262 AD

Ice Caves and Glacier

Öxará

Öxarárfoss

The Law Rock

Lake
Þingvallavatn

Skalli's Farm

Þhorgeir – The Lawspeaker's Hall

Freya and
Njal's Farm

Hallr's Hall

Trade Route Up River

Port/Landing

The Sea

Vestfirðingafjórðungur
(Western Quarter)

Norðlendingafjórðungur
(Northern Quarter)

Austfirðingafjórðungur
(Eastern Quarter)

Sunnlendingafjórðungur
(Southern Quarter)

Contents

Part One

Part 2

Prologue

The blood looked black in the moonlight. It had saturated the snow that had fallen in the early hours, pooling in a trail that led off into the valley. Kneeling, Gunnlaugr Egilsson grabbed a handful of the blooded ice and brought it to his nose.

He cast his gaze before him, straining to see where the trail disappeared. The wind was flowing across the plains, sweeping up the powdery snow into devils that twirled across the vista. The Northern Lights were bright tonight, bright enough that the green and purple tendrils could light the way. They snaked across the sky with their slow, undulating ribbons, a comfort to the trapper. Unsure of the time, he tried to find the tell-tale spokes of Odin's Wagon; if the constellation was high in the sky, then there would be many hours until dawn, and a midnight hunt would be dangerous. Luckily, he found it slowly tapering away to the east. Sunrise would not be far off. He unsheathed his axe and began to follow the trail.

Two sets of tracks carved their way through the snow. The wounded man had been followed. Given the blood loss and the erratic path of the wounded, the assailant could easily have caught up and overpowered their prey. Gunnlaugr surmised that the attacker had waited and followed their target; perhaps they wanted to see where their victim ran to. He picked up his pace as the pools of blood grew larger and larger, until he found the source.

It was a young man, no more than eighteen winters, by the looks of him. He lay on his back, glassy eyes reflecting the green river in the sky. He looked like one of Skjalti Olafsson's thralls; Gunnlaugr recognised him from the nearby farm. Under the moonlight, the killing blow was visible—an axe wound to the gut. It would have been slow and painful. His eyes were drawn to the token that lay clutched in the thrall's hand. A wooden cross. He plucked it from the corpse and ran his fingers over the coarse wood.

Standing sharply, he looked around for the second set of tracks. They continued onwards and down towards a longhouse—a small, earthen-roofed building by a frozen stream. After the snowfall, it looked like any other hillock, but there was no doubt that was Skjalti's farm. With a parting look at the shocked face of the young thrall, Gunnlaugr took off running, his long dark hair whipping against his face. He headed for the farm and hoped he was not too late.

He found Skjalti's front door open, its large, weather-worn timber creaking lazily on unoiled hinges. Wind had brought snow across the threshold and damp footprints were imprinted in the earthen floor. Slowly, Gunnlaugr entered the farmhouse, axe raised. It was no warmer inside; the hearth fire had gone out. Ice crystals were already forming on the scorched logs and the last of the embers had long since faded.

His eyes adjusted as best they could as he moved deeper inside. The silence of the house was punctuated by the gentle ringing of hanging pots and pans moved by the wind. Making his way towards the sleeping area, he tried to remember how many people lived in Skjalti's house; including immediate and foster family, along with thralls, there should have been twelve people here tonight.

He found them.

Grimacing, Gunnlaugr reached out and touched the first body. Even in the darkness, he recognized his old friend, with his balding head and distinctive scar across his crown. He had earned it as a boy when the two of them had stolen a horse and Skjalti had fallen off in their mad dash for freedom. Now, the head flopped in an ugly way. Gunnlaugr eased Skjalti's body on to its back, prying it off Jofrid, who lay equally still in the cot. Skjalti had lain over her. Frozen blood and entrails covered the sheepskins between them; they had been disembowelled. A low moan escaped Gunnlaugr's lips as he released the body of his friend.

Moving further through the hall, he made his way to where the children slept. Tiny limbs, twisted and covered in blood, hung loosely from their cots. The strength in his legs failed him, and Gunnlaugr knelt beside the cot. Gently, he attempted to straighten the bodies of Ask and Embla, Skjalti's son and daughter. Running his hand through Embla's mouse-brown hair, he used his growing tears to try to wipe away the blood from her face.

There was a change in the air behind him, a subtle shift that drew his attention back to the room. Whipping about, he brought his axe to bear. It was too late. The blade cut deep into his left calf, severing the tendons and sending hot blood gushing. Screaming in shock and anger, he swung wildly, his left leg buckling. He missed his attacker, who dropped back into the darkness.

"Coward!" he screamed. "Murderer!"

The response was another blade sinking into his arm, splicing flesh. He managed to hold his axe and counter with a thrust of his own. He hit his mark this time. The assassin let out a startled cry and fell back momentarily.

Gunnlaugr had to get outside. With his one good leg, he limped and crawled out of the sleeping area. He tried to push off the ground and leap towards the door, but his strength failed him. He crashed into the frozen hearth fire, sending the ashen wood and cooking pots flying. Managing to use the momentum of his fall to roll towards the exit, he attempted to get back to his feet, but he found he could no longer feel his left leg at all.

The third blow struck then, right between his shoulder blades. He felt the sharp edge embed itself in his flesh, sinking several inches before hitting bone. His scream filled the longhouse and he collapsed to his knees, dropping his axe. He knelt there, stunned, his lungs burning as he fought for breath. He felt a boot in the small of his back as his attacker prised his weapon free. With a wet sound, the offending blade came clear of the wound and Gunnlaugr fell, face first, across the threshold and into the cool snow.

Weak, confused, but determined to get away, he used his one good arm to drag himself all the way outside, leaving a trail of blood smeared across the ground. Hearing footsteps coming up behind him, he rolled on to his back, staring up at the doorway. Slowly, casually, the killer emerged and stood over Gunnlaugr. His face was shrouded, covered by the hood of his cloak, and he wore a strange garment underneath. It was heavily embroidered, and the pattern seemed familiar. In his stupor, however, Gunnlaugr struggled to place it.

His throat was filling with blood, and his breath came in ragged bursts. "Who are you?" He coughed over the words.

A shake of the head was his only response. The killer sheathed his weapons and leant down next to Gunnlaugr. He collected the fresh blood from the ground and began to paint across the door with his hands. Seemingly satisfied, he turned to face his victim. He searched Gunnlaugr's broken form, ignoring the weapons, animal hides and silver coin, until he found what he wanted: Gunnlaugr's cross. Ripping it from his neck, he cast it aside.

The murderer never did say anything. Instead, he rose to his feet and walked off, his form disappearing into the early morning sun that had begun to crest the horizon. Gunnlaugr could only watch him leave; gasping for breath, he tried to form words, but he choked on the fluid in his lungs. As his consciousness began to fade, the morning light lit up the scene before him. There, on Skjalti's door, the killer had left a message. His vision darkened and his breathing weakened, but he strained to make out the words:

False God.

Chapter One

The white winter sun hung low over the horizon, its light dancing on the surface of the Öxará as the river tumbled its way from the mountains and into lake Thingvallavatn. Speckled light caught in its foam as the waters cascaded down the Öxarárfoss waterfall. Arinbjorn took a deep breath of crisp air, enjoying the biting sensation in his lungs. He watched as his flock slowly ambled down the riverbank, their thick woollen coats picking up snow as they went.

"I blame you for this," Arinbjorn said. He began to tie back his dark-blond hair so that it would not obstruct his vision. His horse, a black mare with a thick mane, shuffled beneath him. He steadied her.

"How is this my fault?" Sigvaldi answered as he guided his horse to Arinbjorn's side. He turned and faced Arinbjorn, his green eyes bright in the morning sun. "You're the one who lost the sheep."

"Yes, but you were the one who convinced my father to give us this job."

"How hard is it to herd sheep?"

The pair turned from the vista and back to the dozens of sheep making their way downstream towards the lake and Arinbjorn's father's hall. The tendrils of smoke rising from the longhouse were visible even from here, and several people milled about close to the farm. Arinbjorn tried counting the sheep again: thirty-eight, just like before, and *definitely* two down.

"Apparently very." Arinbjorn sighed. "We cannot go back without the other two."

They had left late in the morning, but the sun was only just rising by the time they made it up into the Thingvellir valley and set about finding his father's flock. Letting them roam was risky during the winter, but they were a hardy sort and could withstand the cold comfortably, provided they had access to plenty of grazing land. It was normally a simple enough task to find them, but they had proven surprisingly difficult to spot after the snowfall from the previous night. Arinbjorn and Sigvaldi had scoured the plains about the lake for hours before stumbling upon a small copse of ash trees. They found the herd there, sheltered from the wind and snow, grazing on the grass beneath.

"Are you sure there were forty of them?" Sigvaldi ran his hand through his brown hair, pushing the strands out of his eyes as he looked about.

"Very."

"Then we had better head back up there, I guess." He gestured upriver, towards the copse.

Arinbjorn eyed the land between them and the ash trees. The morning light cast purple shadows across the ravines and crevices, illuminating the twisting streams that criss-crossed the Thingvellir valley. "Race you?" He smiled.

"Ari, we are already in enough trouble as it is." Sigvaldi fixed him with a level stare as he manoeuvred his horse about. "It would be best for all if you just accepted defeat now." He grinned and spurred his colt.

Arinbjorn watched dumbly for a moment as his friend charged off upriver. Laughing, he kicked the sides of his mare and chased after him.

Like all Icelandic horses, their animals were short, stocky beasts. Arinbjorn used his powerful and hardy mare for everything from travel to tilling, and, should she get old or sick, she would prove delicious roasted. She had been a stalwart companion for many years, and, while she was nearing the end of her usefulness, she was a beauty. She was not, however, speedy. The poor girl strained beneath him, her breathing laboured, and, despite his shouts of encouragement, he watched as Sigvaldi pulled further and further ahead of him. He was managing to weave his way about the shallow streams that fed into the river, bounding towards their goal.

Arinbjorn sighed and slowed down to a trot. He was not going to win this one and he saw no reason to risk the horse.

Shaking his head, he carefully wound his way up towards his victorious friend. Sigvaldi had come to Arinbjorn's farm when he was a child; his parents were from Norway and had no land to speak of. Thorleikr, Arinbjorn's father, had offered to foster the boy until his parents had set up a farm of their own. They had grown up together and stayed close even after Sigvaldi had returned to his family. There was no better man, in Arinbjorn's opinion, but he knew Sigvaldi would not shut up about this victory for days.

His horse whinnied in shock, snapping Arinbjorn out of his reverie. He looked down to see her front legs disappearing into snow that slowly collapsed, revealing a gulley underneath. His mount abruptly halted, managing to stop herself from falling. Arinbjorn was not so lucky. He was thrown out of his saddle, tumbling forward, and crashed into the hard pebble bed of the shallow waters below. He cried out as he landed on his side, pain shooting up his right arm as it collided with stone.

He lay there for a moment, stunned, letting the water wash over him. It was freezing, but it was numbing the pain. A shadow fell across him as his mare leant over the edge and stared down into the gulley.

"Anyone else would eat you for this," he scolded. Gingerly, he stood up, cradling his arm. He flexed his fingers and stretched the joints. It ached, but he could move it. Trying to focus, he looked about the ravine. It was shallow, only a couple of yards deep, but the obsidian walls were slick and icy. He knew it would have to merge with the Öxará eventually, so he began to follow the trickle of water downstream. He made it only a couple of yards before he noticed two snowy mounds ahead, blocking the path. Shuffling over to them, he let out a resigned sigh. Sigvaldi's head appeared over the top of the ravine, concern etched into his face.

"Ari! Are you all right?" he called down, his voice echoing in the confined space.

"I'm fine, Sig." He looked up and gave a weak grin. "I found the sheep."

Arinbjorn kicked the soft mound before him and the snow dropped away, revealing two matted corpses. Their legs jutted out at an awkward angle and their glassy black eyes stared out blankly.

"Shit," Sigvaldi cursed. "Come on, I'll get you out."

"We need to take them with us." Arinbjorn gestured to the dead ewes.

"Right," Sigvaldi agreed. He disappeared and reappeared a moment later, a rope in his hands. "Better get them tied up. I'll haul them out."

Nodding, Arinbjorn set about his task. It was difficult with his cold, rigid hands, but he managed to secure the sheep. One at a time, Sigvaldi pulled them out, until finally he brought Arinbjorn up and over the edge. They sat there for a moment, both catching their breath, the sun bathing them in a low light.

"That went well," Sigvaldi said.

"At least I found the sheep." Arinbjorn stared down the valley towards his longhouse. The shadows were getting longer already.

"Truly, the gods must favour you." Sigvaldi got to his feet and offered his hand to Arinbjorn.

"You have no idea." Arinbjorn smiled at his friend and took his hand as he got to his feet. "Come on. It is getting dark and we have to get back in time for the feast." With that, they mounted their respective horses and began the long ride back to the farm, reuniting with the rest of the flock as they did so.

*

The sun was beginning to set when the pair reached Thorleikr's longhouse on the edge of lake Thingvallavatn. It was a long, low building with wooden walls and a thatched, earth-covered roof. Large enough to provide shelter for Thorleikr's family and extended compliment of thralls, it had been home to Arinbjorn all his life. Covered in snow, it blended in almost perfectly with the surroundings.

They secured the sheep in their pen and made their way to greet Arinbjorn's family. The air was thick and warm, the dense wooden walls and earthen roof keeping most of the heat from the hearth fire inside. It lit the room in shades of gold and red, and the hot dry smoke was welcome after the biting evening air.

Gudrun, Arinbjorn's mother, had been preparing the feast; she stood at the hearth fire barking out orders to the thralls, who rushed around preparing the main table. Upon her son's entrance, she stopped shouting at them and began shouting at him.

"Frig cursed me the day she gave me you. To have so stupid a son…" Her smile belied her anger and she rushed over to embrace him. Despite her own impressive stature—she was as wide as she was tall—she only came to her son's shoulders. Her round, rosy face beamed up at him as she buried herself in his chest.

"What are you talking about?" He held her tightly.

Her response was cut off by his father, whose advanced years had not taken their toll; thick white hair framed a wrinkled face, which creased with the warm smile that peeked out from his beard. "Of my two children, you are the one that will drag me to Valhalla."

"I always try to bring you honour, father."

Thorleikr's smile faltered.

"It is not my fault the sheep fell down the ravine," Arinbjorn protested, "and I brought them back so that we could at least use them."

"It is not the sheep of which I speak. Racing across the valleys? You could have been killed for your recklessness."

Arinbjorn turned to Sigvaldi, his friend standing a polite distance behind.

"You told him?" He could not hide the anger in his voice.

Thorleikr struck his son about the head. The act was fast, belying his old frame, and his thick meaty fist was like a hammer striking upon the exact spot he had struck his head in the ravine earlier. "Sigvaldi told me nothing. One of the thralls watched you galloping upriver."

The revelry behind them hushed a moment, and the various members of the household found somewhere else to be. Sigvaldi disappeared from Arinbjorn's side.

"It was just a bit of fun, and we found the sheep!" Arinbjorn squared up to his father, his face red.

"You were lucky! You could have fallen to your death." Thorleikr gestured about the room. "And then what would we do, without you to help?" He pointed towards a young girl, still only a child, who sat in front of the hearth fire. "Your sister has just been returned to us by Kjartan—would you see her raised without a brother?"

Arinbjorn looked at his sister, Jorunn. A helmet, far too big, sat upon her head—one of his father's, from his adventures in his younger days.

"You have only just become a man; would you be struck down so early in life?" Thorleikr pressed. "Would you?"

"No, father." Arinbjorn meant it.

"Good." Without a further word, he guided his humbled son to the high seat and sat him down. The household assembled about them and took their places. "Today, we honour my son. Who, foolish though he is, has managed to survive twenty winters this day. Please—eat, drink, and praise Odin for sparing my son from his own stupidity."

A shout rang out from somewhere and a dozen cups were raised, clashed in mid-air, and a torrent of mead fell about the table, covering the gathered feast.

"To Arinbjorn the Brave!" A cheer.

"To Arinbjorn the Shameless!" Laughter.

"To Arinbjorn the Bloody Lucky!" This last one came from Sigvaldi, who approached from the hearth fire carrying a flank of roasted pig. A chorus of agreement spread among the assembled crowd.

"You slander me!" Arinbjorn cried in mock defiance. "It was my finest hour."

"Oh, I agree," Sigvaldi countered, a smile beaming out from his trim beard.

The sting of wood smoke caused Arinbjorn to blink as he took another swig of mead. It hung heavy in the air, obscuring his vision of those at the other end of the high table, and carried with it the scent of roasted and honeyed meats. It was almost enough to cover the earthy, peaty smell of the roof.

The celebration continued long into the night, with Arinbjorn talking mostly with his family and Sigvaldi. His mother had clearly spent much of the afternoon preparing the food, lining the table with salted fish, roasted swine, sausages, and lamb stew. Jorunn bustled about her mother's legs, pleading to join in the celebrations and drink like her brother. Being ignored was not enough to dissuade her, and she started stalking the high table in the hope of finding more pliable adults.

Arinbjorn allowed the mead to numb his mind, glad to ease his thoughts about the day and forget. As the evening wound to a close and the crowd prepared to leave, Thorleikr gathered the household about him, calling for silence. Gradually, the laughter and conversation died down and all attention was focused on him. He looked about the room, taking in the faces of his family and friends.

"Today, I could have lost a son." The crowd shifted uncomfortably as the thought passed among them. "I ask that you all join me in offering our thanks to the All-Father, for sparing us grief this day."

Jorunn ran up to her father, blond tousled hair flying wildly from underneath the helmet she had insisted on wearing all evening. It sat huge and unwieldy on her head, contrasting with the simple dress she wore, obscuring most of her face. She looked up at him, bright blue eyes shining.

"Would you like to lead the prayer, Jorunn?"

She nodded enthusiastically and the helmet rocked up and down on her head.

Pleased, Thorleikr picked up his daughter and placed her on the table, helmet and all. The others all rose from their seats and waited for her to start. She recanted the prayer they all knew so well.

"Hail to you, Day; hail you, Day's sons; hail Night and daughter of Night, with blithe eyes look on all of us, and grant to those sitting here protection. Hail Aesir, hail Asynjur. Hail Earth that gives to all."

The crowd repeated her words in unison, raising their cups one final time before turning to each other and beginning to say their goodbyes. Thorleikr and Gudrun took their daughter down from the table and began to escort her back to their sleeping quarters.

Together with Sigvaldi, Arinbjorn drank the rest of the mead and watched the others depart, until it was just the two of them tending to the embers of the dying hearth fire. They wiled away the early hours, swapping stories as they warmed themselves by the low flames. Arinbjorn was falling asleep by the fire when there was a knock at the front door. It was frantic, irregular, and shocked the two out of their alcohol-induced fugue.

"Has Hel come to claim us?" Sigvaldi shouted, jumping up and grabbing his sax knife.

"Why would Hel knock?" Arinbjorn asked, as he unsteadily picked up the hand axe from the hearth fire.

The knocking continued and the pair advanced on the door, weapons raised.

"Who calls at this hour?" Arinbjorn shouted out.

"Hrapn Illugisson!"

"Hrapn?" Easing a little, Arinbjorn released the bolt locking the door and opened it to the night air.

A flurry of snow carried across the threshold as they were greeted with the haggard face of Hrapn, their neighbour. His long black hair was damp with snow, and his grey eyes shone manically in the firelight. After seeing Arinbjorn, he relaxed his gaze and replaced it with one of relief. "You're alive!" Hrapn reached out and grabbed Arinbjorn, pulling him into a tight embrace. "Thank the gods."

"You scared us half to death old man," Sigvaldi said. "Of course he's alive, it was only a slight fall."

"What are you talking about?" Hrapn gave Sigvaldi an utterly perplexed look. He crossed the threshold and wiped off the snow that clung to him. "I'm here about your foster-father, Ari."

"What about him?" Arinbjorn had only spent a few years in the care of Skjalti, but he had fond memories of the old man. He had not seen the farmer in some time, not since he had taken to the new religion coming across from Norway.

"Skjalti is dead, Arinbjorn."

Chapter Two

The water rose slowly, but inevitably, up the rocky *sker*; the seaweed that adorned it buoyant against the rising tide. The water that rolled into the sheer granite cliffs that lined the Lysefjord looked as bright and clear as the sky above them, darkened only by the deep shadows cast out by the flanking monoliths. Gulls flew high above, adding their cries to the sound of waves crashing. The *sker* was beginning to disappear now, the temporary island vanishing into the icy waters. It would have been a beautiful scene of the Norwegian fjord, were it not for the screams.

"How much longer until the tide swallows the sker?" King Olaf Tryggvason asked aloud. He was kneeling behind the tiller of his ship, the *Ormrinn Langi*, trying to focus on his rosary. The cries of the condemned made it difficult to concentrate on praying for their salvation.

"Not long now, sire." It was the coarse and assertive voice of Thorer Klakka, captain of the *Ormrinn Langi*. Thorer stood at his side but was facing the opposite direction, out across the deck of the great ship, barking orders to his men, who ran about intently. His face was red from shouting and he ran his hand through his thick, dark beard repeatedly. It was a tick Olaf knew well.

"Why so concerned, captain?" Olaf asked.

Thorer stopped shouting long enough to face his king. "We should just kill these witches." He gestured out to the slowly flooding *sker*. "They could use their *seiðr* any moment to upset us."

"Death is not enough." Relenting from his prayers, Olaf stood. "We must send a message."

He could tell Thorer remained unconvinced. The pair watched as the chained figures on the *sker* began to thrash about in the water, writhing like worms. They seemed to slither across the briny outcropping as they tried to escape their fate, each one desperate to break free of their bonds. Their struggle was as horrifying as it was satisfying; it was good to know their gods did not favour them over his own.

*

Despite knowing the futility of it, Kjartan struggled against his bonds. They had hamstrung him, cutting his tendons and binding him to this rock. His arms strained in their binds behind him, and his head ached from the parting blow that bastard Thorer had given him. Blood dripped down his brow and into the pools of seawater that lay about him.

He looked across at his companion, Steingerd. She lay on her side, arms and legs bound behind her, and stared back at him mutely, a look of resignation fixed on her face. They had taken her tongue to ensure she could not use her magic on them. Her short, mouse-brown hair was damp and clung to her scalp, obscuring most of her face. As the water level rose, her hair flowed about her like seaweed.

There had been three of them originally, bound to this rock to await their sentence. Ogmund, however, had grown tired of waiting and had crawled across in his chains to the edge of the islet. The pair of them had watched as he disappeared beneath the waves and never returned. He did not even scream.

Kjartan screamed though. He screamed and shouted until his lungs were coarse. He cursed Olaf, the king who had welcomed him and his companions to court, only to turn on them when they had refused to convert. He cursed the sailors who had mutilated him and his friends under the orders of their mad ruler. Finally, he cursed this new god who would seek such punishment against him and his companions.

Throughout all this, Steingerd had remained placid. The water had risen sufficiently now to fill her mouth and nose. She was retching and coughing as the salt water coursed down into her lungs. Despite her seeming resignation to her fate, Kjartan watched as she tried to raise her head out of the sea. She could not maintain it; she kept disappearing repeatedly underneath the rising waves. Each stolen breath was followed by two deep gulps of salt water, until eventually she did not reappear.

Steingerd's body was slowly washed away. The water was now up to Kjartan's neck, the tide pulling him off the rapidly disappearing islet. It was ice cold, forcing his breath out of him in quick bursts. He tried to remain afloat, using what control of his legs and arms he had to tread water. The tide, however, was too strong. He continued to scream his curses until he, too, sank beneath the waves.

*

A southernly wind had begun to rise, carrying with it the scent of salt. It caught the sails of the *Ormrinn Langi*, puffing out the image of the dragon emblazoned on them, and Olaf felt his great ship begin to edge away from the scene. The cries of the marooned rang across the winds. He was almost sure he heard his name being cursed. In the absence of their gods striking him down, however, he smiled. Eventually, the screams were drowned out, either by the wind or the sea, and the *sker* disappeared under the waves. Olaf turned from the fjord and looked out across the deck and down towards the dozens of men who crewed his ship.

There was a grunt of approval from Thorer. "The wind is on our side, my king. We leave at your command."

"I think we have been waylaid long enough by *vǫlur*. Take us out, captain."

Nodding, Thorer shouted new orders and drumming filled the air. The beat was shortly accompanied by the shouts and curses of seventy or so men, sitting upon their rowing benches, heaving their oars to the rhythm of the drummer. The great *drakkar* lurched as it turned into the wind, granting the ship an added boost, and once again Olaf felt the call of the sea as the *Ormrinn* cut through the waters.

"I'll never be as happy as I am out here, Thorer," Olaf sighed. "How long do you think it will take for us to reach our destination?"

"Three weeks at the most; the weather is fair."

Olaf allowed the wind and spray to wash over him, coating his finery: the red and purple tunic trimmed with gold, the green cloak with blue embroidery. He ran his hand through his short, blond hair. It came away with a few greying strands that were caught by the wind, flying off into the sea.

"I've rarely seen you so contemplative, my king," Thorer said, evenly.

"I will try not to take that as an insult," Olaf replied wanly. "Have I ever shown you this?" He reached into his tunic and pulled it down over his shoulder, revealing his bicep and the gold ring that banded his upper arm. It was simple, with a dragon motif and worn inscription.

"You've had that as long as I have known you," Thorer said.

"Geira gave it to me. On our wedding day."

"Your first wife?" Thorer asked.

Olaf simply nodded and began to slide it down his arm until it was free. He held it in both hands for a moment, running his thumb over the inscription. There was a time when he had thought nothing was more important than Geira, once raiding a hundred villages in mourning for her death.

"She would be proud of what you have achieved; Norway has never been so united."

"She was pagan." With one final glance, he took the ring and threw it overboard, watching it disappear beneath the waves. "Increase the tempo. We are needed in Iceland, Thorer."

The sound of drums filled the silence between the two of them.

Chapter Three

Arinbjorn watched as the snowflake floated lazily on the morning breeze. It twisted and twirled through the air, catching the early light before coming to rest on Embla's pale cheek, sticking there. It was followed by another. And another. Soon her whole face would be covered. He reached out and gently brushed them away, his calloused fingers rough against her smooth skin. He watched as the snow continued to fall.

It had taken him many hours to get to Skjalti's farm; by then, the closest neighbours had already arrived and begun the process of removing the bodies and laying them next to each other in the snow. Twelve men had come to help. Heads of local households and a few choice thralls. Arinbjorn sat on a nearby embankment beside Embla's rigid form. Her brother, Ask, lay beside her. Arinbjorn fancied that their arms seemed to reach out to each other. He brushed some more snow off her face.

A series of low grunts brought his attention to the house. Sigvaldi was helping Hrapn carry out Jofrid's body. She had been a slight woman, but indomitable and fiercely protective of her family; he remembered earning many a strike from her bony hands. Now she lay slack in his friends' arms, covered in frozen blood. Hrapn and Sigvaldi shuffled across the ice and snow and brought his foster-mother to rest next to her children.

"We could use your help." Sigvaldi's voice seemed far away, muted, but Arinbjorn turned to face him. He was gesturing to the house. "With Skjalti."

Arinbjorn nodded and rose from the ground. He followed his friend into the house and tried not to breathe too deeply. The air was still. Great arcs of frozen blood stained the walls and floor; he assumed it had come from Gunnlaugr, the trapper, who had been found frozen outside. The floor was lined with broken detritus: pots, plates and food lay scattered about, mixed with coals and ash from the hearth fire.

"If they were killed in their sleep, why is the place such a mess?" It was Hrapn, from behind. He stood in the doorway, his face dour.

"Maybe Gunnlaugr smashed the place up after killing them," Sigvaldi suggested.

"Gunnlaugr was a good man," Hrapn barked. He walked over to Sigvaldi. "I have known him since he was a boy and will not have his name dishonoured."

Arinbjorn reached out and touched Hrapn's shoulder. He flinched at the touch, but his stance eased.

"I cannot speak to his honour," Arinbjorn said, "but I know he worshiped the Christian god, like Skjalti." He looked about the farm. "He would not have done this."

"You think this was a religious killing?" Hrapn asked.

In response, Arinbjorn pointed towards the farm door and the words painted there.

" 'False God'? That could mean anything."

"I think Gunnlaugr walked in on the murderer." Arinbjorn gestured to the scattered hearth fire. "It looks like one of them fell through the fire and tried to flee." He pointed to the floor and the trail of blood that led outside. "Look here, see the tracks in the blood? Gunnlaugr crawled outside and was followed. Yet all of Skjalti's household are accounted for in the dead. Someone else was here." Kneeling down, he picked up the bloodied ice and sniffed it. "It has been days, by the smell of it. The murderer must still be out there."

Sigvaldi gave a small cough. "Well, speaking of gods, we need to decide what to do with the bodies."

"What do you mean?" Hrapn said.

Arinbjorn, still squatting down on the floor, brushed some ice and dirt off a small wooden horse. Skjalti probably carved it himself for one of his children. "He means, how should we honour Skjalti and his family?"

Hrapn nodded in understanding. "I will order my men to begin making a pyre."

"Skjalti would want to be buried," Arinbjorn stated.

"The ground is frozen solid!" implored Hrapn.

"I will bury them myself if I have to." Arinbjorn's voice was sharp, cutting off the reply from Hrapn. He raised himself from the floor, still holding the wooden horse, then turned from his friends and walked deeper into the building. The longhouse seemed darker here, the air close. Finally, he came to Skjalti himself, older and greyer than he remembered, but his foster-father all the same. Kneeling, he ran his hand over Skjalti's bald head, his fingers tracing the scars that lined the skull. Someone had already closed the eyes.

He looked at his old foster-father for some time before he called back to his friends.

"Help me move him."

*

The blade of the shovel barely pierced the earth on his first attempt; on his second, he only managed to scrape a layer of permafrost off with it; by the third, he had found his rhythm. It was slow work, but Arinbjorn refused to stop. Not even when the wood of the handle wore through his hide gloves and began to chafe his palms. He simply placed his hands in the snow until the pain eased up, before tearing some linen from his tunic to cover the slowly reddening flesh.

After all the bodies had been removed from the house, most of the local farmers returned to their homesteads to continue with their daily routines; they had objected to the concept of burying Skjalti and his kin. Arinbjorn, as the only living relative, had the last word. They left him behind, along with Sigvaldi and Hrapn.

It was late morning by the time they had finished digging the first grave. It was shallow, but it would have to do. Gently, Arinbjorn picked up Embla, while Sigvaldi carried Ask, and they brought them over to the grave. They had dug it overlooking the small stream that ran down the back of Skjalti's farm. It was mostly frozen, but water still tumbled and bubbled over the rocks in the centre of the stream as it made its way west. He had loved to play here as a child, leaping across the stream and trying to catch the fish, pretending he was Thor catching Loki.

Arinbjorn stared at the small grave, the wind whistling along the tundra before him.

"What's wrong?" Hrapn asked.

Arinbjorn looked down at the still form of Embla in his arms. "I don't know which way she is supposed to lie." The words caught in his throat.

"South-west to north-east." Sigvaldi's voice, calm and quiet, cut through his mental fugue. "With the head at the south-west."

After a brief pause, Arinbjorn nodded. He lay Embla down in the earth, and Sigvaldi eased her brother in beside her. Both were wrapped in whatever clean linen sheets they could find on the farm. Their tiny frames barely filled the grave. Kneeling beside their bodies, Arinbjorn placed the small carved horse between them.

"Stand aside on this one, Ari," Hrapn said gently. "Allow us to bury them."

Arinbjorn retreated from the grave as Sigvaldi and Hrapn began to refill the hole. He watched as the frozen earth was methodically piled atop the two children. It did not take them long to cover the bodies.

"I believe we are supposed to say a Christian prayer," Sigvaldi said.

"I don't know any," Hrapn replied gruffly.

"Me neither," Arinbjorn whispered. Instead, he stood at the base of the grave and cleared his throat, his voice quiet yet firm. "I swear, by your god or mine, that I will find who did this to you and kill them." With that, he turned from the grave and made his way over to the still-waiting corpses, tears filling his eyes.

*

The white of the sun was kissing the horizon when the final body was laid to rest. They had saved Skjalti till last. While Arinbjorn and Sigvaldi dug the grave, Hrapn was sent inside to find any items Skjalti might have wished to have buried with him. Arinbjorn had barely spoken a word all afternoon. Instead, he focused on digging the holes. Despite his precautions, his hands had developed blisters and his back ached from the labour, but still he continued. He was so focused on his task that he did not hear the footsteps approaching.

"Arinbjorn." It was a soft voice, low and gentle, but it cut through the evening breeze.

His back stiffened slightly, and he paused to drive the shovel into the ground, embedding it. He turned to face the new arrival. "Freya."

She was wearing a long hide overcoat wrapped around her linen dress. She pushed her headscarf back, revealing her soft, sad face. He smiled up at her from the grave. She smiled too, but it did not reach her honey-coloured eyes. Strands of blond hair were stuck to her flushed cheeks, her small nose was red, and her chest heaved through the thick coat as she caught her breath.

"It's good to see you, Freya," Sigvaldi said, walking up to her. He placed his hands on her shoulders. "I need to help Hrapn find some more treasures for Skjalti's grave." He departed for the farmhouse, leaving Freya and Arinbjorn alone.

She stood above him, looking down into the grave.

"I'm sorry," she said eventually.

"This isn't your doing." He left the spade in the ground and climbed out of the hole. He tried to dust off the ice and dirt, but only succeeded in rubbing it further into his clothes.

A genuine smile flashed across Freya's lips. "I would have come earlier, but—"

"How is your husband?" Arinbjorn interrupted. "I'm surprised I didn't see Njall here."

"He had to go out on a hunt." Her smile hardened. "He said I could come and pay my respects once he got back."

"I'm glad he gave you permission." His chest had tightened, but he maintained his level gaze.

Snowflakes peppered Freya's eyelashes. She blinked and turned away to look at the almost finished grave. Arinbjorn watched her shoulders sag. When she looked at him again, the softness had returned to her eyes.

"Now is not the time for this," she said.

He felt her hand on his arm and he flinched despite himself, before easing into her touch. He placed his right hand on hers, feeling her soft cool fingers through the gaps in his gloves.

"Gods, what happened to your hands?" She pulled both his hands out. Gently, she pried away the bloodied linen bandages and looked them over. His flesh was cracked and split, with deep crevice-like wounds and blisters lining each palm. They were purple and angry. Her fingertips traced the worst of the damage.

"I needed to bury them." It was all he could say. Now he had stopped working, he could feel the pain in his hands; each beat of his heart made them swell and ache.

"You have to get inside; the frost could take them."

"We are almost done—Skjalti is the last." He eased his hands from her grip and began to wrap the linen back around them.

"Oh no you don't. I can finish for you." Before he could argue, she jumped down into the hole, hair tumbling out of her kerchief, and pulled the spade from the ground. "Unless you plan to fight me for it?"

Despite himself, Arinbjorn smiled. "My father always said, 'Only pick fights you can win.' "

"Your father is a wise man." She shovelled the last of the soil from the hole as Hrapn and Sigvaldi returned from the farmhouse bearing whatever arms and valuables they could find.

Hrapn seemed to have favoured weaponry, carrying back two swords and a heavily worn shield. Sigvaldi had found some jewellery—a collection of gifts and rings Skjalti had received on his adventures as a youth.

"We found all we could," Hrapn said. He dropped his goods next to the grave. "Freya, showing Ari how to do it, I see."

"Someone has to." This came from Sigvaldi.

Freya stopped digging and threw the spade out of the hole. "Come on, one of you men can help me up." She held her arms out expectantly. Hrapn and Sigvaldi looked at each other and grinned; they reached down and grabbed an arm each, hoisting her up out of the hole. She dusted herself off and gave them both a hug. "Thank you. For helping him."

"It was the least we could do for Skjalti," Hrapn said.

"That's not who I meant." She gestured over to Arinbjorn.

The two men nodded in understanding.

"Are you three finished?" Arinbjorn asked. "I need help laying him down."

The four of them picked up Skjalti's body together. He was wrapped in several cloaks, the only clean garments left. With great care, they moved him into the grave and began adorning him with his life's treasures.

As Hrapn lay down one of the swords, he stopped to admire it for a moment. "I remember when he came back with this. He said it was a gift from Jarl Hakkon, after he beat his best man in single combat," Hrapn said.

"He told me it was a gift for reciting poetry to Queen Gunnhild," Arinbjorn countered. The two men stared at each other before bursting out laughing.

Freya and Sigvaldi looked on, bemused.

"Skjalti? A skald? The dead would rise in disgust," Hrapn said through his laughter.

"I knew I was an idiot for believing him." Arinbjorn took the blade from Hrapn and stared at it a moment longer, his smile slowly fading. "He always told good stories though."

"Then does it matter if they were true?" Freya asked.

"No. It does not." Arinbjorn lay the sword by its former master and the others began to cover the body with soil.

Dusk had fallen by the time they had finished, and a chill wind brought flurries of snow. Sigvaldi found some wood from the house to make a rudimentary crucifix. He tied two pieces together with some twine and planted it firmly at the head of the grave.

"I think that's how you do it," he said.

"It will do," Hrapn replied. "Come, it's time to go home."

"I think I will take the river route back," Arinbjorn said. The group looked at him with incredulity. "I need time to think before I head home to face my father."

"Your hands are ruined, Ari," Freya said sternly. "You need to get inside as soon as possible."

Arinbjorn ignored her. "I believe the killer is still out there."

"You think the murderer fled down the stream," Freya said, comprehension dawning on her face.

"It is just a thought, but it *would* have hidden his footprints. If he did, he would have to leave the waterway at some point. I may yet find some trace."

"I am coming with you," Freya said.

"Is Njall not expecting you back?" Sigvaldi's tone was more curious than judgemental.

"He can wait."

"Are you sure?" Arinbjorn asked. He watched Freya tighten her hide coat about her and cross her arms.

"East or west?" Hrapn asked.

Before Arinbjorn could answer, Freya interjected, "West—there are more homesteads there."

All nodding, and with one final look to the graves, the four of them set off towards the river.

The walk was not arduous, but they still had to be careful. The snow had obscured the boundaries of the stream and twice Arinbjorn put his foot through thin ice into the shallow waters below. The sky above was muted, the gathered clouds a dark grey, but at least the snow had stopped. Arinbjorn hoped this meant that some trace might be found.

They walked for an hour before Freya found something. They had come to a farm that was even closer to the river than

Skjalti's. The longhouse sat on a small hill overlooking the frozen waters and a stable backed right up against the water, providing easy drinking for sheep and horses.

"Wait!" She had fallen behind the other three and had to shout.

"What is it?" Arinbjorn asked as he slowly made his way back to her.

"Look!" She pointed to a series of ash trees that lay between the river and the farmhouse.

Arinbjorn squinted, but he could not make out what she was pointing to. "What?"

Sighing with frustration, she grabbed Arinbjorn's arm and dragged him over to the nearest ash. Finally, when he was practically upon it, he saw it: a small piece of cloth, caught on the low-hanging branch. It fluttered in the wind and, as it twisted and turned, he saw the dark tell-tale stain of blood. Reaching out, he tore it from the tree.

He held it in his hands for a while.

"Who lives here?" he muttered.

No one answered.

"Who lives here?" he shouted this time, turning to look at his friends. "Tell me!"

Even in the darkness, Arinbjorn could see Hrapn's reticence.

Eventually, he spoke. "Thorgeir." Hrapn swallowed. "The lawspeaker."

Chapter Four

Thangbrander felt the satisfying wet crack as his opponent's jaw buckled beneath his fist. His knuckles met cleanly with the lower jaw, connecting with an already disjointed chin. The crunch reverberated up his arm and he watched as the head snapped sharply to the right. A single gnarled tooth flew out and arced away on to the beach, trailing blood. Howling in pain, his attacker retreated a few steps, leaving Thangbrander free to deal with the accomplice.

The second attacker was warier. A young man, with tiny arrogant eyes, he circled Thangbrander from a distance, hoping to close quickly with a few swift strikes before backing away again. This was foolish; it gave Thangbrander more time to prepare. He cast his eyes about the beach. The tide was low but had begun to turn, the grey water forming an icy froth as it washed up against the snow and sand. Where the snow had cleared, black rocks slick with seaweed jutted out. He began to back slowly into the water, wary of his footing on the slippery surface.

The assailant was forced to choose between meeting Thangbrander head on or entering the sea himself. He chose the former. Coming in with a wild series of punches, the young man lashed out. Thangbrander blocked easily, luring him deeper into the shallows. He watched as his opponent overextended and lost his footing in the high water. Now, Thangbrander thought.

Parrying the blow, Thangbrander retaliated with a few well-placed punches to the gut. The youth let out a muted grunt as the air was forced out of his lungs, doubling over in pain. Seeing his chance, Thangbrander drove his hands into the man's hair, gripping tightly. He pulled as if to tear it from the scalp and brought his face down upon his knee, where a burst of blood and snot signalled a crushed nose.

Releasing his grip, he watched as the attacker floundered in the low tide and attempted to drag himself up the beach. Slowly, he moved about this would-be assailant and raised his leg, bringing it down hard on the man's lower back. The screams were choked out by sea water. Keeping his boot on the man's back, he watched him writhe.

"Enough!"

Thangbrander looked up towards the sound of the command and saw Hallr Thorsteinsson making his way towards the beach. His bloated form was barely concealed by the heavy fur cloak he wore. He was unsteadily climbing over the rocks and snow, stumbling a few times, before coming down to the beach proper. Thangbrander gave one last kick to the young man before turning and wading back to land. He emerged from the water just as Hallr arrived to meet him there.

"Priest Thangbrander," he wheezed. "Training goes well, I see."

Thangbrander looked over his shoulder at the two men; they were helping each other up off the beach and retreating to a polite distance to sit and lick their wounds.

"Your sons couldn't even hurt an old man," he said. He looked down at his hands and saw his knuckles were raw and bloodied. "Excuse me." Kneeling down, he ran his hands through the water, wincing slightly as the salt stung his broken flesh.

"They are young and eager to join your cause."

"Faith in Christ is not a cause. It is a necessity." Thangbrander rose from the sea and began to walk slowly up the beach, with Hallr following. He was soaked through, his tunic and trousers clinging to his meaty form. He felt the weight of his crucifix on his chest, a comforting feeling in the cold. "Why are you here, Hallr?"

"When you did not return, I thought maybe my boys got the better of you."

Thangbrander's laugh was as deep as it was unexpected. It seemed to echo along the shore. Hallr recoiled slightly before easing into a grin of his own. Thangbrander found a suitable rock and gingerly lowered himself down on to it. His muscles ached and his knees were slow to bend. He looked out over the roiling sea to the horizon, where the dark, grey-green waters met with an equally unfriendly sky.

"Olaf is coming here, isn't he?" Thangbrander said, more as a statement than a question.

"Yes." There was a pause. "He will be here in the next few weeks."

Thangbrander ran a hand through his wet black hair, slicking it back.

"He expects progress," Hallr said tentatively.

"I know what he expects." Thangbrander looked at Hallr. His blubbery, red face was puffy in the chill wind. The chieftain finally looked away.

Thangbrander reached for his crucifix on his chest and held the wooden cross before him. The small, emaciated figure of Christ nailed to it never failed to bring him comfort. Some blood from the fight had stained it. Frowning, he ran his thumb over it repeatedly.

"We should make our way back to my hall; you have a sermon to give," Hallr said after a while. His high-pitched voice grated on Thangbrander.

"Yes," he sighed. "We must not forget our flock. No matter how few they are." Cold, damp and weary, Thangbrander rose from his perch and returned the crucifix to his chest.

The stain had not shifted.

*

The walk back from the beach to Hallr's hall took longer than Thangbrander would have liked. The cold caused his knees to ache, slowing his progress. He refused help from Hallr or his sons, insisting on walking and feeling the pain. The wind had picked up, whistling across the grasslands, bringing the scent of the sea, chilling his bones. He wrapped his cloak tighter around himself and eased his way across the plains.

By the time they arrived at Hallr's hall, a squat rectangular building with a triangular roof covered in grass, his congregation had already gathered. A deep throng of people huddled together outside. Even from a distance he could tell they were riled up; loud voices in heated debate carried on the wind.

"We cannot sit idly by while we are murdered in our own homes!"

"What would you have us do, Kormac, attack our brothers with no evidence?"

"We know those who reject our faith. We should rout them out."

"More violence is not the answer. We should take trial to the assembly."

"The laws do not respect our faith. Our suffering means nothing to them."

"I worship Christ, this does not mean I forget myself or where I come from, Kormac. We must proceed according to the law."

"Then the law must be changed," Thangbrander shouted above the arguing throng. His voice, deep and coarse, brought them all to silence. He strode forward confidently, trying to hide his wince at the stabbing pain in his knees. The crowd turned to face him as one, and he attempted to make out the source of the argument.

He spotted Kormac, a short man with unwashed hair and a pockmarked face. His thin frame belied a wiry and taut physique. Thangbrander had baptized him only a few months ago. He was a lonely man, with no wife or family, and Thangbrander suspected he only became a Christian to feel part of something. No matter, Christ can make use of everyone.

His opponent was Gizurr the White, one of the first Thangbrander had baptized when he came to Iceland two years ago. He was older than Kormac, with a shock of white hair that belied his actual age. Gizurr had proven a passionate and thoughtful proponent of the faith here in Iceland, proving many times his command of oratory. Thangbrander had come to rely on him a great deal, one of the few capable men he had found on this forsaken island. He hated lying to him.

"Priest Thangbrander," Gizurr said, emerging from the crowd. He walked forward and embraced Thangbrander, his strong arms holding him tight. He whispered in his ear, "Do not let the others see you hurt."

Thangbrander smiled warmly and allowed his friend to take his weight and escort him into Hallr's hall. Crossing the threshold, he was immediately hit with the warm dry air of the roaring hearth fire at its centre. The hall was small by the standards of most farmsteads, barely tall enough to stand in. It meant, however, that the single fire warmed the space comfortably. Aside from Hallr's sleeping area at the far end, tucked away into a discreet alcove, the majority of the room was taken up by seats and tables, all angled to face the high seat.

As much as he could irritate him, Hallr was truly generous of spirit; he had offered up his home freely as a place of worship for Christians, clearing out his own retinue in order to allow the slowly expanding flock to congregate here. Thangbrander chastised himself for getting mad at Hallr. He could not have achieved even this much without him. Typically, he led two sermons a week in these halls, but also regularly held confession for his new charges. He had not considered that the hardest part of his role would be to convince them to abandon many of their old traditions. Time and again he had found some of the newly converted eating horse meat or exposing their newborn children if they could not afford to keep them. Confessions kept him busy.

Gently prying himself from his friend's grasp, Thangbrander smiled at Gizurr and walked to the other end of the hall, easing himself into his chair. The high seat, a simple wooden construct with intricate patterning, had been given up by Hallr. Instead, he would sit at the priest's right. Thangbrander watched as the throng slowly entered the hall and took up their usual positions. He looked about at each of the gathered, taking the time to mentally record their faces. They were silent, but anxious. He noticed Kormac sat as far away from Gizurr as he could.

There were no new converts. This was taking too long.

Once they had settled, he began to speak.

"Two years." His voice filled the cramped space and he watched the look of mild confusion spread across the crowd. "Two years I have been on this island. Two years I have spread the Word of God, bringing enlightenment and salvation to you happy few. It has not been an easy task. The people here are proud and set in their old ways."

There was a snort of derisive laughter from Kormac.

"I have watched you all struggle to accept the way of Christ, and to bring your friends and families to the faith. We have fought. We have preached. We have begged those we love to join us. But we have failed. Now, we find ourselves once again at the mercy of barbaric heathens."

The group grew restless before him, shuffling and looking about at each other.

"What can we do?" Gizurr asked from his position at the front of the crowd.

"We must take the fight to them!" Kormac stood sharply and shouted, "For too long we have let them beat and mock us!"

"Christ was beaten and mocked. Did he turn to violence?" Gizurr retorted calmly.

"We must defend ourselves!"

Thangbrander raised his hands; Kormac eased up slightly but remained standing.

"I agree that we must defend ourselves; that's why I ask for every able-bodied man to join me in training." Thangbrander gestured to the two bloodied and bruised sons of Hallr, who smiled weakly. "The law on this island will not be changed through reasoned debate with unreasonable people. When Jesus went into the temple and saw usurers, did he meekly turn away?"

Murmurs of "No" spread about the hall.

"When Moses came down from the mountain and saw the golden calf, did he meekly turn away?"

"No!" More confident now, the crowd swelled. All except Gizurr.

"When Korah, Dathan and Abiram led a rebellion against Moses, did he meekly turn away?"

"No!" There were cheers now. Shouts and cries filled the hall.

"Their false gods have no power here. Make them listen to us!" someone shouted.

"It is the law that must be changed!" Gizurr shouted against the throng.

Thangbrander watched as his friend turned to him with horror across his face.

"We will change the law Gizurr, I promise you that."

Gizurr said nothing, but the hurt on his face was palpable. He turned from Thangbrander and made his way out through the braying congregation.

Thangbrander forced himself to smile. "Go out from here. To your neighbours, your foster families, your friends. Cry out for justice. And if they will not listen, *make* them listen. Demand that assemblies meet to discuss your faith and the wrongdoings brought down upon you. I will train you how to defend yourselves and, when the time comes, to attack."

Confident shouts of agreement spread throughout the hall.

"Christ is with us. Our suffering is as nothing compared to His. These challenges are only His way of testing our faith. We will resist these attempts to chase us away."

They were animated now, smiling, holding on to each other in solidarity.

"We will bring the light of God to this island. We will find our salvation at the hands of Jesus Christ, our Lord. Amen."

"Amen." Their cheers filled the room.

*

It was not until the last person had left the hall, leaving on a rapturous high, that Hallr spoke.

"You didn't tell them about King Olaf."

"My king wants results. He will have them."

Thangbrander watched Hallr slowly rise from his seat.

"You play a dangerous game, priest, lying to these people. What more would you do in the name of your king?" He left, leaving Thangbrander alone with his thoughts.

"You have no idea," Thangbrander whispered.

Chapter Five

A heavy tear of glistening fat popped and spat as it glided down the steadily browning rump of the colt. It had been skinned and spitted, its legs removed so that the beast would fit over the fire, then it was hoisted into place. Thorgeir watched the meat slowly darken as the flames licked the flesh, browning at first before splitting and cracking. Marbled fat pooled out of the seams and dropped into the fire below. The scent of the rosemary-and-salt salve filled his hall. His stomach rumbled.

"I can hear your hunger from over here."

The sing-song voice of his wife brought his attention back to the moment. Gudrid had finished basting the colt. She was smiling at him, grey eyes staring out from a round, pink face. Strands of her hair, once golden but now greying, clung to her forehead.

The sweat glistening on her brow stirred a hunger of an altogether different kind in Thorgeir. He rose from his high seat and made his way down the long table. "I am hungry."

He watched as she mopped the sweat from her brow and wiped her hands on her apron.

"It won't be ready until tonight." Her eyes shone brightly, and the dimples in her cheeks glowed.

"It's not the horse I want."

"What do you want?"

He reached out and pulled her towards him. After a moment of resistance, she fell willingly into his arms, laughing as she did so. She was slight and his arms could wrap around her fully.

He held her close to his chest. "My dear white fox."

"I haven't been that in years, my love."

"A few grey hairs do not blind me to your beauty." Tracing a hand down her face, he moved a few wisps of her hair out of her eyes, his fingertips running across lines and wrinkles she had acquired over their long years together. He could still see the young girl who had teased him into swimming in the hot springs at night, their naked bodies pink in the cold air and hot water, the stars their only witnesses.

Cupping her face, he leant in for a kiss.

A knock, heavy and rapid, beat against his hall door.

Gudrid pulled out of their embrace, shock and annoyance spreading across her face as she turned to face the door. "Now, who could that be? We are not expecting anyone for hours."

"They better have a good reason for interrupting us."

The aggressive knocking continued. Thorgeir went over to the hearth fire and pulled a hand axe out of a log. Inspecting it briefly, he made his way to the door.

Wind whistled through the crack beneath the door, chilling his feet as he approached. The wood buckled with each heavy knock. He raised his axe and tensed.

*

"Who comes to my hall?" A voice shouted from behind the door. Arinbjorn recognized it as that of Thorgeir. He stopped his banging.

"It is Arinbjorn, son of Thorleikr."

"Arinbjorn?" Thorgeir said through the door. Then, more quietly, as if to someone else, "It's Thorleikr's youth."

"What does he want?" A woman's voice. Probably his wife. An image of Jofrid appeared in Arinbjorn's head. He banished it quickly. He had to focus.

The sound of poorly oiled metal dragging across wood signalled that Thorgeir was opening the door. Arinbjorn went for his axe, only to feel Sigvaldi's hand catch him. He turned sharply to his friend. Sigvaldi was staring at him, eyes wide and intense. It was just the two of them now that he had sent Freya home with Hrapn as escort. She had not been happy, but he would not risk a confrontation with her present.

The door opened slowly and Arinbjorn pried his arm from Sigvaldi's grasp but did not reach for his weapon again. Before

them stood Thorgeir, short yet muscular, topless, with one arm
behind his back. The evening sun lit up his speckled hair, but no
light seemed to pierce the two black eyes that narrowed upon
seeing Arinbjorn.

"What is the meaning of this?"

"We were worried you may have been attacked." He tried to
keep his voice level. He could almost feel Sigvaldi's stare burning
into the back of his head, encouraging him to remember that he
promised not to act without further proof.

"Why would we have been attacked?"

"After burying the Skjalti family, we followed some suspicious
tracks. They led us here. And to this." Arinbjorn drove a hand
into his tunic. He watched Thorgeir tense. Smiling inwardly,
Arinbjorn pulled out the small piece of bloodied cloth they had
found by the river. It was made of a thick wool and dyed blue.
He held it before Thorgeir, hoping he wouldn't notice the shake
in his hands.

Tentatively, Thorgeir reached out to take the cloth. After a
moment of resistance, Arinbjorn released it. Thorgeir studied it
for a moment in the low evening light.

"Do you know where it came from?" Sigvaldi asked.

"Why would I?"

"It was found on an ash tree in your field. Down by the
river," Sigvaldi provided.

Thorgeir turned the piece of cloth over. "This looks like it
came from some form of cloak," he offered. "Although it has
intricate patterning."

"We were hoping you would know whose cloak it came
from." This all came from Sigvaldi. Arinbjorn simply kept
watching Thorgeir for his reactions. His eye was twitching, and
he still had not revealed his other arm.

"I do not have any blue cloaks."

"What are you men talking about?" The female voice
revealed itself to be an older woman. She emerged from behind
Thorgeir, a long thin dagger in her hand. If only Jofrid had been
given such time to prepare.

"Gudrid, these men think they tracked Skjalti's killer to us," Thorgeir said. "They found this." He offered her the scrap of cloth.

"The killer made his escape down the river," Sigvaldi said. "He emerged here."

"We don't know anything about that," Thorgeir said, squaring up.

"This is *murder*." Arinbjorn made a move towards him, but, before he could cross the threshold, Thorgeir whipped an axe from behind his back and held it up to Arinbjorn's face. The blade hung inches from his eyes.

"Be careful with your next words, son of Thorleikr."

Arinbjorn felt Sigvaldi's hand on his shoulder. It pulled him gently away from the blade.

"I will find this killer. Perhaps I have *already* found him."

"How dare—"

"Come to dinner tonight." His wife's suggestion caused Thorgeir to stop dead.

"What?" Arinbjorn spat.

Gudrid deftly placed herself between her husband and Arinbjorn.

"Gudrid, what are you—?"

"We truly do not know who this belongs to," Gudrid said, cutting Thorgeir off and gesturing to the cloth. "But my husband will kill you if you slander him again."

"Then why invite us to dinner?" Sigvaldi asked. He, too, was now positioning himself before Arinbjorn, gently moving him aside.

"Because tonight we are hosting a feast for the local chieftains, including Hallr and his priest. One of them may know who this belongs to." She looked pointedly at her husband. "He is the foster-son of the murdered. He has a *right* to pursue the killer."

"You're inviting the Christians too?" Sigvaldi queried.

"We all have to live on this island," Thorgeir said, lowering his axe.

"Then why the roasted horse?" Arinbjorn asked. "I recognize the smell."

"They are welcome to live here, they are our neighbours, but I'll be damned if they take away my way of life," Thorgeir said proudly.

"He likes to see them uncomfortable."

Thorgeir shot his wife a look.

"But that doesn't make him a murderer," Gudrid said swiftly.

"No," Arinbjorn said at last. Now the moment had passed, a bit of the energy had left him.

"We accept your offer," Sigvaldi said, finally. He turned to look Arinbjorn dead in the eyes. "We will return for dinner."

Arinbjorn nodded.

"Good. Now, leave us to prepare for the night."

"Bring better manners later." Thorgeir crossed his arms.

"We will, thank you."

Sigvaldi took Arinbjorn by the shoulders and guided him away from the lawspeaker's farm.

*

The walk back to his father's home was quiet. Arinbjorn had no words for Sigvaldi. Instead, he simply kept his gaze ahead, studying the landscape leading out from Thorgeir's hall. The low, undulating hills glistened in the sun. The sound of their boots pushing through the ice filled the silence between them. Thorgeir's family had been one of the first to arrive in Iceland. His great-grandfather built their farm close to the Ljósavatn lake, far to the north-east of Iceland. Upon becoming lawspeaker, however, Thorgeir had relocated to the Thingvellir valley so that he could be close to the Law Rock. This new hall was built close to the Ölfusá river, providing a shipping route all the way to the sea. During the spring and summer, the land was rich and fertile, but, with a few more weeks of winter left to go, the earth was white all over.

After a while, Arinbjorn spotted what he was looking for. A rocky outcropping that jutted out of the hills like iron teeth. It was a vantage point that overlooked the entire river basin of the Ölfusá. Deviating from his route home, Arinbjorn began to climb the black rock.

"What are you doing?" Sigvaldi asked. "We haven't got long before we need to return to your farm and change for tonight."

"We can be late." Arinbjorn continued to climb.

Sigvaldi let out an audible sigh and joined him in climbing the rock face. It was slick with ice, but Arinbjorn managed to find his way to the top with little difficulty. Aside from a few curses from Sigvaldi, who kept losing his footing, the climb was uneventful.

"Why are we here?" Sigvaldi's question came through his panting and heaving. He lay on his back on the top of the rock, eyes closed.

"I can see everything from here. Skjalti's farm, the river, Thorgeir's hall." He pointed them out as he said them. "The Ölfusá goes straight into the sea, and past many farmsteads. So why did the killer get out at Thorgeir's?"

"He was running in water at night. His feet would have frozen if he kept going."

"I know. But the lawspeaker's farm? Considering the butcher wants to hide, it's a dangerous place to emerge."

"Accusing him was stupid. Even if he is the killer. If you are wrong, you could get killed for slander."

"Unlike this murderer, I respect the laws and traditions. I will not hide from my intent."

"A little more subtly might help."

Taking his gaze away from the river, Arinbjorn found Sigvaldi smiling.

"I *was* being subtle." Despite himself, Arinbjorn laughed. Sigvaldi joined him. "All right, I will try."

"Come on, if you want to talk to these people, we had better move."

Sigvaldi began his descent, but Arinbjorn stayed a moment longer, casting his gaze out over the farmsteads below. He knew he had been foolish to accuse the lawspeaker so brazenly. If he and Sigvaldi were to survive their dinner with the chieftains tonight, he would have to learn to hold his tongue.

Chapter Six

The wind and rain hurled themselves against the hull of the *Ormrinn Langi*. The great *skeid* lurching violently against the relentless battering. The storm had formed quickly; a dark sky, purple and bloated, greeted them as they left the relative safety of the fjords. Thorer had wanted to turn back, but Olaf overrode him, citing cowardice on his captain's part. Now, as Olaf watched the boatswain get swept off the deck and fall into the black waters, he regretted his decision.

He watched as the young man fought against the writhing waves, his head surfacing briefly before being smothered by the next blanket of water. He cries for help were drowned out by the storm.

"Man overboard!" Olaf shouted, his voice disappearing in the wind.

"No time!" Thorer shouted back. He was at the tiller, bent over and straining to keep the ship on an even course. "More drums!"

The drummers, who had lashed themselves to the deck, began beating their drums with more intensity. The rowers in turn heaved their great oars to the new rhythm. Olaf watched as dozens of oars rose in unison before diving into the roiling waters. The ship pressed on into the storm, and the boatswain's figure disappeared behind them.

"My king, stay back from the edge!"

Thorer's cry brought Olaf back to the moment. He released his grip and unsteadily made his way over to the captain.

"You were right, Thorer. This is madness."

"I'd much rather have been wrong, my king." Thorer wore a manic grin, but he maintained his gaze on the sea ahead. "I think I see the storm clearing."

Olaf turned to look out across the bow; all he could see was purple cloud and an endless black sea.

"I see nothing."

"Go below." This came out quietly, almost resignedly.

Olaf nodded slowly and left Thorer at the tiller. Just as he was about to take the stairs below, a squall caught the sails and the ship lurched violently to starboard. Olaf lost his footing and fell, head first, down the stairs into the hold. He managed to slow his descent by grabbing on to the rails, but they were slick with water. His head struck the floor, and white-hot light filled his vision.

*

The rain lashed at Thorer's face, blurring his vision. His skin felt raw and swollen as he stared down the maelstrom. The wind was deafening; he could barely make out the drums behind him, nor the cries of his men as they gave all their strength to the oars. Focusing on the horizon, he desperately fought to keep the ship angled into the waves. He watched as the waters rose up to starboard, a blanket of ink that reached up to the sky before crashing down on to the deck.

"Brace!"

The water careened across the deck, and Thorer felt the whole ship tip to port. With all of his strength he fought the tiller, his muscles screaming for him to stop. His left arm tore under the strain. He cried out.

Eventually, mercifully, the ship righted and Thorer could ease off the tiller. If this continued, they would lose the ship.

"The king is dead!" The cry cut through the wind like a bell.

Thorer tore his gaze from the bow to see who was shouting. He saw an older man, lean and haggard, climbing out from the hold. His eyes were wide with shock and his cries revealed few yellowed teeth.

"He has angered Aegir and killed us all!"

"Restrain him!" Thorer shouted. Two oarsmen, young and able-bodied, leapt from their bench and tackled the hysterical sailor. "Leif! Take the helm!" Thorer released the tiller to young

Leif, his first mate, and made his way over to the sailor. He grabbed him by his sodden tunic and shouted. "Where is the king?"

"With Hel!"

Frustrated, Thorer threw the sailor back to the deck and made his way to the hold. The deck was slippery, and he lost his footing a couple of times as the ship continued to rock violently. He looked back to the tiller, where Leif appeared to be handling the navigation well, a grim expression fixed upon his aquiline face.

Finally, Thorer reached the hold stairs and looked down below. There, in the darkness, surrounded by a dark stain, lay Olaf.

"No." It came out a whisper.

Holding on to the rails, Thorer rapidly took the stairs and landed at his king's side. Olaf lay face down in a pool of seawater and blood. Gently, Thorer turned him over. A low moan escaped Olaf.

"He is alive!" Thorer shouted. He looked above and called for men to join him.

Holding his king's head in his lap, Thorer began to examine him. The blood was coming from a head wound.

A moment later, several oarsmen had surrounded them. Looking about, he did not recognize any of them, save an older sailor called Illugi.

"Illugi, help me get him to his bed. And find me someone who can heal."

"We left the healers clinging to that rocky sker." Illugi knelt and helped raise Olaf from the floor. The pair made their way quickly to Olaf's cabin.

"What about that Icelander we have in the cell?"

"The hostage?"

"Bring him to me." Thorer did not have time to argue.

"What if he won't help?"

"If Olaf dies, the hostage dies."

*

It was pain that brought him back to consciousness—a dull ache that seemed to reverberate around his entire skull and spread out to his body. It was cold. Tentatively, he opened his eyes. The world gradually came into focus and he realized he was on his bed. A low light from a couple of lanterns cast his cabin in a yellow pallor. He winced as a stabbing pain pierced his eyes. Gradually the pain receded as he acclimatized to the low light.

He thought back to the last thing he remembered, the fall into the hold, and raised his hand to his head. He felt a bandage that had been wrapped tightly about his temple. Pulling his hand back he saw it was wet with both water and blood.

"Ah, you're alive. That's good for me, I imagine."

Sitting up, Olaf looked for the source of the voice. He found it. Towards the back of the cabin, in a darkened corner, a small man sat in a chair. He was old, with white straggly hair that framed a weathered and tan face. He was slight, his clothes hung loosely on him, with thin bony hands that lay interlaced on his lap. Olaf recognized him immediately.

"Einar Geirleifsson."

"My king."

Even in his weakened state, the sarcasm was unmistakable to Olaf.

"Where is Thorer?" He tried to get out of bed, but pain from his head shot through his body and he eased himself back down.

"I wouldn't move too much, if I were you. I've seen men die from head wounds such as that, days after the fact."

"Why are you here?"

"It turns out, in your haste to kill all those witches, you also killed anyone who may have been able to help you. They unfettered me to heal you. Under pain of death, of course."

Olaf sighed. "Of course."

"I will alert Captain Thorer to your recovery."

Olaf watched as Einar rose from his seat, joined by the clashing of chains, and made his way to a little bell that lay on a side table. With a smile that did not reach his eyes, Einar rang the bell. Olaf winced.

Moments later, the door to the cabin burst open and Thorer Klakka came bounding into the room. His heavy muscular form barged past Einar, and he threw himself to his knees at the side of the bed.

"My king, you live!" The genuine joy in his voice was in sharp contrast to Einar's sarcasm.

"Thanks to you." Then, after a moment, "And Einar."

Thorer looked over to a theatrically bowing Einar. "I'm sorry I used him, but I could think of no other way."

Olaf reached out and squeezed his friend's arm. "You did well. Thank you."

Thorer smiled warmly.

"What news of the storm?" Olaf asked.

"We have passed through the worst of it."

"Why don't you tell him how the storm ended?" Einar said.

Thorer's smile faltered. He turned to Einar and called out, "Get him out of here! He lives, for now."

Two men came and escorted Einar out of the room, hoisting him off the floor and dragging him away.

"What did he mean by that?"

"Nothing, my king."

"Thorer, you are a great captain. But a terrible liar." Olaf stared at Thorer. He watched him swallow and spend time considering his answer.

"The storm was heavy and I saw no way out of it. I sent you down below to keep you safe for as long as I could."

Olaf nodded, he remembered as much. "But we made it through."

"Yes."

"Then, what happened?"

Thorer rose from his kneeling position and looked away from Olaf. His great shoulders were tense.

"One of the men found you down in the hold. Barely breathing and blood pouring from your head. He thought you were dead. He came out screaming about your hubris in defying the old gods, and how it had killed us all."

"Go on."

"I ordered him restrained while I came to help you. I summoned Einar." Thorer was visibly shaking now. "As I watched Einar tend to you, the storm seemed to abate. As if from nowhere, Leif found a route through the waves and managed to escape the worst of it."

"What is wrong with that?"

"It is Einar. He prayed to the old gods the whole time he was treating you. Praying for your recovery. Praying for the storm to end. Several of the men had gathered to pay their respects. They all saw it."

"He defies me even as he heals me." Anger began to replace confusion. Olaf rose from his bed, resisting the pain in his head.

"He saved your life. And the storm abated." Thorer returned his gaze to Olaf.

"Don't tell me you believe him?" Venom filled his voice.

"I am just relieved you are alive."

Olaf could hear the vulnerability in his friend. It calmed him. A little.

"Old friend, it is only by the grace of God we live." After a moment's thought, he continued, "Einar's son is in the hold too, is he not?"

Tentatively, Thorer responded. "Yes, my lord."

"Good. Bring him and Einar to the deck at once. Let us see whose gods are greater."

*

The sense of calm that had fallen over the sea was matched only by the rising disquiet on board the *Ormrinn Langi*. Olaf stepped out of the hold and into the late afternoon. The dark bloated sky had passed, leaving only grey clouds that hung high above. The sun was setting. Streams of golden rays burst through the breaks in the cloud and lit up the sea. The ship rocked listlessly in the waters, the creak and moans of the wood palpable in the relative silence.

Some members of the crew were using buckets to empty the ship of water that had been taken on during the storm. The air smelled of salt and vomit; clearly someone had been sick during the storm. More than one someone.

As he emerged from the hold, all activity on deck paused for a moment. The oarsmen and drummers looked up at him, a mixture of relief and fear on their faces. They knew what was to happen. Thorer was behind him, along with Einar and his son. Four guards flanked them.

Olaf made a show of walking slowly across the deck until he made it to the edge of the ship. He leant over and looked down into the water. He spat.

"I am alive."

No one spoke.

"I was saved by this man." He gestured to Einar, whose brown eyes narrowed in suspicion.

"I was promised that, if I saved you, I would be spared," Einar said.

"You were."

"Then why are we here?"

Raising his voice so that all could hear him, Olaf faced down his crew: "He claims the old gods saved me and quietened the storm."

The sailors all shifted uncomfortably.

"What does it matter what I believe? You are alive."

"It matters because you are wrong. And I will prove it."

"How?"

Olaf smiled. "Bring him to me."

Einar went to protest, but found no one was grabbing him. Instead, he watched his son, Afli, get taken before the king.

"Father!" Afli cried.

"Leave him!" Einar attempted to break free.

Swiftly, a guard struck him about the head and sent him to his knees. He was dragged back and restrained.

Two of the guards brought the boy before the king. Olaf grabbed Afli's chin and inspected the young runt. He couldn't have been more than ten years old, but he was tall for his age, and handsome. He wriggled and squirmed beneath his touch. He reminded Olaf of the eels he would catch as a young man.

"If his gods had any power," Olaf's voice was now louder than the sea, "why would they save me? I am their enemy. No, it is only the one true God who has any power in this world. It was He who saved us."

"We came willingly to your hall, we did you no wrong!" Einar was screaming as he struggled against his captors. "Let him go!"

"Your people refuse to accept God into their hearts; until they do, you are mine to do with as I please." Olaf pulled out a dagger from his belt. It was short and mostly used for carving, but it would do.

"I curse you!"

"You have no power here." Olaf smiled. "But maybe, if your gods are real, they will save your son." With that, Olaf drove his blade into the young boy's stomach. He felt the blade pierce the flesh and plunge deep into his bowels. The boy's scream was stifled by the guard holding his mouth. Olaf drew the blade slowly across Afli's gut, opening a wound from which his entrails came pouring out. Red hot blood gushed forth and covered his hands. Einar screamed.

Olaf looked up at the guards holding the boy and gestured overboard. Nodding, they hoisted his still wriggling form up and threw him into the waters. A moment later, there was a small splash.

Einar threw back his head and screamed a wordless howl. The sailors looked on.

"I guess not," Olaf said. Wiping his blade on his tunic, he shouted, "Let this be a reminder to you all. There is no god but ours, and He gives no quarter." He finished there and addressed Thorer directly. "Captain?"

Thorer's face was ashen. He was staring at the pool of blood and organs on the floor. Eventually, he turned his gaze to Olaf. "Yes, my king?"

"Clean up this mess."

With that, Olaf left his crew and made his way to the bow of the ship. He wondered if he could see Iceland yet.

Chapter Seven

Darkness fell early in Skálholt. Thick clouds hung low and heavy in the sky, their bulbous pink forms rising to block out the moon. Arinbjorn could see a curtain of heavy snow slowly advancing upon their position. It had already fallen over Thorgeir's hall in the distance. He pulled his cloak tighter about himself.

"I don't like the look of this," Sigvaldi said. He was slightly ahead of Arinbjorn, standing atop a small rock and looking down into the valley before them. His shorter brown hair was whipped up by the slowly increasing wind. "If we go through with this, we may be trapped within Thorgeir's walls."

"Someone in there knows who killed Skjalti."

Sigvaldi grimaced. "Then we had better hurry."

It took them a further half hour to make it down into the valley. They paused before the encroaching wall of snow. It had encompassed the fields before them. If they went in, there was a danger they could get turned around and lost. Many men and women had disappeared in one of Frey's storms.

Arinbjorn did not hesitate. "We press on." He plunged into the wall of snow.

The horizon disappeared and their world was reduced to the few feet in front of them. "Stay close to me," Arinbjorn said to Sigvaldi as he waited for his friend to catch up. The fall was heavy, and their walk became a crawl. Thankfully, the wind was not yet high. Snow clung to their faces and beards, obscuring their vision yet further as they attempted to navigate their way through. Arinbjorn knew the route through the valley well enough to continue in the general direction, but these snowstorms had a way of disorientating those trapped within them.

It was quiet. The cloud about them was dense and the flurries of snow danced in silence. The pair made their way to what they hoped was their destination, and soon shapes began to appear ahead. Tall shadowy forms, misshapen and blurred, loomed out at them. One, a black shadow hunched on all fours, seemed to have a hideously wide maw that screamed silently at the sky. As they approached, its tortured pose revealed itself to be nothing but an ash tree, gnarled and weathered, standing alone in a field. Arinbjorn stopped before it.

"What's wrong?" Sigvaldi asked.

"For a moment, I could have sworn I saw Fenrir."

"It is just an ash tree."

Arinbjorn nodded. "We must be close. They line the boundaries of Thorgeir's land."

"Then keep moving, my hood has frozen to my hair."

Arinbjorn smiled back at his friend, then moved past the tree and deeper into the ice and snow. A further ten minutes passed. He was about to stop walking, convinced they were going in the wrong direction, when another shape emerged. This one was far larger, squat and bowed, like a ship that had beached upside down. They had found Thorgeir's hall.

"Thank the gods," Sigvaldi sighed.

"Let us introduce ourselves."

The heavy snowfall had covered the turf roof and walls completely; it blended in seamlessly with the landscape and cloud behind it. All that could truly be seen was the wooden entrance door. As they approached, they could hear laughter and singing coming from inside. Giving Sigvaldi one last look, Arinbjorn raised his fist and beat heavily upon the door. It took several moments before it opened before them.

The face that greeted them was worn and gaunt, like someone had drawn too-thin parchment over the skull. The only colour to his pale skin was the blue of the thick veins that lined his forehead, and the wisps of hair that adorned his skull. He was dressed in a clean yet basic tunic, and brown trousers. He wore no jewellery, his only adornment the carving knife on his belt.

"You're late." His voice was guttural and carried a strange accent.

Before Arinbjorn could respond, Sigvaldi stepped in. "Please extend our apologies to your master. The road was long." He gestured to the heavy snow as it fell about them.

The thrall nodded, then moved back from the threshold and gestured inside.

Thanking him, the pair moved into the light and warmth of the hall. When they were here earlier, Thorgeir had stood in the doorway, blocking their view of his home. Now, they could truly take in the lawspeaker's hall. Compared to many of the farmsteads that dotted the Skálholt valley, this hall was massive. The main room, the *skali*, had been decked out with long wooden benches and tables. They were lined with people—mostly men, but a few women too—who were in deep and loud conversation. Many ignored the arrival of the newcomers, but a few faces turned and appraised them both before returning to their meal. Two rows of pillars ran down the centre of the space, bisecting the hall, and a large hearth fire glowed with bright yellow flames at its centre. The wind from the open door caused the flames to roar as the pair entered, but settled down when the thrall closed the door behind them. The air was hot and thick inside. It would have been stifling, were it not a relief to be out of the snow. At the back of the hall, towards the *stofa* living space, Thorgeir and Gudrid were sitting at the largest table Arinbjorn had ever seen. It was laden with food and drink, and perhaps a dozen people sat around their hosts. The lawspeaker looked up from his meal and eyed Arinbjorn steadily, before whispering something into Gudrid's ear. Gudrid then excused herself from the table and made her way over to Arinbjorn and Sigvaldi.

"Don't get me killed by being disrespectful in here," Sigvaldi whispered.

"I will be respectful if they are."

Gudrid had tied her greying hair into a long braid and was wearing an ankle-length linen dress, dyed red, which she had fastened at the neck with a bronze brooch. It fitted her well, Arinbjorn noted.

She flashed them both a smile. "I am glad you could make it. You must be frozen solid. Leave your cloaks with Eogan here and come to join us on the high table." She gestured to the thrall who had let them in.

"The high table?" Sigvaldi asked, stunned. "We would be just as happy down here."

"Nonsense. You are honoured guests this evening." She leant in closer and lowered her voice. "If you truly wish to find out who killed Skjalti, then the men who sit with my husband are your best chance of learning anything. Nothing happens on this island without their knowledge."

"We would be honoured," Arinbjorn said.

He removed his cloak and shook off the worst of the snow from his hair and beard, before handing it over. Sigvaldi followed suit. Gudrid passed her gaze over them both.

"I hope we are appropriate?" Arinbjorn said, gesturing to his clothes. He had borrowed his father's red tunic for the occasion; it hung a little loosely on his frame. Sigvaldi wore a green tunic he had brought over from Norway.

"You both certainly look the part. I am pleased you didn't see fit to bring any weaponry."

"Sigvaldi insisted," Arinbjorn replied evenly.

"Your friend is a wise man."

"I get told that a lot."

Gudrid smiled. "If you will follow me."

She placed them at the furthest end of the high table, between two men Arinbjorn had not met before. To their left, closest to the roasted colt that took pride of place, sat Hallr, a red-faced man with too high a voice and too large a belly for Arinbjorn's taste. He was talking passionately with someone Arinbjorn did not recognize—a man who was probably as old as his father, yet had a head of thick black and white hair, with a beard to match. Despite his age, he was powerfully built. He drank slowly and stared at the colt that lay presented before him on the table with barely disguised disgust on his face.

"He must be the Christian Thorgeir told us about," Arinbjorn whispered to Sigvaldi as they sat down.

"I heard he was one of their priests. Thangbrander, I think they called him."

"Was he the one who baptized Skjalti?"

"I think he is the only one who can."

To their right sat Ingolfr, a widower who owned much of the land between Øxárfoss and Skálholt. He was old and wiry, with a thin, droopy beard that kept catching in his soup. He greeted the pair with a disinterested nod before returning to his meal.

The rest of guests at the table were some of the most respected chieftains in all of Iceland. Arinbjorn felt his nerve weaken.

"I find your presence here insulting." The words cut through the chatter at the table and a hush descended over the gathered chieftains. Arinbjorn tensed in his chair.

"Thankfully, I am not here at your invitation, Teitr," Priest Thangbrander retorted.

Arinbjorn let out a breath.

"We all know it is you riling up our farmers, Thangbrander!" Teitr Gunnolfsson, a farmer and trader whose salt-and-pepper beard was stiff with sea spray, was staring angrily at the priest.

"Only today I caught a thrall attempting to set free my pigs and sheep!" This came from a younger man at the end of the table. He was shorter than most, with thick red hair that flowed down his head in ringlets. His green eyes flashed with drunken anger.

"I am not responsible for the actions of those who struggle under your tired ways, Gellir," Thangbrander retorted evenly, his gaze steady.

"And where is Gizurr? He decided not to take advantage of our hosts' hospitality."

"We know he is close to you."

"Ah, Arinbjorn. Thank you for coming," Thorgeir said loudly, cutting off Thangbrander's reply. Twelve faces turned to stare intently at Arinbjorn and Sigvaldi. "Everyone, this is Arinbjorn Thorleiksson. Foster-son to Skjalti."

The anger died down only to be replaced with a tense silence as the table absorbed this information.

"We are sorry for your loss," Hallr said, after a pause.

"Thank you. But loss is the wrong word. Skjalti was taken from me."

"Why have you brought him here, Thorgeir?" Gellir asked.

"Because a murder has been committed."

The table stirred uncomfortably.

"He has a right to pursue the murderer." Thorgeir passed his gaze slowly over each of the chieftains.

"Your pursuit has led you here?" Ingolfr asked.

Arinbjorn was stunned for a moment. He had not expected Thorgeir to be so open.

"He came to me for help," Thorgeir interjected, while giving Arinbjorn a knowing stare.

Arinbjorn felt his face redden.

"As lawspeaker, I could not refuse."

"Why have you surprised us with this?" Teitr asked.

"Do you have something to hide?" The accusation was light, but pointed.

Teitr bristled and the table erupted into heated argument. The other tables in the room quietened.

"I meant no disrespect," Arinbjorn said at last. "Thorgeir was kind in letting me come here. I only wish to beg your help in finding this killer."

"From what I can see, it is only Christians who have been targeted. Why should I worry?"

"Are we not all the same here, Teitr?" Hallr shouted, his high-pitched voice surprising in its intensity.

"How is your horse, Hallr?" Teitr replied. His mouth, filled with horsemeat, grinned out from his straggly beard.

"Chieftains, please," Gudrid said calmly, interjecting before her husband could. She took a deep gulp from her cup and placed it down slowly and purposefully. "What affects one affects us all. Murder is murder. You would do well to remember that, Teitr."

The men were quiet at her words, pensively staring at their food.

"Your wife shows great insight, Thorgeir," Thangbrander said at last. "I appreciate the support." He turned to face Arinbjorn directly and appraised him with cold black eyes. "If myself or my flock can be of any assistance in finding this murderer then you need but ask."

Arinbjorn nodded evenly. "Thank you."

"What would you have *us* do, lawspeaker?" Gellir asked.

"Eat your meal and enjoy the entertainment. When the evening allows, simply answer his questions. Then he will leave." Thorgeir looked pointedly at Arinbjorn.

The group shuffled uncomfortably, but Arinbjorn watched as they each slowly resigned themselves to the situation.

"Very well," Gellir said finally, and the chieftains eased slightly and settled down into discreet conversation among themselves.

"The entertainment had better be good or this will be the last meal we ever have," Sigvaldi whispered, before downing a flagon of mead.

*

As the evening wore on, Arinbjorn spoke to several of the gathered chieftains. Most greeted him with mild disinterest. Gellir and Teitr both argued that they did not know who had killed Skjalti, that it wasn't their problem, and they wouldn't stop a Christian murderer if they saw him in the field anyway. Arinbjorn dismissed their bluster; arrogant and unpleasant though they were being, he was sure they wouldn't break the laws of the land. They had too much respect for tradition. He showed the scrap of blue cloth about the table in the hope someone would recognize it, or at least react, but got nothing except a cursory inspection from Thangbrander.

"Blue is an expensive dye, young man. Who here can afford such?" Thangbrander offered.

Arinbjorn thumbed the cloth and sighed, exasperated. He had not considered that. The priest was right; whoever wore cloth of blue dye must be wealthy, or at least the servant of a wealthy patron. For all their relative power and authority here, none of the chieftains could be said to be that wealthy.

He was beginning to get frustrated and was about to leave when he felt a hand upon his shoulder. Hot, wet air was breathed into his ear as Hallr whispered, "Do not leave just yet; stay for the entertainment."

"I haven't got time for poetry."

"The storm is still raging outside; it is not safe. We will speak to you *after*." Hallr released his grip and returned to his mead.

"What was all that about?" Sigvaldi asked.

"I don't know. But it looks like we are staying for a while longer."

*

Odin was going to lose. Everyone knew that. Yet, no matter how many times he heard the tale, Arinbjorn wished it ended differently. He watched, enraptured, as the skald, Skuli Thorsteinsson, recounted the tale of Völuspá, the seeress. Skuli was a talented poet, known throughout Skálholt for his command of language and oratory. That Thorgeir could call upon him for entertainment was testament to the lawspeaker's standing.

Skuli was a small and slight man with a trim beard that was greying in patches. Standing before them atop the raised *set* dais, he cut a striking figure with the hearth fire glowing behind him. He wore a leather cuirass over his tunic, a piece of armour said to have been gifted to him by a jarl on his travels, and a helmet. It was the helmet that caught Arinbjorn's eye. It was basic in comparison to the cuirass, nothing more than steel fashioned into a conical shape and some eye guards, yet Skuli had gilded the inside of the right socket. The flames of the hearth fire were reflected by the gold paint, lighting up Skuli's right eye in a fiery red. From Arinbjorn's vantage point at the far end of the high table, Skuli looked like the manifestation of Odin himself.

Arinbjorn studied those gathered about him, trying to make out faces in the crowd. It was dim, with flickering light dancing across the features of the guests. He fancied that, if he looked hard enough, he could see Skuli's poem play out in the shadows. The wind outside shook the building and the hall itself seemed to groan. Skuli's voice, low and melodic, carried across the room as he recited his poem. He spoke of the release of Skoll, the dread wolf, and Arinbjorn remembered the vision he'd had outside in the storm. He shuddered. Shackled and chained, Skoll, along with their brethren Hati, would one day break free of her confines and swallow the moon. This act would mark the beginning of the end for the old world, and darkness would fall over mankind. Skuli's poem came to an end and was greeted with applause from the crowd. Arinbjorn rose with the rest and added his cheers to the chorus. Skuli bowed slightly.

"That was inspired, Skuli!"

"Tell us another!"

"The Lay of the High One?" Laughter and cheer greeted Skuli's suggestion.

"How about something different?" The voice, deep and raspy, cut through the throng. The crowd slowly stopped applauding and turned to face the source of the voice. It was Thangbrander, still in his seat and staring stoically at the colt before him. His face was in shadow as he drank slowly and deliberately.

"Do you have a suggestion, priest?" Thorgeir asked. Mead coated his beard and it glistened in the low light.

Thangbrander finished his drink and placed his cup upon the table. "Tell us of the death of the gods."

"Ragnarök?" Skuli looked to Thorgeir.

"Yes." Thangbrander finally turned to face Skuli directly. "Tell us of Ragnarök."

To Arinbjorn, it felt like everyone in the room was holding their breath. He swept his gaze around the hall, noticing as two thralls discreetly took up position behind Thangbrander, their hands resting on the hilts of their sax knives. He caught Gudrid staring at them, her small thin hand gripping her husband's arm. Outside, the wind howled; the walls creaked and moaned violently in the silence of the group. One of the thralls left the back wall and advanced slowly on Thangbrander.

"I, too, would like to hear of Ragnarök!" Arinbjorn exclaimed. The thrall paused in his advance and looked at Arinbjorn, his hand dropping to his side.

"Who are you," a croaky, phlegm-filled voice asked, "to make requests in Thorgeir's hall?" It was Ingolfr. He cast his dull grey eyes about the room, searching for the author of the insolent request.

"I thought that it was good manners to welcome one's guests. Priest Thangbrander is as much a guest as us, is he not?"

"Ari, what are you doing?" Sigvaldi whispered from his side.

Arinbjorn silenced him with a gesture. The group shuffled uncomfortably.

"Do not make me regret inviting you into my hall," Thorgeir said to Arinbjorn, before turning to a visibly distressed Skuli. "Give the priest what he wants. He could do with the education."

The group let out a collective sigh and eased back down into their seats as Thorgeir took his place. Reaching over to the colt, the lawspeaker grabbed some steak carved from the carcass and proceeded to eat it noisily before the priest. Thangbrander dutifully ignored this and instead subtly raised his cup to Arinbjorn, who nodded in return.

Skuli, easing once the tension dissipated, recovered some of his swagger.

"Very well!" He drank deeply from a cup of mead before continuing. "Most of us here know the stories of the gods. But what becomes of them, in the end? Why are we called to Odin's hall in Valhalla? It is because of Skoll and Hati? When the end comes, they will break forth from their fetters and consume the sun and moon. Not even the All-Father will be able to stop them. Or is it because of their father, Fenrir?" After this introduction had got the crowd's attention once more, Skuli launched into his poem. His voice, sonorous and rhythmic, wafted above the entranced crowd. He described the final fate of the gods. The crowd cried out when Yggdrasil, the world tree, was bowed and broken before the onslaught of Nidhog the wyrm, his poisonous fangs digging deep into its roots. Teitr actually howled when Surtr, the giant who bore a sword as bright as the sun, marched down on the Aesir with Jǫrmungandr, the world serpent, whose writhing body caused great waves that flooded the earth. Finally, when all was silent and his audience were enraptured, Skuli came to the moment all dread: the fall of Odin.

> "Now comes a new hurt to Hlín,
> Now Odin dares to battle with the wolf,
> And Beli's just slayer seeks Surtr,
> For there will fall Frigg's joy."

Silence greeted this last stanza, with the guests staring down into their food and drink, mourning just like Odin's wife, Frigg. All except for Thangbrander, who held his head high, and Hallr, who copied him.

"So, your All-Father dies in the end." It was not a question.

"I would not celebrate too soon, priest," Thorgeir stated. "He is not dead yet." Murmurs of agreement spread across the table.

"His death will not be the end." Sigvaldi's voice, normally so sure and calm, wavered slightly. Arinbjorn shot him a look, but Sigvaldi continued, "His death will galvanize the other gods who will defeat Fenrir and his father Loki. In Odin's stead, a new world will be made."

A chorus of agreement rose up towards the end of Sigvaldi's speech.

"Besides, didn't your Christ die on the cross?"

Thangbrander's eyebrows raised in mild shock. "Impressive. It would appear some of my teachings are getting out."

Hallr barked out a laugh.

"If you came to my church, however, you would also know that Jesus came back to us three days later. You cannot kill the true God."

"Shall we put that to the test?" Gellir asked, his eyes glassy and unfocused thanks to the mead.

"I think we have had enough entertainment," Gudrid interjected swiftly. "I grow tired, husband; perhaps we should draw our evening to a close?"

"Yes. I think so too."

The gathered guests nodded in agreement and started to depart the table. Thralls appeared and the crowd began to collect their cloaks and shawls. Arinbjorn and Sigvaldi waited at the table for a moment and watched the majority leave. Hallr and Thangbrander remained.

"You did a brave thing tonight, standing up for me as a guest," Thangbrander said, once everyone else had left.

"If you are a guest in someone's hall, you have a right to be treated as all others."

Thangbrander leant in closely. His breath was hot and carried the scent of mead. "I knew Skjalti. Come to my church. I have information that will help you in your search for his killer."

"What do you know?" Sigvaldi asked.

"Not here." Thangbrander lowered his voice. "We do not know who else may be listening." He cast his eyes about the room and then refocused them upon Arinbjorn. Nodding, he stood up. He was a full head taller than Arinbjorn and cast a deep shadow. "Until we meet again, young man."

Arinbjorn and Sigvaldi watched him depart with Hallr. Once they were gone, a lighter voice greeted them from behind.

"I trust you are happy with your answers tonight, gentlemen." It was Gudrid. She had their cloaks in her hands which, rising from the table, they accepted gratefully.

"We appreciate your kindness in allowing us to be here," Sigvaldi answered.

"These are good men; they would not lie to you."

"Which only means my killer is that much further away," Arinbjorn sighed.

Smiling, Gudrid came in to hug them both. She held tightly for a moment and lowered her voice: "I know Thangbrander has invited you to speak with him. Be careful." She pulled back and walked away.

Arinbjorn stared after her.

"Does it strike you as convenient that Thangbrander suddenly has information that may help us?" Sigvaldi asked.

"I knew helping him would garner favour, and gods know we needed allies at that table, but still…"

"So, what do we do now?"

"What else? We go to church."

Chapter Eight

The darkness just before dawn was her favourite time of day. The farm was at its quietest. Her husband, Njall, had yet to wake and the few thralls that were starting their chores were too busy to bother her. Here, on the edge of the farmstead, past the hall and barn, she could look out across the valley and be alone. She looked up; Odin's Wagon was high in the sky and the stars shone brightly. The storm from the previous night had passed, leaving the few ash trees that dotted the landscape covered in thick snowfall. The plains leading down to the Ölfusá river sparkled in white.

The air was crisp and cool, and the wind was biting against her exposed arms. She took in a deep breath, smiling at the pain as the wind cut into her lungs, and hugged herself tightly. The farm was beginning to wake up; she could hear the excited cries from the chickens, pigs and horses as the thralls went about feeding them. The earthen smell from the stables and sty was comforting, reminding her of home—her real home, before her father had sent her away with Njall. A low crunch from behind her let her know she was no longer alone.

"Good morning, Failend," Freya said, without turning.

"Good morning, miss," Failend replied. She came to a stop behind her. "I have brought your cloak."

She felt the cloak as it was placed over her shoulders. She stiffened under the touch.

"Thank you."

There was silence for a moment before Failend continued, "Bad dreams again, miss?"

Freya did not respond. Instead, she waited until she heard the tell-tale crunch of snow that marked Failend's departure.

Yes, bad dreams. She had been having them ever since she heard about Skjalti's murder. In her dream, she was standing on the edge of a restless sea. A beluga whale had washed up on the shore, its ice-white flesh covered in black sand; it lay there moaning, with its tired mournful eyes staring out listlessly. She watched as half a dozen white foxes attacked the whale, tearing at its flesh. As they tore at its festering carcass, she realized the whale was already rotten and bloated, the foxes' mouths teeming with maggots. The waves rose ever higher; she tried screaming to the foxes to leave the whale alone, to escape the rising waters. They did not hear her. The frenzied foxes drowned even as they continued to eat the whale. Their high-pitched cries became the sound of rushing water.

She had woken up each night, crying.

She tried to shake away the mental image and took in another deep breath, the pain a welcome distraction, and her attention returned to the valley before her. A red glow began to creep into the sky over in the east. Her moment alone had passed. Time to go and greet her husband. She about-turned and walked back towards the farmstead.

When she crossed the threshold, she took stock of the *skali*. Njall's hall was modest, but was well maintained. Looking at it now, it was about the same size of Skjalti's. She tried not to think about that. The hearth fire was already roaring, thanks to the thrall that tended to it, and last night's stew was bubbling away, filling the air with the scent of rosemary. Njall emerged from the *stofa*, pulling a dull grey tunic over his head.

He was older than her by a good two decades, and the wrinkles that lined his face came from years of toiling outside in harsh wind and rain. He smiled at her, his brown eyes soft when set against the harshness of his features. Ringlets of brown hair fell about his face.

"Good morning, my love."

She smiled and went over to him. "Good morning, husband." She ran her fingers through his hair and tucked it back behind his ears.

He took her hands in his and held them gently. "You look weary. And your hands are frozen."

"I went outside to check on the animals."

"You did not sleep well last night. I felt you waken."

"It was just dream nonsense; I'm sorry I disturbed you."

Njall stared intently into her eyes for a moment. She held his gaze until he broke away.

"I am going down to the coast to hunt walrus with Tongu-Oddr," he said at last.

"So soon? You only came back from the last hunt yesterday. The farm needs you here."

"Their ivory is too valuable an opportunity. It could feed us for months."

Freya removed her hands from his.

His face hardened. "We may be gone a few days, this time."

"I understand."

They spent the rest of the morning collecting Njall's hunting gear. As they loaded his horse outside, he detailed his plan to her—how he intended to stay with Tongu-Oddr on the coast, their hunting strategies, how it would benefit the farm. She let it all wash over her like water in a babbling brook. By the time they had finished packing, the sun had risen comfortably above the horizon.

She finished stuffing his leather-working tools into a satchel, patting the mare softly as she whinnied against the weight being put upon her. Freya watched as Njall got into the saddle.

"Must you go again?" she said at last, looking up to him.

"We have been through this."

"I know. But…" She took a while to formulate her thoughts. "People are beginning to ask questions."

Njall leant down and ran his hand against her cheek. "Let them ask, my love." He leant back and settled into the saddle, ready to depart. "You should see that Arinbjorn fellow. I know you are lonely when I am gone." He spurred his horse on and began to trot out of the farm compound. "And see a witch about your dreams. See if they really are nonsense."

She watched his form slowly disappear down into the valley and out of sight.

"Do you really not know, or do you simply not care?" she whispered to herself.

*

The remainder of the morning passed slowly, with Freya resigning herself to her duties. First, she ensured the remaining thralls were fed and watered, instructing Failend to distribute the stew from last night's dinner. She sent Aesgir, a younger thrall, awkward and gangly, up to the fields to herd their flock of sheep. It was not a hard job, but the weather made it miserable and few of the older thralls could handle it. Aesgir accepted his task with glum silence. She kept Conall and Fergus, two brothers who were sold to Njall together, back at the hall to help with some repairs to the barn.

Conall was a brute of a man, almost as wide as he was tall, with a mane of red hair that fell down a hard face. It was possible that he had been beautiful once, but, thanks to years of fighting and abuse, his nose was squashed and jutted at an odd angle. His brown eyes poked out from under a swollen and hooded brow. Fergus was the opposite of his brother, small and slight, with a wiry frame that bordered on the skeletal. He kept his red hair long too, but it masked a much more gaunt and withered face. They were older than Freya, by more than twenty years, but accepted her orders in good humour. Njall had promised to make them free men once this winter had ended; as the end date approached, Freya found nothing could dampen their spirits.

"What can we do today for you, miss?" Conall's voice came out with a slight lisp, thanks to a split-lip wound that had never fully healed.

"The roof of the sty has collapsed. I need you two to repair it."

"Spend the day covered in ice and shit?" Fergus smiled.

"Of course," Conall said.

Freya looked at them hesitantly. "There is some old wood left over from the last shack that collapsed. You can patch it with that. And I'd like it finished before Njall gets back."

"When will he be back, miss?" Conall asked, already moving about the hall to collect various tools.

Freya paused. She didn't realise she had balled her hands until the pain from her nails bit into her. She eased them open.

"Miss?" Fergus prompted.

"A few days. You have time."

"Great!" Fergus shouted. "Come on, you big oaf, the sooner you start and all that!"

She watched the pair of them leave the hall, singing a song she had heard them sing a hundred times but never recognized. She should ask them about it one day. Once the brothers had departed for the sty, Freya sat down and looked around the empty hall.

She could hear the wind whistling outside as she watched the flames of the hearth fire dance and writhe. The logs seemed to spit and cackle at her. She passed her gaze over a pile of torn clothes: tunics, cloaks and trousers that were victims of Njall's zealous hunting lay sprawled over the end of their bed. She was supposed to mend them. The leather-work needle lay before her atop a small barrel used as a side table. She picked it up and held it between her thumb and forefinger lengthways. She squeezed. She winced as blood began to pool on her finger. She watched it dribble slowly down her hand.

A loud banging on the front door made her drop the needle. Quickly, she grabbed one of the tunics and wrapped it about her hand before approaching the door. As she got nearer, she could hear voices on the other side. She placed her hand upon her sax knife.

"This is highly improper!" It was Failend.

"Get away from me, thrall." Freya knew that voice, too. More banging.

"Miss is out!"

Freya opened the door and watched as the knocker stumbled mid-knock and fell to the floor. He let out a satisfying yelp.

"Kormac Vekellsson," Freya stated evenly.

Kormac's pockmarked and scarred face looked up at her from the floor, with black, beady, eyes. "Freya! I thought you weren't in." He glanced at Failend before standing, running his hands through his thin, greasy hair.

"I just got back." She straightened the tunic to make it look like she was carrying it. "Why are you here?"

"I saw Njall leave for a hunt again. I thought I would come and make sure you were safe."

"You cannot keep coming here when my husband is away."

"I don't see a problem with a neighbour offering to help another, especially during these troubled times." He had regained his composure and stepped more confidently over the threshold and into her home. He seemed to favour his right leg, a barely noticeable limp in his gait.

Freya stood her ground. "You clearly know nothing of these troubles; the murderer is only attacking Christians."

"We know nothing for sure," he said with a smile.

She felt the wet, fishy stench of his breath upon her face as he spoke.

He looked about the hall. "Don't you think it irresponsible of Njall to leave you alone?"

"I assure you, Kormac, should anyone attack me in my home, I will not be the one in danger." A shadow fell about the two of them as Conall and Fergus appeared behind Kormac. "Besides, you would not be fit to protect anyone—you're hurt."

A pleasing look of confusion spread across Kormac's face. "Hurt?"

"Your leg. I can see you limping."

He gave a small laugh as he stepped back. "My stupid horse threw me off on the way here."

"Then your horse and I are in agreement."

Kormac started to retort, but he was cut off by Conall from behind.

"Everything OK, miss?" Conall asked.

"Everything is fine. Kormac was just checking up on me like a good neighbour. He is leaving now."

Kormac's broken, yellowing teeth formed a crescent as he smiled. He walked up to the brothers and stared into Conall's eyes. "What would you do if I wasn't leaving, thrall?"

"Miss?" Conall's jaw tensed. His hands curled into balls.

"No. Let him answer, Freya," Kormac interjected, his gaze never wavering. "What *could* you do?"

Freya stared at the back of Kormac's head, acutely aware of the sax knife in her hand.

"Nothing," Conall said at last.

"Yes. *Nothing*." The joy in Kormac's voice was sickening. He turned to face Freya. "As it happens, I do have to leave now. Do not worry; for as long as Njall is gone, I can come here to protect you." He leant in as if to hug her, before leaving a hot, damp kiss upon her cheek.

Freya watched as he turned from her and walked past the two brothers, whistling as he went. It was not until she was sure he was gone that she let out a small cry. Failend immediately ran to her side, catching her as she buckled.

"You two watch the house, warn us if he comes again!" Failend shouted, concern and fear manifesting as anger.

Conall and Fergus's sheepish faces disappeared behind the closing door.

"Thank you, Failend." Her breathing was short and sharp.

"Come, miss," Failend wiped away Freya's tears. "The brothers will keep an eye on you."

"No, no." Freya straightened herself and used Njall's tunic to dry her face. "I don't want to stay here. Can you get my horse ready, please? And have Conall grab two chickens and some eggs."

"Where are you going?" Failend fussed about her as she moved to grab her travel cloak from the stand.

"To see a witch."

*

Her horse was actually a pony called Aki, named after a foster-brother she particularly disliked. It pleased her to use his name for a beast of burden who must do her bidding, although she quite liked the pony. Her path led up and out of the Öxará basin, towards the Haukadalur valley. Bordered to the north by the Langjökull glacier and mountains, Haukadalur was a remote place. When not covered in ice and snow, the ash-black dirt was fine and brittle. Little grew or lived out here. Freya tightened her cloak against the wind. The journey to the witch was a long one, but she found herself greatly appreciating her solitude. Failend had tried to insist on coming along, but Freya would not have it.

It was a clear day; the storm from the previous night had blanketed the ground and cleared the sky. The light from the low sun was almost blinding against the snow. Freya used her hood to shield her gaze as best she could.

Yngvildr, the witch, liked living in isolation. It was as much for her own safety as for the privacy of the people who used her services. The use of magic was often considered a necessary evil by those ill equipped to understand its uses—mostly men. Freya's great-grandmother had been a witch, known throughout the region for her ability to predict good or bad harvests. One year, a group of angry farmers blamed her for their poor crop and burned her in her home. Freya could still remember the smell and the screams.

A quick burst of wind caught her off guard and she was almost blown out of her saddle. Tightening her grip with her thighs, she managed to avoid falling off. She held fast to the reins and instinctively reached back to the goods secured to Aki's rear. Two dead chickens, bound by their legs, and a pouch of eggs dangled off to the side. Good, they were still safe. It did not do well to ask for the advice of a witch without payment.

Content that her goods were safe, Freya repositioned herself on the saddle and made sure to lean into the wind. She looked out upon the glistening flat plains and the mountains that bordered the glacier, with nothing but the sound of Aki's footsteps through the snow filling the air. She took a deep breath. She liked it here.

The rest of her journey was uneventful. The last hour of her trip was spent trying to find out exactly where Yngvildr's hut was. She came across a couple of thralls shepherding sheep, who directed her to a lake formed by the glacier's water. The path down from the ice shelf was steep and slippery, the snow giving way to stones and black sand by the shoreline. The lake itself was still, its surface a mirror of the sky and landscape about it. There, on the far shore, Freya spotted a cave going deep into black rock. Wood and earth had been placed over the entrance to create a seal. She had found Yngvildr's home.

Once she was close, Freya dismounted Aki and left him drinking at the water's edge. She unhooked the offering from his back and made her way slowly to the front door. She was greeted by the sound of a pair of bone chimes as the wind whipped over the lake. They had been hung from a post on the side of the entrance, and had runes carved into them. A crunch beneath her feet drew her attention to the floor. She had stood on a bone, snapping it in two. Scattered about the floor she could see the remnants of chickens and pigs, their carcasses piled up and left to rot.

Grimacing, Freya did her best to step over them and strode to the door. Before she could get there, however, it swung open and a young woman came bursting out. She was carrying a pile of rotten and dirty linens that she unceremoniously dumped on the ground before straightening out her dress. She found something untoward sticking to it, which she wiped on the mossy doorframe. She was younger than Freya, barely an adult, with a thin frame and a round face that was red and puffy. Her thick, curly hair had been blown by the wind into wild proportions. Brown ringlets spiralled off in dozens of directions.

She spotted Freya.

"Can I help you?" It was practically barked out.

Freya stood for a moment, confusion overriding all sense. "Yngvildr?" she finally asked.

"Oh gods, not another one. No, I'm not Yngvildr." She stepped aside from the doorway and gestured into the cave. "I'm afraid you're about a month too late."

Freya tentatively approached the entrance and looked inside. The first thing she noticed was the smell. The air was stale and rotten; she suppressed a gag. A pile of skin and bones, collapsed and foetal, lay in the corner with a mass of grey hair covering its face. The old witch, Yngvildr.

"What happened?" Freya asked.

"She died," the young woman said plainly, before barging past Freya, back into the cave home. She went over to several piles of goods—foods, pans, clothes—and began rifling through them.

"How did she die?"

"She lived in a cave buried beneath a glacier. She died of cold. Stupid woman—I'd warned her so many times. Liked the cold and the solitude, she said. Well, now look at her." The young woman's rant was interspersed with the sound of pots and pans being picked up, inspected, and then cast aside.

"Who are you?"

"Bera Thrandssdottir." She stopped for a moment. "Her granddaughter."

"I'm sorry."

"Don't be. She was mad to stay here, and those who sought her council were also mad." She caught herself.

"No. No. It's OK. I understand. I guess I will be going, then." Freya stumbled over her words and began backing out of the cave. Her heel caught the hem of her dress and she tripped and fell over a pig carcass, tumbling into the black sand. After a moment's stunned silence, she began to cry. Tears fell freely down her face and her chest heaved uncontrollably. She couldn't help it; she found it hard to catch her breath. She breathed in sharply, only to let it back out again in a bark. She gripped her sides tightly.

A red-faced Bera appeared at her side and knelt before her. "I am sorry. I did not mean to slander you."

"It's. Not. That." Freya could barely get her words out. Each one was a fight against her own breath.

"You hoped she could help you. I can do that: don't take advice from women who live in caves." A warm smile spread up and across her rosy face. It immediately made her look her age.

Freya managed to cough out a laugh. With some gentle coaxing from Bera, she got her breathing down.

Bera went and filled a cup with lake water before returning to Freya. "Drink this."

Freya took the cup and sipped gently. The water was fresh and crisp, cutting into her throat.

"What was it you came here for?"

Freya looked up into the young woman's face and felt foolish. Bera must have been a few years younger than her, yet she was striding around this remote hovel and her dead grandmother without bursting into tears. "Dreams."

"Ah. Well, I'm not my grandmother, thank Thor, but I know a thing or two about dreams." Bera positioned herself next to Freya in the sand.

"What do you know about dreams?"

"That, if they affect you, they mean something, and, if they don't, then you probably ate some bad cheese."

Freya frowned in confusion before bursting out laughing. A proper laugh, this time—one that echoed out across the lake. Bera joined in.

"Bad cheese?"

"You'd be surprised."

"I'm sure I would be."

"What are you dreaming about?"

Freya considered not telling Bera, but then became acutely aware of the fact she was sitting below a glacier, outside a dead witch's home, covered in soil, bones and viscera. What did she have to lose at this point? She described the white whale and the foxes drowning as they feasted upon its corpse.

"I can see why you'd want help with that one," Bera said after listening.

"I've been having it for days, now." She picked up a stone and threw it into the lake. She heard the satisfying splash and followed the ripple as it spread across the surface, distorting the reflection.

"Dreams are Odin's way of communicating with us; maybe he is trying to warn you. Seen anything dangerous lately?"

Freya thought back to Skjalti, watching as Arinbjorn buried him, his tight back muscles quivering with exhaustion and grief. Arinbjorn. Then her mind filled up with images of Kormac. She shuddered. "Plenty of dangerous things."

"You must lead an interesting life," Bera said evenly.

Freya laughed. "You could say that."

"If I were you, I would focus on the here and now, not on your dreams. They will go, in time." She paused, before standing and heading inside the cave. She emerged a moment later with a small, flat stone in her hand. "But, if you really want to take something back, have this. Place it under your pillow. It should ward off the dreams."

Freya took the stone and flipped it over; it had a series of small runes carved into its base.

"Yngvildr used to give them to me. They helped sometimes."

Freya nodded in appreciation.

"You're welcome. Now, if you will excuse me, I need to finish cleaning out the cave. I want to get home before nightfall."

Freya stood and dusted off the dirt from her dress. She wiped her face with her sleeves. "Thank you, Bera. Do you want any help?"

"No, I'll be fine. Besides, you don't want to go through her stuff, trust me." She made a gagging face.

Smiling, Freya gripped the pebble token and made her way over to Aki, who was contentedly drinking the lake water. She pocketed the pebble and then went to mount. A shout from behind stopped her.

"Wait!" Bera's voice was shrill.

"What's wrong?"

"Can I still have the chickens?" She held up the freshly killed chickens and pouch of eggs that Freya had dropped on the ground when she fell.

Bursting into laughter, Freya nodded her consent and then jumped into Aki's saddle. The path back home would be a long one, but she felt better. She would focus on the here and now—and, right now, she wanted to see Arinbjorn.

Chapter Nine

This was not Iceland. Olaf looked out across the sea and towards the grey mist-covered isle that lay before the *Ormrinn Langi*. The grey waters frothed and foamed against jagged pieces of obsidian rock that climbed out of the sea and towered over their ship. Seagulls circled above, their cries carrying on the bitter wind. He thought that he could smell their shit even from here—it covered the tops of the stone monoliths, the basalt rock giving way to yellowing white stains. Further away, past the crumbling towers, a muddy shore awaited them.

"Where are we?" Olaf asked.

"Orkney," Thorer replied.

The captain had been mute since the disposal of Afli the day before. Olaf watched as Thorer guided the ship through the passage between the rocky outcrops and towards the shore. His grip was white and he stared hard ahead.

Since the storm of the previous day had passed, the waters surrounding these isles had become much calmer, but the ship had taken on substantial water and Thorer Klakka was concerned there may be damage to the hull. He wanted to find a safe haven to inspect the ship before continuing the journey.

Olaf was frustrated by this, but found it hard to argue, and he was not totally blind to the mood among the crew. They were all solemn and quiet. He had successfully demonstrated his strength over the old gods, but he was aware that his crew might benefit from light activity and relative rest to relax them. Orkney was as good a place as any to rest, he supposed. He had been here once before, five years ago, but all these islands looked the same.

As the ship approached the shore, Olaf spotted a small party making their way across a cliff edge. They rode small stout horses and gazed down upon the *Ormrinn Langi*.

"Sigurd the Stout rules these islands, does he not?"

"Yes. He and his family have dutifully served the King of Norway for several generations."

"Whomever that king might be," Olaf stated pointedly.

Thorer looked briefly at Olaf before returning his gaze ahead of the ship.

"Where are you taking us?"

"There should be a small village just around the back of that cliff." Thorer gestured to a large cliff face that arced around to the right.

As the ship neared the high cliffs, they gave way to a small bay with a long beach. The sands seemed grey in the morning light, the only colour coming from the grasslands that peppered the tops of the hills behind the shore. Not far from the water's edge was a small settlement no bigger than a farming village in Norway. From his vantage point on the deck, Olaf could only make out one larger building, presumably the hall of Sigurd, towards the back and away from the beach. Several smaller wooden buildings surrounded it. Soil covered their roofs and grass had been planted in the dirt. This gave the impression that these buildings had sprouted from the earth, their floral crowns still attached.

Olaf's attention was drawn to a building just off to the side of the main settlement, back and away from the beach. It was built of wood, much like the others, but several loads of stone bricks had been piled up at the base. He would recognize a boating house anywhere. He studied it for a moment.

"The *Ormrinn Langi* will not fit in there," he said at last.

Thorer handed over piloting the ship to his first mate before going to join the king. Olaf watched him study the boating house and enjoyed the look of frustration that passed across his captain's face.

"I feared as much. This is a great ship, Your Majesty, but it does make it difficult to get repairs. We will have to anchor here in the shallows. Repairs will take longer."

"How much longer?"

"To be safe? At least three days."

"Three days! We are already behind schedule thanks to that storm. Thangbrander is expecting me."

"The priest will have to wait. I will not take this ship out on open waters until all repairs are completed."

"Then perhaps I should find a new captain. One who is not a coward."

"Then you will drown with an idiot for a captain," Thorer said evenly.

Olaf stared, incredulous, at Thorer. In all their years together, the captain had never spoken to him in this manner. "You must really mean this, Thorer, to speak to me so."

Thorer nodded, and for the first time Olaf took note of the dark rings under his old friend's eyes.

"My king, I have fought by your side for many years. I have helped you unite all of Norway, and now I want to help you unite all the lands under Christ. We cannot do that dead."

"Very well." Olaf softened his voice and put his hand upon his friend's shoulder. "Take the three days. I will impose myself upon Jarl Sigurd. If he is a friend to the crown, he will not object."

Thorer raised his hand to grasp Olaf's still resting on his shoulder. He squeezed gently.

"I am sorry, my friend, for my behaviour of late," Olaf said. "Know that I would do anything to bring Christ to these lands. I am simply eager to bring Iceland to heel as soon as possible. I cannot allow the old gods any quarter. We have greater enemies than some sheep farmers with delusions of grandeur." He allowed a smile to play across his face.

"I will get you there as soon as I can, my king. I promise you that."

"I'm sorry I doubted you." With that, he turned from Thorer and walked across the deck towards the bow. As he passed the rowing berths, he took note of the men manning them. They looked haggard, their faces sallow. Each one steadfastly avoided his gaze and focused their efforts on rowing. Just before him, a young deckhand was on his hands and knees, violently scrubbing the deck. He was trying to get the stain of Afli's blood from the wood. It had flowed surprisingly far, and the stain looked like a wound upon the great ship.

*

"You should not have come here." The statement was one of fact, delivered without aggression or judgement.

Olaf stood knee-deep in the sea, facing his host, Jarl Sigurd Hlodvirsson. The icy waters lapped at his knees, the silty sand beneath his feet shifting unsteadily. The jarl had come down from his hall, no doubt alerted by the locals of the arrival of a warship in his bay. He was a tall man, yet slight of build, belying a physique built for running; he was sinewy and lithe. He could only just be at the end of his fourth decade but already he was completely bald. The only hair on his head came from a bright, if trim, ginger beard. Two green eyes shone intently at Olaf; their gaze moved to just over his shoulder and then back again.

A small retinue of guards and advisers accompanied the jarl, perhaps half a dozen men, of various ages. They were dressed in courtly tunics and cloaks, and stood close by their liege lord. They were armed, their hands resting gently on the hilts of their swords.

"You presume to speak to your king that way?" Thorer asked from Olaf's side. He had taken the king ashore personally, their small skiff bobbing listlessly behind them. Thorer held a length of rope in his hand, the other end tied to their boat. He grunted as the waves began to take the boat out to sea. None of the jarl's men stepped forward to assist.

"I presume to save the king's throne," Jarl Sigurd responded evenly.

With a gesture, he sent two of his men to help Thorer stabilize the boat and drag it to shore. Sigurd stepped forward into the sea and knelt before Olaf. The rest of his retinue followed suit. After a moment, the group rose again and Sigurd extended his hand up the beach, beckoning Olaf to lead.

"Welcome to Orkney, my king."

Olaf nodded and waded the rest of the way to the shore, the jarl falling into step beside him.

"You have a strange way of greeting here, Sigurd."

"I had to be sure it was you first; I cannot go kneeling to everyone who goes around claiming they are the King of Norway."

"You would forget the face of the man who baptized you?"

"I was underwater for most of the time," Sigurd said evenly, before breaking into a wide smile and embracing him while they walked.

Olaf laughed. "You have aged since we last met. Has it really been five years?"

"Five years of hard-fought battles, my friend."

Olaf's words seemed to weigh on Sigurd, his brow furled slightly before once again brightening. "Your ship is impressive. I had heard tales of the *Ormrinn Langi*—great serpent that stalks the waves. There is only one man who sails her: Olaf Tryggvason."

"There is no greater vessel." Olaf beamed with pride. He knew when he was being flattered, but, in this instance, it was not wrong. There was no larger vessel in the whole of the northern realms, and he had not lost a battle with her yet.

They walked into the town proper, where the earthen streets were lined with people going about their business and the air carried the familiar scent of hay and soil. Farmers and traders moved out of the way of the approaching jarl, but several stopped to observe the newcomer.

A loud crash to his left made Olaf start, his hand reaching for his sword instinctively. A hand fell on his shoulder, light but firm. It was Sigurd, who smiled thinly and directed Olaf's gaze to the culprit. A young girl—a child, really—was busy cursing as she chased after a number of carrots and parsnips that came rolling down from a broken barrel. She had dropped it. Olaf released his grip.

"The only danger you will find here is from soiled vegetables," Sigurd said warmly.

Olaf nodded, hoping his embarrassment did not show. Without commenting further, Sigurd led them up to his hall.

*

It was not the grandest hall Olaf had ever seen and he privately hoped that his own hall in Nidaross could lay claim to that. Nor was it the largest. It was, however, a very comfortable hall. The tables and benches seemed to be carved from reclaimed wood, the salt of the sea baked into them. They gave off a pleasing aroma as the hearth fire warmed up the room. It was already hot enough to take his cloak off, and he found his trousers were drying quickly in the heat. Sigurd had given him the high seat, before taking his place just to his right. The rest of the retinue followed suit, taking up their respective places. Thorer took a seat at the far end of the table. He would have had the right to sit at the king's side, but Thorer liked to sit with the lowliest members of any court they visited. He said he found drunken housecarls to be far better sources of information, and better company. Olaf envied him.

"Would you like some mead, Your Majesty?" A young woman with red hair tied neatly into corn rows appeared behind him. She had eyes the colour of dark honey. Beautiful.

"I would be delighted." He proffered his cup; she began filling it. "Who are you?"

"I am Olith."

"She is my wife," Sigurd said from his other side.

A brief flash of anger passed through Olaf. Of course she was taken. He could take her anyway, if he wanted to. The anger passed.

"Thank you, my dear." He returned his attention to Sigurd.

"She was a gift from High King Malcom."

"The Scotsman?"

"The very same. A trade to ensure I would stop raiding his lands." Sigurd looked over at his wife. "A more than worthy offering."

Olith blushed before walking around the rest of the table filling cups.

After a moment's pause, Sigurd asked, "Why are you here? We cannot be baptized again."

"My fleet and I were heading to Iceland. There are those who have not yet accepted my message of faith and I would use them in my campaign against Burislav."

"You would fight the King of the Wends with those farmers? What does it matter if they do not follow your ways?"

Olaf noticed the slip, but let it pass. "It matters because they believe themselves above Norwegian law, above Christian law." He spoke quietly, as if confessing. "But, more importantly, I need men."

"Still, I would advise postponing your conquest of them. You have bigger threats far closer to home." Sigurd spoke evenly, but Olaf could hear the entreaty behind his words.

"What do you mean?"

"I have heard word King Sweyn of Denmark moves against you."

Olaf stopped drinking. Down the table, he noticed that Thorer and stopped talking with his hosts and was listening intently. Conversation around the table slowed to a halt.

"He never forgave me for marrying Tyra..."

"He has placed a sizable bounty on your head." The table tensed. Olaf looked at the men who sat about him, a good dozen now. While their swords had been taken from them before dinner, each man carried his sax knife. More than enough.

"Do you intend to claim it?"

Sigurd drank languidly from his cup, his gulps seeming to echo throughout the hall. He finished his mead, burped, and placed the cup gently before him, his hands clearly above the table.

"I will not betray my king for mere gold, and I doubt Sweyn has a woman the equal of Olith." He looked evenly at Olaf. "You are safe here, but you are not safe. You must return to Nidaross to prepare for his plans."

"What is he planning?" Olaf asked, trying to keep the rising concern out of his voice.

"I do not know. I only know from passing traders and raiders who use us as a port: Sweyn is amassing a flotilla."

"I do not wish to abandon my efforts in Iceland. Priest Thangbrander is expecting me."

"We can attend to that duty, Your Majesty. I will send a ship to aid this Thangbrander."

Thorer rose from his seat at the far end of the table. "With your permission, Your Majesty, I will see to the repairs of the *Ormrinn Langi* immediately."

Olaf nodded solemnly. "I would appreciate your haste in this matter."

Thorer bowed, and then was gone—a chill wind entering the hall as he opened the door. It seemed to linger long after he had departed.

Olaf passed his gaze over the amassed retinue of Sigurd, acutely aware that he was now alone. They were an ugly bunch. He suspected most of them were not that old, but the seafaring life had left them looking haggard, their skin tired and leathery. Were it not for the different lengths and colours of their beards, he would barely be able to tell them apart. They looked evenly at Olaf.

"Which of these men would you trust the most, Sigurd?" Olaf asked, speaking clearly and confidently. Hoping to portray strength.

"Gunnar Steinsson." Sigurd gestured to a man at the far end of the table, who stood to attention. He was short and squat, but seemed to be solid muscle. He had a long brown beard, which he had braided, and it flowed seamlessly into his hair. A long scar across his forehead served to give him a formidable appearance. "He is the finest captain of my fleet."

"Would you serve your king?" Olaf asked Gunnar directly.

"It would be an honour." The voice was deep and raspy, as if someone had cut his throat and failed.

"How soon can you depart for Iceland?"

"I have a ship that can leave today. We will find this Thangbrander and assist him."

"Good. I suggest you get started."

Gunnar nodded and departed the table, a few housecarls leaving with him.

"Until my ship is ready, I will remain here in your hall," Olaf stated.

"Of course, Your Majesty." Sigurd made a small gesture behind him and food began to arrive on the table, thralls appearing from the shadows to dispense drinks.

"While we wait, tell me everything you have heard about Sweyn."

*

The sea had begun to turn again, the dark grey waves growing larger in size. It took the better part of half an hour to row the skiff back to the *Ormrinn Langi*. His brief examination of the ship before going to shore with Olaf had revealed some minor damage to the hull, and the main sail was torn in a few places. Most of the work would simply be emptying the vessel of the water it had taken on. Still, it was slow work out at sea.

Once aboard, he set about issuing orders to the crew and examining what repairs had already begun. As he strode about the deck, he came across the red stain that lined the port side. Afli's blood. He stopped for a moment and observed it. The scrubber had done a good job, but he could see where the boy's organs had spooled out. He suppressed a gag at the memory.

On a whim, he abruptly changed course and headed down into the hold, making his way to their brig. He stopped outside the only occupied cell. At first, he could not see Einar, the darkness of the hold obscuring his vision. Eventually, he heard a small rustle, and the gaunt grey man stepped out from the shadows. With his long white hair, bony physique, and tattered clothes, he looked like a pale wraith. Einar simply stared at him, grief and anger spread across his features. He had not spoken since his son's death.

"I wanted to say I am sorry," Thorer said, after a long silence.

Einar did not respond.

"Your son did not deserve his fate."

Einar simply stared at him.

"If you had just kept your mouth shut…" Thorer ran his hand through his hair agitatedly. "Why did you have to bring the old gods into this?"

Still nothing.

"Gods damnit, man—say something!"

Einar approached the cell door.

Despite himself, Thorer backed off, bumping into the hull behind him.

Einar's old, wrinkled face was slack, but his eyes shone brightly. Cracked lips parted to reveal yellowed teeth. "I curse you, Thorer Klakka—you and your king." He spat the last word. "All you have built will be taken from you and the sea will be your grave, as it was my son's." With that, Einar retreated once again into the darkness and disappeared.

Chapter Ten

The church was small to Arinbjorn's eyes. Hallr's hall, converted into this place of worship for the Christians, barely counted as such. It was squat, and the earthen roof sagged in the middle, the weight of the snow causing it to bow. It looked like a sea slug he had once seen, black and slick with slime, washed upon the shore when he was a boy. It had lain there, rotting in the ice and sand. Even then, he had thought it an ill omen.

"Welcome, friends." The priest's voice was deep and gravelly, yet his tone was joyous. He stood outside Hallr's hall, draped in a simple white robe and holding a shepherd's crozier. It looked like he had carved it himself from a large branch. The morning wind caught his robe, causing it to billow out; Arinbjorn saw glimpses of a sax knife still affixed to the priest's waist, and a longer blade discreetly tucked away under the folds.

It had been an early start. A day had passed since the invitation to Thorgeir's hall and his interrogation of the local chieftains. They had returned home, the storm having abated enough to warrant the journey, and Arinbjorn preferred to face down Thor's wrath than stay any longer as Thorgeir's guest.

They had slept poorly that night. Sigvaldi had been restless, tossing and turning in the bed next to his own. Once or twice, he had let out a low moan as his dreams got the better of him. Arinbjorn had simply lain still, staring at the roof beams and watching the shadows of the dying hearth fire dance across earth and hay. He was exhausted, yet sleep would not come to him. Instead, he had thought about their encounter with the chieftains and this Christian priest.

He was concerned about the ease with which Thangbrander had proffered information, and the general recalcitrance of the chieftains. He wondered whether they would be so difficult had it been one of their own families murdered. These political troubles were supposed to have been left behind in Norway.

Sleep eventually claimed him in the early hours, but, tired as he was, he knew he had to come to see Thangbrander and hear his claims. He returned his attention to the priest before him. While he could not see it, the biting wind brought with it the smell of salt, which meant the sea could not be far. He cast his gaze about the rest of Hallr's farmstead, eager to see if anyone had watched their arrival with interest. There were a few people who had arrived ahead of them, greeting the priest warmly, before disappearing inside the hall. The outbuildings were still being used for the animals; he spotted half a dozen pigs and more sheep. The clucking coming from a small shack behind the hall implied chickens too. His farmstead, while small, was surprisingly well stocked. He had not known Hallr was so wealthy.

As he thought this, the man himself emerged from the hall, red faced and wheezing, and approached the priest. He whispered something in his ear before returning back inside. Looking at the size of the man, Sigvaldi reconsidered his disbelief at the abundance of livestock. He had a peculiar gait that favoured his left leg, and his short, thinning, hair clung to his scalp as though it feared a light breeze might take it off completely.

"I am glad you both could make it," Thangbrander said as Arinbjorn and Sigvaldi stopped before him. He stretched out a hand towards Arinbjorn. "God be with you."

Arinbjorn stared at him mutely for a second.

Thangbrander retracted his hand. "Perhaps a little early for that."

"We have not come to learn about your god," Arinbjorn stated flatly.

"You said you had some information for us?" Sigvaldi said, a little more gently. "Would you prefer a more private meeting?"

Thangbrander nodded in appreciation. "Indeed. Perhaps you could stay for Mass? I will be able to speak freely afterwards."

He paused and addressed Sigvaldi directly: "And you may learn something more of our God."

Sigvaldi recited, "*Anima Christi, sanctifica me. Corpus Christi, salva me. Sanguis Christi, inebria me.*"

"Soul of Christ, sanctify me. Body of Christ, save me. Blood of Christ, inebriate me," Thangbrander translated, eyes wide. "You know Latin?"

"You are not the first missionary I have met."

"Indeed? Perhaps I will be more successful. Please, come inside; I believe the last of our congregation has arrived for the day." Thangbrander used his crozier to gesture inside and began herding the pair of them within.

"Are you done showing off?" Arinbjorn said quietly to Sigvaldi.

"It never hurts to understand the enemy, Ari."

"So long as you don't become them."

Sigvaldi stopped dead, just before the threshold, and placed his hand out to stop Arinbjorn moving in further. The priest almost walked into the back on them.

"Would you mind going ahead of us, Thangbrander? I would speak with Arinbjorn."

"Not at all." He looked between the two of them. "I need a moment to prepare, anyway." He moved on ahead of them, casting a curious glance behind him.

Once the priest was out of earshot, Sigvaldi turned to face Arinbjorn, his face hard and his mouth pulled taught into a snarl. Arinbjorn had only rarely seen Sigvaldi's anger, and it had never been directed at him. It shook him.

"Do not speak to me like that again." Sigvaldi's words were laced with his hurt.

"What—?"

"I have been nothing but supportive of you and your endeavours. To imply that I may turn against you, or our ways here, is an insult to my name."

Arinbjorn watched as his friend squared to fight the point, his jaw clenching and his green eyes focusing in anger. The look faded, and his face eased into a softer, sadder, aspect. Arinbjorn could see the darkness under his friend's eyes.

"I am sorry, Sig." His whole body seemed to quiver. "I forget myself." He cast his gaze towards the floor and hung his head.

Sigvaldi brought his arm back, releasing Arinbjorn. "I know. That is why you need the council of those you can trust. Forget them and you really are lost."

"It will not happen again." He meant it.

Sigvaldi smiled gently and placed his hands upon his Arinbjorn's shoulders. "We will catch this murderer. Together."

Arinbjorn grasped Sigvaldi's arms and held them tight. "Together, then."

With that, the pair broke apart and entered the church.

The hall was densely packed with a good fifty people. Arinbjorn had no idea Christianity was so popular. The small space and dense crowd meant the smell of sweat and damp clothes hung heavy on the air. He shuffled uncomfortably as he cast his gaze about the crowd, wondering whether he would recognize anyone. The benches and tables had all been turned to face the far end, where two seats and a small wooden table faced out. As such, it was mostly scalps and hair lines he could see. He did spot Gizurr the White, his thick white hair giving him away almost immediately. He was standing towards the front but at the furthest edge of the room with his wife, Saehild, and another man. Their faces were in profile, but somewhat obscured in the dim light; nonetheless, Arinbjorn thought he recognized the man. It was Hjalti, a tall, almost skeletal figure, whose shock of red hair made him stand out among the congregation. If Arinbjorn remembered correctly, he had married Gizurr's daughter recently.

Sigvaldi seemed to have noticed also.

"What are Gizurr and Hjalti doing hiding in the dark? Shouldn't they be right at the front?" he asked.

"Gizurr doesn't look very happy. He is not talking to anyone."

"He was absent from Thorgeir's gathering, too."

Their conversation was interrupted by the booming voice of Thangbrander. Deep, coarse, but full of joviality this morning, it reverberated throughout the hall. He was standing before the small table at the head of the room, with Hallr behind him to his right.

"In the name of the Father, the Son and the Holy Spirit." He made a cross-like gesture before the gathered flock.

"Amen," the crowd replied in unison.

"The Lord be with you."

"And also with you." The rhythmic recitation by the gathered farmers unsettled Arinbjorn.

"Welcome, one and all, to another Mass here in this beautiful space." He turned to acknowledge Hallr, who smiled brightly through his rosy face. "Today I see we have some new faces—don't be shy; all are welcome here."

The crowd turned to face Arinbjorn and Sigvaldi, a ripple of smiles and nods spreading about them. The pair nodded politely and shuffled on their feet. The crowd returned their attention to the front. All except Gizurr, who stared intently at the two of them. Arinbjorn looked into the old man's eyes and held his gaze. Eventually, Gizurr broke contact and turned away.

"Brethren, let us acknowledge our sins, and so prepare ourselves to celebrate the sacred mysteries." Thangbrander retreated behind the table and took his seat before the congregation. Once he was sitting, everyone joined him, Arinbjorn and Sigvaldi taking a moment to follow suit. Now they were all seated, Arinbjorn could see the makeshift altar more clearly. It had a small wooden cup and bowl, with a jug off to the side with a loaf of bread.

"Are we going to watch him eat?" Sigvaldi whispered to Arinbjorn, who could not help but smile.

Thangbrander began again: "Have mercy on us, O Lord, for we have sinned against you. Show us, O Lord, your mercy and grant us your salvation. May Almighty God forgive us our sins and bring us to everlasting life. Amen."

"What is this about everlasting life?" Arinbjorn uttered.

"I assume it's like going to Valhalla."

"But you have to die to go to Valhalla."

The pair of them spent the remainder of the Mass confused and lost. There seemed to be a lot of movement, with people standing and sitting seemingly at random and lots of repeating whatever Thangbrander happened to say.

Arinbjorn decided to spend the time observing those around him. He saw now that they were mostly thralls, or poorer farmers—those who tilled the land of the more powerful chieftains. Only one of whom was present here: Gizurr.

Gizurr was proving interesting to watch. He spent most of the time staring straight ahead, as if ignoring Thangbrander, and when the crowd was uttering one of many recitations, his lips barely moved.

"Something is wrong with Gizurr," Arinbjorn stated.

"How do you mean?"

"He seems distracted."

"Wouldn't this bore you, too?"

"Yes, but Gizurr was the first ever chieftain to be baptized and has been a vocal supporter of Christianity ever since."

"So why would he look so unhappy in church?"

"Exactly. I should speak with him once Mass finishes. If it ever finishes."

"And what of Thangbrander?"

"You speak with him." Before Sigvaldi could respond, Arinbjorn continued, "You are the smartest man I know, Sig, and it is clear you are more learned in his faith than I. See what the priest has to say—I trust your judgement in this matter."

"If you are sure." Sigvaldi smiled thinly and looked up to the still-proselytizing priest.

Arinbjorn stared at the side of Gizurr's head. "I am sure."

*

Eventually, finally, the Mass came to an end. Arinbjorn broke away from Sigvaldi, leaving him to speak with the priest alone, and quickly made his way outside. He wanted to get ahead of the crowd and seize the opportunity to speak with Gizurr when he emerged. The sun had risen significantly since they entered, its cool bright rays reflecting off the snow that blanketed the farm, and Arinbjorn winced as his eyes adjusted to the light. He waited by the sty, propping himself up against the wall to watch the crowd leaving the hall.

They came out slowly and formed large, chattering groups. The priest stood outside, shaking hands and laughing heartily to whatever was being said. The stream of people came to a low ebb. There was no sign of Gizurr. Confused, Arinbjorn moved away from the sty and the sound of squealing pigs, rushing over to a thrall who was carrying some grain.

A voice, light yet strong, came from behind: "Looking for me, son of Thorleikr?"

Arinbjorn whipped around, his hand instinctively reaching for the sax knife at his waist. He stopped. Gizurr stood before him, calm, hands raised. His blue eyes seemed bright in the mid-morning light. He was not that old, but the combination of weathered skin and pure white hair made him look far older. He was smaller than Arinbjorn, and wider. Unlike Hallr, however, his breadth was clearly more down to muscle than fat. Arinbjorn eased out of his stance and straightened himself up.

"Why do you ask?" He felt foolish bluffing.

"Because you were staring at me during the whole Mass."

Arinbjorn gave up the pretence. "How did you even get out?"

"Hallr's hall has two doors," Gizurr stated evenly.

Arinbjorn groaned and ran his hand through his hair.

"So you *were* looking for me."

"I just wanted to talk. You did not seem very happy in there."

Gizurr smiled a thin smile and began walking away, but Arinbjorn fell into step beside him. He was heading over to the pitching post where his family had tied their steeds. Saehild was brushing down a chestnut beast twice the size of her, while Hjalti was busy tightening the straps on his saddle.

"It just seemed strange; you have been such a supporter of Christianity here. I thought you would be happy."

Gizurr stopped in his tracks. "Why should I be happy when Christians are being murdered and the flock is being called to yet more violence?"

"You disagree with Thangbrander's methods?"

"Christ is about forgiveness. Not violence."

"Then why are you here?"

"Because I believe in Christ. He is our only hope in these dark times."

"I don't believe you."

Gizurr bristled, his body tensing under his cloak and tunic.

"Not that you don't believe in Christ," Arinbjorn hastened to add. "But you are renowned for being a practical man. An honest man. You are here for more than just vain hope."

Gizurr did not answer for a moment. Instead, the wind whistled past, carrying the scent of manure and hay from the barn.

"Why are you and your friend here?" he asked at last.

"Thangbrander offered me information on the murderer."

Gizurr's eyes widened. "Did he, now?"

"This surprises you?"

"Why would a priest know anything about the identity of a Christian killer?"

Before Arinbjorn could reply, he was cut off by Hjalti: "We must leave here, Gizurr."

Gizurr's son-in-law was tall and lithe, and his angular face regarded Arinbjorn with suspicion before looking back upon Hallr's hall. Arinbjorn followed his gaze, but saw nothing but the talking priest disappearing inside with Sigvaldi.

Gizurr acknowledged his son-in-law with a nod and began to ready his horse.

"Wait! Perhaps he doesn't trust the chieftains to act if he brought this information to them."

"Perhaps." Gizurr mounted his horse, patting its black mane gently. "I respect Thangbrander a great deal, but these murders have made him too ready to deal out death and violence. His sermons grow more aggressive." Gizurr and his family began to move away from Hallr's hall, with Arinbjorn walking beside them.

"You're concerned he will encourage others to lash out?"

"I worry you are caught up in something far larger than the tragedy of Skjalti. You are angry and looking for somewhere to bury a blade. That can be easily appropriated."

Arinbjorn opened his mouth, but, before he could ask further questions, Gizurr cut him off.

"No more. Not here. If you wish to speak further on this matter, you are welcome on my farm. But be careful." With that, Gizurr spurred his horse onwards.

Arinbjorn watched as they rode off towards the south-west. Frustrated, he made his way back to the hall.

Sigvaldi practically ran him down as he came barging out of the main entrance.

"Ari! I might have something." He continued to stride away from the farm, fidgeting with his sax knife and holding a large bundle of cloth in his hands.

"You have something? What did Thangbrander tell you?" Arinbjorn asked, trying to keep up with his friend.

"He gave me this." He tossed the cloth to Arinbjorn, who caught it awkwardly.

Arinbjorn stopped and stared as his friend made haste away from him. He turned around to look back upon Hallr's hall; Thangbrander was standing on the threshold, leaning on his crozier and watching them leave, his face impassive. Arinbjorn gave him one last look before casting his gaze down at the cloth. It was a woollen cloak, inlaid with an intricate diamond pattern on the outside. Down the middle, filling the length of the cloak, there was a golden cross with hand-stitched images of figures Arinbjorn did not recognize. He unfurled it, holding it before him, and allowed the wind to catch it. He stared at it as it flapped in the breeze.

"What is this?" Arinbjorn rushed to catch up with Sigvaldi.

"That is one of the priest's vestments." Sigvaldi struggled to say the foreign word.

"I don't understand."

"It's the cloth the Christian priests wear during their ceremonies. Thangbrander showed me his collection. He said one had been stolen, along with some other items of value. A *blue* one."

Arinbjorn stopped. *Blue.* The same colour as the rare cloth they found outside Thorgeir's hall. He looked to Sigvaldi, who clearly saw the recognition upon his friend's face.

"Yes. We find that vestment, Ari, we find our killer. We find that vestment, and you can avenge Skjalti.

Chapter Eleven

Conall let out a roar as he heaved the final log beam up to Fergus. His younger brother, the lighter of the two, had clambered on to the roof of the collapsed pigsty, where he was taking the replacement beams and securing them in their rightful place. It was a long process and the pair were working up a sweat. Despite the cold, Conall had removed his tunic. It had been a dry day, the snowstorms of the previous few nights having given away to a bright, cloudless sky. Still, it was brisk, and the scars that criss-crossed Conall's torso were bright pink in the chill.

It had taken them the better part of the morning to find and trim appropriate pieces of wood that could be repurposed to reconstruct the collapsed roof. The beams that Freya had directed them to use had been rotten and brittle in places. They had decided it would be best if they carved out the rot and lashed the good lengths together to ensure a more stable long-term solution. If the roof collapsed again and, gods help them, killed a pig, Njall would never make them free men.

Conall may have had the strength, but his brother had more finesse with a blade, so Fergus had taken charge of the whittling while his brother hacked and heaved the old beams out of their original slots in the abandoned shack. In this way, they made good progress and, by late afternoon, they had finished half of the roof. Failend had come out repeatedly to bring the men some broth and bread; she kept shifting her gaze to the east, down to where Kormac's farm lay.

"Don't worry, Failend," Conall said through a mouthful of bread. "We will see him coming."

"I'm just worried about Miss Freya being out on her own."

"She is a smart one; she will be OK."

"She should be back already."

Conall looked about the farm. It was getting dark. The tip of the white sun was already disappearing below the horizon and long shadows stretched about them. He suspected they would have to finish the roof the next day now. It would be unwise to continue.

He wiped the sweat off his brow with his tunic before putting it back on.

"Would you like me and Fergus to go looking for her?" he asked.

"Why are you dragging me into this?"

Conall ignored his brother. "Failend?"

She turned back to face him, the concern palpable on her face. "Would you?"

"Of course!" He shouted it in an effort to reassure. "Come along, brother."

"Walking around on the plains at night is a bad idea."

"And Miss Freya is out in it."

Fergus stopped arguing, a look of contemplation passing over his angular face. Conall usually found it comical to see him think. "I will saddle the horses," he said at last. He shuffled to the edge of the roof and dropped down next to Conall and Failend, kicking up a cloud of fine snow on his landing.

Conall slapped his brother on the back. "Good man. We do this, we may even be free men before the next harvest." He gave Failend his most reassuring smile and set off towards the stables.

*

The moon had only just risen when Conall realized they were being followed. The ride out from Njall's farm had been slow going. They were not allowed to take the best horses, and so were left riding two older, tired mares. Conall's was all skin and bone, her poor mane flat and balding. He had called her Máire, after their mother; she too had been an indomitable beast who refused to die. He had loved her dearly. Fergus rode a reddish

Icelandic horse, who was squat yet hardy, renowned more for brute strength than speed.

They had set off down into the valley before turning north-east towards Freya's destination. While the sky was the clear and the moon bright, the snowfall from the previous few nights had blanketed the ground, making it a slow journey through the glittering ice fields. Stars began to emerge in the sky, a beautiful band of diamonds that reminded Conall of the Bifröst, the rainbow road that linked Midgard, the human world, and Asgard, the land of the gods. He had stopped to take in the vista when he heard the tell-tale shuffling of a horse making its way through the snow behind them.

"Fergus," he whispered. "Stop."

His brother, who had been ahead of him carving a way through the packed snow, came to a halt and gave him an exasperated look. "What?" He hissed.

"Listen."

Fergus cocked his head, his red hair falling off his face.

Conall did the same, listening more carefully this time. The horse was going slowly—slower than it had to if it was following the trail they were leaving behind them.

"What is that?" Fergus asked.

"Someone is following us," Conall whispered, while making a hand gesture for his brother to quieten down.

"Could it be Freya?"

"Why would she be behind us?"

"Good point. What shall we do?"

Conall thought for a moment and cast his gaze over the moonlit fields before him. The wind had picked up and flurries of snow danced across the low undulating hills. A small copse of ash trees caught his eye, a hundred or so yards off to the right, where they dipped down into a small valley flanked by some of the larger hills.

"There." Conall pointed to the copse. "We will wait for them in there."

Fergus simply nodded and the pair of them changed course, now heading directly east judging by the position of Odin's Wagon in the sky. It was still slow going, thanks to the densely packed snow, but they managed to reach the trees with some time to spare. Acting quickly, they dismounted their horses, tying them to a tree on the edge of the copse so that their tracker could easily spot them, and then ducked down low to the ground. The ash trees loomed over them; their spindly branches were devoid of leaves, but long icicles had formed, spiking out sideways as the wind had caught the limited moisture and formed daggers. It looked like the trees were wrapped in blades.

They laid low for a time and kept an eye on the trail they had left through the snow. Their horses whinnied listlessly and attempted to find something to eat, their mouths nuzzling at the ground. Eventually, they heard the crunching of earth and snow as something made its way down the path. Conall put his finger to his lips and pulled his sax knife from his belt. Fergus already had his out.

The figure continued to approach. It wasn't until it was practically upon them that they identified it. It was another horse, taller and stouter than theirs, and clearly in better health. It was pure white and seemed to radiate a blue hue in the moon's light. There was no rider, the saddle empty. She made her way down to their charges and joined them in looking for food.

A snap of a twig right behind them caused Conall to flinch, and he rolled on to his back just in time to see a blade come flashing down, digging deep into the earth where he had been a moment ago. A figure, hooded and cloaked, loomed over them, his face obscured by the darkness.

"Fergus!" Conall shouted.

The hooded figure leapt back and swung out a second time, the moonlight glinting off the steel. It was an axe. The blade buried itself in Conall's thigh. He screamed. The attacker yanked the axe out and pulled back for a third strike as blood gushed from the wound. Conall could simply stare.

The blade never fell, as Fergus threw himself at this would-be murderer, careening into his side and tackling him to the ground. The masked figure let out a surprised grunt as he fell back into the snow.

Conall began to drag himself away from the fight. He was surprised that he wasn't feeling much pain, but there was no strength in his left leg. It was going numb. Turning on to his front, he used his arms to crawl through the snow, leaving a slick, wet trail behind him.

He could hear the shouting and cursing of his brother as he fought, the thwacks of flesh against fist filling the small wood. Conall did not stop to look back; he knew his brother was a good fighter. He pawed frantically at the ice and dirt, his fingers wet with his own blood, heading for their horses. They had been spooked by all the noise and were adding their own cries and stamps, but so far had not managed to break free of their tethers.

He had just made it to the edge of the copse when someone yanked his wounded leg. He let out a cry and tried to turn on to his back, arms thrashing wildly, hoping to hit anything. The attacker was dragging him into the woods. Conall looked about desperately for his brother. He saw him, lying against a tree, breathing sporadically. An axe was buried deep in his chest. He was staring, wide eyed, at Conall.

"Brother…" It was barely a whisper. Blood seeped out of the sides of Fergus's mouth.

Conall howled. Summoning what strength he had, he reached for the murderer's hand and pulled him down. With a loud grunt, the attacker hit the ground, his hood falling away, revealing the face.

"You!" Conall should have known. Of course it was him.

The figure smiled—a yellowed, broken, smile that seemed to fill his whole pockmarked face. His two black eyes didn't even blink.

Conall headbutted him. The crack sent white-hot light through his vision, but he could feel the killer's nose give way as warm blood spurted out all over his own face. The killer pulled back, snarling. Conall looked about him. There, just to his left, lay a discarded sax knife—his brother's or his own, it did not matter. He reached for it.

His fingertips graced the hilt, but the snow and blood gave him little purchase. He tried to wiggle out from under his attacker, but his strength had left him. He could no longer feel his leg at all and his mind was growing dim. He turned to look one more time at his brother. Fergus's eyes were open, but they were still and his chest had stopped moving, the axe blade no longer rising and falling with his ragged breaths. Conall had never before wept as an adult. He wept now.

With one last heave, he dragged himself towards the sax knife. He looked back up at his killer and saw that he had managed to recuperate, his bloodied face a black mask in the moonlight. Fingers gripping tightly, Conall sat up and, harnessing every drop of power left in him, he drove the blade deep into the attacker's side. The look of shock on his killer's face would carry him over into darkness. A sense of calm fell about Conall, as the last of his energy drained away and the edges of his vision closed in.

*

The trek back from the glacial lake, and her unexpected encounter with Bera, had been an intentionally slow one. Freya's mind was still reeling from her conversation with the young witch. She had not been what Freya had expected, but she had given her much to think about. So, instead of heading straight back, Freya had decided to take a longer route through the hills. It had been a beautiful day—one of those rare days when she could not see a cloud in the sky, the blue so perfect she thought she could see the edge of Ginnungagap itself.

It was not until night when she finally came within sight of her farm. She knew it was dangerous being out alone, but Njall had *left* her alone. Besides, she had Aki. The young horse had been happy enough on the trek out to the old witch, but was now tired and belligerent. Gods help anyone who came between him and his rest, Freya thought with a smile.

The stars were out and the green curtain of aurora light ducked and weaved its way across the sky. She came to the top of a hill across from her home and looked down into the valley between them. The limited light drew her attention to a set of tracks that were heading out towards her, before veering sharply to the east. At first, she thought they were hers from when she had set out in the morning, but even from this vantage point she could see they were fresh. Besides, she had not stopped in the copse of trees that lay at the end of the trail. As she continued to gaze at the tracks, she saw something moving: two figures were running about wildly. She frowned. They were horses. *Her* horses. The ones she had given to Conall and Fergus.

She felt a weight in her chest and her hands held firm to Aki's reins. She watched as the two horses ran about the valley below, tossing their heads back and neighing. Something was wrong. With a firm kick to Aki's rump, she set off towards the copse of trees.

As she approached, the wind whistled through the frozen trees. Howling. Screaming. She stopped and dismounted Aki, stroking him to keep him calm before setting off towards the rogue horses. They had clearly been tied to a tree but had managed to break free in their distress, their leads whipping about them as they ran around frantically.

Freya was going to reach out and try to bring them down when the sound of snapping wood dragged her attention to the copse.

"Who goes there!" She tried to keep her voice calm and assertive. "This is my husband's land. Show yourselves!" Her hand had been resting on her sax knife. She unsheathed it now. A snow-white figure leapt out of the forest and dashed about her feet. Freya screamed and leapt out of the way as the tiny white fox ran off into the night. She began to laugh at the absurdity of being scared by such a small creature, but caught herself as she saw something in the beast's mouth before it disappeared. It looked like a finger.

Her chest was tight now and her breathing rapid. She tried to steady herself, but a sick, heavy feeling lay in her stomach. Holding the sax knife ahead of her, she approached the copse, her hand shaking.

Slowly, her eyes adjusted to the gloom. The silver light of the moon through the branches froze the scene before her as if in glass. Freya looked out upon the dead and mutilated bodies of Conall and Fergus. She screamed.

Chapter Twelve

The arrow hit with such force it pierced the young sailor's skull and embedded itself in the mast, pinning him in place. His body twitched and convulsed, his one good eye wide open in shock. Olaf watched as he went slack, his longbow clattering to the deck. The king had been mid instruction to the sailor when the first volley hit the *Ormrinn Langi*. He had told him to get down. Too late now, idiot.

Olaf crouched behind the taffrail as another volley arced over his head. He watched as the sunlight momentarily darkened, as if a cloud had passed above, before the hail of arrows fell down upon his ship and crew. Most of his men were beneath their shields, but there were still one or two cries of pain as some arrows found their mark.

"More speed!" Thorer Klakka shouted from his position up on the forecastle. He was piloting the ship, refusing to leave for the relative safety and cover of the taffrail. The drummers, whose beat was deep and rhythmic, found a quicker pace, one that shook Olaf's bones. The sixty seamen in the rowing benches cried out as one as they tried to match the pace. Their arms were straining, muscle and sinew stretching to breaking point as they heaved their great oars and dragged the *Ormrinn Langi* through the water.

"We cannot outrun them!" Olaf shouted. "We are too heavy." Wind buffeted the ship and spittle coated his face.

Thorer turned to look at his king and gave a manic grin. "We are not trying to outrun them."

Olaf stared at his captain and understood the implication. God Almighty.

"Brace!" Olaf shouted, his instruction lost on the roar of the wind and battering waves.

Daring to peer over the taffrail, Olaf raised himself slightly and watched as Thorer began to angle towards the nearest attacking *knarr*. The two longships that had ambushed them were smaller and lighter than the *Ormrinn*, relying on speed rather than brute strength. If Thorer could just get *close* enough…

*

It had not meant to go like this. The departure from Orkney had been a relaxed affair. Sigurd had been the consummate host, sending Captain Gunnar immediately to Iceland to collect Priest Thangbrander and providing food and warmth for Olaf's exhausted crew. In the end, they had spent two days in the company of Sigurd. He proved to be an entertaining sort, putting on wrestling competitions and encouraging his court skald to write a verse in honour of their kingly guest. Despite his rising anxiety about the news of King Sweyn's designs against him, and his frustration at having to turn back from Iceland, the two days passed by pleasantly enough. Still, when Thorer reported at the end of the second day that he was content with the repairs, Olaf began recalling his men and ordered that the ship be made ready to sail immediately.

"It is unwise to leave for a journey at night, especially around these isles," Sigurd had said as he stood upon the sandy shore surrounded by his retinue. He made no move to stop Olaf, but equally had not instructed his men to help the preparation either. The wind had picked up during the day and the waves were crashing upon the cliff face behind them. The water was ink black in the low, evening light.

"You have been a loyal and generous host, Sigurd," Olaf began. "But I will wait no longer. If what you say is true—"

"It is true, Your Majesty."

"Then I have little time to waste," Olaf finished curtly.

Sigurd simply nodded and turned to whisper to his wife, Olith. She was stood beside him, red hair billowing out behind her, looking resplendent in a green dress. Not for the first time this trip, Olaf envied Sigurd.

Olith walked forward carrying an item wrapped in cloth. She stood before Olaf and smiled. "For you, our king. To remember that Orkney and its isles are loyal to the true King of Norway." She opened the cloth and revealed a sword. It shone brightly, even in the half-light of the dying sun. The blade curved out in the shape of an elongated leaf, the hilt a dark red wood inlaid with gold bands. It was beautiful.

"Thank you. It is almost as beautiful as you."

Olith blushed and returned to the side of her husband.

"And thank you, Sigurd. This will not be forgotten."

Sigurd nodded his bald head. "If you insist on leaving, do so now, before the tide turns. And watch out for raiding ships— these isles present a good opportunity for ambush. A lot of rock for cover." He gestured to the cliffs and exposed stacks of rock about him.

Thorer Klakka had spoken then, his coarse voice hard even against the sound of waves: "Come, my king. We are ready." He gestured to waiting boat that would return them to the *Ormrinn*. Olaf gave one more glance to his jarl before wading into the sea.

*

The attack, when it came, was at dawn. The journey out from Orkney had been simple enough, despite Sigurd's warning. Leaving at night *was* dangerous, especially with the broken rock stacks that peppered the water surrounding the isle, so Thorer had guided the ship south and east, out and away from the main islands and into open water, before angling the ship due east and back home. As eager as he was to return, Olaf did not want a repeat of the journey that landed him in Orkney, so he instructed the men to take shifts on the rowing, ensuring that they would be well rested for a storm, or worse.

While the wind had been heavy during the night, and the waves powerful, the sky was clear. Olaf stood at the bow of the ship and stared up at the band of gold that stretched across the sky. He never grew tired of the view. Once, long ago, when he had been held prisoner as a young boy by Estonian pirates, he had looked up at the stars from the deck of their ship. Ever since then, the sight of Odin's Wagon or Aurvandill's Toe brought him comfort.

He felt he needed comfort at the moment. Too many things were going wrong: first, the failed journey to Iceland and Thangbrander's limited inroads there; second, the threat of Sweyn. While he was convinced Sweyn could be dealt with, he didn't like this seeming turn in fortune. So, he stared. He was looking at the bright Toe when he spotted something at the very edge of his vision.

Red was just beginning to colour the horizon, casting a warm glow over the black waves, when two shapes formed in the growing morning light. It was hard to see what they were, but Olaf instinctively knew they were ships. They could be nothing else.

"Captain!" Olaf shouted back along the ship. The cry made the rowers jump and one or two pulled unnecessarily heavily. The ship lurched.

Thorer began to make his way down the length of the ship, passing his men and issuing instructions. He had taken Sigurd's warning seriously and ensured the men were fully armed and armoured since their stay in Orkney. Those who were principal combatants rose from their rest and took positions along the side of the ship. By the time Thorer had reached the bow, the ship was on full alert. Olaf was once again reminded of the efficiency and capability of his captain.

"What do you see?" Thorer asked. His voice was steady, but Olaf could hear the tension.

"Two ships. Coming right for us."

Thorer looked past his king and eyed the approaching vessels. "Looks like two *knarrs*."

"Trading ships?"

"No. They are riding too high on the water. No trade captain would leave without a full complement of wares." He gave Olaf a hard stare. "Raiders. Possibly Sweyn."

"How did they find us?"

"I do not know. Shall I turn us about?"

Olaf considered it for a moment. The ships were approaching fast; he could begin to make out details on the vessels. There were around thirty oars each, and their respective sails bore red and white stripes. If the *Ormrinn Langi* continued straight, it could be easily surround, and, if it turned about, the raiders would be upon them before they could regain momentum. He looked around for inspiration. To the north, a few knots away, the last of the Orkney islands was coming into view.

"Take us towards Hollandstoun."

"You intend to beach?" Thorer asked, incredulous.

"No, but we may be able to hem them in against the coast."

Thorer grinned. It was a manic, violent grin. He began issuing orders and the great ship turned to face the last of the islands. Olaf unsheathed his new blade—now was as good a time as any to try it out.

*

"Brace!" Thorer shouted again.

The crew of the *Ormrinn* shouted their confirmation. Those who were rowing held tight to their oars, and the archers on deck ducked behind the taffrail, steadying themselves for the impact. Olaf looked out at the bow of the ship, the serpent head at the prow angled straight towards the attacking *knarr*.

Thorer was a fine seaman, and a clever tactician, but it wasn't until this moment that Olaf appreciated his captain's terrible genius. Olaf had suggested they bring the ship into the shallower waters around the isle of Hollandstoun, hoping that they might be able to use the island for cover and limit the ability of the attacking ships to surround them. This had worked. Their attackers were forced to stick to their starboard side as their port was angled towards the rocky shore. They were still outnumbered, but at least they were not surrounded. Volleys of arrows had been fired between the ships, but, thanks to the thicker hull of the *Ormrinn Langi*, casualties had been limited. Olaf counted eight dead on his ship, and had spotted perhaps a dozen spread among their attackers who had fallen. In the game of attrition, the attackers still had the odds. Olaf needed a miracle.

Thorer had provided that miracle.

Thorer feinted a last desperate retreat, angling the *Ormrinn Langi* out to sea and abandoning their cover. With their port side now exposed, the attacking *knarr* ships attempted to circle around them. Which is exactly what Thorer had hoped they would do. The moment the first ship crossed in front of the *Ormrinn* on its pass around, he turned the ship back towards the coast. He used the sail as a wind break and ordered the rowers to turn sharply. The port sailors stopping their rhythmic rowing while the starboard side increased in tempo. The great ship lurched sharply to port, tipping violently in the water. Olaf watched the waves crash up on to the deck as it went almost vertical, before the ship righted itself. As it fell back into the water, the serpent at the prow was now angled *ahead* of the circling *knarr*, which had already committed to its course.

"Ramming speed!" Thorer shouted, his roar carrying over the waves and wind. The seamen shouted and hurled obscenities as they gave all their strength to the rowing. The circling *knarr* could not turn away, as it was now hemmed in against the coast. All it could do was watch as the *Ormrinn* bore down upon it, the howls and cries of the sailors sounding like the great dragon Nidhogg itself was crawling up from the depths of the world tree to consume the *knarr*.

The *Ormrinn Langi* collided with the *knarr* vessel. The sound of thunder filled the air as wood splintered, metal warped, and masts buckled. The sailors on the other ship were catapulted out of their vessel, dozens of archers flung out into the roiling waters, their cries lost in the chaos. The *Ormrinn* had hit with enough force to almost bisect the ship, the two halves held together only by the presence of the embedded *skeid*. The creaking and moaning of the buckled wood filled the air as water began to rush up between the cracks, foaming and bubbling angrily beneath. Those who were still left on the shattered *knarr* looked about, stunned, fear and confusion on their faces.

Olaf looked down upon them from his position at the prow, one hand steadying himself on the serpent figurehead, the other wielding his sword. He looked behind him; his crew were shaken but steady, and were gathering their dropped weapons readying to attack. He stilled his shaking hands and raised his sword above his head. He screamed—an angry, joyous scream, filled with violent intent. The crew replied in kind.

Leaping off the prow and into the broken and compromised *knarr*, Olaf began to cut through the enemy. Blades met flesh as he struck down the wounded and shaken attackers. Behind him, he heard the cries of his men as they boarded.

"For King Olaf!"

He ducked to avoid the swing of an axe, the blade passing mere inches above his skull. He reached up and grabbed the arm that wielded it, pulling his attacker closer and driving his sword into his gut. Warm blood spat out like a geyser, coating his hands. Olaf embraced the dying man impaled on his weapon; to anyone observing, it would have looked like he was holding him. Instead, he lifted him up on his blade, his battle frenzy gifting him hitherto unknown strength, and charged with the man into the waiting archers behind, using the body as a shield.

Arrows flew at Olaf, but they embedded themselves harmlessly in the man he had skewered. One arrow erupted through the skull, showering blood and viscera all over Olaf as the face disintegrated. Screaming, Olaf wrenched his sword free and threw the now useless body on the floor.

He fell upon the archers. In close quarters, they did not have the time to react. Some stood by in dumb horror as they were cut apart by the wild slashing of the Norwegian king. Even in the midst of battle, Olaf began to appreciate the sword Sigurd had given him. It cut through flesh, tendons, and bone like a heated knife through deer hide. He knew where to place his strikes; the armour these sailors wore was similar to that of his own crew: sturdy in the face of a frontal blow, weak at the joints and neck.

Those archers who were attempting to grab their short swords were cut down before they could unsheathe them. Not all were killed by Olaf. Several of his men had formed a defensive perimeter around him and were striking down any who tried to attack their king. Olaf had just carved off the top of a man's skull, brains tumbling out in an explosion of red and grey, when he heard Thorer's cry from back on the *Ormrinn Langi*.

"Fall back! The ship is sinking!"

It took Olaf a moment to realize his feet were wet. Looking down, he could see he was knee-deep. Limbs floated about in the rushing red water.

"Fall back!" Thorer called out again.

Olaf nodded, his battle rage fading now and exhaustion beginning to set in. His boarding party fell in beside him, grabbing him and escorting him back to the *Ormrinn Langi*. He did not resist.

Arms reached down from the *Ormrinn* and dragged him aboard, dumping him unceremoniously on the deck. He sat and watched as the rest of his impromptu boarding party were brought aboard. Looking back into the shattered hull of the *knarr*, he saw the water bubble and froth, the two halves of the ship disappearing beneath the red and black water, leaving nothing but splintered planks and severed limbs. A few of the sailors had managed to get away and swam desperately towards the shore of Hollandstoun isle. His archers took swift care of them, leaving their bodies to float listlessly on the waves.

A hand fell on Olaf's shoulder, pulling him back to the moment.

"Are you all right, my king?" Thorer asked, his windswept face mere inches from Olaf's, concern etched into his features.

"What of the other *knarr*?"

"Fleeing. They saw your heroic charge and turned tail."

Olaf let out a satisfied bark. "Is that all Sweyn can throw at me?"

"We must make haste. Sweyn is still stalking these waters."
Thorer paused. "You have been cut!"

Olaf looked down. His chest had been sliced from left to
right, like someone had carved a bloody smile into his tunic.
Blood pooled beneath him. How had he not noticed? He began
to feel dizzy.

"Bandages! I need bandages quickly!" Thorer was shouting,
but he sounded very far away.

The sound of rushing water filled Olaf's ears. He could feel
his heartbeat reverberating inside his skull. Shadows fell about
him as the crew brought aid to their captain and king.

"Olaf! Olaf!" A slap to the face from a firm, calloused,
hand brought the King of Norway back from the brink of
unconsciousness. "We need to get this wound cleaned and
stitched up. You have to stay awake." Thorer's words were
distant and muted, like someone talking underwater.

Olaf felt strong arms lift him up from the deck and begin to
carry him below into the hold. "We…need to keep…" But he
could not finish the sentence. He suddenly felt very weak, his
arms and legs leaden. He was grateful to be carried.

"Do not worry, my king. We will get you healed. I promise."
The words were said to comfort, but Olaf could hear the
desperation and fear in Thorer's voice.

"Don't be afraid. God will protect me."

Olaf was not sure if he said these words aloud or whether he
had just thought them. Light and noise began to fade to oblivion
as he slipped away into darkness.

Chapter Thirteen

The two heads stared dumbly up at Arinbjorn, their clouded blue eyes frozen in states of shock and anger respectively. They had been cut—no, hacked—from their bodies and left to stand watch over the snowy copse, embedded in the roots of an ash tree. The bloodied cruciforms that had been carved into their foreheads looked dull in the early morning light. Blood crystals formed at the edges of the wounds. Arinbjorn clenched his fists, feeling his fingernails digging into his palms, and turned away from the faces of Fergus and Conall.

Freya stood a little way away, her thick hide coat contrasting with the pure white background of snow and ice. Her back was to the trees and she stared out across the valley. Her honey-coloured hair blew wildly in the wind and she hugged herself tightly. He could see her trembling slightly—either from cold or upset, it didn't matter. He wanted to go to her. Instead, he turned to face the eviscerated bodies of the two thralls, where Sigvaldi knelt amid the frozen blood and organs.

Sigvaldi normally took his appearance absurdly seriously, keeping his hair and beard trim in the Norwegian style. Here and now, however, he looked tired and dishevelled. He ran one hand repeatedly through his hair, while the other used his sax knife to pore through the remains of the thralls.

"What do you think?" Arinbjorn asked.

Sigvaldi gave him a tired look, the black rings under his eyes having grown larger by the day. "Conall and Fergus may have been taken from Ireland, but they exhibited no Christian leanings." He gestured to Freya. "According to her, they were good and loyal men."

"I met them a few times. What she says is true."

If Sigvaldi was in any way concerned by the implication, he did not pursue it. "Then, at first glance, it looks like someone was making a retaliatory strike," he said.

"Against Njall?"

"Against pagans." Sigvaldi rose from his crouching position and stretched his legs.

"But why these two?"

"They're just thralls. Their only value is as a commodity. If the killer is found, it won't count as murder."

"They are not *just* thralls." Freya's voice cut through the close, dense silence of the copse. It was cold and laced with venom.

Sigvaldi looked like he had been slapped. "Of course, Freya," he said slowly. "I did not mean to undermine their value as people—merely to highlight their appeal to a killer."

Freya did not turn to face them, instead returning to her silent watch.

"Do you think one of Thangbrander's flock did this?" Sigvaldi asked.

"He *has* been riling them up on the back of Skjalti's murder," Arinbjorn replied. Gizurr's warning about the priest still played in his mind.

"Can you find the killer?" Freya said at last. Her voice was low, tired. She had ridden through the night to Arinbjorn's farm to find him and Sigvaldi and bring them here.

Arinbjorn surveyed the scene of death on the valley floor. Aside from the path through the snow that they themselves had taken, there were two other sets of tracks that wound their way across the valley. The first seemed to belong to Conall and Fergus; the second to whoever had fled the murder.

"We will find him and kill him," Arinbjorn stated earnestly.

Freya whipped around. Tears streaked from her bloodshot eyes and her chest heaved violently. Her reddened face, covered in dirt and ice, scowled at Arinbjorn.

"You think that kind of talk is comforting?" she cried out. "More killing!" Her voice broke against the bitter wind. Hugging herself tightly, she fell to her knees in the snow. Flurries of ice whirled around her in the pale morning light. She was trembling, her head bowed. "You and your killing."

Arinbjorn stared at her for a moment, before kneeling in front of her. He put his hands on her shoulders and gripped her firmly, yet gently. "I am sorry, Freya."

She looked up at him then, honey-coloured eyes staring intently. A few strands of her dark gold hair clung to her wet and puffy skin. He brushed them aside, careful not to let his callused hands linger.

Her thin red lips curled into a half smile. "Sorry for wanting to avenge me?" Her voice was barely above a whisper, but Arinbjorn could hear the sarcastic tone.

"For showing a lack of respect. I know these men meant a lot to you. No mere act of vengeance will bring them back. I know that."

"Do you? Finding Skjalti's killer won't return *him* either."

Arinbjorn sat back upon his heels and looked past Freya's shoulder. The mutilated remains of Skjalti's children flashed into his mind and he forced himself to shake away the image.

"I cannot teach Ask to wield an axe or show Embla what runes can teach us." His voice hardened. "But I can ensure the murderer never hurts another again."

He felt her hand upon his cheek, her fingertips lightly tracing the contours of his face.

"You are an idiot, Arinbjorn Thorleiksson." Freckled cheeks rose into a smile. "I do not need a hero." Remembering herself, she pulled her hand back. "I understand your need to act. But does it have to be you who finds these killers?"

"If not me, then who?" He gestured to the wide expanse of white hills about them. "There are not so many people here who would act."

"The chieftains would act," Freya insisted. She reached out and grabbed his hands.

"We have already spoken with several chieftains," Sigvaldi said from behind them.

Turning, Arinbjorn saw that he was busy gathering kindling for a fire.

Sigvaldi stopped and stared at a small, moss-covered log in his hands, before dropping it and addressing Freya directly. "So long as their laws are respected, the death of Christians and thralls will not move them to act."

Freya shook her head. "They *must* act. The lawspeaker cannot have two separate rules for Christians and the rest of us!"

"Thorgeir is tacitly supporting us in our hunt. But he cannot do anything without proof. By then, we could be facing more death." Arinbjorn cupped Freya's face and rubbed away some of the dirt on her cheeks with his thumbs. "Sigvaldi and I are the only ones doing anything. We might be the only ones who can stop this happening again."

"But you are no fighter!" Freya brushed his hands aside and got to her feet, anger and disbelief colouring her words. "You are a *farmer*, and not a very good one at that!"

Arinbjorn clambered after her, grabbing her arm as she tried to walk off.

"Let go of me!" Freya shouted.

Arinbjorn pulled her close, holding her as she struggled against his grip.

"You are such a bastard." She quit trying to break free and looked up at him. He could feel her breath on his lips. "You'll get yourself killed and I don't want to mourn you." Her breathing slowed and she eased into his grip. "I said let me go."

Arinbjorn did so. "I do not want to die, Freya." He stepped back to increase the space between them. "But I have to do this."

"I know," Freya said, after a pause. She looked away from him, towards the bodies of Fergus and Conall. "I don't want to see you like that. Will you keep him safe, Sigvaldi?"

"Almost certainly not," he said seriously. "But I will be by his side the whole way."

Freya barked out a laugh. "Could you not have lied, at least?"

Sigvaldi's smile did not reach his eyes. "It is not my way."

"Two honourable men." She shook her head in disbelief. "You know what happens to honourable men in the sagas." It was not a question.

Arinbjorn walked back to Sigvaldi's side and began to help him pile the wood into a pyre.

*

The group of mourners stood together in silence, the ash and smoke from the burning bodies of Fergus and Conall rising into the sky and merging with the gathering clouds. Failend, Aesgir, and the remaining farmhands had joined them to watch the fire consume the two thralls. Freya wanted to say something, but could not come up with the words. Instead, Failend sang. The tune was slow, melodic, interrupted only by her trembling voice, and the words were strange—Arinbjorn could not make them out.

"What does it mean?" he asked, when she had finished, the last notes of her song dying out on the wind.

"It was a song they used to sing when they worked," Freya offered. "They never told me what it meant." Something about this statement caused her to buckle, and Arinbjorn went to grab her. She steadied herself and waved him away. "I am fine."

"It speaks of a young maiden," Failend said. The others stared at her, waiting. She did not acknowledge their stares; instead, she had fixed her eyes on the slowly blackening bodies of the thralls. "And how one day she would marry her love." There was something in her voice, a bitterness that edged the words.

"Failend..." It was all Freya could say before Failend turned and walked off, back towards the farmstead, her red, snow-speckled hair and mud-brown cloak flowing out behind her. Aesgir and the rest of the thralls followed, their eyes cast low and their shoulder sagging. This was not rebellion. Freya did not give chase, nor did she admonish. She just watched them all go.

"They all like you, Freya," Sigvaldi said, once the last had departed and they were left alone again. "A rare thing among thralls."

"Njall should be here." Her voice had hardened.

"Where is he?"

"Where do you think, Ari?"

"Tongu-Oddr?"

Freya simply nodded, her fists balled. For a moment, Arinbjorn thought he could see a thin trickle of blood appearing on the palm of her hand, but, before he could ask, she turned to him and Sigvaldi and said, "Thank you, both, for your help." Wiping her eyes, she straightened her hair and dried her face. She took a few deep breaths. "I should return to the farmstead. There is more work to be done."

"Freya, wait—you cannot spend the night alone, after all this."

"I have Failend and Aesgir."

"Would they fare any better than Conall and Fergus against an attacker?"

"Perhaps you should return to your father's hold. At least until Njall's return?" Sigvaldi proffered.

Arinbjorn shot him a look; his friend's green eyes were fixed and level with his own, his face neutral.

"I will not let some coward murderer push me from my home." She would not be budged.

"Then let us stay with you," Arinbjorn offered.

Freya was still for a moment, her amber eyes studying Arinbjorn intently. He was suddenly aware of just how close she was. Her chest rose and fell rhythmically, her breath formed in the frigid air from thin red lips.

"That would be inappropriate," she said finally, her gaze locked on his.

"Yes. It would be," Sigvaldi cautioned.

Arinbjorn faced his friend. "Would you rather we left her alone?"

"You know how it would look to others."

Arinbjorn shook his head and turned back to the burning pyre. The fire was a deep orange now, and the light danced across the frozen trees.

"Do you care what others think?" Arinbjorn asked Freya.

"You expect me to say no?"

"I expect you to prize safety over wagging tongues."

"It is precisely those wagging tongues that provide me with safety, Arinbjorn." She squared up to him now, her body tense and resolute. "You think they don't know that Njall is away all the time with Tongu-Oddr? You think they don't know that it is I who manages the farm? It is only the flimsiest of pretences that keeps them from rounding upon me and my husband." She put emphasis on the last word, hardening it. "If I spent the night with another man, no matter the reason, they could well remove me and Njall from our home."

"But is it worth your life?"

"It *is* my life!" she shouted. "My life, and all I have of one! Njall may jeopardize it, but I will not." Her face was red; sadness had changed to anger.

Arinbjorn raised his hands and took a step back.

"Then we will escort you back to your farm," Sigvaldi offered to Freya, before addressing Arinbjorn: "And check on her in the morning."

Arinbjorn nodded to his friend. He did not like it, but he knew Freya was right. There were dangers in the world other than this killer.

"Thank you, Sig." Freya may have spoken to Sigvaldi, but she never took her eyes off Arinbjorn.

The three stood in silence while the last of the embers died on the pyre. The blackened bodies of the thralls slowly collapsed into ash and the wind carried them off into the morning sky.

Chapter Fourteen

The low afternoon sun was blinding as it reflected off the freshly fallen snow. It was painful to look out across the plains towards the coast; Thangbrander could barely make out the grey waves and black sand that lined the shore. He stared for as long as he could, straining to see any sails on the horizon, but found none. He closed his eyes and pulled his cloak tighter about him. Taking a deep breath, he allowed the cool air to cut deep into his lungs. He held it there a moment before letting it out slowly. He watched his breath disappear before him, carried away by the wind.

The wind was biting today and his knees ached. Each step out on this morning walk had been hard fought, but he embraced the pain. It kept his mind sharp. This island does not welcome outsiders, Thangbrander thought. If it was not the treacherous seas, then it was the frozen earth with its winding, tumultuous rivers and rocky crags hidden beneath the snowfall. The cold *burned* here. Even the red rock that spewed forth from the black mountains in the south could not help but freeze in the face of this desolate land.

Then there were the people. An obstinate, brash race of sheep herders. Farmers who thought themselves above kings. God himself would struggle to convert these heathens. When he had first arrived here, he had been greeted by some of the local chieftains, led by Thorgeir. They had invited this emissary of Olaf, King of Norway, to join them in a meal. Thangbrander readily agreed—he felt fortunate that he was meeting with such renowned men so soon—but it rapidly became apparent their agenda was not benign.

Dinner was horse, much like it had been only the other day when he met that young Arinbjorn. He still remembered their yellowing smiles, their teeth filled with the rotten flesh of the poor beast. Greasy, bloodied, bones lay cast upon table. After this orgy of consummation had passed, one of the chiefs — Gellir, if he remembered correctly—encouraged him to speak of his God and explain to them how He was the only one worth worshipping.

He began speaking at length about the nature of God, the Son, and the Holy Spirit, how He was all things to all men. Thangbrander was halfway through his impromptu sermon when he noticed the chieftains chuckling among themselves.

"Why do you laugh?" he asked.

"This is a good sermon, priest. But we have a better way of seeing who is worth our worship." Gellir rose from the table, disappearing for several moments. The group continued to laugh together and cheered when Gellir returned. He was carrying something large in his hands. In the oppressive darkness of this sheep herder's hall, Thangbrander could barely make out the shape. Not until the thick, meaty form had been thrown on his plate did he recognize it for what it was. A horse's cock.

The group's laughter filled the hall. Thangbrander felt his face redden—not with embarrassment, but anger. The air was thick with smoke and the scent of horse meat. It was hot and the chittering, bawdy laughter from his hosts bore into his skull. Under the table, his fist curled around his sax knife. He stared at Gellir as the chieftain returned to his seat, receiving slaps on the back from those around him.

"What am I supposed to do with this?"

"Hold it!" one shouted.

"If your God is as powerful as ours, surely you can get it up."

"Look, I will show you!" Teitr, the trader, with his purple face and greying beard, rose from his seat and took the appendage from Thangbrander's plate. His grey, liver-spotted hands could barely grasp the base. He swung it before him and began reciting a poem, an ode to their false god Odin.

To Thangbrander's amazement, the poor beast's appendage began to engorge and rise until it was stiff in Teitr's hands. The group laughed uproariously.

"Even the priest is impressed!" Gellir shouted. Thangbrander watched as he picked his teeth with a bone. "Your turn, Thangbrander."

Teitr dropped the cock back on Thangbrander's plate and sat down.

Releasing his grip on the sax knife, Thangbrander picked up the penis and held it before him. If these farmers could do this, his God certainly could. He began to recite a prayer in Latin. To his horror, the cock deflated, rapidly shrinking until it lay cold and limp in his hands. The group were screaming with laughter now, banging the table and tossing their mead about the floor. Thangbrander's anger got the better of him. He threw the cock down upon Teitr, pushed back from the table, and stormed out of the hall. Shouts and jeers followed him outside into the night.

To this day, he could not figure out how they had managed to inflate the cock. He assumed they had stuffed it with a bladder full of air that needed to be held in a certain way to maintain the illusion. Innovative, certainly, but about as far from holy as you could get. If anything, that brazen display of cruelty and base humour only solidified his resolve to try to convert these petty people.

He continued his walk along the coast, trying to ignore the whistling wind that sounded too much like Gellir's high-pitched laughter.

*

Not until the sun had passed its zenith, its white light cutting across the pale sea, did Thangbrander catch sight of that which he dreaded. A red sail on the horizon. The ship was arcing into the bay from the south-east. It had at least thirty rowing benches, sixty oars moving rhythmically into the ice and foam, and that large red sail embossed with a design he could not make out at this distance. He let out a breath he did not realize he was holding. This was not the *Ormrinn Langi*. Still, it was a ship built for one purpose. In his heart, he knew it had been sent to collect him, even if Olaf himself was not here. He would have to answer for his lack of progress. His letters to the king these last few years had contained precious little good news.

Thangbrander estimated that the ship would make it to the beach in an hour or so. He should not keep them waiting. The walk back to Hallr's hall was slow and painful. The ache in his knees, which at first he had welcomed, was now just a burden as he attempted to navigate the snow-covered hills. He tried to remember where the ice beneath his feet would give way to crags and fissures.

His mind raced with thoughts about what he would say to King Olaf's emissary. He had been here for three years; in that time he had managed to convert only two of the chieftains that oversaw the farmers here, and only one of true importance: Gizurr the White. A man who had become his friend. A man he had betrayed. He could still see the look of loss and anger on Gizurr's face when he had used the death of Skjalti and his family to encourage more violent means of protest. He regretted that pain, but felt it was necessary.

He remembered when he had baptized Gizurr, almost a year to the day after he first set foot here. It had been a clear spring day, the pale blue sky above turning purple at its ceiling. The winter ice had finally begun to thaw, the first green shoots had begun to poke through the ice, and the air was still with the fragrant scent of heather.

This being the first ritual in Iceland, there was no church or consecrated ground. Instead, Thangbrander had decided to utilize the Öxará river, emulating the baptism of Christ in the Jordan river. He felt it was fitting. The bank was lined with Gizurr's entire farmstead: his wife and children, his thralls, and some of the lesser farmers who tilled his land. They all had gathered to watch this momentous occasion—the first man to be baptized in Iceland.

Gizurr had stood before Thangbrander, his ice-white hair tied back in a simple braid. This was a man who had come to truly *believe* in God the Father.

After his first disastrous meeting with the other chieftains, Thangbrander had taken himself away from their farmsteads and travelled further east, inland. He came across Gizurr, who was kind enough to offer sanctuary on his farm. They spent many an evening lost in debate about the metaphysical nature of God, His Son and the Holy Ghost. Thangbrander was amazed by Gizurr's keen intellect and sharp questions. He had to admit, in some instances he had struggled to answer the farmer's queries.

Yet, there he had stood, the first chieftain in Iceland ready to accept Christ into his heart. It had been a glad day for both men.

"Do you believe in God the Father Almighty, maker of heaven and earth?" Thangbrander asked.

"I do." The reply was loud and firm, carrying all the way to the people watching on the embankment.

"Do you believe in Jesus Christ, his only begotten Son our Lord, who was born and suffered for us?"

"I do."

"Do you believe in the Holy Ghost, the communion of saints, the forgiveness of sins, the resurrection of the flesh, and life everlasting?"

"I do."

Thangbrander smiled at his new friend, before gripping Gizurr's shoulders and guiding his head beneath the icy water. He held him under and fancied that the rushing water was stripping Gizurr of his sins and dumping them downstream, into the sea. With one hand, Thangbrander made the sign of the cross over Gizurr's head.

"I baptize thee in the name of the Father, and of the Son, and of the Holy Ghost."

Easing his grip, Thangbrander pulled his friend up and out of the water.

"Welcome to the Church, my friend."

The crowd erupted in applause.

Since then, Gizurr had always promoted law as the means of conversion. He was convinced that the people would respect the rules made by their chieftains and that all they needed to do was convince enough of them to force the issue at the Althing. Gizurr argued that you didn't have to convert the entire island, just enough chieftains to be able to bring the issue to the court. Of the thirty chieftains that governed Iceland, so far Thangbrander had managed to convert two, and Hallr barely counted. His rotund ally's holding was small, but well stocked; Thangbrander had ensured that any supplies that came his way from Norway went to Hallr. It helped boost his status within the community and improve the cause for conversion—or that is what he hoped.

The court of the Althing was a difficult process to navigate. These free folk would gather and discuss issues that affected the whole isle and rule on personal disputes. A convincing argument was only half the battle; if one did not have the weight of numbers to support a motion or legal claim, then one could not sway the law. It was an ineffectual means of making decisions, in Thangbrander's eyes; without a king to guide them, change came slowly or not at all. He had to work to a faster timetable than the Althing's deliberations would allow.

Hence his betrayal of his friend's ideals. Gizurr still had not spoken to him since he had rallied the congregation. He still came to Mass, but always left before Thangbrander could speak with him. He hoped, one day, that Gizurr would understand why he had made the decisions he had. Maybe, if Thangbrander was lucky, his friend might even forgive him.

*

"Captain Gunnar," said a wall of a man clad in an ill-fitting chain shirt, by way of introduction. "Are you Priest Thangbrander?"

"I am."

Thangbrander stood on the black sand, looking down into the tumultuous grey waters. The warship had beached and the crew were busy securing the great *skeid* in place. Before him stood the self-described Captain Gunnar. He was powerfully built and would have given Thangbrander pause twenty years ago, never mind now. He was scowling, and the thick scar across his forehead only seemed to heighten the disdain.

"Jarl Sigurd, on behalf of King Olaf Tryggvason, has sent me to collect you and return you to the king."

"What?" Thangbrander could not hide his surprise. He had known Olaf was coming, but he had assumed it was to condemn him for his lack of progress, maybe offer support, not to remove him entirely.

"The king would like a report on your progress."

"I can provide you with all the information you need; you can take it back to the king."

Gunnar's scowl deepened. "I am not a messenger. Your king has commanded your return." He stood at ease, but his right hand lay upon the hilt of a sword he had sheathed away. His fingers flexed idly.

"Do you know why I am here?" Thangbrander had to try something different if he was going to remain in his position. He did not like the idea of returning to Olaf empty-handed. He just needed more time.

"No. Nor do I care. You will gather your things and meet us here at nightfall."

"I am here to convert these pagan sheep-fuckers. To bring them the way of Christ. You say you are one of Jarl Sigurd's men? That means you are Christians, yes? You are duty-bound to assist me in my endeavours."

"I am loyal to the king first, my faith second."

"These are one and the same! King Olaf needs me to convert these heathens, and I have just begun something that will ensure he can finally see his efforts rewarded. I cannot leave now."

"You must—"

"But, if you help me, not only will you be doing your king a favour, you will also be doing right by your God!"

Gunnar breathed deeply, his gaze never wavering. "What do you need?"

"Time. And your steel."

Gunnar broke eye contact and stared back at the beached longship and the darkening skies. The tide was coming in, and the roar of the waves as they crashed upon the beach filled the silence between them.

"It will be difficult to get out of this bay. The tides are strong. Perhaps it would be best to wait a day or two until the weather is more favourable…" Gunnar's voiced trailed off.

Thangbrander seized his chance. "Help me. I guarantee you will earn favour with the king. Help me, and you will earn favour with God himself."

Gunnar unsheathed his blade and held it before him. Grey light reflected off the steel. He turned to face Thangbrander. "You have a week. Then, no matter what happens, I am taking you to Olaf."

The roar of the waves seemed to grow louder, as if the beat of a war drum.

Chapter Fifteen

The ebony sky began to lighten as the first rays of the morning sun merged with the ribbons of green and blue aurora above. Slowly, the stars receded into purple shadow and the waterfalls of diffuse light vanished. The figure that stalked along the frozen hill became clear. A slight limp hindered his gait, and he moved haphazardly, cutting left and right through the snow; every so often, he would attempt to drop behind what few trees or shrubs lined the ascent to Njall's farm. In his dark cloak, he looked like an ink stain oozing up the hill.

Arinbjorn's eyes were heavy with snowflakes, his eyelashes practically frozen. He blinked rapidly to clear his vision and attempted to refocus on the target. From his vantage point on the other side of the low valley, he could see both Njall's farmhouse and the copse of trees where they had found the murdered bodies of Fergus and Conall. He stood and dusted the powdery snow off his tunic. Flexing his fingers inside his gloves, he tried to encourage warmth into them, then reached down to the sax knife on his belt. He watched the black shape continue towards Freya; he was halfway up the hill now, making slow, snaking gains towards the summit.

"Who do you think it is?" Sigvaldi asked. He was still in the hide tent they had brought out from Arinbjorn's farm, with only his head protruding outside. His trim beard was white with frost and snow. He had several layers of heavy hide draped over him, yet he still trembled with the cold. The wind was only slight, but it was biting.

Arinbjorn felt guilty for keeping his friend out all night, but he was sure the murderer who attacked Freya's thralls would return. They had spent the night huddled up together for warmth, with one of them checking outside whenever they heard anything. It has been a cold, painful, and restless night.

Now, however, it appeared Arinbjorn was right. The killer was back.

"I cannot tell."

"Are you sure it is not just Njall?"

"Why would he sneak up on his own farm?"

"Then we had better get going." Sigvaldi disappeared inside the tent and emerged a moment later without the hides, rubbing his hands together. His breath hung heavy in the air. Arinbjorn noticed he had buckled on his axe. Good.

Without further words, the pair of them started away from their tent and moved down into the valley surrounding Njall's farm. The morning sun cast long black shadows across the snow, and ice crystals shone red in the early light. To Arinbjorn, it was like they were wading through fields of frozen blood.

They made quick work through the valley and began their ascent of Njall's hill. Their target was still creeping up on the hall, preferring stealth instead of speed, allowing them time to catch up. Arinbjorn and Sigvaldi carved their way through the snow, hoping that their prey was too focused on his task and would not hear them. They closed the gap.

They were maybe fifty yards away when the cloaked figure reached the front door of Njall's hall. Hunching over, he began working on the lock. They had to move quickly. They were almost upon him when a cry came out from one of the side buildings—a cockerel proclaiming the dawn. Arinbjorn turned in shock towards the cry; when he looked back, the hooded figure was staring down upon them. The sun breached the horizon and bathed them all in its light.

For a moment, no one moved. The figure before them was heavily cloaked to protect against the wind, and he wore a woollen kerchief pulled up to his nose, but Arinbjorn could still see two black eyes scowling back at him from under the hood. It was not the eyes that commanded Arinbjorn's gaze, however. Beneath the black cloak, covered in ice and blood, was a heavily patterned vestment. Just like the one Sigvaldi had shown him. Only this was blue.

"Murderer." He did not shout it, but the word carried across the space between them, merging with the sound of the wind. He unsheathed his sax knife.

Skjalti's killer unsheathed a short sword and backed away from the door, moving towards the pair of them. He was still limping slightly, but the sure grip and comfortable stance warned Arinbjorn against rash action.

Hearing Sigvaldi pull out his hand axe, Arinbjorn said, "Careful, Sig."

"Don't worry, I was planning on throwing you at him." Despite the joke, there was no humour in his friend's voice. The pair of them separated and began to circle their target, who eyed them keenly.

Arinbjorn raised his knife and braced himself. "You are a coward and a murderer. Show your face!"

The figure leapt and swung his sword in a low arc, kicking up powdery snow as he did so. Arinbjorn leant back and narrowly avoided the blade slicing into his chest. He moved further away to draw the attacker towards him and give Sigvaldi an opening, but his foe was not foolish; keeping his back to the farmhouse, he moved out and away from them both. Sigvaldi went in with a quick strike, clearly hoping to hack the sword out of their opponent's hands, but he was too fast. Pivoting, he knocked Sigvaldi's blade aside and brought his sword down in a swift stroke. He caught Sigvaldi on his arm and cut deeply enough for blood to spurt out across the snow. Sigvaldi barked out in pain.

Arinbjorn closed the distance between them, hoping to drive his knife into the killer's side while he was distracted by Sigvaldi. He got close, too, before he was struck about the head by the pommel of the short sword. His vision flashed white and he stumbled. He flailed about with his knife in the hope of hitting something, then saw the glint of steel as the blade caught the sun's light, arcing down towards his head.

Sigvaldi's axe clanged against the blade and knocked it off its course. Still holding on to his injured left arm, Sigvaldi then took up a defensive position in front of Arinbjorn as his friend regained his composure. Arinbjorn looked about himself and noticed that somehow they had all been turned around with the assailant's pivoting and blade work; now he was free, while the two of them were hemmed in against the wall of the farmhouse. How had he done that?

"This isn't going so well," Sigvaldi said breathlessly, as he strained under the wound to his arm.

"He is no farmer; I haven't seen anyone fight like him." Arinbjorn had regained his composure and stood by his friend.

"Do you not speak?" Sigvaldi shouted.

The door behind them opened and light from the interior hearth fire flooded out. Turning, the pair saw Freya standing with a large kitchen knife in her hand. Her eyes were wide with shock at the scene.

"Ari, what are you—?"

"Not now!"

The cloaked figure leapt at Sigvaldi and swung for his head. Arinbjorn kicked the legs out from under his friend. Sigvaldi cried out in shock as he fell backwards, but the blade missed his throat by inches. Standing over him, Arinbjorn parried the blade away with his sax knife and grabbed hold of his enemy's sword arm, pulling him in close and holding fast.

The pair of them wrestled, muscles taught with strain. The murderer writhed beneath Arinbjorn's grasp in an attempt to break free, sinews stretched and bones bent to the point of breaking. Arinbjorn headbutted him. He felt his opponent's nose give way under his forehead and warm liquid sprayed across his face. The assailant cried out in pain and Arinbjorn yanked his hood down. A craggy and pockmarked face stared back at him. Pitted by age and exposure to the elements, it was a face lined with bitterness. Black eyes flashed in anger.

"Kormac!" Freya shouted from behind.

"You?" Arinbjorn looked on dumbly, giving Kormac his chance. He struck out, kneeing Arinbjorn in the groin and weakening his grasp. Pulling free, Kormac looked frantically between the three of them and brought his blade up. Arinbjorn dragged Sigvaldi to his feet and the pair of them moved back to put a barrier between Freya and Kormac.

Kormac only smiled—a thin smile that made him look like a weathered snake. He took a step closer.

"What is going on here?" The voice was male, firm, and deep. It bellowed across the plains from behind them.

All four turned to see Njall Bjarnisson riding towards them on his horse, a smaller, lither man riding at his side. The pair were trotting up the hill towards the farm.

Kormac looked back towards Arinbjorn, Sigvaldi and Freya and scowled.

"You are outnumbered, coward." Seeing his chance, Arinbjorn began to charge towards Kormac.

"Ari, no!" Sigvaldi shouted.

It was too late. Arinbjorn had already committed himself. Crouching low as if to tackle Kormac, Arinbjorn readied his sax knife, intent on driving it into Kormac's gut. He watched as Kormac braced himself, easing his weight on to his back foot, blade outstretched. With one slick motion, Kormac whipped his blade up, slicing deep into Arinbjorn's forearm. He barely felt the cut, but the blood that flowed from the wound told him it was bad. The sax knife tumbled from his grasp. In shock, he continued his run into Kormac, who took the brunt of Arinbjorn's shove and moved with him, spinning around and flinging him low. Arinbjorn felt the second strike then, rougher than the first strike, cutting a jagged groove into his back. He cried out and tumbled into the snow, face first.

He lay there, shocked, his mouth full of ice and dirt, his body hot with pain. Blood pooled about him. Somewhere, in the distance, behind the heartbeat that seemed to roar in his ears, he heard screams and shouts. He strained to look at what was happening, but the dawn light seemed all too bright. Darkness crept in around the edges of his vision and the shadows fell upon him.

*

It was a scream that woke him up. A loud, ragged shout, filled with pain and fear. It took him a moment to realize he was the one screaming. He was on his front, his open mouth gnawing on a mattress; hay and feathers tumbled out from the seam he had torn with his teeth. A sharp, jagged pain arced up his back and seemed to light his whole body on fire. He cried out.

"Somebody stop him from moving; I need to clean the wound." It was a voice that Arinbjorn didn't recognize. Soft, yet terse. A woman's voice.

He tried to open his eyes, but even the dim light of the farm hall seemed too bright.

Firm hands grasped his shoulders and pressed him into the mattress, restraining him. "Ari, stop. It's all right." Sigvaldi's voice was soft, almost tender. It was then Arinbjorn knew his wound must be grave.

"Sig, what—is happening?" He could barely get the sentence out. His breath came in rapid gasps and each intake caused his lungs to burn.

"Shut up." That woman's voice again. Young. "Don't talk. Don't move."

He felt something dig into his back, dragging a white flame down the wound. He screamed again.

*

"Is he going to be OK?"

"I don't know. Wounds like that can prove fatal long after they are inflicted."

"He is a stubborn one; if anyone can survive, it would be him."

"I don't want platitudes, Sig. I want him to be all right."

"I know, Freya."

"Freya…" Arinbjorn's mouth was dry, and her name came out as a cracked whisper.

"Ari!" The gasp and joy in her voice made him want to smile.

Instead, he summoned what energy he had to lift the weights of his eyes. Gummed shut, he had to fight to pry them open and take in the scene. Slowly, the figures around him resolved themselves out of the shadows.

He was staring up at the soil ceiling of Njall's hall. The air was thick and warm, carrying the faint scent of rosemary and earth, and the crackle of the hearth fire filled the silence.

Sigvaldi was sitting at his right side, smiling brightly. His tunic was rolled up on his left arm, which was bandaged heavily. To his left, Freya sat with a needle and thread in her hand, and a red tunic lay half-finished in her lap. It took him a moment to realize it was his tunic, stained by blood. She was trying to repair it.

He felt her cool hand upon his and she gently squeezed, running her thumb over his knuckles. "Are you OK?" The concern and joy in her voice were palpable.

This time, he did smile. "I am now." He blinked a few times to clear his vision. Suddenly, images of the blade that cut him filled his mind. "Where is Kormac?" He tried to rise from his lying position, but Sig reached across and held him down gently.

"Gone, my friend." He kept the pressure on Arinbjorn until he relented and eased back. "You held him off long enough for Njall and Tongu-Oddr to get here."

Arinbjorn looked down on his right arm, remembering the swift flash of light as the steel cut into him. "How am I alive?"

"The gods clearly see fit to have you live a while longer," Sigvaldi said.

"The gods had nothing to do with it." That new voice again. The woman. Arinbjorn turned to face the source. He saw a young woman, no more than eighteen years old, tending to a pot over the hearth fire. She had a mess of brown curly hair that sat wildly on her head. Her round face was red with the heat of the fire and she scowled into the flames. She turned to face him. "You would have died were it not for my grandmother's salves."

"Ari, this is Bera. From Haukadalur," Freya explained.

"Haukadalur?" His mind raced. "One of the witches?"

Bera let out an exaggerated sigh. "By default, if not by choice. You're welcome, by the way." She rose from the hearth fire and came over, moving Sigvaldi out of his seat. Assuming his spot, she held a cup before him. "Drink this; it will help with the pain."

He took it. The scent was bitter and sharp, with a strong note of garlic, and made him retch.

"Come on, brave hero, drink up."

Arinbjorn decided to drink just to get rid of Bera's smug smile. "Thank you," he said, after forcing the drink down.

"I believe I also owe thanks to you." Njall moved about from behind him.

Freya let go of Arinbjorn's hand.

"You kept my wife and farm safe while I was away." There was something in his voice—not anger, but something. The man was trying very hard to keep his emotions in check, that much was clear. His brown eyes seemed sad in the low light and his weathered features made him look far older than he was.

"He got away," Arinbjorn said quietly.

"And he killed Conall and Fergus," Freya said evenly. She stared coolly at her husband.

Njall nodded. "But he did not get you. For this, I am eternally grateful."

"It should not have been *him* defending me, husband." Freya's voice was low, laced with hurt, and she laboured over each word.

"I could not have known—"

Freya stood sharply, the needle and thread tumbling to the floor. "You were away! When I needed you, you were away!" Her face was red, now—not with sorrow, but fury.

"Freya—"

"He came here, you know, right after you left," Freya continued. "The very *moment*. You are gone so often, our neighbours think I run this farm! He had ample opportunity to strike; I am just lucky Arinbjorn was passing by."

Passing by. There it was. Njall did not know that he and Sigvaldi had camped out overnight. Did not know that he had been there the day before for the funeral of the thralls.

Njall lost whatever fight was in him. He nodded at Arinbjorn and took himself away. The sudden gust of cool air told Arinbjorn that he had left the hall entirely.

Freya stood for a moment, watching him leave. She used the sleeve of her dress to wipe away the tears that had formed at the edge of her eyes.

"Here, drink this." Bera walked over and gave Freya a cup.

"More pain relief?"

"In a fashion. It's mead." Bera smiled warmly.

Freya a barked laugh before drinking deeply. The two took their seats.

Deciding that now was not the time to address what had just been said, Arinbjorn changed the subject. "Do we know where Kormac has gone?"

"I saw him fleeing north, deeper into the valley," Sigvaldi answered. "He may intend to hide out in the caves of Thingvellir."

"Now he has been exposed, he has no choice but to face trial or be outlawed," Bera stated evenly.

"He doesn't fear outlawry." Arinbjorn remembered the look of calm in Kormac's face, the look of smug superiority, as he was cut down.

"What I don't understand is why he attacked here. Isn't Kormac Christian?" Bera asked.

"Maybe it was a revenge attack for the killing of Skjalti?" Sigvaldi offered.

"No. He killed them all." Arinbjorn's statement was met with silence.

"That doesn't make any sense, Ari," Freya said.

"Did none of you notice what colour his vestment was? It was blue, the same colour of the cloth snagged on the tree outside Thorgeir's hall. The same colour as one supposedly stolen from Thangbrander."

They all considered this.

"Then this isn't about the Christians?" Bera asked.

"I do not know. I just know he is the killer. We have to find him." Arinbjorn attempted to rise from his bed again, but the pain that raced up his back dropped him down.

"You are not going anywhere," Freya said sharply. She addressed Sigvaldi: "You are both welcome to stay here until his wounds heal."

"We can't let him hide!"

"We won't. Njall will address the chieftains tomorrow and, by the end of the day, he will not be able to go anywhere on this island without fear of death." Venom dripped off Freya's words.

A sudden fear gripped Arinbjorn. "Bera, I will heal, yes?"

"If your body is as stubborn as your spirit, I would say so. But you do have to rest for a few days."

Arinbjorn nodded, the fear not quite abating.

"Could I have a moment with Ari?" Freya asked.

Sigvaldi and Bera exchanged glances. They waited the briefest of moments before nodding and removing themselves. If they felt it inappropriate for Freya to be left alone with Arinbjorn, they did not speak it. When the tell-tale gust of wind told him that they had left the hall, Arinbjorn found himself staring into the golden eyes of Freya as she leant over him.

"You are an idiot." She whispered it, but it was tender. She reached down and held his hand freely again. She felt cool against his skin. "I told you I did not want a hero."

"I couldn't let anything happen to you." He could feel her breath upon him, lightly scented with honey. A droplet of mead hung on her lower lip, then dripped on to his chin.

"*I* could have lost *you*." She was close now, her chest rising and falling to the rhythm of her breathing. "And if anyone saw you lurking about the farm…"

"I know. I—"

She kissed him and he fell into a different kind of oblivion.

Chapter Sixteen

The gull circled lazily above, silhouetted against the white sun. Olaf watched as it floated on the warm air, its shadow coursing over the low waves, then abruptly tucked in its wings and dived towards the surface of the sea. It plunged into the water, droplets and foam bursting out in its wake, before emerging a moment later with a fish in its beak. The stunned and confused look on the gaping fish made the king smile grimly. He had always assumed he was the seagull, but, after the attack a few days ago, he now felt more like the fish.

He turned away from the scene, his right arm cradling his gut. He could feel the tender wound across his stomach. He tried not to touch it too much, but it was sore and itchy. He distracted himself by looking out upon his ship. The *Ormrinn Langi* listed under his feet; the sea was calm this morning and he found the gentle creaking of the wood to be comforting. The ship had taken some damage in the fight against Sweyn's raiders, but her crew was patching her up nicely. Their victory had changed the mood of his men significantly. Dour ever since the sacrifice of Afli, now they went about their work with the pride and succour of those who had faced death and won. The only person who was not happy was Thorer.

"This is taking too long." Thorer's hands were white as he gripped the tiller. The captain of the *Ormrinn Langi* looked tired to Olaf; his face seemed more stretched, his skin too tight against his skull. Blue eyes, dull and speckled with red, never left the horizon. It was a clear and crisp day; if there was a ship out there, it would be easily spotted.

"There is no one coming, Thorer. Sweyn's thugs turned tail and fled."

"How did they know where we were?" Thorer took a break from staring at the horizon to stare at Olaf, who found the slightly manic look disturbing.

"You look tired, my friend. Have you slept at all these last few days?"

"While you were being healed and rested, I took it upon myself to ensure there would be no more surprises."

Olaf decided to let the accusatory tone pass. "It has been *five days*, Thorer. You need to rest."

"I will rest when we get to Nidaross."

Olaf considered ordering his friend to go and get some sleep, but he knew better than to challenge him in this matter. Thorer had saved his life, and the lives of the men of the *Ormrinn Langi*, with his manoeuvres during the battle. If he needed this, Olaf would let him have it. For now.

"How long until we get there?" Olaf asked, changing tack.

"I would have expected to see the shores already." His hands fidgeted at the tiller.

"Then I have no doubt we will see home shortly."

Thorer grunted in response and returned his gaze to the horizon.

Olaf took one last look at his exhausted friend before turning to leave. He walked down through the ship and to the bow, taking the opportunity to observe and appreciate his crew as he passed the rowing benches. They were operating on a reduced capacity, and many of the men were bandaged or scarred. Still, they were in good spirits, and, as the drummers beat their rhythmic instructions, they filled the air with song.

When he was halfway down the ship, he almost tripped over a young sailor who was on his hands and knees, scrubbing the deck. He could not have been more than eighteen summers, with a mop of blond hair that covered a sunburned and wind-blistered face. Two brown eyes looked up in alarm as Olaf almost went over him.

"My king, I am sorry!" The young sailor pulled back, out of Olaf's way, and bowed his head low. The movement was so swift the young man scraped his knees across the wooden deck, leaving small rivulets of blood in his wake.

Olaf was surprised by the strength of the fear in the sailor, but then he saw what the young man was scrubbing. Faint, but still visible, was the darkened stain left behind by young Afli. Now that he was looking, he could see the tendrils of dried blood snaking out from the desiccated pool that the sailor was desperately trying to scrub away. They wormed their way deeper into the sailing benches, dropped into the hold, and merged with the more recent pools of blood that had been spilled during the fight. The whole ship looked like one open sore. He knew this was what the sailor saw too.

"What is this?" Olaf used the tip of his boot to point to the fresh blood from the sailor's knees. "Are you supposed to be cleaning the deck, or dirtying it?"

"I am sorry, my king."

"How old are you?" The sun was low in the afternoon sky, causing Olaf's shadow to fall long over the young man.

"Nineteen, my king."

"How long have you been part of my crew?" Olaf became aware that the singing had stopped and now there was just the beat of the drums.

"This is my first voyage with Captain Thorer. He took me on at Nidaross." The downcast gaze and quivering told Olaf everything he needed to know. This young man was afraid, but he was more afraid of Afli's blood than of his king. This would not stand.

Turning to address the now silent crew, Olaf raised his voice, looking as many men in the eye as he could: "God granted us safe passage through the storm. He provided a safe port with Jarl Sigurd, and now he has granted us victory in the fight against the pagan, Sweyn. Sing! Cheer! And remember that God is with you."

The crew let out a chorus of cheers and the drumming resumed.

Returning his attention to the deck scrubber, Olaf leant down and cupped his face, forcing the young man to stare directly into his eyes. He lowered his voice: "If you wish to survive until your twentieth year, you will scrub away all the blood that stains my ship." He released him, took one last look at the deck, and continued his way to the prow of the ship.

The cheers and singing of the crew continued. Closing his eyes and feeling the spittle and spray of the sea, Olaf basked in the sound for a moment. Yes. God was with them. He had to be.

*

It was a sight he never grew tired of: the shallow islands at the mouth of the fjord giving way to the limestone and shale cliffs that rose out of crystal-clear waters. Like towering guards, the monoliths flanked the waterway as it carved its way out into the sea. With crowns of green that seemed to pierce the pale blue sky, their shadows were long and deep no matter the time of day. From his vantage point at the prow of the *Ormrinn Langi*, he could see the boundary of the great river, where the waters seemed to instantly settle, as if signalling its welcome to the ships and men of Norway. It told them that they were home.

Olaf stood for a moment longer, just taking in the sight. Thorer had been right: it had only been a matter of hours before they spotted familiar land. The captain had taxed the men in the approach, demanding full speed from the rowers. He had been desperate to make it to the relative safety of the fjord. While Olaf didn't think it was necessary, he had to admit that finding himself in the shadows of the towering rock sentries did bring him comfort. From here, it would not take long to navigate upstream to Nidaross.

As the ship bore down the channel, and the sea gave way to the glacial waters of the river, an almost instantaneous calm fell upon the crew; they had been struggling against hard tides and now suddenly found themselves gliding through the shallow waves. The relief was palpable to Olaf. This whole expedition to Iceland had been a ridiculous endeavour, a failure from beginning to end. He should never have left Norway and allowed the likes of Sweyn to rise in his absence. This was his home. This was where he belonged.

That did not mean his campaign was wrong, only that his zeal to pursue it personally had been a mistake. That was what missionaries like Thangbrander were for. He was bitterly disappointed in his priest's lack of progress in the conversion and would make him acutely aware of this fact when he was brought before him. He wondered how Captain Gunnar and his crew were doing. If they were on schedule, he would expect to have his wayward priest home within the month.

A shout from the boatswain drew him out of his reverie.

"*Skeid* ahead!"

Olaf turned his gaze to the channel dead ahead and saw the approaching ship. Smaller than the *Ormrinn Langi*, it was still a sizeable vessel. The coat of arms upon the sails chilled him: a golden dragon, with the rear of a sea serpent and a crown upon its head, on a red background. There was only one man who sailed with those colours: Burislav, King of the Wends.

Olaf turned to look for Thorer. He saw that his captain was already shouting orders to the crew, the tired manic look in his eyes now seemingly mirrored in those of the rest of the men. Suddenly, Olaf became acutely aware of how exhausted everyone looked. They were worn out from the recent fight, and flagging from Thorer's fast pace, their movements sluggish. Many were injured.

"To arms! Bows to starboard. Drummers, give me more speed."

"No!" Olaf's shout cut through the activity on the deck and the crew paused mid order.

Thorer looked stunned. "My king, we need to prepare!"

"Get the men armed, but keep it slow. That is King Burislav's vessel; let us see what he wants first."

"You know what he wants, Olaf!" Thorer's shout carried over the heads of the crew and hung accusingly in the air.

"Well, he can't have her!" Olaf shouted back. He was not a man afraid of a fight, but he was depleted here, with a bloodied crew and an exhausted captain. He needed to buy time. "Now, arm the men and bring us alongside his ship!"

Thorer nodded. He issued his orders and guided the tiller accordingly.

Olaf reached down to feel the comforting grip of his short sword; as he did so, he felt the wound in his gut tear slightly and he winced. A moment later, a small red stain spread out across his blue tunic. He let out a low moan. He was in no shape to fight, but he could not let Burislav see that he was weakened.

"You!" He pointed to a deck hand running up behind the rows of archers, filling buckets with pitch.

"Yes, my king?"

"Fetch me my cloak."

The deckhand nodded and turned to run below decks.

"And be quick about it!"

"We are pulling in alongside them!" Thorer shouted. As he said this, the rowers reversed their direction and the sails were pulled up. The ship began to slow and eventually came to a stop a few hundred yards away from Burislav's vessel.

Olaf returned his gaze to the rapidly approaching *skeid*; he could make out individuals on the deck now. They, too, had arranged their archers on their port side, ready to let loose a volley at a moment's notice. A figure, tall and immobile, stood at the head of the line. A thick fur cloak obscured most of his form, but even from here Olaf could make out the bald head and hard features of Burislav. He had black, sunken eyes, and a hooked nose, jutted and angular, as if broken and rebroken repeatedly, dominated his face. Olaf had always thought he looked like a living skull.

"Where is my damn cloak?" Olaf shouted. The deckhand practically threw himself out of the hold and presented Olaf with the garment. He took it quickly and pulled it tightly about himself to try to hide the bloodstain on his tunic. "Get out of here." The young man scurried away and continued his job of preparing the pitch.

Burislav's *skeid* finished its approach and glided effortlessly beside the *Ormrinn Langi*. The captain left a good twenty-five yards between them; if this did turn into a fight, it would all be down to the archers. Olaf gave one last look over his men; he hoped none of them would be stupid enough to fire first.

"King Olaf Tryggvason! I would have words with you." The deep, resonating voice of Burislav carried across the water. To Olaf, it always sounded like he had rocks in his throat.

Trying not to wince, Olaf stepped forward and addressed his enemy directly. "You dare to enter my waters and make demands of me?" He attempted to inject his words with as much anger and strength as he could.

"You are a fine one to speak. You took something from me! I would have it back."

"It has a name. And you cannot have her. She chose me, Burislav, not you."

From experience, Olaf knew that Burislav was not a hot-headed man. Ruthless, cunning perhaps, but rarely openly angry. If Olaf were a hammer, Burislav would be a knife. So, it unnerved Olaf to see the king turn purple with rage.

"She was promised to me!" Burislav's shout sent a ripple through his men, their bows going taught in response to his anger.

Olaf had to resist the urge to duck behind cover. He saw his own men pull back on their bows. "No!" His shout across the deck was almost a scream. "Do not fire!"

"A rare thing indeed to see you acting wisely, Olaf," Burislav goaded.

"Be under no illusions, Burislav of the Wends, I stay their hands only for your sake," Olaf replied, regaining his composure. "You are here, in my country, in my fjord. I have a dozen ships out in the bay; even if you defeated me here, you would not make it to the sea before my vengeance was upon you."

"I see no ships, Olaf. Only you."

"Then you are as blind as you are stupid." As Olaf said this, he brought himself up to his full height and stared evenly into the eyes of his opponent. He felt his belly would tear yet further if he held the pose for long. The silence between them then was as loud as the crashing sea upon the cliff face. Only the creaking of the listing ships, and the cries of gulls filled the air.

"I did not come here to fight." The words came out through clenched teeth. "At least not yet." With a gesture, he instructed his men to lower their bows.

A collective sigh spread throughout the *Ormrinn Langi*.

With a nod, Olaf gave Thorer instruction to do the same. "Then why did you come?"

"I came here to offer you one last chance to be a man of honour and return Tyra, my wife."

"I see no reason to do so."

"Is open war not a good reason? Would you risk the lives of your men over your pride?"

"My forces outnumber yours two to one, and my pride is my men's pride."

"Then it is as I feared. Be warned, Olaf, son of Tryggve— this is the last time we will meet on friendly terms."

"Then this is the last time your vessel will be allowed passage through these waters," Olaf countered. "Take your ship and crew and leave my realm immediately."

Burislav merely narrowed his gaze before turning to his captain and issuing orders Olaf could not hear. Then the opposing crew unfurled their sails and began rowing.

Once the *skeid* was sufficiently far away, Olaf let out a long breath and collapsed to the floor, cradling his gut.

Thorer rushed over and grabbed the king, lowering him to the deck and holding him. "Bring me water!" he shouted.

"It is OK, my friend." Olaf lay back and stared up at the sky as Thorer poured water into his mouth.

"Our list of enemies grows long," Thorer stated, lifting Olaf's tunic to survey the wound. "You have torn the stitches."

"They fight without God."

"They fight with ships and men." Thorer pulled out a bone needle and thread from a pouch and began to sew up the wound.

Olaf let out a small cry. "I was not lying to Burislav—we outnumber him."

"Is Tyra really worth the lives of so many men?"

Olaf reached up and grabbed Thorer's tunic, pulling him close. He could taste the hot fishy breath of his captain. "Tyra is a woman of God. That is why *she* chose *me*." Olaf let his anger colour his words. "She is the only one who truly understands why we must bring the Word of God across these isles."

Thorer pried himself out of Olaf's grip. "She will be the death of you," he said at last, as he resumed stitching up Olaf's stomach. "Then what will your people do? I joined you because I believed you were the right man to unite and rule our broken kingdom. You cannot do that dead."

Olaf's anger subsided and he attempted to smile through the pain. "Old friend, I promise you, with God on our side we cannot fail."

With that, he lay back upon the deck and let Thorer finish his work. Looking up into the pale blue sky, his last sight was of the gulls circling above.

Chapter Seventeen

The thick vein of red flame flared and popped. An ember, dull and orange, curled out of the blackened wood and landed at her feet. She watched it darken and turn to ash before using the poker to stir up the remnants of the hearth fire before her. A gust of wind briefly whipped up the flames before they died down again. Sighing to herself, she placed another log upon the fire. Footsteps, slow and gentle, came up behind her.

"Do the flames reveal anything to you, my wife?" Njall asked. He walked around and knelt beside the fire, leaving a polite distance between them.

"Only that we need more wood."

Njall let out a small grunt. He passed his fingers through his hair, brown ringlets tinged with more grey than she remembered. The orange flames flickered in the deep brown of his eyes.

"Where is Arinbjorn?" Njall's voice was quiet, subdued.

"In the sleeping area." She gestured behind her, far to the back of hall, behind the sleeping screens. "Sigvaldi is keeping an eye on him."

Njall nodded. For a while, there was only the crackle and spit of the flames to fill the silence between them.

"I am sorry I left you," Njall said at last.

"Where is Tongu-Oddr?"

Njall's face flushed red and his hands clenched briefly before easing. After taking a deep breath, he replied evenly, "He has returned to his father's farm. He offered to stay and protect the hall, but I felt it best he return home."

"So now you two consider protection? After the fact?" She could not hide the pain in her voice. The anger.

"I have said I am sorry, Freya."

"What good is a husband who cannot protect his wife? Who cannot protect his lands?" Her voice was low, but she ground out the words through clenched teeth.

Winds, strong and fierce, howled outside. The door to the hall shook violently and the flames briefly flared again.

"I will not leave you again."

"I have every cause to leave *you*, Njall."

"Will you?"

That was the question that had been on her mind ever since her illicit moment with Arinbjorn. She had not chosen to marry Njall. As with all marriages it had been arranged. Her father and Njall had been lifelong friends, and when Njall visited the family, he would comment on how beautiful Freya, the only daughter, had become. When she came of age, Njall had approached her father in the proper way and asked for her hand in marriage. The men of her house had sat around and discussed the marriage proposal— her father, her brothers, and the party of men Njall had brought with him. Tongu-Oddr had been at Njall's side even then.

They had gathered around her father's hearth fire, not too dissimilar from the one she stared into now, and recounted the marriage deal. Njall had offered his *mundr*, the bride price: two hundred ounces of silver. Quite the offer, it must be said, one that was matched by her father, who offered sixty hundreds as her *heimanfylgja*, or dowry—the equivalent of eighty cows. That was no small contribution. It had made her smile to think she was worth so much.

She had listened in silence as her father promised that she was without flaw, that she had no impediments to diminish her value, and these two great men shook hands and signed the deal without once asking her opinion.

"I honestly do not know, husband," she said at last.

"I know ours has been an…unconventional marriage. But it has worked, hasn't it?"

Unconventional? She was not sure whether to laugh at that or slap him. Her father had hosted their marriage ceremony in his own hall; several days of festivities had been planned and her father gave lavish gifts to the guests who came to celebrate and witness the union. Swords, rare weapons he had acquired in his youthful travels, fine cloths, and rings to be worn about the arm. As if eighty cows were not enough of a gift to get rid of his daughter. Still, she had to admit, back then she had been excited. No, she would not have chosen Njall for herself, but of all the men her father could have married her off to, he was the best candidate. At least she had not been given to an old enemy as a peace offering, like her friend Thoris had been. Forced to spend her life among strangers.

The moment she knew her marriage was going to be a difficult one, however, came at the end of the celebration. Six of her father's men, good men of fine social standing, had taken Njall and her to the sleeping quarters and watched as the newlyweds got into bed for the first time.

She had been nervous. Terrified, even. She still felt a tightness in her chest as she remembered the look on their faces. The slightly glazed expression brought on by too much mead. Their flushed red cheeks and sweat-covered brows. Six pairs of eyes staring intently at her as she got undressed.

All her discomfort, however, seemed to be surpassed by Njall's. He was not a young man, but he had never married before. It made him an oddity in the community, and his taking Freya as a wife had been met with a collective sigh of relief by those who knew him. As he got naked before her, he seemed utterly at a loss as to what to do. It had taken some gentle coaxing, and a lot of patience, before they could consummate their marriage to the satisfaction of the men around them.

It had been a cold and passionless union, yet it gave her strength to realize she was not the only one who had been made uncomfortable. She hoped that, once the men observing were no longer necessary, their lovemaking would improve. She had been wrong. In the year they had been together, Njall had barely touched her.

"It was *your* weakness for Tongu-Oddr that left *me* vulnerable." Bile laced her words. "Do you think Kormac is the only one? The only one who looks at me and thinks I can be taken? You are lucky he is only the first one to have *tried*."

"It will not happen again." He turned to face her now. He looked so much older in the flickering firelight, which caused deep shadows in the creases that lined his face. Old and tired.

"It *cannot* happen again. Do you understand?" She reached out and grabbed his hand, holding it perhaps too tightly. "We have to come out of this looking strong or they will circle us both."

"What of Arinbjorn?" The question she had dreaded.

"What of him?"

"I am many things, Freya Hoskuldsdottir, but blind is not one of them."

"There is nothing there."

"While I am grateful that he was here to protect you, it is convenient timing that he happened to be passing our farm at that exact moment." There was no anger in his voice.

"I do not pay attention to his movements."

He picked up the poking iron and proceeded to move the smouldering logs until their flames caught again. He placed another log on the fire. "I was selfish when I asked for your hand in marriage."

This statement caught her off guard. She pulled her cloak tightly about herself.

"I knew your father of old. Helped him more than once. I knew if I asked for your hand, I would be granted it," he continued. "I thought I could offer you a comfortable life. One removed from the petty feuds and one-upmanship that seem to dominate the families here." He prodded and poked the fire; the flames hit a knot in the wood and a huge pop shook them both. "I have tried to want you."

Freya realized she was crying, slow tears moving down her cheeks. She rubbed her nose on the hem of her dress.

"If Arinbjorn——"

"If Ari what?" Freya cut him off. "Wants to fuck me?" Her anger had returned. "Where is your pride? That you would let your wife sleep with another man to preserve your lie?"

Njall seemed genuinely shocked. "I would have thought you would be happy—"

"I would be happy with a husband that wanted me. With a husband that could *protect* me. Why should I settle for less? Why don't I go and tell everyone what they already suspect: that you bugger Tongu-Oddr, that you let him bugger you, and you *like* it?" Her anger and hurt were getting the better of her. She could not stop now. "How dare you suggest I live a lie to protect yours."

"What would you have me do?" He was pleading now, and the winds outside had reached a crescendo.

"I don't know!" She was crying freely.

"I am sorry, Freya."

"Be better! Help me find and kill Kormac, the man who would have taken your wife."

"I am no fighter."

"You are a hunter. He has fled north into the mountains. I am a good tracker, but you are better. Help Arinbjorn find him."

For a moment, she stared into those tired old eyes of his. Seeing his mournful expression robbed her of the last of her energy. She collapsed in on herself and wiped away her tears.

"Tomorrow, the lawspeaker and other chieftains have agreed to an assembly. We will present our evidence that Kormac should be outlawed. Afterwards, I will help Arinbjorn find him."

Freya simply nodded. She did not have the strength to argue any further.

"I will go and double check the pigs are secured. The winds sound fierce." With that, Njall rose from the fire, took one last look at Freya, and left, a gust of chill wind signalling his departure from the hall.

*

He was an ugly sleeper. His mouth lay agape and drool puddled around his chin. His breathing was harsh and ragged, perhaps brought on by the wounds, but more likely this was just how he breathed when he lay down. Every so often he would let out a snore that made him sound like one of the swine outside. Freya chuckled to herself.

She sat at the side of the bed with a needle and thread, repairing Arinbjorn's tunic. There was nothing she could do about the bloodstain, but she could at least mend the holes. Sigvaldi had left to get his own rest and she had offered to keep an eye on the bloodied hero. Bera had given Arinbjorn something to ease the pain and it had knocked him straight out. So now he lay there, sprawled out and mouth open. What a ridiculous sight. Was this the man she desired so?

Young. Reckless. As capable a farmer as he was a poet. He would be an unsuitable match for anyone. They had grown up together; her father and his had both been land men to the same chieftain. While their families were not officially allies, they weren't enemies either, and the relationship was civil enough. From a young age, she always thought him foolish and arrogant. Yet, for all of that, he always came up with the best games and was the only boy who included her. When they got older, and they came of age, her father would not let him visit her anymore. He did not deem him a worthy suitor and did not want him scaring off potential applicants. They saw each other at the market though, and at the various assemblies. She found herself going along, just hoping to see him.

Then she had married and all that had stopped. It was improper for a married woman to be left alone with a man who was not her husband. They had drifted further apart. She considered herself lucky with Njall, in a way. He seemed more interested in his hunting than his husbandry. She might not have had a choice in her marriage, but she had become master of Njall's farm. It was she who arranged all the duties with the thralls, and her responsibilities grew further than the threshold of their hall. All the farm's successes, its failures, were hers. It was her life. Not Njall's.

If she left him, she would lose it all. Undoubtably her father would find someone else for her to marry soon enough. She would be sent somewhere she did not have as much freedom and control. Would she give this life up because of her husband's incompetence?

Despite all of this, her mind still lingered on their kiss, and she looked down now at Arinbjorn's lips. He was younger, to be sure, but Freya doubted Njall had ever been in such good condition. As he lay there, she traced the contours of his body with her eyes. He was muscular, but defined rather than broad. It was the body of a man who tilled fields for hours on end. She watched his chest rise and fall with his breathing.

It was warm in the hall, dry and smoky thanks to the hearth fire, and Arinbjorn was sweating. She watched a droplet of sweat trace its way down his neck, tumbling through the sinuous valleys and on to his chest. She reached out and wiped it away, her fingertips catching the gentle curls of his chest hair. She left her hand there, cool against the heat of his flesh, and felt the beating of his heart. It seemed fast to her.

She curled her fingers and ran the tips across his chest, feeling the salt and sweat of his body catch beneath them, before running them down his chest and to his abdomen. He was not hairy like Njall; he had some chest hair, but it was thin and wiry compared to the sheep's hide her husband had. It simply tapered to a small line that ran down the centre of his stomach and continued further below. Her hand lingered over his stomach, feeling his taut muscles beneath.

"Please, keep going."

Freya snatched her hand away and turned to find Bera staring at her, a wry smile upon her lips. Freya felt her cheeks redden.

"No need to blush on my account. I snuck a peak myself when I was healing him. Quite the man, huh?" She grinned a wicked smile that made Freya want to smack her.

"I haven't seen what kind of man he is." She returned her attention to the tunic and attempted to push the bone needle through.

"Liar." Bera picked up a small stool and moved to the other side of Arinbjorn. "You did more than kiss him earlier." She had a bowl filled with herb-scented water, which she dipped a cloth into and proceeded to wipe down the cut in his right arm.

Freya's chest tightened in panic, "You saw?"

"Heard, more like. You are lucky I was the only one." There was no judgement in her voice.

"I am married."

"Did you die when you married?"

The needle got caught in the tunic. Frustrated, Freya attempted to force it through and caused it to tear a hole in the stitching she had just finished. Growling, she tossed the bloodied mess on the floor.

"No," Freya said at last, "I didn't die."

"There we are, then. Is this what all your dreams have been about of late? The ones you came to my grandmother to talk about?"

"What do you mean?"

"When a person is torn in two, the spirit is at war with itself. You want Arinbjorn, that much is obvious."

"What if I do?"

"What else do you want, Freya?" Bera finished administering to Arinbjorn's wound. She passed the bowl over to Freya and gestured to the series of minor cuts and scrapes that covered Arinbjorn's body. "If you're going to touch him, may as well make yourself useful." She grinned.

Freya took the bowl. She couldn't help but smile back.

"I want a life for me, Bera." She began to rub Arinbjorn's cuts with the cloth.

"Easy, he is not a floor to be scrubbed. Be gentle," Bera admonished. "Is this life not yours?"

"It is Njall's."

"Such is the way of married women, I am afraid."

"But I have made so much of it *mine*. This farm, I am the one in control here. I am the one respected by the thralls. Last spring, it was me who oversaw the largest crop to be harvested on these lands in a generation."

"You are afraid to lose what little control you have?"

"Arinbjorn is a good man. But he is a traditionalist. He believes in honour and duty; he would give his life for mine. But he has this mission. I can see it in him. He so desperately needs to avenge Skjalti that he would chase this murderer all the way to Hel's domain."

"You're afraid that, if you give up on Njall and throw in with Arinbjorn—"

"That he would leave me too. Not to hunt, but to avenge. I'd be left alone all over again, only without the life and small measure of control I have built here."

"And here I was thinking all you wanted to do was fuck him." Bera's smile seemed to fill her whole face.

Freya couldn't help but laugh. "Well, I—"

Arinbjorn gave a loud snort and jerked at her touch.

A cry from outside, loud enough to defy the raging wind, shook them both. It was Njall. Freya dropped the bowl and stood, grabbing a knife from the cooking supplies and heading outside. Bera was not far behind her.

It was night, but the sky was clear, the waxing moon providing a pale blue light over the farm. The wind was fierce, blowing the fallen snow across the fields, and it whipped at them mercilessly. Looking about, Freya quickly found her husband. He was at the foot of the valley, staring into the copse of trees where Fergus and Conall had been murdered.

She took off at a run, the wind fighting her, almost blowing her off her feet. She practically fell down the hill. When she got to the bottom, she found Njall on his knees, weeping.

"Husband, what is it?" The question died on her lips. She looked up and into the copse and saw what had made him cry out.

Someone had taken the fallen branches of the ash trees and used them to make two rudimentary stick men. One was bending over, while the other stood behind. It took no leap of imagination to intuit its meaning. But the thing that caught her attention, the thing that chilled her more than the winds about her, was that the ash branches were blackened and scorched. She watched as the last orange embers winked out in the wind. The fire was gone, but she knew what it meant. Someone knew about Njall and this was a warning. They were coming to burn him.

Chapter Eighteen

Thangbrander was going to have to break them. These sheep herders and farmers respected only one thing: force. He had been reasonable. He had been patient. But now his time was up, and so was theirs. Olaf wanted results. If Thangbrander wanted to live, he had to provide them. He looked about at the group of men and women before him. They were a scrawny, haggard-looking lot. Sheep herders, thralls, freed men—they were the lowest of the low in what counted as a hierarchy around here. He had gathered them in Hallr's hall to hear reports of their acts of rebellion against their pagan masters.

Gunnar, the scarred and constantly scowling captain of Jarl Sigurd, sat off to one side. He and a selection of his men had taken up a portion of the hall all to themselves. They had commandeered one of the long tables and were busy eating supplies they had brought with them. They had not taken off their armour and they kept their weapons close. The farmers maintained their distance, clearly made uncomfortable by the warriors from Orkney. Thangbrander did not blame them; they unnerved him too, although for entirely different reasons. He wondered if Olaf had instructed them to kill him if he refused to come back.

He tried to return his attention to the congregation.

"A number of us have thrown down our tools on Gellir's lands," a farmer was saying. He was an older man, with grey parchment-thin skin drawn too tightly over his bones. Thangbrander could not tell if he was forty or sixty, so deep were the creases of his skin. Despite his frail form, his voice was resolute: "We have said we will not work again until this Christian murderer is caught."

A murmur of agreement passed among the gathered host.

"*You* may be able to throw down your tools, but what of the thralls among us?" a woman, young and portly, asked of the group. "They risk death and outlawry if they refuse to work."

"We must protect them, slave or not," another agreed.

Hands were shaken and arms were squeezed as the freedmen lent their solidarity to the thralls among the collective.

"I managed to release the entire herd of swine that my chieftain had locked away. I watched him chase them over hill and dale for hours." A chorus of laughter answered this revelation from one of the thralls, a younger man, not even out of his teens, with long unwashed hair. "He still hasn't found them all."

"How did you avoid punishment?" Thangbrander asked.

"I did not." He held up his hand to show that his small finger was missing. A bloodied tourniquet was wrapped around it. Despite this, he had a look of pride upon his face, back straight and chin high.

"Would you risk such an act again?"

"I have nine more fingers and ten more toes."

Thangbrander barked out a laugh. "This is a true man of God!" He rose from his high seat and moved down to the thrall. Placing his hand upon his shoulder, he continued to address the crowd. "One who knows the value of his life lies not in this world, but in the next. You will be one of the first to enter the gates of heaven." Thangbrander smiled as the collective cheered, and he meant it.

He took the time to pass his gaze over the gathered throng. They were looking up at him with pleading eyes and clasped hands. Most had seen too many harvests; they were old, broken things with yellowed eyes and red, wind-whipped skin. They were not fighters. Some could barely stand.

His smile faltered. This was not going to work. Freed pigs, lazy farmhands? This was not going to force the chieftains to address their needs. These people might be his flock, but they were not capable of bringing about the change he needed.

He missed Gizurr. He had stopped coming to the gatherings of late, attending only the mandated Masses and then not staying to talk. Gizurr was so well liked by the people here, his power and influence among the other chieftains had not diminished, even after his conversion. He was the one best placed to enact change from within. He was also the one who objected to Thangbrander's disruptive methods. Thangbrander understood his reticence, and Gizurr really did believe in Christ and redemption. His disapproval wounded the priest. Gizurr had been the only one who treated him with respect upon his arrival here. Thangbrander simply did not have the time to do it his way.

Doing this without him was going to be a much bloodier affair. He looked again at Captain Gunnar. He only had one more day before the captain would take him away from this island, whether he had succeeded in forcing through a conversion or not. He could not hope to baptize the whole isle in that time, but, if his plans had been put into motion, he could leave knowing the seeds had been sown. Hopefully that would be enough to stay Olaf's blade.

A chill wind burst into the hall, and the congregation turned to see Hallr come bustling in from outside. He was flushed, his face red from the chill air. He hastened to the front of the hall and stood before the priest, wheezing.

"What is it, Hallr?" Thangbrander asked. The last thing he needed was this simpleton bothering him.

"We have been summoned to the lawspeaker's hall," Hallr replied. A complex mix of panic and derision played across his face.

"Why?"

"Thorgeir claims to have new evidence regarding the Christian killer. He is holding an assembly of all the chieftains in the area."

The crowd burst into quiet mutterings as this information was digested, then turned to look at Thangbrander. An expectant pause filled the room.

"No." The words escaped his lips as a whisper.

"What was that, priest?" Hallr asked.

"We must go at once." He tried to put as much force and conviction into his voice as he could. "Come, Hallr. Let us see what justice looks like to these godless folk."

Thangbrander caught whispers of conversation as he left the throng and made to get his travelling cloak.

"Is it true?"

"Have they caught him?"

"Can we trust them?"

"Does this mean we should stop?"

There it was. That was what he was afraid of. These farmers did not have the necessary conviction behind them; only the fear of this Christian killer was driving them to act out. If Thorgeir really did have information on the murderer, Thangbrander's revolution could be over before it ever really began. He gave one last look to Gunnar. The captain was sitting on his bench, sax knife in hand, carving an apple. He returned the priest's stare.

No. He would not let this happen. He grabbed Hallr by the shoulders and pushed him ahead, out into the low morning sun. It was dark, darker than it should be for this time of day. As Thangbrander's eyes adjusted to the light, he passed his gaze over the horizon to the south. Hallr's hall was positioned high up on the headland and he could see the grey sea from here, peeking out on the horizon. The winds had whipped the waves up, and dark, purple clouds hung over the waters. Even from here, he could see the sheets of sleet and snow falling like a curtain ahead of the clouds. They did not have long before the storm front reached them. Tightening his cloak about him, Thangbrander turned to make his way towards Thorgeir's hall.

*

Thangbrander stood by the hearth fire in Thorgeir's hall, together with the few local chieftains who could make it. The tables and chairs from the last time he was here had been cleared away and now the hall seemed oddly cavernous. The only chair was for Thorgeir himself, set upon a raised dais.

Hallr was by his side, sweating profusely in the heat. He kept mopping his brow with his tunic and wringing it out on the floor.

"Would you stop that?" Thangbrander hissed.

Hallr looked at him sheepishly and proceeded to keep his arms at his side.

Thangbrander had to admit it was hot in here. He wondered if Thorgeir had done it on purpose to make his guests uncomfortable. Hallr was certainly not alone in his discomfort. Gellir, red hair plastered to his skull, had moved away from hearth fire and was attempting to use the breeze from under the door to cool down. Teitr was the only one who seemed unfazed by the heat. He stood silently waiting for their host to finish, head hung low and eyes closed, listening intently.

"As you know, our farms have been plagued of late. If it is not Christians," Thorgeir turned to look directly at Thangbrander, who simply smiled in return, "it is this murderer who had been targeting them."

"At least, that is what we thought until now," Gudrid, Thorgeir's wife, interjected. She had emerged from the sleeping area carrying a wooden tray of drinks. She went to each man in turn, her husband first, and offered a cup to them. All bar Thangbrander accepted. He waved her away. Now was not the time for mead; he needed to be able to focus.

"What do you mean?" Gellir asked from the back of the room.

"We mean that we suspect the killer may be just that—a killer. Not a pagan with a grudge against your god." Thorgeir addressed Thangbrander directly.

"We all saw the blood-daubed warning on Skjalti's door," Thangbrander scoffed. "How could it possibly be anything other than a pagan with a grudge?"

Thorgeir's smile unsettled Thangbrander—it did not reach his eyes; it was like looking into the maw of a shark.

"Because, two days ago, that same killer struck a pagan farm. That of Njall Bjarnisson and his wife, Freya."

"How can you be certain it was the same man?" Thangbrander replied. He felt an icy cloud form in his chest.

"We have spoken to witnesses of the event—Njall himself, and his bondsman, Tongu-Oddr," Thorgeir continued. "Both are men of high standing and I accept their account of events."

"Surely you are not basing your judgement on the testimony of known deviants?" Gellir asked.

Thangbrander was surprised to find himself agreeing with Gellir.

"Rumours surrounding Njall are unsubstantiated," Teitr said. "I have known his family for some time. He was late to taking a wife, but he is a good man."

"I would not come to this conclusion based solely upon testimony, priest," Thorgeir continued. "Their account matches that of the young farmer, Arinbjorn. He came to this very hall looking for answers. As you all know, he found a blue piece of cloth, torn from a cloak, and erroneously pursued the killer here."

"Who cares about the colour of the cloak he was wearing?" Gellir stated.

"How many blue cloaks do you own, Gellir?" Gudrid asked. "One of the richest men in all Iceland..." Her voice was quiet, her tone one of a mother educating a child.

"None," Gellir said at last.

"And you, Teitr? Most wise and powerful merchant that you are?" she continued.

"None."

"Blue is a very hard dye to make. Especially given the resources of this island. Only the wealthiest of men, foreigners, tend to wear blue garments. Even then, they tend to be of a king's court."

"Are you suggesting, Gudrid, that this killer is an agent of Olaf Tryggvason? Sent to do what? Kill farmers?" Thangbrander scoffed.

"I am suggesting only that the rarity of the cloak implies a single agent. The same man who killed Skjalti attacked Njall," Gudrid stated evenly. She had walked to her husband's side and now stood with her hands clasped before her, staring intently at the gathered men.

"If this is true, then you have riled up your flock for no reason, priest," Teitr said. "We face a common enemy."

"Well put, my friend," Thorgeir stated. His gaze never once left Thangbrander. "You will instruct your followers to cease their disruptions immediately."

"Are we to take the word of you pagans that it is not a pagan who is the killer?" Hallr interjected, his high-pitched voice surprisingly forceful in its conviction.

"Would you accept the word of the killer himself?" Gudrid asked.

Something about the question made Thangbrander uneasy. "Do you know him?" he asked at last.

"No, dear priest." The venom that laced Thorgeir's words made Thangbrander instinctively reach for his sax knife. There were no snakes on this godforsaken island, but right now the lawspeaker was doing a very good impression of one. "But *you* do. It is Kormac that Njall claims to have seen raiding his farm."

"Kormac?" Hallr scoffed. "That is impossible. He attends Mass every day; he is a good man."

"We resent the accusation that one of our own could be so vile and treacherous."

"I'm sure you do, Thangbrander. Yet you are more than happy to believe it of us," Gellir retorted. He moved away from the door, towards the assembled men. "This murderer is most convenient for you."

The chieftains were lining up against Thangbrander and Hallr. Smug faces, red and swollen in the heat, bared down upon them.

"What are you implying?" Thangbrander attempted to put as much anger into his voice as he could.

"Only that these killings have given you plenty of material for your righteous sermons," Gellir snarled. With his yellowed teeth and greasy red hair, he looked the very image of a devil.

"Where is Kormac now?" Thangbrander asked, trying to keep his voice level.

"Fled into the hills. This meeting was to decide whether to make Kormac an outlaw," Thorgeir answered.

"Surely he must be present to defend himself?" Hallr asked.

"We will not stand down our disruptions until we have had time to question him, hear his confession," Thangbrander said quickly. "If he is indeed guilty."

"What?" Thorgeir rose from his chair. Gudrid placed a gentle arm upon his shoulder. He stopped mid-rise and resumed his seat.

"You want us to just believe you? You who would have every reason to lie about it?" Thangbrander spoke rapidly, mind racing. "If we are to believe this of one of our own, we must hear it with our own ears. Kormac must be found."

The others in the room looked to each other and finally to Thorgeir. His chest was heaving rapidly, hand gripping his sax knife. For now, it remained unsheathed.

"You agree to stop the disruptions if we find Kormac and prove he was the killer?" Gudrid asked.

There was a pause while Thangbrander considered his options. He did not see any.

"Yes."

"Gellir, Teitr, rally your men. Good hunters and riders. We set off as soon as you're ready." Thorgeir's instructions carried across the hall.

The two chieftains nodded and made their way to the exit.

"I believe the young Arinbjorn and Njall would also like to be there, husband," Gudrid stated. "It is they who are most aggrieved."

"Agreed. Send one of the thralls to inform them of our decision. There will be no outlawry judgement until Kormac can be brought here to defend himself. Invite them to join the hunt." Thorgeir looked to Thangbrander. "I trust this meets with your approval?"

"It does, lawspeaker. If you will grant me leave, I will return to my church to pray for Kormac's safe return."

Thorgeir studied Thangbrander for a moment, then, with a wave of his hand, he dismissed the priest.

Nodding, Thangbrander turned to Hallr. "Come."

The pair made a swift exit from the lawspeaker's hall. It was midday, but the sky was almost black; the storm front he had seen on the horizon had arrived. Sleet fell heavily from above and Thangbrander had to shout over the wind.

"We must move quickly, Hallr." Thangbrander's words almost disappeared on the wind.

"What shall I do?"

"Find Captain Gunnar. Tell him to bring twelve men for a hunt."

"You intend to join the lawspeaker?" Hallr's incredulity was palpable, even through the storm.

"No. We must find Kormac first."

As the pair moved through the sleet, Thangbrander could see the rapidly disappearing figures of Teitr and Gellir. They were making their way back to their halls.

"Who knows what those pagans would make him say?" Thangbrander's voice cracked. "We leave *now*."

As the storm raged about them, Thangbrander's mind raced. He could not let that idiot Kormac destroy everything he had worked so hard to build. How could he be so stupid as to attack one of the pagan farms? Was it his zeal, or was it something else? Either way, he had jeopardized everything. Thangbrander did not like what was going to happen next, but he saw little choice in it. He would find Kormac before the others got their hands on him. Then, when he had learned everything he could from him, he would kill him.

Chapter Nineteen

The world seemed to come into existence one piece at a time around Arinbjorn. It was the scent of *blóðberg*, the artic thyme that grew abundantly in sandy and gravelly soils, that first came to him. It had a potent aroma, but the smell was so strong his head swam in it; it masked other smells as well, the tell-tale scents of earth, sweat, and smoke that permeate every farmhouse.

Smells were followed by sounds. He could hear the gentle crackle of a hearth fire, wood spitting and popping, and the clink of pots and pans as someone busied themselves over the flames. There were low murmurs, hushed yet frantic conversation between several people. He could not make out what they were saying, but he recognized some of the voices. Sigvaldi, with his deliberate way of speaking, and Freya, with her sing-song voice that carried the words around the hall in waves. The witch, Bera, and Njall also seemed to be about still. The conversation was heated, that much was clear, and there was someone else in the room. A voice he did not recognize.

He decided to open his eyes. They were gummed shut, and it took a moment to force them open. He looked about to try and get his bearings. It was almost always dark in a hall; the majority of the light came from the hearth fire or candles, so there wasn't much to look at. He was in a sleeping area, far to the back of the hall, behind a low screen that separated it off from the main area. The light from the fire bathed the earthen ceiling in a dull orange and long shadows. Looking down, he could see he was topless and covered in sweat and oil. At least he now knew where the *blóðberg* smell was coming from—he was covered in it. The witch must have used it as a salve.

His body ached, especially his back and right arm. He remembered Kormac's blade cutting into him and flinched at the memory. Still, it was a dull ache and he managed to push himself upright. He felt weak, his muscles stiff, as if they had not moved in days. He wondered how long he had been unconscious. Slowly, gingerly, he rose from the bed, but he stumbled as his legs gave way beneath him and dropped down to a knee, waiting a moment to summon his strength. Finally, he used the sleeping cot for leverage and hauled himself up to his feet.

Once up, he could see over the screen to the gathered members of Njall's farmstead surrounding the hearth fire. They were in deep conversation with two people Arinbjorn did not recognize—a youth and an older man. Freya was busy handing out pots of stew that had been bubbling over the flames. As she handed a bowl to Sigvaldi, he looked over her shoulder in Arinbjorn's direction. He broke out into a broad smile.

"The bloodied hero lives, it seems," Sigvaldi said.

The rest of the group turned to see him, and he suddenly remembered he was topless.

Bera hurried over to him. "You should not be up yet." Her tone was one of admonishment, but he could hear the relief in her voice. "Your stitches could come undone."

"Thank you, witch." His mouth was dry and his lips cracked. His voice came out as barely a whisper.

"Most people just call me Bera." She came around to his side and propped herself under his arm, taking his weight. "Come on, you're not strong enough yet. Back to bed."

"What is going on?" he asked, continuing to push forward towards the collective.

"Nothing that can't wait until you're healed." She tried to coax him around, back to the sleeping area.

"Sig!" He tried to raise his voice, but it just came out as a mumble.

Thankfully, his friend heard him and came over to his other side. Sigvaldi put his good arm around Arinbjorn's waist and gave Bera a look. She rolled her eyes but stopped trying to guide him back to bed. Instead they practically carried him over to the fire. They sat him down and Sigvaldi threw a cloak over him.

"It is good to see that you live," Njall said, once he was comfortable. "We owe you a great debt."

"Indeed, we do," Freya added. She had stopped handing out stew and now stood by her husband. Her golden eyes stared at Arinbjorn intently and she was biting her lower lip, but she said no more.

"Are you all right?" Arinbjorn's question was for the room, but he stared at Freya.

She looked away.

"Everyone is alive and safe, thanks to you," Sigvaldi said. "Do you remember what we said to you when you first woke up?"

"Kormac escaped," Arinbjorn whispered. There was a moment of silence between them all.

"Yes, but we have petitioned Thorgeir the lawspeaker to declare him an outlaw." Njall did not seem happy about this.

"What is wrong? Surely he has enough witnesses and evidence now?"

Njall gestured to the two new faces Arinbjorn did not recognize. The younger boy must have been in his mid-teens. He was scrawny, and his face was pockmarked with acne. Dry, hay-like hair tumbled back off his face.

"This is Trian, a thrall to Thorgeir."

The young man bowed his head.

"And Corcc, one of the lawspeaker's freed men."

The older man did the same. He was bald, but patches of stubble on his head were tinted red.

"May I have some water?" Arinbjorn asked. His mouth was so dry, it hurt to talk.

Bera jumped up and grabbed a small clay cup filled with water. She passed it to him and watched as he drank it all in one. "Careful, you'll drown." She smiled.

When he was done, he set the cup down and turned to face the visitors. "What news do you bring from the lawspeaker?"

The collective exchanged glances.

"Is Kormac to be made an outlaw?" Arinbjorn did not understand the reticence.

"Not yet," Corcc said at last. "The lawspeaker and the local chieftains are putting together a hunting party. They intend to hunt Kormac and bring him back to defend himself at an assembly."

"What?" The little strength Arinbjorn had seemed to vanish, and he was glad he was already sitting down. "What more evidence does Thorgeir need?" He could not hide the anger in his voice.

"It appears that your friend, Priest Thangbrander, argued that Kormac should be able to defend himself." Disgust infused Sigvaldi's words.

"Thangbrander?" Arinbjorn was incredulous. "Why does he care?"

"Kormac is one of his new Christians," Njall explained. "He must be trying to protect him."

"But Kormac killed Skjalti, a Christian!"

"I know. But the death of Skjalti has galvanized his followers; they are disrupting the way of life around here," Freya said. She moved around the fire and sat next to Arinbjorn, placing a hand upon his shoulder. "It appears Thorgeir attempted to get the priest to put an end to the disruptions."

"He refused," Trian said. "He did not believe my master that Kormac could be guilty of such crimes and believes it to be 'pagan lies'. He will not stop their rebellious acts unless it is proven that Kormac is the killer."

"I never understood why Thorgeir did not just kill Thangbrander the moment these disruptions started," Njall said. He was pacing the room, clearly distressed.

"Many of these Christians are old friends and family. The land is being split in two. If Thorgeir were to move against Thangbrander without good cause, we could have a civil war on our hands," Sigvaldi countered.

"Are the acts of his followers not enough?" Njall asked. "*He* should be tried for Kormac's murders." There was something more to Njall's anger. He was fidgeting, running his fingers over the hilt of his sax knife again and again. Arinbjorn could see the dull, polished sheen on the hilt where Njall had made this gesture many times.

"Has something else happened?" Arinbjorn asked.

Njall looked at him and shook his head. "Nothing."

"You know our laws, Njall," Freya said to fill the growing silence. "Kormac is a free man and landowner, albeit of a small farm. He does not answer to Thangbrander in the eyes of the law and is responsible for his own actions. The priest will certainly argue that is the case for all his followers."

"So, he whips them up into a fury and sets them out against us, but is not responsible for their crimes?" Njall spat into the fire. "Quite the system he has here."

"I met with Thangbrander," Sigvaldi interjected. "He took me aside and showed me his collection of vestments."

"What are they?" Bera asked. She was busy making another poultice by the fire; Arinbjorn could smell the *blóðberg*.

"Special cloaks worn by the Christian missionaries. One was missing."

"So, you think this Kormac stole the cloak?" Njall asked.

"I am sorry, Sig, but that does not make any sense," Arinbjorn said. "When it was just Christians being targeted, the theft of a cloak to do the deed could be seen as an extra insult."

"That is certainly how Thangbrander presented it," Sigvaldi said uneasily.

"But now that Freya and Njall have been attacked," Arinbjorn continued, "it just looks like misdirection."

"You think the priest is involved somehow?" Freya asked.

Arinbjorn went to reply but let out a small cry as his stitching pulled and a wave of nausea passed through him.

Bera practically leapt across the hearth fire to check his wounds. She passed him a drink of water that stank of the *blóðberg*. "Drink." It was not a request.

Arinbjorn did so. "I do not know what to believe," he said at last. "But I do not trust the priest."

"We have been invited by Thorgeir to join his hunt for Kormac," Njall explained. "If there are to be any answers, they must come from him."

"When does the hunt leave?"

"Now," Corcc said. "The chieftains will be amassing their men at my master's hall as we speak. They will not wait long."

"Then we better get going." Arinbjorn went to rise, but found several hands placed upon his shoulders.

"You are in no fit state to ride," Bera said sternly.

"You will wait here while we go," Njall said. He cast a brief look at Freya that Arinbjorn could not interpret.

"No." Arinbjorn pushed Bera and Sigvaldi away and summoned all his strength to stand. "I cannot fight, I grant you that. But, with so many men present, I won't have to. I can be propped up on a horse."

"The weather is turning out there, Ari," Sigvaldi said tenderly. "A storm has come in. It is too dangerous."

"No!" Arinbjorn stunned himself as much as them with the force of his shout. "He killed Ask and Embla. I will be there when he is found."

The others passed a look among themselves.

"Well then, you'll need me along too," Bera said at last.

Arinbjorn turned to look at her, this small, round-faced woman with flushed cheeks and manic hair. She held his gaze.

"And me," Sigvaldi said. "I made a promise to be by your side, no matter what." He looked pointedly at Freya, who looked away.

Njall coughed. "Then we have little time. Bera, prepare him as best you can for travel. Sigvaldi and I will saddle the horses. Corcc, Trian, return to your master with all haste and let him know we are coming."

The group dispersed to their duties, leaving Arinbjorn with Freya and Bera.

"I have to grab some supplies for the journey." Bera gave the two of them a look before disappearing to the back of the hall.

Freya stood on the other side of the hearth fire, arms folded about herself, staring off towards the door after her husband. "I can't convince you to stay here, can I?" Her voice was low, resigned.

"I have to see this through, Freya." Arinbjorn moved across to her and reached out. She did not take his hand, so he pulled it back.

"I know." She attempted a smile, but it did not reach her eyes, which shimmered in the firelight.

"I will be coming back. I promise."

"This time." Her body shook.

Arinbjorn closed the gap and held her. She remained tense. "What do you mean?"

Freya looked up at him, her expression cool. "You will have to follow this to the end."

"I will always come back."

"You expect me to be waiting for you?"

"But, last night—"

"Was a mistake!" Freya pulled herself out of his arms and wiped her eyes. "A foolish hope."

"What are you saying?" Hurt now infused his words.

"Look at you." She gestured to his body, his wounds. "You nearly *died*. I cannot rely on a man who so effortlessly throws his life away." She straightened now, her gaze stoic.

"I almost died *protecting* you! Now, you expect me to let Kormac escape?" He was angry, confused. His voice raised and filled the hall. "After everything he has done?"

"There are two dozen men assembling to deal with Kormac as we speak, but you still insist on going." Freya's voice was calm, but her eyes were wide and red.

"I *have* to see this through."

"I know, Arinbjorn Thorleiksson. I know." She smiled at him. "But I cannot give up my life for a man who may not come back to me."

Bera returned to the fire. She was fully dressed to travel, with several leather satchels about her person. She presented

Arinbjorn with his tunic and cloak. "It is time for us to leave," she said, casting her gaze to Freya quickly.

"Yes. It is." With that, Arinbjorn turned from Freya and gingerly donned the tunic and cloak. He heard the door open and a burst of cold wind flowed through the hall. Freya had gone.

*

It was early afternoon when they joined Thorgeir's hunting party, and clouds the colour of bruises hung thick and low. What was sleet over the ocean became curtains of hail and snow on land. The wind roared in Arinbjorn's ears, and he struggled to keep his horse moving in a straight line. The wind was often the most unpredictable element of the weather in Iceland; it could scour the earth bare, uprooting whole fields, and it piled snow high up into dunes. All too often, a person could be blown off their course and down into a crevasse hidden in the ice. Travel during storms like this was tantamount to suicide. Which told him everything he needed to know about the desperation of the chieftains to find Kormac and end the Christians' revolt. So long as they helped him avenge Skjalti, he did not care.

Thorgeir had assembled quite the group. There were twelve of his own men—farmers that tilled his lands known for their proficiency in hunting. Teitr and Gellir had brought six men each, and, when combined with Njall's party of Arinbjorn, Sigvaldi and Bera, that brought the total up to thirty. Thorgeir insisted on single-file riding through the storm, with Corcc, the freeman who had come to deliver the news to Njall, taking point. He was a skilled navigator and he knew the safest routes through the ice floes and ravines that bisected the journey north, hidden beneath the freshly fallen snow.

Arinbjorn was on a horse lent to him by Njall. It was a small, stocky creature, with a thick chestnut mane, but he lacked the strength to guide it, so instead he shared it with Bera, who proved an adept horsewoman. He clung tightly to her back and ignored some of the looks he received from the other men. At least he was here. Bera had insisted on double-cloaking him, and they were all wearing hide gloves and thick boots to keep out the worst of the storm. They were in the middle of the party, following on the heels of Njall, with Sigvaldi immediately behind. The wind was too loud for conversation, so they trudged on in silence, stopping every now and again when Corcc put up his hand to change direction, seemingly unhappy with the route ahead.

It was slow going. With the sky so dark, it was impossible to know how long they had been out, and time seemed to stretch endlessly. Arinbjorn's back ached and his right arm felt weak; he could barely hold on to Bera, but did not wish to let her know for fear she would fuss over him. Every time he felt like he might topple, he hauled himself forward into the wind until he righted himself. The snow and hail passed over them in waves, briefly obscuring their vision enough to lose sight of Corcc and those at the head of the trail, before clearing again. The mountains to the north inched ever closer as they made their way through the Mosfell valley.

When they had arrived at Thorgeir's hall, the lawspeaker had revealed to them his plan. Kormac fleeing north was a dangerous and reckless move; there were no farmsteads up towards the mountains, only icefields and glaciers. There was, however, a network of ice caves that criss-crossed through the Langjökull glacier. These were dangerous, unpredictable places, but they could be used for shelter. Several men who had been made outlaws had fled there; all died in the end, but some lasted longer than others. Thorgeir believed Kormac would have gone there first.

It was a guess, but a guess was all they had. The group had agreed and set out accordingly. It took them hours to make it to the foot of the glacier; night was almost certainly coming. Not that Arinbjorn could tell the difference right now.

As they made their way through the ice fields, and passing sheets of hail, his mind wandered. He thought of Freya. Her last words had stung him. He had not set out to steal her from Njall, but *she* had kissed *him*, and it was *she* who had instigated far more than that. Now she wanted nothing to do with him because he was trying to right the wrongs of Kormac? It made no sense to him. He found himself thinking about what he should have said to her back at the farm. He wanted to grab and shake her, he wanted to shout at her, he wanted to kiss her.

He was so lost in thought, he almost fell off the horse when Bera brought it to an abrupt stop behind Njall.

"Watch out!" Bera shouted.

Njall turned to them, face hidden behind his thick cloak and tanned hide. "We are here." He had to shout over the winds that coursed across the plains. "Corcc has found something." He gestured ahead of him.

They were now at the foot of Jarlhettur, the Jarl's Hat, a mountain that dominated the horizon. In the current storm, they could not see the top of it. Not far ahead of them, the ground went into a sharp decline into the ice of the glacier. A jagged maw, pitch black and surrounded by blue-white rime, lay at the bottom of it. An ice cave—it opened up the way to Hel's domain.

"Kormac?" Arinbjorn shouted back.

"No, another trail. It looks like several people on horseback came out this way, recently enough that the storm hasn't hidden their tracks."

"Who could it be?"

"We don't know, but Kormac may have help. We are almost at the first ice cave, so we will know soon enough."

Nausea, brought on by the pain in his back, passed through Arinbjorn. They needed to hurry up. If Bera's poultices didn't last, he wasn't sure how long he could remain conscious. Kormac was just ahead, possibly with a group of co-conspirators; Arinbjorn had to press on. He gripped tightly to Bera and gestured for her to continue. She whipped the reins in her hands and dug her heels into the horse, urging it forward and passing Njall. The group followed suit and the hunting party made their descent beneath the ice.

Chapter Twenty

Thangbrander regretted his decision to come out almost immediately. The journey to the Jarlhettur mountain had been mired from the start. Hallr had rounded up Gunnar and twelve of his best men, getting them horses from his stables, and they had assembled outside Hallr's hall. They were a motley group, and it was clear that Gunnar's men were not familiar with horse riding. They found the stocky, low horses difficult to control. It would have been comical had Thangbrander not been so desperate. They practised guiding their mounts around the farmyard while Thangbrander spoke with the captain.

"Why must we find this Kormac, priest?" Gunnar gestured to the dark clouds above and had to shout over the rising wind. "Especially in this weather?"

"He could undo everything I have accomplished here." Thangbrander was busy affixing his short sword to his steed. Once he was happy it was secure, he mounted the horse. He felt heavy in the saddle; he had got rid of his traditional vestments and instead wore a chain mail shirt over his tunic. Over that, he wore a hide cloak to better keep out the weather.

"This is the last day you have here, Thangbrander," Gunnar warned. He had mounted his own horse and now sat waiting for the priest. He was a squat man, broad and heavy, and to Thangbrander's eyes he looked more like one of the horses than a man. The thick scar across Gunnar's brow was now slick with sleet, and the way it glistened made Thangbrander sick. "Are you sure you want to spend it doing this?"

"If they get hold of Kormac first, they will make him say whatever they want. A Christian murderer could set back Olaf's plans for conversion by years. Do you want to explain that to him?"

Gunnar appeared to consider this for a moment. He passed his gaze over the assembled men. They seemed to have mastered their horses, for the moment, and now stood waiting to set off.

"Conversion is not *my* mission, priest."

"It is everyone's mission who serves our king." The hail had begun then—waves of sharp ice stinging their ears and faces. Thangbrander had to shout over the noise. "Help me find Kormac and then we will leave immediately for Norway."

Gunnar held Thangbrander's gaze a moment before turning to lead his men out. Thangbrander followed. The captain's men were well-trained combatants and heavily armed, but they did not know the lay of the land at all. They had to rely upon an elderly thrall of Hallr's, Mael, who had not left the farmstead in many years. He must once have been a portly fellow, but years of ill health had drained him of his fat, leaving him looking like a pile of creased cow skin draped over bones, and his is yellow eyes were tinged with blood. He led the pack at a slow pace.

"Can we not go any faster?" Thangbrander had asked, desperately. He was sure they had managed to get out ahead of Thorgeir and his hunting party, but he knew it would be only a matter of time before the pagans caught up.

"The Langjökull glacier is littered with ravines and boulders," Mael replied, his voice raspy and phlegm filled. He coughed his way through the words. "A horse could break a leg; you could fall to your death."

It turned out that Mael had been right to set a slow pace. It was two hours into their journey north to the mountains when they suffered their first casualties. They had just made it to the base of the glacier and the beginning of the ice fields when Mael called a halt to their party. He stared across the sea of ice and snow. Thangbrander could not see anything to be concerned about; the route seemed relatively flat and even, aside from the giant obsidian boulders that poked out of the ice sheet like black teeth. After a moment, Mael gestured to the group to move wide to the left; before he could take point, however, one of Gunnar's men moved ahead.

They got about a hundred feet before they let out a wail. There was a sound like a crack of thunder as the ice sheet gave way beneath him. Thangbrander could do nothing but watch as the sailor disappeared beneath the surface in an explosion of ice and snow. His scream, and that of his horse, was muted the moment he fell from sight. Two others leapt off their horses, grabbing rope from their satchels. They ran over to where the sailor had disappeared, crying out his name.

"No, wait!" Mael shouted. "You don't know where—"

He did not get to finish his sentence. As the men rushed to save their fallen comrade, the ground gave out beneath them and they, too, went below the ice, their shouts drowned out in the wind.

"Mael!" Gunnar was raging. He brought his horse alongside the ancient thrall and struck him about the face. Thangbrander thought his meaty fist would knock the elderly man's head clean off. "You said you knew where you were going!"

"Your man went ahead of me! You must stick behind me and travel single file!" Mael's rasps were barely audible.

Gunnar turned to face Thangbrander. "You will pay for their deaths, priest!" Only his eyes were visible beneath his thick hood, but the rage and hurt were palpable.

"They died for King Olaf." He kept his gaze steady and stared down the captain.

Muttering something beneath his breath, Gunnar turned his horse away.

"Continue to lead us, Mael," Thangbrander instructed.

Nodding, the thrall resumed the march.

Their journey slowed to a crawl as their guide took them on a circuitous and seemingly random route across the icefields. They criss-crossed their way closer to the foot of the black mountains ahead. They did not lose any more men, but Thangbrander was conscious of the time. He looked behind him to see if he could see the other hunting party coming up after them. The storm obscured his vision, however, and he saw no one. Still, they could not be far behind now. As the shadow of the mountain joined the dark, bruised skies above, Mael brought the group to another stop.

"What is it this time, thrall?" Gunnar asked.

"There are numerous ice caves that line the base of the mountain. Which one do you think Kormac has fled to?" Mael asked.

"Which one is closer?" Thangbrander asked.

"There used to be one over there, but it could have collapsed years ago." He pointed to a dip on the ice, around two hundred yards away.

"Does it lead to others?" Gunnar asked.

"Occasionally, but not always. The routes are unpredictable and change."

"This is madness, Thangbrander!" Gunnar shouted. "We could be here for weeks!"

"No, Kormac can't have got far. Especially on foot. Take us to the nearest cave; let us hope he fled there."

Mael nodded his understanding and began leading the group off in the direction he had pointed out.

*

Kormac knew he had made a mistake. Normally, this stretch of tunnel was close enough to the surface to allow the sunlight to penetrate through the ice and light up the interior with a dull, diffuse light. Today, however, the blue-white cave was dark. The rime walls were slick like a gullet, and he felt that he had been truly swallowed by the earth.

There was a dull howl coming through the ice and he suspected that a storm had blown in. He crawled back into his linen tent. He had managed to drive two iron nails into the opposing walls of the cave and run a rope between the two, draping the cloth over the middle before pegging the sides down. It proved to be quite an effective shelter. The floor was slick and cold, but he used the priest's thick woollen vestments as a mat to keep the worst of it at bay.

His flight from Njall's farm had been hectic, but his route here had taken him back past his own hall. This had given him the time to grab camping supplies and more cloaks before the inevitable hunting party tried to follow him. He lay there in the dark, swaddled in several layers, and thought about his predicament. He had been a fool to go after Freya. He knew he may have jeopardized the priest's mission by attacking a pagan farm as well, but it wasn't about faith. He had been watching Njall's farm for months, observing as that degenerate farmer went off with his lover Tongu-Oddr.

How could anyone prefer the company of a man over Freya? She was as beautiful and vicious as the god she was named after, a prize of a wife, going unvalued and forgotten. Kormac knew he could be a better husband; he would show her what it felt like to have the warmth of a man upon her. So, he had watched, waited, and, when the time was right, he had gone over to see her—only to be rebuffed and humiliated before those ridiculous thralls. If only she knew what he was capable of. He was no simple farmer. His father had fought alongside Haakon the Good against Erik Bloodaxe and his children. Kormac had joined up with Olaf before the king had even converted to Christianity. In his own, limited way, he had helped the king defeat Haakon Jarl, the Danish vassal. Slaughtering a family of farmers and a tracker was nothing compared to that. He would show Freya what kind of man she was dealing with.

To be fair to them, the Irish thralls had proven to be tougher than they looked. Scrappy, if not trained, and they managed to get a good few punches in before he took them down. With them out of the way, he knew she would be alone except for her female thrall, scared and vulnerable. In desperate need of a man to protect her. His plan had been to go to her then, when her need was greatest, and show her his strength.

Then Arinbjorn had shown up. That stupid sheep farmer had ruined everything.

A low murmur that rose in pitch as it reverberated through the ice cave cut through Kormac's reverie. He snapped up, grabbed his waiting short sword, and popped his head out of the tent to listen. Voices. Someone had come to find him.

He crawled out of the tent and straightened himself. His back gave a loud crack, the cold causing his muscles to seize. He let out a small grunt and rubbed his hands together, trying to get feeling to return to them. He would need all his skill to get out of here. He was not sure how long he had before they reached him; the tunnels had a way of amplifying or muting sounds, making it hard to guess.

He had pitched his tent in the middle of the tunnel that linked to several cave entrances. One was still open, but most had collapsed or became so tight he would have to crawl out. He would take his chances with one of the smaller exits and try to double back behind the hunting party, maybe steal a horse and return to the coast.

He was about to leave when he heard a clear shout reverberate down the tunnel.

"Kormac!" It was the priest. "It is me, Thangbrander." The priest's voice, low and powerful, carried through the ice. "We have come to get you out of here."

Relief spread through Kormac. He had not been abandoned. Even though he had made mistakes.

"Priest!" Kormac tried to shout, but it came out in a broken whisper. He had not spoken in days and his throat felt swollen and constricted. He would have to go to him. Quickly gathering his things and abandoning the tent, Kormac set off towards the sound of Thangbrander's voice. The caves were not one continuous size and he often had to crawl from one chamber to the next, before standing and resuming his march. He was weaker than he realized. His muscles were seizing up and his breathing was laboured as he clawed his way to the surface.

He had managed to get most of the way back to the main entrance when he saw the light from their torches, the yellow flickers of flame lighting up the ice from below. He was tired now, and his legs lacked the strength to keep going. He had to lean against the wall and slowly slid down to a seated position.

He could not shout, but he could get their attention. He took his sword and started beating it against the ice. It was a dull sound, but he hoped it was enough.

It was.

"Priest Thangbrander, we have found him!"

Kormac did not recognize the voice, but he did take note of the accent. It sounded more guttural than his Norwegian brethren, maybe from one of the islands, like Shetland or Orkney. A small, squat figure hacked his way around a bend in the ice, preferring to carve his way through rather than crawl. Even heavily cloaked, it was clear he was a well-built man. He approached the prone Kormac and knelt before him.

"He looks in pretty bad shape," the islander said.

A moment later, the tall, broad figure of Thangbrander came up behind him. He, too, was heavily cloaked, but Kormac caught the glint of chain mail over the priest's tunic. He was expecting trouble.

"Well done, Gunnar." Thangbrander knelt before Kormac and gently cupped his face with a callused hand. "Your eyes are black and your skin pallid, Kormac."

"I…" Kormac summoned what strength he could. "I am sorry, priest."

"Now is not the time for apologies." He gestured to Gunnar to lift Kormac up. "Let us get you out of here."

Gunnar hoisted him to a standing position, smiling warmly, before taking up position on his right side and carrying him out.

It took them a little while to reach the widest point in the tunnel system, just a short distance from the mouth of the cave. Kormac could now clearly hear the storm outside, and the wind howled through the tunnel. As the trio rounded the final bend, he saw a group of men sitting waiting, all heavily armed. They stood as Thangbrander and Gunnar placed him down upon the ground. He felt their gazes upon him. Instinctively, he reached for the comfort of his sword and found it missing from his scabbard. They must have taken it during the walk.

"What is going on?" Kormac managed to whisper. He was exhausted, but something about this situation seemed wrong. A cold knot was forming in his chest.

"We came out here to find you, Kormac," Thangbrander said. He turned to the other men. "Go and wait outside, and do not let anyone in."

The men looked uneasily at each other.

"Do as he says," the islander said.

Reluctantly gathering their gear, they moved into the storm outside.

Once they were gone, Thangbrander squatted before Kormac, his face contorting into a wince. His knees must be paining him, Kormac thought.

"Who were those people?"

"This is Captain Gunnar, a housecarl to Jarl Sigurd of Orkney." As Thangbrander spoke, the islander removed his hood and Kormac could see clearly the man underneath. It was his forehead scar that stood out the most. "He and his men have come to take us back to Olaf."

"Then our work here is done?" Kormac coughed, phlegm filled his throat and his breathing felt raspy.

"Yes, my friend, we can do no more here." Thangbrander unsheathed his sax knife and brought the blade close to Kormac's neck. He flinched, but the priest merely cut the strings on his cloak, easing the pressure on his swollen neck. "There, that should help you speak."

"Why all the weapons?" Kormac asked.

The priest let out a long sigh. Kormac had always found Thangbrander to be an indomitable figure, especially for a man his age. His black hair was long and thick, with only the grey in his beard giving away his long life. Right now, however, he looked very old. His face was weather-beaten, red raw from the wind and ice that was raging outside, and his eyes seemed sad.

"It appears there was an attack upon some of the pagans. The lawspeaker seems to think that it was you." He paused for a moment while he looked Kormac up and down. "A hunting party has been sent to find you. I wanted to find you first."

Kormac felt his chest and throat tighten, and he began to cough violently. He doubled over from the pain of it. He felt a weighty hand upon his back. When the fit was over, he looked up at Thangbrander. "I am sorry," he repeated.

"So, it was you." The words were muted, whispered. Thangbrander let out a long sigh, shaking his head.

"Now you know. We must hurry," Gunnar interjected.

"A moment, Gunnar," Thangbrander commanded.

"I had to have her—" It was all Kormac could manage before a coughing fit took him again.

"You have jeopardized our entire mission here." Anger now infused the priest's words. "And you have put me in a very difficult position."

The sax knife was still out of its sheath, Kormac noticed. He shifted uncomfortably.

"I did everything you asked. Picked a target that would galvanize the rest of the Christians. I even wore the vestments so I could bless them on their journey to Christ. I saved their souls."

"And you did well." Thangbrander leant forward, placing a heavy hand upon his shoulder. He squeezed a little too tightly. "The death of Skjalti and his family has set things in motion that cannot be stopped."

Kormac had another coughing fit; Thangbrander held on to him as he doubled over violently, bringing him in close and putting his arms around his neck to support him, allowing him to rest his head upon his shoulder.

"But, by attacking Njall's farm, you have brought undue attention to us, and if they ever found out what we did—"

There was a loud cry from outside.

Kormac looked up towards the cave entrance. He could hear men shouting.

"They have found us," Gunnar said, unsheathing his sword. "We must go now, priest."

"I really wish it had not come to this, Kormac." The priest's face was so close that Kormac could smell his breath; it was stale and hot.

Kormac went to speak, but Thangbrander tightened his arms about his throat and placed his hands over his mouth. Kormac gripped tightly to the priest, his body shaking, legs spasming as he fought for air. Using what strength he had, he pulled himself upright to look into his priest's eyes. As he tried to breathe, hot liquid bubbled up from his throat, and he felt his lungs burn. Thangbrander held him close. Black spots filled Kormac's vision and he clawed at the priest's back. He began to cry.

"May you find yourself in the embrace of God."

They were the last words Kormac heard.

*

"Who stands before us?" Thorgeir's shout was barely audible in the storm; Arinbjorn had to strain to hear him. The lawspeaker had dismounted from his horse and stood at the front of the hunting party, looking down into a rift in the ice.

The black clouds had descended fully, darkening the skies and blanketing them in whirling snow. Arinbjorn urged Bera to get them closer, and she reluctantly agreed, bringing them nearer to the ravine where the lawspeaker stood.

He acknowledged them with a nod. "Looks like we might have trouble," Thorgeir shouted over the howl. "Form a line about this ridge." He gestured back to the thirty-strong party, who began to fall into position at his command, forming a tight circle around the ravine.

The horse beneath Arinbjorn and Bera whinnied unhappily, and Arinbjorn dismounted, leaving Bera to steady it. He fought the wind to make his way over to the ledge.

"What are you—?" Bera's cry was lost to the wind.

There, at the foot of the crevasse, was the ice cave. Seven figures were standing before the entrance, swaddled in hides, their heavily armoured forms creating gross silhouettes in the snow whipping about them. Arinbjorn could not make out their faces, but he could see their blades easily enough. They looked up at him, swords unsheathed, but made no moves.

Thorgeir took up position beside him and shouted down into the ravine, "Who are you that dare wield open arms against a chieftain of these lands?"

"They do not bear arms against you, Thorgeir; they merely protect me." Even through the howl of the storm, Arinbjorn recognized the deep, bass voice of Thangbrander. The priest emerged from the cave, his thick black hair billowing in the wind. He was followed by another man with a prominent scar upon his forehead.

"What is the meaning of this, Thangbrander?" Thorgeir demanded.

"If you would speak with me, speak. Do not bray like a dog." Thangbrander took up position in the middle of his party and stared up at the lawspeaker.

"You must think me a fool to treat with you so armed," Thorgeir shouted.

"Where can we go in this storm? Come and see what you have wrought." The priest's black hair whipped about him wildly, his face flush from the cold. He raised his hand, and his party sheathed their swords.

With a grunt, Thorgeir waved over to Corcc, who approached with Teitr and Gellir. "Come, but carry your weapons. I fear treachery."

Arinbjorn watched as the two chieftains dismounted and left their horses in the care of Corcc.

"I am coming with you too," Arinbjorn said.

"I care not," Thorgeir replied. "But do not get in our way."

The trio of chieftains began to make their slow way down the icy slope. Around the edge of the ravine, the remaining farmers shifted uncomfortably. Those that had them began to take out their axes.

Before Arinbjorn could make his own descent, he was yanked back by Bera.

"Let them deal with this." Bera's eyelashes were covered in flakes of snow, and her round face was red from the cold.

"I have to see this through." He shrugged off her grip.

"Look around you—these men are getting ready for a fight!" Her voice was getting hoarse from the shouting.

"All the more reason to find Kormac before this turns violent!" Bracing himself against the cold, Arinbjorn followed after the chieftains.

It was quieter in the crevasse, the black rock providing protection against the storm raging above, and the heavy snowfall muffled the footsteps of the descending party. Free from the snow devils, Arinbjorn could get a better look at the men who awaited them. They were heavily armed and covered in chain mail, wielding swords and...bows and arrows? No one he knew in Iceland had a bow and arrow. This meant they were foreigners. They stood still, seemingly impervious to the cold, their hands resting on their now-sheathed swords.

Thorgeir and the other two chieftains came to a stop a couple of yards away from the cave entrance, halfway up the incline, allowing them to look down upon the priest. Arinbjorn and Bera took up position just to their left, Bera steadying him as the wind buffeted them on the ice.

"What are you doing here?" Gellir spat, his red hair plastered across his scalp.

Thangbrander did not acknowledge him; instead, he turned to Arinbjorn. "Have you come to right a wrong or merely punish a Christian?"

"I have come for the truth," Arinbjorn replied. "Where is Kormac?"

"Why are you even here, Thangbrander?" Thorgeir interrupted. "You were asked to join my hunting party, yet you have formed your own."

"You expect me to trust you to treat a man of God with dignity?" Thangbrander scoffed. "I have seen how you deal with emissaries of Christ first hand, lawspeaker."

"He is a poor man of Christ, priest. I saw Kormac attack with my own eyes," Arinbjorn said. "I still carry his wound."

"You must be mistaken," Thangbrander replied. He began to pace back and forth, protected by his ring of guards. "But I am a man of honour; I came here to ensure Kormac would receive a fair Christian trial."

"Do Christians deliver justice at the tip of a blade?" Teitr asked, pointing to his heavily armed guards.

"No more than you do. Thirty armed men, for one man?" Thangbrander gestured to the men above. "You did not come seeking justice."

"Enough of this," the man with the scar across his forehead interjected. "We are leaving here; you would do well to let us pass."

"Quiet, Gunnar!" Thangbrander commanded. "We agreed we would do this my way."

The man called Gunnar stepped up beside the priest, nocking an arrow in his bow. "You do not command *me*, priest," he spat.

"Your men would protect Kormac?" Gellir was getting agitated, shuffling on the balls of his feet, his fingers clenching and unclenching over his axe hilt.

"He is protected by Christ now," Thangbrander shouted, clearly agitated, and he tried to position himself back between Gunnar and the chieftains.

"He is dead?" Thorgeir's face dropped, his voice low.

Thangbrander turned his full attention to the men stood atop the ravine, his voice carrying over the wind. "Kormac died of exposure, cold and forsaken in this empty cave. A victim of slander!"

"No!" Arinbjorn shouted. "I saw him wearing the blue vestments that you yourself claimed were stolen from your church."

"Your eyes deceived you; I have seen no such vestments on his person."

"Let us see the body," Arinbjorn demanded.

"You would have to go through us," Gunnar stated evenly.

"I will not let you defile his bodily person," Thangbrander said, giving Gunnar a harried look. "He is to be buried according to Christian tradition." The priest brought himself to his full height and Arinbjorn caught a flash of silver beneath his cloak. The priest was wearing chain mail. But, as Arinbjorn inched closer, he saw something more—a dark, bloody stain upon his collar.

"Your god has no power here, Thangbrander," Thorgeir retorted. "Kormac was a man of Iceland, and we would see his body to learn the truth of the matter."

"Are you wounded?" Arinbjorn interjected, pointing to the discolouration. "Surely a dead man could not have hurt you?"

The priest ruffled, looking down upon the stain. He frowned. "An old wound."

"I saw you this morning, priest," Thorgeir added, his eyes narrowing. "You bore no such stain…"

"Blood freezes quickly on the glaciers," Arinbjorn added. "*That* looks recent."

The arrow was loosed before the priest could respond. The wind whipped up the snow about them and, for a moment, they were obscured by white cloud. The arrow flew above them, caught in the sudden updraught, and arced out of the ravine and into Corcc's neck. He sat upright in his saddle, a look of surprise etched upon his face, before tumbling into the snow. Blood spurted from his neck like the geysers not far from Arinbjorn's home. Nobody moved; they were all too stunned to react.

The priest's face lost its colour as he turned to look at the culprit. Gunnar was already nocking another arrow.

"No—"

The priest's protest was lost on Gunnar, who fired again. This time, the chieftains and Arinbjorn dropped and dived for cover, while Thangbrander's guards unsheathed their weapons and advanced. Within moments, the priest's men were upon them, flashing steel and manic grins. Arinbjorn reached for

Bera, and the two of them began to crawl away from the fight, Bera's cries lost to the storm raging about them.

Looking back, Arinbjorn saw the lawspeaker hack the head off one of the attackers, his broad axe embedding itself in the spine of his foe. He ripped it out before driving it back in and severing the head completely. The head rolled back down the incline and into the cave entrance, a trail of blood running all the way behind it.

The cave. He had to find Kormac's body.

"Bera!" he shouted over the violence behind them. "Roll with me." He gestured to the cave.

She shook her head, her eyes wide with fear.

He did not have time to argue. Grabbing her, he pulled her close before launching them down the incline and into the cavernous maw at the bottom. As they tumbled and rolled past the advancing guards, Bera's screams filled the air. He felt a fire in his back and arm as his wounds tore open anew. His cries joined Bera's.

When they reached the bottom, he tried to pick himself up, but he stumbled, dizzy from the fall. He took a moment to regain his strength, looking about to steady himself. The fighting had reached the top of the ridge. Their attackers were fewer in number, but they were well trained. He watched them dispatch a few of the gathered farmers in a frenzy of severed limbs and hot blood.

Thankfully, the lawspeaker and the other chieftains were no pushovers. Many had travelled abroad on raiding expeditions in their youth. He watched Gellir, the flame-haired chieftain, bisect one of the men from shoulder to navel, while Teitr, aged as he was, managed to run a short sword through the screaming mouth of another.

Arinbjorn vomited—a thick, chunky liquid, tinged with red. Nauseated, he turned away from the fight and back towards the cave. Bera was beside him then; she had stopped her screaming and was now practically dragging him into the darkened entrance.

Several horses were just inside, sheltered from the weather. They were clearly frightened by the noises, whinnying and pawing at the rime-covered floor. Carefully, Arinbjorn and Bera made their way past the beasts and into the cave proper. The sound of the battle was muted in here, muffled by the ice and the storm. Arinbjorn could hear his breathing; his lungs burned and he had to fight for each breath. Bera dragged him around a corner, but abruptly stopped.

"Ari...look." She gestured ahead.

Arinbjorn followed her gaze. There, lying slack against the icy walls, blood and vomit around his mouth, was Kormac.

A cry from behind drew Arinbjorn's attention, and he turned to see Gunnar had fallen back into the cave entrance. He was driving his sword into a farmer's stomach, blood and bile rupturing over the blade. Bodies of the hunting party littered the ground. Thangbrander was shouting for it all to stop, and then he turned and looked into the cave, upon Arinbjorn. The two men stared at each other for a long moment, before Thangbrander's black eyes narrowed. His face set.

With that, the priest grabbed Gunnar and made for the incline up and out of the ravine. Arinbjorn tried to follow, but his legs failed him, dropping him at the mouth of the cave. He tried to stand, but his body lacked the strength; all he could do was kneel there and watch as the two men fought their way to the summit. He watched as Thangbrander cut the throat of a farmer that set upon him, sending arcs of black blood spiralling out in the storm. Finally, Thangbrander and Gunnar mounted two, now ownerless, horses.

"Thangbrander!" His shout was absorbed by the wind raging about him, but the priest looked back. "I will find you!"

The priest smiled, a sad smile that did not reach his eyes, before facing forward once more and riding his horse out into the storm. The cries of his men carried on the wind that cascaded through the tunnel, and all Arinbjorn could do was watch as the priest fled across the ice.

Part Two

Chapter Twenty-One

The axe felt heavy in his hands. The wooden grip was polished smooth from repeated use, and he had to hold it tightly as he raised it above his head, ready to strike. He held it there a moment, feeling the weight in his arms. He twisted the throat to better catch the light of the morning sun; he liked the glint of steel. After a few moments, his muscles began to tremble. He brought the great blade down and sunk it deep into the log of ash wood on the ground. There was a satisfying *thud* and *snap* as it drove all the way through, splitting the log evenly. The two sides tumbled into their respective piles of cut wood on the floor. Arinbjorn sighed.

He left the axe embedded in the stump below and took a moment to rest. Reaching down for his discarded tunic, he used it to wipe the sweat from his brow. It was hot today. Spring was upon them now, and the sun was rising earlier. It shone brightly in a blue sky marred only by the passing of white, hazy clouds. The snow had mostly receded, and he could see the green grass stretching out for miles across the plains about his father's farm. The ash trees that stood at the boundary of their land grew tall and strong, their green leaves returned, and they swayed gently in a rare light breeze. They provided some welcome shade while Arinbjorn did his work.

He loved spring and summer. The days were long and a welcome respite from the seemingly endless dark of winter on the island. The longer days meant he had more time to train too. He looked down at his right arm and the jagged scar that ran along the outside of his forearm. A lasting reminder from Kormac. Not that he needed one. It had mostly healed now, much like his back, but the thick, pink line repulsed him. It had left him weak for weeks, and he was only now regaining his strength.

He could only really train with the axe—his father had no sword—logs were all he could aim at, but it helped to envision

Thangbrander's head as he swung the blade down. He had amassed quite the pile of firewood this morning. He looked north across the green plains and undulating hills, back to the Jarlhettur mountain. Just looking at it made his back itch. The glacier was still visible, no amount of sunlight seemed to reduce it in size, and it shone like a silver beacon in the sun.

"Staring at it will not help." His father's voice, low and melodic, came from behind. He strode up beside Arinbjorn and placed a gentle hand upon his shoulder. "Trust me, I know."

Thorleikr had always seemed indomitable to his son. Strong, brave, and honourable. He had seen his farm through tough times, always managing to keep his family fed, and was as respected as a man could be by his peers. Many a man called Thorleikr his friend. He was first to stand by his allies and last to fall away in difficult times. He was everything Arinbjorn wanted to be. Today, however, like most days recently, Thorleikr seemed old to his son.

His white hair was thinning, and the creases of his face, worn deep by hard labour and a lifetime of laughing, seemed to hang listlessly upon him. His blue eyes still shone brightly though, and he smiled warmly out from under his long beard.

"You look tired, father," Arinbjorn said at last.

Thorleikr favoured his son with a withering stare. "I have been tired for the last forty years; you and your sister will be the death of me."

Arinbjorn could not help but laugh. "Come, sit with me." He leant down and wrenched the axe out from the tree stump, which he offered to his father, watching him take his time to sit, knees shaking. Thorleikr's hands were sinewy and clawed, he had long since lost the ability to stretch out his fingers fully, but they were powerful. They held fast to the stump as he eased himself down. Once his father was in position, Arinbjorn sat cross-legged on the grass next to him.

"It is a beautiful day," Thorleikr said, after a moment. "Do not ruin it by spending your time dwelling on the mountain."

Arinbjorn looked down at the ground and began plucking grass from the earth. "I cannot help it, father. For me, the memories are much too near."

"I have been there, my son. I have spent years mourning the loss of old friends. Even now, Skjalti and his family are never far from my mind. But do not let grief consume your life. There is still so much more left here." He gestured at the farmland around them.

"I failed them."

"Oh, how so?"

Arinbjorn hated that tone. It was the one his father used when he was about to reveal that Arinbjorn's technique for gutting fish was wrong. Or to point out that he had managed to round up only half the sheep.

"Kormac did not face justice, and his master got away."

"You mean the priest?"

"Of course. Who else? By killing Kormac, he denied the chieftains their trial. Even now, months later, we are plagued with these Christian disruptors refusing to accept Kormac was the killer."

"Skjalti was a Christian, or have you forgotten? Do not be so quick to blame them." Thorleikr's tone was quiet but firm.

"No. No, of course not. But they were lied to, and now they just won't see reason."

"It is not the Christians that keep your head on the mountain."

"What do you mean?" Arinbjorn threw the grass clippings he had torn up into the wind and watched them drift lazily about.

"How long has it been since you saw Freya?"

There it was. Arinbjorn stood up and walked over to the ash tree they were taking shade under, reaching out to touch the gnarled wood. Running his fingers over the knots, feeling the coarse wood underneath, he cast his mind back to the retreat from the ice cave.

Thangbrander and half of his men had managed to get away; the rest were killed, their bodies left on the ice to rot. The hunting party had been severely depleted too, however, and over half of the men that set out were brought back as slashed husks. It had taken them hours to get out to the mountain. Darkness had fallen while they were treating their injuries and counting their dead, and the storm continued to rage. Rather than risk a flight across the ice, they had spent the night taking shelter in the cave with Kormac's body.

When morning came, and the storm had passed, they found they had lost two more in the night, claimed by their wounds. Of the thirty men who had set off for Kormac, only thirteen remained. Of the chieftains, only Thorgeir and Gellir were relatively unscathed; the older Teitr had lost an eye. Njall lived, albeit with a new wound to his upper thigh that bled profusely. Only Sigvaldi managed to get through the battle unharmed. Bera proved to be invaluable. She used what supplies she had brought with her to treat their injuries, and it was widely believed that, had she not been there, many more would have died—Arinbjorn included.

The journey back had been a sombre one. The group used the spare horses left behind by the priest's men to carry the bodies of the fallen. Without Corcc to guide them, they had to be incredibly careful on the glacier; the pace was set to a walking speed, and it took them twice as long as it had on the way out. Thankfully, the storm had passed during the night, making the journey less daunting.

The chieftains returned to their halls, and Arinbjorn, Sigvaldi, and Bera headed with Njall to his farm. Upon their arrival, they were greeted by Freya and her thrall, Failend, who rushed out to them. Freya helped her husband inside, but made a point of ignoring Arinbjorn. He watched her focusing on the others, never once meeting his gaze. After everything he had been through, all they had lost, she couldn't even bear to look at him. As she disappeared into the hall, his stomach turned and he felt as though his chest would fall out of his body. It was then that he thought he might cry. Sigvaldi, seeing this, had gently coaxed him away and taken him home.

That was the last time he had seen her.

Later, the lawspeaker had called an assembly of all chieftains, farmers, and freed men of the district, inviting the Christians too. There, he had laid out what had happened. There was an uproar and the gathering had almost descended into violence. The Christians believed their priest had been chased off the island illegally, and they refused to accept that Kormac was the killer. Everyone else believed the Christians had brought a killer into their midst and should all be cast out. Rather than solving the problem, the death of Kormac had only entrenched positions. The assembly had disbanded when the Christian camp declared that they no longer recognized the lawspeaker's authority, and they left. Arinbjorn had watched these proceedings quietly, only speaking when answering questions. He had watched with low spirits the splitting of the assembly.

"I have not seen Freya in months," Arinbjorn said, at last. He took his gaze off the ash tree and looked down upon his resting father.

"Yet you think of her every day." Thorleikr was staring out across the farm and the valleys. His hands, peppered with blown spots, lay folded in his lap.

"I try not to think of her. She wants nothing more to do with me."

"Nor should she; she is a married woman." His father's words were biting.

Arinbjorn felt a spike of anger—he wanted to tell his father to leave it well alone—but, as soon as it came, it passed. He felt deflated and what energy he had seemed to leave him. He returned to his father's side and dropped down to the floor, dejected.

"I know what you feel, my son, but you must let it go. No good comes from loving another man's wife."

Arinbjorn merely nodded and began plucking at grass again. For a moment, there was silence between them, filled only by the sound of the trees rustling in the wind. A gust brought with it the scent of the *holtasóley* flowers that grew on the plains— white star-shaped flowers whose aroma always made Arinbjorn think of summer.

"I did not come out here to admonish you," Thorleikr continued. "I have something for you."

Arinbjorn looked up at his father, but could see nothing except the clothes he wore.

Thorleikr must have seen his searching gaze. "It is not something physical I offer, but an opportunity." His face hardened. "Did you really wish to avenge Skjalti, or did you just want to get into the bed of a woman?"

"Were you not my father, I would strike you for saying that." His anger, and his energy, returned anew.

"Good." Thorleikr stared his son down. "Because what I offer is not for some childish endeavour. I have word from Teitr, the trader. Since he lost his eye, he has retreated into his work and cares little for the affairs of his farm. He has spent these last few months planning his summer expeditions; I think he intends to leave Iceland with his ship."

"What is this to me?"

"Teitr trades all over the world. His ship has come back laden with spices from countries I have never heard of. I happen to know he has need of a few men to join his crew, and I know which port he will be calling at first."

"Where is he going?"

"Nidaross, the seat of Olaf Tryggvason."

Arinbjorn stopped playing with the grass and tuned to meet his father's level gaze. "The king of Norway? Why would this interest me?"

There was something to his father's expression—a glint in his eye, a slightly upturned lip—that gave away the fact he was enjoying this.

"Where do you think Thangbrander came from?" Thorleikr said at last.

"How do you know this?" This was not information Arinbjorn was privy to. "He did not sound Norwegian."

Thorleikr shifted in his seat, wincing as he did so.

His back must be hurting him again, Arinbjorn thought.

"The priest himself was not of Norway, but the vessel that brought him here was. It was a trading vessel owned by a man called Eirik Palson. I was there doing business when the chieftains arrived to welcome the priest."

Arinbjorn's mind began to race. It was not much to go on, but, if he could find the ship captain, he might know where Thangbrander came from. "You think Thangbrander fled back to Norway?"

"It is a possibility. Thangbrander never hid the fact that he was an emissary of King Olaf; I do know you will not find him here on this farm." He smiled a warm smile, but behind it was a hint of sadness.

"Are you offering me a place on Teitr's ship?" In that moment, Arinbjorn was glad he was already sitting down. His legs seemed to lose their strength. He looked about the familiar sights of the farm: the trees, the flowers, the plains that stretched north to the mountains. He knew them well. He knew the little stream that cut across his father's land, where he has learned to fish. He knew the ancient ash tree that he had played on as a child, climbing the trunk as though he were Ratatoskr, the squirrel that climbed Yggdrasil. He knew the small rock pillar just south of here, where he had taken Helga Skallagrimssdottir to bed underneath the stars. This was all he had ever known.

"It is not my place to offer it." Thorleikr's answer brought Arinbjorn back to the present. "As I said, he is looking to replace some of the men he lost. If you go to him and offer yourself as a crewman, he may take you to Nidaross. From there, you may find out what became of the man who has done so much to hurt our society."

"Do you not need me here, father?" He wondered if it sounded like more of a plea than a question.

"I have the thralls to help with the farm. They could do with more work." He dropped his tone to a knowing whisper. "Keep them out of trouble."

Arinbjorn smiled at his father and reached across to squeeze his shoulders. He could feel Thorleikr's bones through his tunic, like the ribs of malnourished cattle. When had he lost this much weight? It seemed to have dropped away suddenly, as though food no longer sustained him. In that moment, all worries about Thangbrander melted away. Could he leave his father like this? Kneeling there, as his mind filled with so many conflicting thoughts, he felt his chest tighten and an icy feeling descend upon him. He had been feeling it more and more of late, ever since his encounter with Kormac; it would often strike out of nowhere, seemingly triggered at random moments. In those moments, he just wanted to cling tightly to his own chest and scream. He fought hard to overcome it now.

"Do not worry about me, my son." Thorleikr passed a concerned eye over Arinbjorn. After a moment, he reached forward and brought him into his chest to hold him. Arinbjorn let him. They remained that way for several moments.

"I do not know what is wrong with me," Arinbjorn said, breaking away from his father. "Ever since Kormac cut me with his blade, I have felt weak."

"You look stronger than ever," Thorleikr said.

"It is not a physical weakness that I speak of, although it can take me like one."

"It is possible that his blade was cursed. Have you spoken with the witch who saved your life?" Concern etched itself into Thorleikr's many wrinkles.

"She prefers to be called Bera." Arinbjorn smiled briefly at the memory of being admonished so. "No, she returned to Haukadalur shortly after the flight from the cave."

"Then that will be your next port of call, after Teitr. If you are to leave for Norway, you must make sure no magic was placed upon you. While I will help you seek the closure you need, I would see my son returned to me."

Arinbjorn smiled at his father. He felt the tightness in his chest loosen and his breathing return to normal. "You know the dangers of travel better than most. Do you really think I can do this?"

"There was a time, not too long ago, when you never doubted yourself, Ari." Thorleikr rose from his stump seat, his bones giving an audible crack as he did so. He held out his hand to pull Arinbjorn up as well. "Self-doubt can stop one making foolish decisions; it is not something to be ignored. That being said, I went on Viking raids when I was younger. It is how I earned enough for this farm. I have seen the dangers of this world first hand, and I can tell you now that, if I could survive it, with all my naivety, then you can too. You are far more capable than I ever was at your age."

"I am afraid, father," Arinbjorn said.

"You would be a fool not to be. Now, come, let us prepare what you will say to Teitr so he will agree to hire you. You have never sailed in your life and he may take convincing."

With that, the pair of them ambled slowly to the farm hall, the sun shining warmly upon their backs.

Chapter Twenty-Two

He had loved many women over the years, this was true, but the one he saw before him held his heart like no other. Tyra was tall, taller even than many of the men he had in his retinue, and she carried herself with an easy grace. She wore her blond hair long, with two braids woven about her head like a crown. It was a look he favoured; he thought it framed her aquiline face beautifully. He watched as she brushed a stray strand of hair behind her ear, laughing at some terrible joke a housecarl was telling her. She looked up at him then, her green eyes shining brightly even from across the hall, and smiled. He found himself smiling dumbly back.

He watched as she continued her way about the tables, moving through the throng of men who had assembled in his hall for a feast. She did it effortlessly, often looking like she was floating between spaces. He watched her glide about the court, offering mead and meats to the assembled housecarls, laughing at their poor jokes, listening to their woes, offering council. Everything she heard, she reported back to him; it was a subtle way for Olaf to keep an eye on his men.

"What do you think, my king?"

Olaf's attention was brought back to the high table and the young man next to him. He was a scrawny fellow, wiry, with a nervous disposition. He was desperately hacking away at the flank of a roasted swine that had already been picked clean by the other guests, trying awkwardly to tear off a piece of meat. Olaf watched as bits of pork and gristle flew about the table, landing upon the young man's bald head. He had shaved his crown, but he had a ring of thick brown hair about the sides. It was the tonsure style, traditional to men of the cloth, and it gave the illusion of being far older than he was. Perhaps that is why the clerics styled it so, Olaf wondered, to give weight to their emissaries.

"I am sorry, Thormothr, I missed the question," Olaf responded.

"Apologies, my king." The young priest gave up on the carcass and looked about the high table at the men assembled.

Olaf followed his gaze. These were his most trusted jarls and captains. Thorer Klakka, his closest and best friend, was sitting at the far end with a few of his lieutenants. He was deep in conversation with one of the serving girls, who was busy refilling their drinks. Their end of the table was littered with the detritus of the feast Olaf had laid on; duck bones lay discarded beside them, and the scent of pickled herring was strong enough to pierce through the woodsmoke that filled the room. It was good to see his friend finally enjoying himself.

It was not Thorer that the young priest was eyeing up, however. Thangbrander, broad and tall, sat in silence next to Captain Gunnar. The good captain was feasting heartily on some porridge made of onions and pork, but Thangbrander had barely touched his food. He was staring stoically ahead.

"Repeat your question, Thormothr," Olaf ordered.

"I do not mean to challenge you, my king, but are you sure it is I who should be sitting next to you in this place of honour?" Thormothr gave up his fight with the swine carcass and returned his hands to his lap. Olaf could still see him wringing them beneath the table.

"If I choose to honour you—you who have helped bring the Word of God to my beloved Nidaross—then the others here must accept it."

"But Thangbrander is the more senior—"

"I could care not less for Priest Thangbrander!" Olaf shouted, allowing his anger at the elder priest to infuse his words.

His voice cut across the throng, and the tables before him grew quiet. The housecarls stopped in their conversation and turned to look at their king. Thangbrander himself looked shocked, his face pale.

"Why should I honour the man who has failed me so?" The question filled the hall. Olaf looked about the gathered men, waiting to see if any would dare to answer. As he passed his gaze over each man, he watched them, one by one, drop their gaze and stare at their chests.

"Perhaps Thangbrander should tell the hall what happened in Iceland?" Tyra's voice, calm and melodic, answered Olaf from the back of the hall. She walked up between the tables, her delicate footsteps loud in the sudden silence, her silk dress red as flame in the firelight. She came to stand behind her husband's seat and placed a hand upon his shoulder, squeezing gently. She leant in. "So that the men may better understand your decision."

Olaf reached up for his wife's hand and held it, but he kept his gaze firmly on Thangbrander. "Very well, tell them all how things faired on the island. Explain to them why it is a mercy that you live."

"My king, this isn't what—"

"Be quiet, Thormothr," Olaf snapped.

The young priest silenced himself and returned to fidgeting with his brown robes.

Olaf watched as Thangbrander nodded and rose from his seat. His black hair seemed to have more grey in it than when he arrived, but he was still a powerfully built man. He strode around the front of the high table and bowed before Olaf. The hearth fire crackled, its orange flames lighting up the priest from beneath. He stood for a moment, surveying the hall, passing his gaze over the men and women who had gathered there. When he spoke, his voice was broken and weak.

"I was sent by our king to Iceland, to bring the Word of God to the heathens there."

"How long were you there, Thangbrander?" Olaf asked.

"Just under two years, my king."

"And how many of these farmers and sheep herders did you manage to convert in that time?"

There was an expectant pause and the hall waited to hear Thangbrander's response. Olaf saw one or two discreet smiles pass across the faces of his jarls.

"I could not say how many, my king, but a great portion of the population listened to my word. Even chieftains, such as Hallr Thorsteinsson and Gizurr the White, both men of good standing."

"Yet the pagans still outnumber them?"

"Yes, my king." Thangbrander slowly turned about the room, raising his voice so that all could hear. "I tried several methods, from peaceful sermons to lawful challenges. I did everything within my power to get them to see the light of God."

Olaf stood then. Slowly, but with purpose. It was times like this he was grateful his hall was designed so that the high table was on a raised dais, a step above the rest of the room. It meant he could look down upon Thangbrander.

"In two *years*, you have barely made any headway. I needed men for my campaign against Burislav, and now even Sweyn knocks at my door. I sent you because of your reputation. You were not afraid to use force of arms to convert. How did these sheep fuckers defy you?"

Thangbrander cleared his throat, and this time he addressed his response to Olaf directly. Olaf knew what he was going to say. The priest had reported to him the moment he was dragged back by Captain Gunnar. He knew the excuses to come. He wanted the hall to hear them, to learn they were not good enough.

"From the moment I arrived, I was mocked, ridiculed, and barely tolerated. The chieftains took great delight in my misfortune, from putting on feasts of horseflesh to tormenting me with severed penises."

A low chuckle spread throughout the room and Olaf had to suppress his own smile.

"In the end, I tried to use fear to bend them to your will. I sacrificed much, killing my own flock to stoke the discontent and prejudice of both sides."

The hall burst into heated conversation then. This was information the jarls did not know, and it sat uneasily with them.

"You killed an innocent Christian?" Thorer Klakka's voice, loud and gravelly, cut through the din. He stood up sharply, the high table shaking with the force of it, and looked between Olaf and Thangbrander. Olaf could hear the shock and anger in his friend's voice as he turned to face him and said, "Did you authorize this?"

"Silence!" Olaf ordered.

Reluctantly, the jarls quietened. Thorer stood for a moment longer, his face red, before retaking his seat.

"Did this strategy work, Thangbrander?" the king asked.

"I was undone by the greed of one of my agents. He drew attention to the plan and was made an outlaw. He would have testified before the assembly of chieftains to the truth."

"So, tell my court what you did to the man who failed you."

Thangbrander waited a moment, his head bowed low, staring at the floor. His fists lay balled at his sides. "I killed him," the priest answered.

"You killed a man who failed you, who jeopardized your plans." Olaf wondered if the rest of them had figured out where he was taking this. "So, why should I not kill *you*?"

Thangbrander looked up, his face white and his black eyes wide.

Olaf turned to address Thorer. "Captain, if you please." He gestured to Thangbrander. Thorer rose from his seat, slowly this time, his face pinched in a frown. He looked about the hall and nodded to several men distributed throughout the tables. Six made their way to the high table, taking up positions behind Thangbrander.

"No! My king, please, I did everything you asked of me!" Thangbrander looked about the room for support.

None of the men would meet his gaze. None except Gunnar, who was still merrily picking at his bowl of porridge. He smiled disinterestedly.

"You cannot do this!" Thangbrander continued. "I am a man of God!"

"Do not presume to tell a king what he may or may not do, priest," Olaf retorted. He nodded to Thorer and the men behind Thangbrander unsheathed their swords.

"I say it is beyond all expectation that Christianity might be accepted there!" Thangbrander shouted. It became a scream as the first of the blades pierced his back. It erupted through his chest, a stream of hot blood spraying across the room and landing at the foot of the high table. Shock passed across Thangbrander's face as he looked down at the protruding blade. For a moment, he just stood there dumbfounded, blood pooling at his mouth. The next sword came through his gut, spilling his bowels out upon the floor.

The guards piled in then. Olaf watched as Thangbrander collapsed and his men continued to stab, hack, and cleave their way through the priest's body. His screams became gurgles and his black eyes turned glassy. When he was finally still, Olaf raised his hand for the guards to stop.

The roar of the hearth fire was almost deafening in the silence that followed. The scent of faecal matter joined that of the roasted meats, woodsmoke, and dried fish. Thangbrander had died shitting himself.

"Thorer," Olaf said at last.

"Yes, my king?" Olaf thought he detected a slight tremble in his captain's voice.

"I want you and your men to round up every Icelander in Nidaross. Every trader, raider or farmer who has come to our shores. Bring them to me. Until Iceland accepts Christianity, I will show them what it means to defy God."

There was just the briefest of hesitations before Thorer replied, "At once." He gestured to the guards standing over Thangbrander's body and the seven of them departed the hall.

"And somebody clean up this mess!" Olaf ordered. He sat back down and resumed his eating.

A couple of serving girls hesitantly walked over to the corpse of the priest and began putting pieces of him into a bucket, which made a satisfyingly wet sound as they dropped in.

Olaf turned to Thormothr, who was positively shaking in his seat. "There you are, priest. Now you are the most senior cleric in my court."

*

Olaf's head ached. He sat on the edge of his bed, rubbing his temples, willing the pain away. His closed his eyes and concentrated on his breathing. After a few long breaths, he felt the tension in his chest ease. He should not have killed Thangbrander. That had been a mistake. One made in the heat of his anger. He could not care less about the priest's life, but he was a vessel for God; could Olaf lose God's favour? He looked down at his torso, his tunic long since discarded, and ran his hand over the thick scar that cut across his belly. It had healed fully in the months since the attack by Sweyn's raiders, but it was an ugly reminder of the forces aligned against him. He tried to shake away the creeping anxiety.

He stood and walked across to his wooden dresser. There, one of the thralls had left a jug of mead. He poured himself a cup and drank it rapidly, its thick honeyed taste sitting favourably on the lips. He felt it burn his throat for a moment.

"You look worried, Olaf."

He turned to see Tyra emerging from behind her dressing screen, her red dress abandoned, standing naked before him. He stood there for a moment, just staring, his mind suddenly blind to all else. She had undone her braids, and her hair fell in wild golden ringlets all down her back. She was almost two decades younger than Olaf, but he felt like a youth again just looking upon her. He had long ago committed every line and contour of her body to memory; her skin, the colour of honey in the candlelight, was a map, and he knew all the landmarks: the dimples on the backs of her shoulders, the series of small moles on her left breast that looked like the stars above, the small brown birthmark on her right buttock.

"How can I be worried with you at my side? I can focus on nothing else." Olaf smiled and strode towards his wife, collecting her up in his wide arms and kissing her. Her red lips tasted of cinnamon and ginger and her tongue teased his playfully. He took a deep breath in and the scent of almond oil, patchouli, and saffron flooded over him. After a moment, she pulled away, grinning. "You're wearing the perfume I got you?" he asked.

"Of course! Now, come to bed, my husband." She broke free of him and made her way over to their bed, where she lay atop the covers. It was still hot in the hall, the woodsmoke from the hearth fire permeated every aspect, and her sweat made her glisten in the low light. She patted the straw mattress beside her. "Tell me what is on your mind."

Shirking off his linen trousers, Olaf joined her on the bed. Holding her with his right arm, he played with her hair while she ran her fingers across his chest.

"I regret killing Thangbrander."

"Why? He failed you, and now the jarls and housecarls will know the price of failure." She kissed his chest and her hand continued its explorations, moving down to his exposed stomach. Despite himself, he felt his excitement grow.

"Did I ever tell you when I became a Christian?"

"No." She kissed his chest, slowly, delicately. "What happened?"

"I had just lost Geira, my first wife, and I could no longer bear to stay in Wendland. I decided to take out my sorrow raiding the outer isles. From Friesland to the Hebrides, I dealt with my grief by plundering."

"Would any amount of plunder ease the pain of my loss, husband?" She moved across his body and lay atop him. She was tall, but light, and the feeling of her body pressed up against his was intoxicating. He could feel her nipples harden.

He ran his hands down her back, trying hard not to let his coarse hands mar her smooth skin. "I do not know. Perhaps if I took all of Denmark..." he teased.

She scowled at him in mock frustration and bit his chest lightly. He let out a small yell and pulled her up to kiss her.

"What happened on these many grief-filled raids?"

"I met a seer off the coast of Sicily. I had heard about her prowess in fortune telling and wanted to see what the future had in store for me. For I could see none without Geira."

Tyra pouted slightly then and moved to get off him.

He grabbed her and pulled her down forcefully. "Do not be sad, my love; were it not for the seer, I would not have met you."

"A likely story." She struggled in his grip for a moment, only half attempting to escape him, before easing back on to his body. She grabbed his wrists and held them down, then began to kiss his neck.

"It is true. She told me that I would become a great king and do celebrated deeds, that I would convert many men to Christianity. I laughed at her, of course. Back then, I was still a worshiper of the old gods. But she warned me that I would be attacked by my own men and would suffer grievous injuries."

"What happened?" Her kisses continued down his neck to his chest, and he arched his back, desperate to feel her.

"Not long after my meeting with her, my crew mutinied against me. I survived, but I got this wound." He pointed to an old scar on his right shoulder; he always thought it looked vaguely like a squashed spider. "I converted soon after. I knew then that there was only one God, for His seer had truly seen the future. He needs me to be His champion."

Tyra kissed the scar. "You have survived much, my husband. And you have brought many into the rightful faith."

She sat up then, her legs gripping his waist, and ran her hands down his chest, leaving claw marks through the oil and sweat. Olaf held tightly to her thighs, his thumbs leaving little bruises as he pulled her down upon him. She gasped as he entered her. Smiling, she threw her head back and began to rock slowly against him.

Olaf forgot the rest of the story and his anxiety melted away as he lost himself in his wife. Yes, God must still favour him, for He had given him Tyra. He held fast to her then, and the sounds of their lovemaking echoed throughout the hall.

Chapter Twenty-Three

The Öxará river had swelled of late. Its milky white waters, fuelled by the melted ice and snow, tumbled and foamed downstream. From his vantage point on the riverbank, its roar almost deafened Gizurr. He watched the waters cascade between the jagged and coarse rocks that flanked the river. The small, exposed cliffs of obsidian ran its length here in Thingvellir, tapering off gradually as the river got closer to the lake at its end. The waters were high today, rising high enough to flow over the causeway. The stone shelf was normally a foot or two above the surface and was slick and treacherous at the best of times, but now it was almost impossible to cross. This made it a great place for a trial.

Gizurr shifted uncomfortably in his saddle. He had brought his horse, a young, pitch-black mare, to the edge of the bank to graze upon the fresh grass there. He ran his hand through her thick mane, scratching behind her ear, and she whinnied softly in reply. It had been a long ride out to this meeting spot, taking him several hours, and he had ridden the poor beast hard. She was still young, and not quite ready for longer rides, but none of his other stock had her stamina. He may have to call upon her to take him away swiftly.

He heard them before he saw them—the first of the two parties that would assemble here. A large group of riders approached from the west, making their way down the gorge and into the river basin proper. They were led by Runolfr Ulfsson, a small man with greying hair and a pinched face. He had brought almost twenty men to this assembly, as far as Gizurr could tell from where he observed them approach and take up position by the causeway. The sound of that many horses always reminded Gizurr of his time abroad. The morning raids charging into the enemy. It was a show of force, that much was clear, and it chilled him.

Runolfr was taking no chances; he placed two of his men to guard the carved rune stones that marked the beginning of the crossing, before instructing the remainder of his host to dismount and begin to cross the causeway. It was a delicate task, and the party shuffled their way into the middle of the river. It was too much to hope that one or two may slip and be washed away. There they awaited the arrival of the other half of this trial.

Runolfr was an interesting man. He was a chieftain, much like Gizurr, but he kept to his own lands mostly, rarely engaging with the larger assemblies or attending the lawspeaker's feasts. Still, he was said to be respected by his freedmen, and Gizurr had only seen him acting fairly. It was the only thing that gave him hope that this would be a fair trial.

Despite the roar of the water, it was an otherwise quiet day; the winds had died down of late and Gizurr could smell the *holtasóley* flowers that his mare was currently feasting on. She had left a trail of destruction across the bank, the white aromatic petals of the flowers lying scattered and half gnawed across the grass. He liked watching her eat; it was surprisingly relaxing observing her lazily chew her way through whatever was in front of her. He was brought back to the moment by the sound of hooves reverberating across the ground. Looking up, he saw a lone rider galloping towards him from Runolfr's party. He braced himself.

"Chieftain Gizurr!"

It was an older man that Gizurr recognized as Runolfr's housecarl, a freeman named Thrain who had dedicated himself to serving and protecting Runolfr thanks to some unspecified debt. He had come dressed for a fight today, wearing chain mail over his tunic, and Gizurr was sure he saw an actual sword dangling at his hip.

He slowed down and came to a stop next to the chieftain. "Good day to you."

"Good day to you, Thrain." Gizurr bowed slightly in his saddle, wary of showing any slight to this man.

"Have you come to watch the proceedings?"

The pair of them now looked upriver towards the assembled men on the causeway. It suddenly seemed very hot to Gizurr under the sun.

"I heard Runolfr was putting a Christian on trial. I came to bear witness." Gizurr felt lying would serve him little purpose, and the truth could be effective at concealing motive.

"I hope you are not planning on disrupting events." Thrain was a tall man, and he dwarfed his mount. It was almost comical seeing his legs dangle so low to the ground. Still, Gizurr did not laugh. Thrain had the presence of a viper, his gangly form gave him reach and he was awfully close now.

Gizurr stared evenly into his square, impassive face. "I respect the laws of our land. Your master knows this. If this were the other way around and I was placing one of *you* on trial, I have no doubt Runolfr would want to ensure things were fair."

Thrain appeared to consider this. "Indeed. Apologies. Runolfr is being overly cautious today, this being the first trial of a Christian."

"I understand. I would be making a liar of myself if I said I was not nervous." His mare shifted beneath him and he had to pull gently on her reins to stop her wandering off in pursuit of more *holtasóley*. "This can only bode ill."

Before Thrain could answer, the second party of men arrived, cresting the gorge cliffs to the east. They numbered maybe half a dozen, and, unlike Runolfr's men, they bore no weapons. Thrain dug his heels into his mount and kicked off, back to his master. Gizurr watched the new arrivals make their way down to the riverbank. They were led by his young, spindly son-in-law, Hjalti Skeggjason—one of the newer converts. They came to a stop beside the river and dismounted. Their faces were familiar to Gizurr—thralls, poor freed men, farmers—he had seen them all attending Thangbrander's sermons. They looked dishevelled and filthy, clearly having had to finish their tasks before attending this summons.

Hjalti walked with purpose and kept his head high as he and his men began to shuffle through the high, cascading water. There was pride in seeing his son-in-law behaving without fear, but Gizurr hoped it would not lead to arrogance. They came to a stop before Runolfr, and for a moment the two parties stared at each other in silence, with only the sound of the river to fill the absence.

With a curt nod from Runolfr, Thrain and his men flanked Hjalti, with several making their way over to the other side of the bank. Despite being trapped in the middle, Hjalti kept his back straight and he stared evenly into the narrowed eyes of the chieftain.

This was a dangerous place to convene the assembly. Gizurr could see that men from both sides were struggling to stand in the rushing water. Which was presumably why Runolfr had chosen it as the site for his trial. Gizurr knew what was going to come next, but he decided to move closer so that he could hear what was being said. He tugged on the reins of his mare and led her upstream until he met the group of men waiting on the west bank. They barely acknowledged his presence, nodding impatiently as he greeted them. That was fine by him, so long as they did not bother him and he could be close enough to act.

He pulled up next to the rune stone, a tall, tapered boulder that had been rolled into position by the causeway, and ran his hands over the heavily eroded waymark stave that had been inscribed upon it. Four bisecting lines formed the eight spokes of a wheel, each ending in a fork or circle. It was meant to ensure that those who utilized it always found their way. Gizurr did not believe in the magics of the runes, but he hoped that he would not lose his way today.

"Hjalti Skeggjason, you have been summoned before this assembly to answer for crimes of blasphemy." Runolfr had to project his voice to be heard over the flowing river.

"I accepted this summons," Hjalti replied, looking to the men about him. "And I am here at the appointed time." It was a ritual phrase, one said aloud to declare to the assembled men that you took the accusation seriously and would defend yourself in the court legally. Still, Hjalti managed to spit it out, sounding disgusted at the mere suggestion that he would be summoned.

Do not anger them, Gizurr thought.

"Why did you decide on this location, chieftain?" Hjalti continued. "Afraid that I would attempt to escape your justice?"

"I could not risk you attempting to flee. You may be Christian, but you are still subject to the laws of this land. I have heard of too many Christian troublemakers escaping their fates of late." Runolfr turned his head to stare at Gizurr on the riverbank, and he had to suppress a flinch.

"Thangbrander did not escape. He left to bring us help," Hjalti said.

Did he really believe that? Gizurr wondered. What had given the young man such faith in the absentee priest? Gizurr had not spoken with Thangbrander before he headed off into the ice caves to the north, but he had heard what supposedly happened there along with everyone else. Many of the younger Christians, like Hjalti, believed it all to be some trick of the heathens—that the pinning of the murder to Kormac was a ruse designed to justify their persecution.

Gizurr did not think so, however. He had seen the way Thangbrander had behaved, how he had taken advantage of the murders to rile up his flock. Privately, he worried that Thangbrander *himself* had encouraged Kormac to perform the killings. At the very least, he believed Thangbrander killed Kormac.

Not that it mattered to the young firebrand that now stood toe to toe with Runolfr. Hjalti was busy shouting out his defiance when the chieftain interrupted him.

"We are not here to argue the crimes of Priest Thangbrander. You are the one on trial here." Runolfr dug a gnarled finger into the younger man's chest. "Thorbjorn Thorkellson, this court calls you forward to sum up the case and stand as a witness."

A large bear of a man emerged from the crowd, his thick brown hair tied back. He strode into the middle of the causeway, the waters of the Öxará barely affecting him, and looked down on Hjalti with a hard, square face. He did not bear any armour, but he had an unwieldy looking axe hanging at his side. Gizurr felt the few men on the riverbank tense.

Thorbjorn addressed the crowd: "You stand accused of composing a verse that blasphemes the gods. Not only this, but you then spoke the verse aloud at the Law Rock itself."

Several of the men let out angry shouts. Barking and braying like beasts, Gizurr thought bitterly. He watched as the two sides became agitated, and he thought he saw several people reach for their weapons.

Runolfr put up his hands and the chorus died down. "I was there when you and your Christians came to an assembly to discuss your disruptions to our way of life. It was there that you uttered the following verse: 'I don't wish to bark at the gods / It seems to me that Freya is a bitch.'"

"Are you really putting me on trial just for saying 'Freya is a bitch'?" Hjalti clearly took delight in repeating the offending phrase. He watched with unhidden glee as anger passed among his accusers.

Gizurr felt his chest tighten; there was no need to further aggravate the pagans. In that moment, he was half-minded to abandon Hjalti, leave him to his fate. He was not sure he had the patience to save such a man, especially from himself.

No, he had to stay. There had been enough death already and he would not let Hjalti die for believing in the machinations of Thangbrander. Besides, his daughter would never forgive him.

"You know well the penalties for slander," Thorbjorn said, "and to slander the gods is the highest crime." He turned to face Runolfr and raised his voice for the crowds on the bank. "He admits it!"

"You freely admit you said these words?" Runolfr seemed surprised.

"I said the words, but I am not guilty of blasphemy," Hjalti replied evenly. "Your gods would have to be real for that to be the case."

Hjalti had to duck as one of Runolfr's men suddenly made to swing at him with his axe. The guard overextended himself, losing his footing, and the water that coursed over the causeway pulled his legs out from under him. He let out a scream and tumbled into the river. Gizurr watched as he disappeared under the water, only to reappear several yards down river, where he promptly disappeared again.

"Your man tried to kill me!" Hjalti shouted.

"And he failed." Runolfr turned to Thrain. "Go see if that idiot washes up downstream. If he does, cut off a finger for defying my orders."

Thrain nodded and waded ashore, passing Gizurr. "As you can see, Runolfr takes the trials seriously. He will have no man threaten the accused until it is decided so." He mounted his horse, his trousers soaked through, and headed off down the river in search of the missing man.

Gizurr did find it comforting. It meant that he might not have to intervene after all, *if* Runolfr stuck to the law.

"It is too dangerous to attack each other here." Runolfr was chastising his men before turning to Hjalti. "You cannot escape, but nor can you be harmed until your trail is completed."

The young man seemed to accept this, and it quietened his temper. "Very well, continue with your trial."

"You have admitted you said the phrase, so it falls to me to decide your fate."

"Chieftain Runolfr!" Gizurr shouted across the waters. The whole crowd turned to look at him in his saddle. "May I step forward and make a case for leniency?"

The scowl that embedded in Runolfr's face told him that the chieftain hated the notion. "Why are you here, Gizurr?"

"This man is my son-in-law. I came to witness his trial and offer aid if I could. I would not hide this."

"Very well." Runolfr sighed visibly and gestured to his men. They parted in the middle to allow a route through. "But only because you are a man of high standing and a fellow chieftain. You may speak your case."

Gizurr dismounted and tied his mare to the rune stone. He then began the treacherous walk across the river. This had not been the plan. He had intended to wait out the trial and potentially pick up a fleeing Hjalti. He saw instead an opportunity to help through his preferred means—the law. Still, as he struggled to find his footing in the rushing water, he knew he had committed himself now.

"We are both chieftains, Runolfr," Gizurr said at last, when he made it to the meeting in the middle. He took up position next to Hjalti and placed a hand upon the young man's shoulder, as much for stability as for comfort. "We know there are ways around this that do not turn our people against each other yet further."

"I have every right to have this man suffer *skóggangur*," Runolfr stated evenly.

There it was, exactly what Gizurr had feared. *Skóggangur* meant Hjalti would be deemed a full outlaw; his lands and possessions would be confiscated, and he would be banished from society. If anyone was seen to be giving him aid, they too could be brought before a trial, and, should anyone kill him, it would not be illegal. He would be a man stripped of his possessions and sent out into the wild without any legal standing as a person. It was tantamount to a death sentence.

"His death would only galvanize the other Christians into further acts of violence and disruption. You must know this."

"What matters is the law, Gizurr. Your son-in-law broke it." Murmurs of agreement passed among the assembled men. "If I forgive his crimes here, we will have anarchy throughout our lands."

"I do not ask you to forgive them. I ask instead that you make him a lesser outlaw."

Hjalti looked shocked, and his few companions began to protest. Gizurr silenced them with a look.

"You would see me banish him for only three years?" Runolfr asked. His eyes narrowed in suspicion.

"His lands would not be confiscated, but for the duration he would still have no legal rights." Gizurr tightened his grip on Hjalti as he felt his son-in-law tense. "You would have three whole years to kill him without consequence."

"But I would still be seen to be showing leniency, in the eyes of his fellow Christians?" Runolfr's furrowed brow belied his musings.

Gizurr turned to look at the gaunt faces of the fellows that Hjalti had brought with him. "We can only change the way of things through the law, my friends. Violence and slander will only turn them against us. They are our family. They may not believe as we do, but they are our people. I ask that you accept this and help me ensure Hjalti's safety."

There was a moment's pause as they considered this, before a chorus of agreement met his request.

Gizurr smiled, relieved. "You have their agreement, Runolfr. What say you?"

"This court finds Hjalti guilty, and sentences him to lesser outlawry."

The shouts of disappointment from Runolfr's men were enough to make Gizurr take two steps away from them, his feet slipping on the slab beneath the water.

"Silence! From the moment you leave this trial, you are banished from our society and have no legal rights. If you are slain by any man, your family will have no right to claim compensation. If, after a period of three years, you return to us. Your full rights will be restored."

Gizurr let out a sigh of relief. Runolfr dismissed the assembled men, and they began to make their way back to the riverbank. Only after they had reached the west bank, and he was sure they could no longer be heard, did Gizurr turn to Hjalti.

"We have little time; we must get you off the island."

Hjalti looked stunned and it took him a moment to reply. "I have a ship, berthed in Thórsárdalr. We can use that." He looked around at his men, then down at the waters. "Where will I go?"

Gizurr tilted the young man's chin up and smiled at him. "We will set sail for Norway."

"We?" Hjalti raised a questioning eyebrow.

"Yes. I believe we will need help in making the necessary case for a law change here in Iceland." Gizurr began to wade back to his horse, who was now happily grazing on some heather. "I would seek the council of King Olaf Tryggvason."

Chapter Twenty-Four

The men pulled hard on the mooring ropes, dragging the giant *knarrs* up the beach. Unlike the *skeids* she had occasionally seen coming to Iceland, the *knarrs* were trading ships. They lacked the rowing berths and were powered only by sails; below the main deck, where the rowers would have been, were the stores for all the cargo they were transporting. From her vantage point high on the cliff, Freya could look down upon the sailors as they brought the two trading vessels on to the black sands and secured them with timber poles on either side of the hull.

It was an impressive operation, and she never grew tired of watching the intricate manoeuvres of the ships as they came here to berth. It had been easy for the sailors today; they had timed their arrival with the tide coming in, and the winds were fair; it did not take the two crews long to mount the beach. These must be seasoned travellers, then; she had seen whole ships topple just as they were getting into the bay, ill prepared for the high winds that often cut across the land. Freya looked up and out across the ocean; the skies were clear and the sunlight reflecting off the water was almost blinding; she pulled her kerchief further over her brow to provide some shade.

The wooden frame of the pack upon her back had begun to dig into her sides; she hoisted the shoulder straps and the weaved basket full of wool shifted into position. Her back ached after the long walk from the farm, but she would have done anything to get out and away from Njall. Trading would normally have been his role, but some of their sheep had gone missing—not enough to be a problem, but Njall was still concerned. He had gone off to try to locate them with Tongu-Oddr. She did not know why it angered her so—still, after all this time—when he had agreed to all her demands.

When he had come back from the ice cave, exhausted and heavily wounded, she had been full of worry. Njall had suffered a nasty leg wound that had been infected for days; she was lucky Bera was on hand to help take care of him. He still walked with a limp now. She had been grateful, in a way. The wound stopped him from going on his many hunts and he was forced to stay on the farm and actually help manage the estate. He bought some more thralls from some of their neighbours—younger men, who could do more of the heavy lifting—and he made a point of patrolling the perimeter of their hall every evening. She had never felt safer, and they spent far more time together than before. So why did she resent him?

She tried to dismiss the thoughts and just enjoy being out, away from the farm. Looking down on the beach, she could see the traders beginning to unload their goods. They would take them up to the temporary market further inland, just outside Smokey Bay. From her vantage point, she could see the steam plumes rising periodically up into the clear sky, signs of the bubbling cauldrons that gave the bay its name. Further along, where the black sand met the green grass of the plains, the first of the farmers were beginning to arrive. She could see dozens of people slowly making their way from their respective farmsteads, hoping to catch the traders early, before they got to the market. She smiled to herself; she was in no rush. Besides, it would take her the better part of an hour to get down from the cliff and into the bay proper.

She began her gradual descent and basked in the heat of the sun. As she continued her walk along the cliff, she began to make out the faces in the gathering crowd. An older man with a long thin beard was busy yelling instructions to the captains of the two vessels. Even from here, she could see he was missing an eye. It was Teitr, the chieftain and most profitable trader in all Iceland. The loss of his eye had not diminished his energy, it seemed; he was really yelling at the sailors.

Many of the farmers' faces she recognized too. Most men liked to come themselves, rather than trust these errands to their wives or thralls, as market day was a good opportunity to socialize and catch up on the events from around the island. Still, she saw one or two women about, with baskets as large and ungainly as hers upon their backs. The traders often brought news from the continent; many people still had family in Norway and elsewhere, and the wealthier individuals could pay for their letters and missives to be delivered. The island had a way of making people feel isolated and alone a lot of the time, but, as summer approached, more and more traders would come to their shores; the markets allowed people to feel like they were part of a wider community.

By the time she made it down off the cliff, the area surrounding Smokey Bay had been transformed. The trading stalls were easy enough to set up—temporary and rudimentary things, made from the crates used to transport goods. As each trader revealed their wares, the space around grew busier. Hundreds of people must have come today, the first real market of the season. It occurred to her that the only other time she had seen this many gathered in one place was at the Althing, the yearly assembly. It, too, was a great social occasion. The lawspeaker would recite one third of the law, and legal disputes that could not be settled in local assemblies were decided. She had heard rumours that the Christians were contemplating legal challenges for the Althing this year.

Freya threaded her way through the gathered throng, taking in the sights and sounds of so many people interacting at once. The sea air was light but briny, the scent of fresh fish mixing with the aroma of *hvönn*, the angelica plant that so many used for medicinal purposes. She wondered whether she should pick some up for Bera.

She had to stop as an older farmer wrestled his way in front of her trailing a horse. The poor beast looked ancient, and the farmer had laden it with wares; it plodded sullenly along after its master. Freya stroked it gently as it passed. A chorus of squeals snapped her attention behind her, where two men were haggling over a very hairy pig; she was amazed it could see, its eyebrows were so thick. It reminded her of her father, and she laughed aloud to herself.

"Freya Hoskuldsdottir?" The high-pitched voice seemed to pierce the air, causing Freya to wince. She turned and was greeted by the bloated sight of Hallr Thorsteinsson, the Christian chieftain. He was only as tall as her, and he seemed just as wide. His red, sweat-coated face beamed at her through a patchwork beard.

"Chieftain Hallr." She moved a little to the side to allow room for people to pass between them while they spoke. "What an unexpected pleasure."

"I just saw you walking through the market and I wanted to offer our sympathies."

Freya felt her face tighten in confusion. "Sympathies?"

"For the dreaded assault upon your farm. We never got to see you, only Njall. It must have been just awful. A shame we have not caught the man who did it." He tried to cross the distance between them, but the farmer who had bought the pig made his move to leave, and Hallr almost tripped over the swine.

"We do know who did. Kormac. I saw his face myself."

"You must have been mistaken. A good Christian like Kormac could never have acted in such a way." He cast his eyes down to the ground, before looking off towards the beached *knarrs*.

"I know what I saw, Hallr." She felt pain in her palms and realized she was balling her fists. She eased them open.

"As I said, you must have been mistaken. I wanted you to know that we Christians take the attacks upon us, and all the people of Iceland, seriously. It is not safe for a woman in your situation; you would be welcome to our church, should you ever need sanctuary."

"Just what situation do you think I am in, chieftain?"

"Your husband, Njall—his fondness for buggery is well known." He said it so bluntly, so matter of fact, that the statement hit her like a stone.

Freya was glad that she could not reach across the divide between them, for fear she would strike him. Then she *would* be in trouble. "You know nothing of my husband, and he will hear of this slander." She tried to put as much venom and threat into her words as she could.

"Freya, please, I just wanted to extend an invitation—there is a place for you and your husband with us. God forgives all." He looked furtively about the amassed farmers. "These pagans do not."

"Does your god forgive Thangbrander? Where is *he* now? How come we have not seen him since these attacks?" Freya watched as Hallr visibly recoiled. She did not hide her smile.

"*Priest* Thangbrander's holy mission took him elsewhere."

Hallr stared at the ground and for a moment Freya believed that she saw sadness and confusion upon his face. He had the manner of a sheepdog that had been abandoned by its master.

He looked back at her. "I did not come here to threaten you. I really am sorry to hear about the attack on your farm. I had hoped that you would better understand the Christian position, as someone who was also under threat. My offer will stand: all are welcome at my hall. Now, if you will excuse me, I am to see Gizurr and Hjalti off." He gestured to the black beach, where, in the distance, the white-haired chieftain and his son-in-law were boarding one of the *knarrs*. He bowed awkwardly and began to amble away.

"Under threat?" Freya whispered to herself, then she shouted, "If you know something, Hallr, I would hear it!"

His only response was a backhanded wave as he disappeared into the crowd.

She suddenly felt very alone and exposed. Looking about, she thought she caught the stares of people making their way past her. Did they all truly know? She must conclude her business and be gone from here.

She tried to remember why she had come, but her mind had gone blank. Soapstone—that was it. She had hoped to trade her wool for some soapstone cooking pots. Soapstone seemingly did not occur in Iceland, so it had to be imported. Only Eindridi, a trader from Orkney, came this early in the year with supplies of the hewn rock. She looked about for the old man. She, like most women she knew, had spent most of the winter months combing, spinning, and weaving the wool into *vaðmál*, or homespun. Aside from silver, it was one of the best ways to pay for goods at market, as it had proven popular abroad. The amount she had on her back should be enough to get the majority of what she needed, and Eindridi always traded fair.

She decided to head closer to the beach. One of the blacksmiths, who primarily dealt in tools and small weapons, had set up his stall there and he often had a small collection of necklaces made of glass beads and amber that she was particularly fond of. He was also good friends with Eindridi and may know where the stonemason was. As she approached the black sands and the two hulking *knarrs*, she heard an all-too-familiar voice a little way ahead of her in the crowd.

"Do you really think he will take me, father?" It was Arinbjorn.

"If you remember the speech we practised."

Freya ducked behind a man trailing two horses and peeked over their short, stocky frames. She could see Arinbjorn walking through the market with his father, Thorleikr. They were ignoring the traders and making their way down to the beach. They were moving at a decent pace and seemed to be heading towards Teitr. The one-eyed chieftain had finished shouting at his two captains and was now standing beneath the prow of one of the ships, busy hollering at some unlucky deckhand who had dropped a barrel while unloading.

She felt her heart quicken as she watched the pair of them meet up with Teitr. The old man greeted Arinbjorn with a hearty handshake and laughed uproariously. Freya didn't think she had ever seen the trader welcome anyone like that. What was going on?

She felt like a small child, standing there, trying not to be seen staring. It had been so long since she had seen him. It had been her choice, the right choice, to put some distance between them, but she regretted not welcoming him back from the tragic encounter in the ice cave. She had been so mad at him for leaving, for pursuing Kormac even though he was so badly wounded. She loved his honour and strength of duty, but he was going out there to die instead of staying with her. If he had stayed that day, if he had given up his quest, she would have left Njall. At least, that is what she told herself. Instead, he had shown that he would pursue his vengeance no matter the cost. Freya could not gamble the life she had built on a man who might never come home. Could she?

Looking over at him now, she could see that the intervening months had been kind to him; he was a little leaner and his brown hair had begun to turn golden in the spring sun. She watched as he and Teitr spoke at length. She could not make out the words, but she could see Arinbjorn shuffling on the balls of his feet. He was nervous—she knew that tell well; he had done it when working up the courage to kiss her as a child. She decided she had to get closer.

She eased the straps of her wooden pack off her shoulders and dropped it to the floor. Her back ached and she enjoyed the brief moment of freedom before removing the basket of *vaðmál*. It was cumbersome, but she could carry it in her arms, and it should obscure her face. Happy, she began to weave her way closer to Arinbjorn and Teitr. It would be difficult to get near where they were standing beneath the prow of the *knarr* without being seen. Thankfully, there was a trail of people moving to and from the vessel, carrying goods. She joined the line heading towards the ship and ignored the stares of the sailors. As she got closer, she heard a laugh she recognized as Eindridi's—it was deep and loud, echoing across the market.

Freya looked about and spotted him setting up his wares close to the second *knarr*. He was busy laughing with someone attending his stall. Perfect. She broke away from the line and made her way over to him, careful to keep her basket between her and Arinbjorn. When she got there, the warm jovial face of Eindridi beamed out at her. He was a stocky man, with a mane of red hair. He dressed well, in hues of scarlet and purple, and he always greeted people with wide arms and a broad grin.

"Freya Hoskuldsdottir! It is a pleasure to see you again!"

Freya winced as his booming voice carried her name across the beach. She looked behind her, but Arinbjorn did not appear to have noticed. He was still in deep conversation. She smiled awkwardly at Eindridi.

"It is good to see you too; I was hoping to buy some soapstone from you." She placed the basket upon one of his many crates, but kept her back to Arinbjorn. "Do you still accept *vaðmál*?"

"But of course!" He pulled out some of the homespun from her basket and held it up to the light. "Excellent craftsmanship as always, Freya. If you weren't already married, I would make an offer myself. Together, we could make a fortune on the continent!"

"You always say that, Eindridi." She couldn't help but grin. "And you have a wife."

He scoffed loudly and leant in with a conspiratorial wink. "She wouldn't have to know."

"Just let me view your wares, you old dog."

Eindridi sighed dramatically. "Oh, to be spurned every time I come to this isle. You're the only reason I come here, you know."

"You say *that* to everyone, too."

He laughed. "The crates over to the left have been opened. Let me know if you see anything you like." With that, he turned to another patron.

Taking her chance, Freya moved to the crate of wares closest to where Arinbjorn was standing and strained to listen in.

"My doubts are not about the boy's honour or courage, Thorleikr," Teitr was saying. "I saw for myself his bravery in battle. Considering the extent of his wounds, he should not have accompanied us on the ice. Then again, perhaps I should not have either." He gestured to his lost eye. Freya could see now there was a nasty scar running from his forehead down to his cheek. "But he has no experience at sea. I cannot afford extra ballast."

"How can I ever get experience if I am never given the chance?" Arinbjorn asked, earnestly.

"You should find another captain with more time to spend on youth," Teitr replied evenly. "My journey is long and hard." He looked down the beach and across the horizon. The tide was beginning to turn. "And I do not mean to return."

"Arinbjorn can find another route back. And what better time to learn than when thrown to the wolves?" Thorleikr pressed.

Teitr sighed. "Why must you make this journey now?"

Freya watched as Arinbjorn and Thorleikr exchanged glances.

"We know that Thangbrander was an emissary of King Olaf. If Thangbrander fled anywhere, it would be there," Arinbjorn said at last. "If not, perhaps someone in Nidaross knows where he came from."

"You would pursue this murderer still?" Teitr looked surprised. "He is gone and no longer welcome on these shores; if he returned, he would almost certainly die. Let it go, child."

"The man took your eye!" Arinbjorn's sudden shout drew the attention of the sailors unloading the ship, and several stopped to listen.

Teitr whirled about then and grabbed Arinbjorn by the scruff of his tunic. "His men did take my eye! I am telling you, I would still not be so foolish as to pursue this matter!" He kept his voice low, but Freya could see his snarl.

"Your fear is well founded, chieftain," Thorleikr said, his hands raised in a peace gesture. "But look what that man left behind: the murder of Kormac, so he could not testify to his crimes; the discord sown between the Christians and us. Our country is divided because of him. It is bigger than us, Teitr."

Thorleikr's softly spoken words seemed to have the desired effect. The chieftain eased his posture and released Arinbjorn.

"I just want the opportunity to try, Teitr. Someone must pay for Kormac's crimes. If I can bring Thangbrander back, maybe we can get him to tell his followers the truth." Arinbjorn looked down and kicked the sand.

There was a long moment of silence as Teitr passed his gaze over the busy market, seemingly taking in the sights. Freya raised her basket to cover her face.

"We came to this island to escape the machinations of Norwegian kings. I would hate to see it fall under another's sway in my lifetime." Teitr returned his attention to Arinbjorn and his father. "Very well, you may join my crew. I will take you as far as Nidaross; from there, you are on your own."

"What about Sigvaldi?" Arinbjorn asked, and both Teitr and Thorleikr looked at him in surprise.

"You want *two* berths now?" Teitr replied, irritated.

"Sigvaldi has sailed before; his family came across from Norway to settle here. He will not need training." He looked evenly at Teitr. "And I will need help."

"You certainly will." Teitr sighed. "Fine, two berths, but no more. And you will have to work the journey."

Freya missed the rest of the conversation as Eindridi came bustling over to her.

"Do you need any help, there? You have been staring a long time."

Freya looked at him dumbly for a moment, forgetting why she was there.

"I changed my mind," she said at last. Picking up her basket, she began to walk away, with Eindridi shouting after her. She ignored him.

Arinbjorn was leaving? Was he even going to tell her? Why should he tell her, after how she ignored him? She felt a wave of dizziness pass over her and her stomach tightened into a knot. As she made her way up the beach, her vision went blurry, a drop of salty water touched her lip. She realized she was crying.

Chapter Twenty-Five

Bera's house in Haukadalur was a small, wonky affair, barely more than a hut. It sat on the plains in the shadow of the mountains to the north, an abandoned farm she had repurposed for herself. Its turf roof was a vibrant green, and the first time Arinbjorn had come calling for her he had mistaken it for a small hill in the grasslands. A plot of tilled earth to the back housed many herbs and plants, and several chickens stalked the property freely.

In the months since their ordeal on the glacier, Arinbjorn and Bera had formed a fast friendship. He appreciated her blunt manner and she relied on him to do some work about her small farm. The young woman had eschewed her role as a daughter to be married off for her father's alliances. Preferring instead to manage her own affairs, she had set herself up as a wise woman and herbalist. Normally, this would have been unthinkable, and it caused no small measure of difficulty for the young witch, but many people had now heard of her prowess healing those wounded in the battle on the glacier. She found herself inundated with callers seeking her counsel.

Today, at his father's request, Arinbjorn was one of those callers. The waves of nausea and tightness in his chest had not abated and his father's worries about a curse hung heavy on his mind. He chastised himself for not examining Kormac's blade when he had the chance; he may have noticed some runes or markings indicating what had been done to him. He found Bera belatedly chasing some hens back into their pen. He could not help but smile as she fussed and cooed over them, only to turn to swearing when they would not listen.

"Fucking get in the fucking pen, you fucking stupid bird!"

Arinbjorn's laugh caught her attention and she turned to face him, her round face flush with frustration.

"Think you can do any better, Thorleiksson?" Bera stared at him, her hands on her hips. She held the gaze a moment before bursting into a wide smile. Arinbjorn returned the grin.

The two met in a brief embrace. He released her and looked down upon her. It had only been a few months since the ice cave, but something in her eyes seemed older. He understood that feeling; he had not been the same either.

"Want me to get those in for you?" Arinbjorn gestured to the three hens that were currently making their way around the back of the hut.

"No, leave them be. If you stress them, the eggs aren't as good." She moved away from him and gestured for him to follow her. "Come inside, I shall make us some tea."

"*They* seem to be stressing *you* out," Arinbjorn said as he followed her. "Is everything all right?"

"Yes, yes. I have just been busy of late, finding it hard to keep on top of things."

That became patently obvious to Arinbjorn as he crossed the threshold of her home. It was a small room, that was true, large enough to house a hearth fire and a single cot, but it was still a mess. A soapstone cauldron lay bubbling over the low flames, and the combined scents of all the dried herbs dangling from the ceiling made his head swim. A small wooden chest acted as both a table and storage, and it was littered with animal bones and runes.

"What in Hel's name happened in here? It looks like the dread wolf himself came barging through."

"Have you come here to talk or just make unbidden comments?" Bera fixed him with a stare before ladling some of the tea from the cauldron into two cups.

He looked about for a place to sit down; finding a small stool, he sat awkwardly upon it. Bera handed him a cup before sitting upon her cot. He sniffed at the tea; it smelled of *blóðberg* and *holtasóley*. Healing tea. He took a sip and for a moment just focused on the feeling of the hot water moving through him.

Arinbjorn looked down into his drink, his energy rapidly leaving him. He did not know why, but the knot in his stomach and the icy cloud in his chest had returned. Suddenly, he just wanted to run away rather than tell her about this curse.

"You're really not all right, are you?" Bera's question came out as a statement.

"You have proven yourself a dedicated healer—"

"And good friend, I should hope." She smiled her broad smile, but it did not reach her eyes this time. Instead, Arinbjorn could see the concern in them.

"Indeed." He took another sip of tea. "I fear I am cursed."

"Cursed?" She barked out the question, an incredulous laugh on her lips. "How so?"

He looked up at her then, his fear turning to anger at her dismissive behaviour, but found she was looking at him intently. He put the cup down upon the chest of runes.

"Why do you laugh at me so?" Arinbjorn asked.

"Oh, Ari." She shuffled across on her cot, opening up a space beside her. She patted the mattress. "Come. Sit."

He rose from his stool, careful not to hit his head on the low ceiling, and moved to sit by her.

"Take off your tunic."

Arinbjorn stared at her dumbly for a moment.

"So I can examine your wounds," she said, replying to his unspoken question.

Nodding, he removed his cloak and tunic and sat there topless while Bera examined him. She held out his right arm, with the thick ugly scar going down the forearm, and traced her fingers upon it. They felt cold in the hot, smoke-filled hut. When she had finished, she turned him away from her and looked upon his back wound. She hummed to herself while she worked. He heard her sigh dramatically.

"What do you see?"

"These wounds are fully healed, with nothing but the scars remaining." She got him to face her once again. She had a gentle smile upon her face. "Tell me why you think you are cursed."

Arinbjorn stared down into his hands and flexed his fingers absentmindedly, remembering how his strength seemed to desert him after being cut. He could not avenge Skjalti like this. He faced an expectant Bera.

"Ever since my battle with Kormac, I have been struck down with feelings of weakness. They seem to happen at random. My chest tightens until I can barely breathe and I just want to double over. Right now, I am resisting every urge to run, even from you. I do not wish to be seen." He could feel the tears forming as he spoke the words. Leaning over, he gripped the side of the cot and closed his eyes.

He heard shuffling as Bera got up from the cot and moved about in the hut. He felt her cold hands upon his. When he opened his eyes, she was kneeling before him, her brown eyes large in the low light of the hearth fire.

"If you are cursed, Arinbjorn, you are a strong man for fighting it as you are." She reached up and wiped away his tears. "And we would be cursed with the same magics."

He sat up straight then, releasing her hands. "What do you mean?"

"I have felt similar feelings since our encounters at the ice cave." She rose from her kneeling position and moved across to the head of the cot. "Why do you think I came out here? Defying my father would have been a death sentence, and the life of a hermit, even a witch, is not easy." She pulled out a necklace she was wearing and resumed her place beside him. Once settled, she held the necklace out for him to see. It was a simple leather cord strung with a piece of bashed lead.

"Rune stones." He held the piece of lead in his hand, running his thumb over the stave inscribed upon it. It was a wheel with eight spokes, each of which had a circle halfway along it and a curved fork at the end.

"It defends me against all sorcery," Bera explained.

"Could you make me one?" Arinbjorn asked.

Bera smiled sadly and removed the necklace from his grip, placing it back beneath her dress. "I could. I fear it would do you no good, however."

"Why not?" He could feel his anxiety rising, turning to frustration.

"Because I still suffer from those same feelings, Ari." She held fast to the lead charm even through the dress. "I have dreams that I die out there in that cave, in the howling storm, Thangbrander's men looking down and laughing at me."

Arinbjorn nodded. He had similar dreams. In his, he was there when Kormac killed Skjalti, and it was him, not the trapper Gunnlaugr, who was killed outside.

"You're saying that I am simply afraid?" Somehow, he found this worse. How could he ever embark upon his journey now? "I am just a coward?

"There is nothing simple about it. You faced a great evil, Ari. To come away unafraid would be the height of foolishness." She reached out and cupped his cheek. "And cowardice is running from your fear."

Arinbjorn stared at the flames of the hearth fire for a moment, watching the steam from the cauldron rise above and ascend into the earthen ceiling.

"I am to leave for Norway in a few days," he said at last. "I am going to find Thangbrander and make him pay for what he did, and anyone else who had a hand in the attacks upon us."

"Would a man who is a coward embark on such a quest?" Bera's smile was that of a parent watching a child come to understand a new task.

Arinbjorn let out a reluctant chuckle. "Perhaps not, but I would feel better if I had some form of protection going out there."

Bera sighed. "Well, if you are insisting upon a magical solution, I am sure I can think of something." She pulled back from him and rose from the cot, moving across to the runes she had on the chest.

A loud knock caused them both to turn towards the door, Arinbjorn instinctively reaching for his sax knife.

"Bera? Bera, it is me." The sound of Freya's voice filled the interior of the hut. "Can I come in?"

Arinbjorn froze, his anxieties forgotten. He stared at the door.

"Of course, the door is open," Bera said.

Arinbjorn wanted to object, but it was too late. With a burst of sunlight, Freya opened the door.

She stood there a moment, underneath the mantle of the door, looking in on Bera and Arinbjorn as a range of emotions passed across her face. Her initial smile was followed by confusion as she saw Arinbjorn sitting there with his top off, then a wince of pain she tried to hide. She immediately attempted to retreat.

"Oh, I am so sorry." She began to close the door. "I did not mean to interrupt…" The words died on her lips.

Bera stopped the door from closing and grabbed Freya by her sleeve, pulling her into the hut. The yelp of surprise from Freya was almost enough to break Arinbjorn from his trance. He just stared at her.

"I was just finishing up with Ari. You can wait here." She dragged a resistant Freya over to the cot and dumped her down beside Arinbjorn. "I will be a moment. Why don't you two catch up?"

Bera went back across to the large wooden chest and knelt before it. She began to work her way through the various pieces of rock, metal, and bone she had laid out upon it.

Arinbjorn sat there, rigid, acutely aware that he was topless. Freya turned the other way, her kerchief hood pulled low over her face to hide. For a long while, there was just the sound of Bera muttering to herself.

"I was not expecting to see you here," Freya said at last. She was still turned away from him, but he could see the golden ringlets of her hair pooling out from under her hood, and her soft white cheek flushed red as she spoke.

"Bera has been kind enough to offer me support." It was not meant as an attack, but he found himself saying the words harshly. He watched her hands dig firmly into the mattress, turning white from the stress.

"I...I am sorry I did not speak to you when you came back."
She seemed to be shaking.

"It is fine. You made your choice quite apparent." He found
himself whispering, hoping that Bera would not hear. "And it
was the only proper choice."

She turned to face him then, and he saw clearly the tears
streaming down her cheeks. They carved streams through the
dust and dirt she had accumulated on the ride out.

"Proper?" It was a plea, not a question.

"You stood by your husband," he explained.

"I stood by my *life*." Her tone was pained, desperate. "I
would have lost everything for you."

Arinbjorn went to speak, but was interrupted by a cry from
Bera. The pair of them turned to look at her. She had taken
off her right shoe, placing her foot upon the chest, and was
using a sax knife to draw blood from her little toe. She saw them
watching, mouths agape.

"If magic was easy, everyone would do it." She laughed.
"Don't mind me." She returned to her work.

Arinbjorn attempted to remember what he had been going
to say, but his mind was blank.

"I never meant to hurt you, Ari." Freya was looking down
into her lap.

"I know." He tried to keep his face ahead, staring at the
witch, but with each breath he found himself acutely aware of
Freya's scent. Unlike the herbal and smoky smells of the hut,
Freya always seemed to have a sweet aroma he likened to dried
fruit. He had always thought he could find her in any room just
by following her scent.

"I should not have kissed you."

"If you had not kissed me, I would have kissed you,"
Arinbjorn admitted. "I very much wanted to."

"Me too." A faint smile graced her lips.

He felt her hand, then, as she reached across and discreetly
laced her fingers over his own. Despite himself, he returned
her tentative grip, and his heart swelled. He turned to face her

and found she was doing the same. They were inches apart. He looked into those eyes, breathing in each of her breaths out, and moved in closer.

A second cry from Bera shocked them both.

"Son of a bitch!" This time, she was drawing blood from her left-hand thumb, near the nail, and was rubbing it over a symbol she had carved into brown coal. "Magic is a bastard."

"What are you making, Bera?" Freya asked.

"It is the sword stave. It will ensure Arinbjorn is never murdered by his enemy." Bera held it out for the pair to see. It was a straight vertical line, bisected by a series of smaller curved and straight ones. It had a cross at the top and a fork at the bottom.

"Do you need this for your trip to Norway?" Freya removed her hand from his grip.

"How did you know about that?" He looked at her with surprise.

"I saw you talking to Teitr, back at the market." She stood then, her head hitting the low herbs that dangled from the ceiling. "Do not go, Ari." Freya made for the door. Arinbjorn reached out to grab her, but she shirked away.

"What do you mean, 'don't go'?" He stood and followed her out.

Bera watched them leave, but made no effort to stop them.

Outside, Arinbjorn found Freya striding off to her horse. The sun was blinding after being in the darkness of the hut and he had to take a moment to adjust to the light. The wind had picked up slightly, but it was still a clear day, and, aside from the rogue chickens, they were alone on the green plains.

"I mean don't go!" Freya shouted back. She was at her horse now, fussing with the saddle. She was crying freely. "You keep almost dying!"

"That is why I came to Bera, for protection!" His protest seemed hollow, even to him.

"Even Bera's magics cannot protect from the evils of this world. You are going up against powerful foes—priests and their kings!"

"Would you have me stay here and let the murders and attacks upon us go unavenged?"

"Yes!" It was a cry—a desperate, pain-filled cry that carried on the breeze.

"Why? There is nothing for me here!"

"You have me!" She gave up on tightening the straps of the saddle and began to run her hands through Aki's mane. The horse was distressed by the shouting.

"You are Njall's," he said, the words coming out as a whisper.

"I can be yours." She looked at him then, her eyes wide with desperation. "Stay. Give up this chase and I will leave Njall."

This was what he had wanted to hear, the words he had coveted for so long, and he could barely believe he was hearing them. They rang like bells in his ears. He took a step back.

"Well?" She wept fiercely now.

All he wanted to do was go to her and hold her. Yet he found himself rooted to the spot. The sound of the grass rustling in the wind filled the silence.

"I can't," he said at last. He tore his gaze from her and looked north towards the mountains. Towards Jarlhettur and the ice cave beneath it. Snow still lined the top of the mountain, but the fields before it were now green and black. "I have to avenge Skjalti. I must stop Thangbrander and his master from doing any more hurt to us. To you."

"I don't care about some Norwegian king! I care about you!"

"You care about Njall, too." He did not know why he said that. Perhaps he knew it would be enough to end their conversation. Maybe he was just reminding himself of the situation. Either way, it stopped Freya.

She looked at him; her face, which had been red and puffy, hardened. "You really would pick this over me." It was not a question.

He stared at her. He could think of a thousand things to say: how he wanted to protect her; how she was the first thing he thought of every morning and the last at night. He could explain how he would take her now and flee from all of this, if only he could banish the images of young Ask and Embla, frozen and pale, from his mind. He could say that he loved her, and always had. Instead, he just said, "Yes."

"So be it, Arinbjorn Thorleiksson." She leapt on to her horse.

Arinbjorn watched her ride away at full gallop, the sound of hoofbeats reverberating across the plains.

Chapter Twenty-Six

Thorer watched as the axe blade was brought down swiftly, severing the man's wrist and embedding itself in the wooden block. He tried not to flinch as the blood that poured from the wound sprayed out and landed on his face. He watched the hand flop to the ground, the fingers twitching momentarily before going still. Einar the Icelander cried out in pain and shock, looking down at his stump, before promptly fainting. That was a blessed relief; the last two men he'd had to watch being maimed had wailed for hours. Their tears and cries still echoed inside his skull. Thorer gestured to the two guards holding the prisoner and they promptly dragged the poor bastard away, dropping him unceremoniously in the cell with the others.

He hated this. It was hot and cramped here in the cells of Olaf's court, nothing more than a converted pig pen. The straw that lined the floor had absorbed a lot of blood, sweat, and shit over the last few weeks. The air was hot, moist, and cloying, and he found it hard to breathe.

"Shall we get another?" one of the guards asked.

Thorer had forgotten his name—he was one of the newer ones who had come looking for fame and fortune serving under Olaf. He was a child, barely eighteen winters—the same age as some of the Icelanders they had maimed.

"No. That is enough for today." He looked into the pen, where half a dozen Icelanders now lay in the dark. Some were missing hands, others eyes. In one case, he had cut out the tongue from an older trader who had been foolish enough to curse Olaf. The group looked out at him with a mixture of fear and contempt. He did not blame them. "Go fetch the healer, tend to their wounds."

There was an expectant pause from the young guard.

"Yes?" Thorer asked, as he bent low to wrench his hand axe from the chopping block.

"Should we be healing them?"

Thorer had to fight to get the axe out; it had been driven deep into the wood. When he finally freed it, he slid his hand across the wooden hilt and a splinter pierced his thumb. His cry of pain became one of anger as he addressed the young guard: "Do as I say or join them!"

The guard nodded and ran off.

Thorer held his thumb to his lips and attempted to suck out the splinter. Thankfully, it was a large one, and he could grip it with his teeth. He tore it free and spat out the wood and blood. He took one more look at the sorry men in the cell before heading outside.

The sun was out, but a light rain was falling from low, grey clouds. He turned his face to the sky and allowed the water to run over him. It was refreshing after being inside the cramped, damp, hot interior of the pigsty-come-cell. The rain cooled him, but it did nothing to get rid of the stench of blood and shit upon him. Sighing, he opened his eyes and began to make his way over to Olaf's hall.

It was a short walk from the prisoner pens to the main courtyard, and he passed by many a trader making his way to and from the king's hall. It was an impressive building, and it dominated the series of longhouses and huts that had grown up around it. Olaf had been taken with the church buildings he had seen on his travels, and he had found a carpenter who could emulate the design, insisting that his hall should look like a place of worship as well as a king's residence. From the outside, it appeared to have two tapered layers, and, unlike the rock-walled and earthen-topped buildings around it, Olaf's hall was made entirely of wood. Its peaked roof was as a sword jutting into the sky and it cast a deep shadow over the courtyard. The sun was setting and it framed the building with a red and gold light.

Thorer stopped as he neared the steps to the main entrance. He was to report back to Olaf on how much progress he had made with the Icelanders, but he found he could not bring himself before his king just yet. Instead, he sat on the low stone step in the shadow of the hall and let the rain fall upon him.

Olaf had built his home at the highest point in Nidaross, overlooking the farm halls, longhouses, and livestock pens that made up the bulk of the buildings in the town. From this vantage point, Thorer could see all the way down to the south bank of the fjord, where the fisherman and traders had beached their ships. Beyond them, the waters of the river Nid stretched off to the east and west, and, to the north, the black cliffs of obsidian dominated the horizon. Thorer had to admire the choice of location; it was a beautiful place to host Olaf's seat of power, but it was also tactically astute. The river twisted in such a way as to create this small peninsular that was easily defended against any land-based assault.

He watched disinterestedly as the traders and farmers went about their business, the pale sands and scrubland filled with crates and barrels being unloaded, traded, and refilled. There would be no more Icelandic ships, he wagered privately. Not once word got out about what Olaf was doing to its countrymen. Thorer did not approve of the imprisonment and maiming of innocent men, but who was he to argue with his king? Especially one with the backing of God. Thorer tried to give the prisoners a chance to convert; if they did, he would not hurt them. The six in the cells, however, had refused, and he had been forced to carry out Olaf's wishes.

The few traders and sea captains that had converted, Thorer had allowed to remain with their ships. Still, they could not leave. No Icelander was to be free in Norway until their countrymen accepted Christianity—so was the decree of Olaf.

"You seem lost in thought, old friend." The sound of his king's voice almost made Thorer jump. He went to rise from his seat, but Olaf stopped him, sitting down next to him instead, and the pair of them looked out upon the beach and its market.

"I was just taking a moment to admire the town. It is testament to all your achievements thus far."

"It is a fine place, one that I would see become the centre of power for a united Christian world." The pride was palpable in Olaf's voice. The surety.

"We have problems keeping our own borders safe; are you sure it is wise to seek more?" The rain had stopped and Thorer looked up into the evening sky.

"Wise? Perhaps not." Olaf placed his hand upon Thorer's shoulder and squeezed. "But it is our duty to God." Releasing his grip, he pulled out a piece of parchment and offered it to Thorer.

"What is this?" Thorer asked, taking it. He began to unravel it.

"It is a missive from Sweyn," Olaf stated simply. He stared ahead, passing his gaze over the crowds down towards the river. He was holding a stem of angelica; the yellow and green starburst flowers were bulbous and bright. He clasped the stem firmly, and Thorer could see his right thumb making continuous circles, as though the hand could not bear to be still.

"Sweyn claims that he has come to terms with King Burislav of the Wends and they wish to see an end to our feud."

"Truly?" Thorer was surprised. Their last encounter with Burislav had been a tense affair; to think that the king might have changed his mind already was suspicious.

"When I married Tyra, Sweyn refused to pay her dowry. As her brother, it was his place to do so, but he and that bitch wife of his took against me."

"They don't call her Sigrid the Haughty for nothing," Thorer said evenly.

Olaf barked out a laugh and it seemed to relax him. "Well, indeed, my friend." He eased his grip on the flowers and took back the letter. Thorer watched him reread it. "It states that if I relinquish my efforts to claim lands to the south, and keep my forces away from Danish and Wendish lands, that *Burislav* will give me Tyra's dowry."

"The lands to the south of the Baltic Sea? Why would he do such a thing? He meant to kill you not three months ago."

Thorer stood from the step, striding forward, and gestured to the Nid. "On that very river! It must be a trap."

Olaf rose and approached his captain. The musky and juniper-like scent of the angelica flowed about him in the light breeze. "It is almost certainly a trap." He seemed anxious to Thorer, and his words came out low and weary.

"You are still considering it though, aren't you?" Thorer could not hide the shock in his voice.

"I have yet to tell Tyra."

"You have yet to tell Tyra what, my king?" The melodic voice of the queen came from behind them. The two turned slowly and found Tyra standing atop the stone steps. She wore a long green dress with golden trim, topped with a simple cloak. She had tied a red kerchief about her hair and was tucking some golden ringlets behind her ear. She looked down upon them, her green eyes narrowed in suspicion.

Olaf put on a broad smile and presented her with the angelica. "I have brought these for you, my love."

She descended the steps and took the flowers. Holding them in both hands, she raised them to her nose and breathed deep. She smiled—a beautiful, bright smile that lit up her face. Thorer knew it hid the viper that lay beneath; he had seen the queen express her displeasure before. She would often smile like this before making an example of the one who had offended her. Thorer found her to be more bloodthirsty than Olaf, she just kept her temper.

"They are beautiful, my king." She leant in and kissed him. "But that was not what you were going to tell me, was it?"

Olaf let out a resigned sigh. "No, Tyra." He held out his arm. "Come with us."

Tyra eyed him for a moment, but took the offered arm. Olaf then led the two of them on a walk down towards the river.

"I have received a letter from your brother, Sweyn, and King Burislav. They are offering an end to our conflict with them."

Thorer watched the queen tense slightly, her grip tightening on Olaf, but she continued her pace.

"What are their terms?" She did not raise her voice and she continued to smile and nod to the people they passed on their route down to the beach.

"Peace and no more war, in return for your owed dowry."

At this, Tyra did stop. They were at the beach now, and the earthen ground gave way to the yellow sands and scrubland. There was more of a breeze here, and it brought with it the scent of the river. The waters had turned golden in the evening sun.

Tyra turned to face her husband. "You are not sure whether you should accept, are you?" The accusation was apparent in the tone, and Thorer took up position behind his king. He braced himself.

"Burislav and Sweyn have not hidden their disdain for our marriage." He gestured out to the assembled ships that lined the shore. "And my raids upon their lands have not made them any more likely to be trustworthy."

"They are *my* lands, not theirs." Whenever Tyra was angry, she would not raise her voice; instead, she would lower it to just above a whisper. Each word was slowly and carefully spoken. It unnerved Thorer more than Olaf's rage. "You were just taking them back for me."

"Your brother would sooner see me dead than legitimize our marriage with a dowry," Olaf protested.

"Since when did Olaf, King of Norway, fear battle?" She did raise her voice now, so that passers-by could hear too.

"Quieten your voice, Tyra!" Olaf ordered.

"Or what? You are seemingly too cowardly to strike. My brother is many things, but not a liar. I would see this for what it is: a chance at peace. Do not allow cowardice to deny us this opportunity." She addressed Thorer. "You, my king's favourite captain—what do you think about my brother's letter?"

Thorer could think of nothing to say. Nothing that would not earn a harsh reprisal. He knew better than to besmirch Tyra before Olaf, even if he was defending himself; if he did that, he would be joining the Icelanders in the pigsty by the end of the day.

Instead, he looked down at the beached ships that lined the shores of Nidaross. There were eleven warships as part of Olaf's dedicated fleet. The largest, of course, was the *drakkar* vessel, the *Ormrinn Langi*, which dominated the beach. Its intricately patterned hull and dragon carving at the prow made it a fearsome sight, but the knowledge it housed sixty-eight of the king's finest warriors was enough to cause dread in any who saw her in battle.

Next to the *Ormrinn Langi* were the *skeids*. While not as large or powerful as Olaf's personal vessel, they were good strong ships in their own right, and could house a complement of sixty fighters each. It was a strong, well-tested fleet, filled with men loyal to Olaf. Still, Thorer knew it would not be enough if they were to go up against both Sweyn *and* Burislav. If there was a chance at peace…

"If it *is* true, as you suggest, my queen, then we would not be looking over our shoulders the whole time. We already have enough issues with Jarl Eirikr," Thorer said at last.

"The bastard son of Haakon is no threat to my king," Tyra said grandly.

Olaf smiled thinly at this, but had to brighten up as a group of traders moved past them on their way up the beach. Each made a show of bowing before the king, and Olaf shook the hands of a few of the more prominent and wealthy traders. He joked with the younger housecarls, and generally made an effort to seem jovial. Once the throng had passed, he returned his attention to Tyra.

"Eirikr and his forces have hampered our ability to expand east," Olaf stated. "And he has always believed that I took more than my fair share of his father's land when I deposed him. I have heard of his emissaries seeking audiences with my jarls in those lands."

"All the more reason to accept this treaty with my brother and Burislav. The jarls only want peace and to live well. The constant raids on their borders cause them justified worry. If it will put an end to your feud, you can assure your jarls of their safety, focus upon Eirikr, and finally claim a Christian Norway all for your own," Tyra retorted.

"If we are to take Sweyn at his word, I would rather we had more men," Thorer said. He wanted to defend his king without offending Tyra. "Eleven ships are not enough."

"I agree," Olaf stated. They had made their way across the sands and now stood before the prow of the *Ormrinn Langi*.

Tyra ran a hand down the exposed hull. "Do you remember where the design for this vessel came from, husband?"

"It is based on Raud the Strong's ship." Olaf's reply was hesitant. He looked away from his wife and walked down the length of the ship, past the timber mooring beams, and came to a stop by the water.

Tyra watched him go, and then followed. The pair stood in the shallows and allowed the river to lap at their feet.

Thorer waited a polite distance behind and tried to look like he was busy inspecting the hull for damage, but he could still hear them.

"And what did you do to that *seiðr*-wielding warlord?"

Even from a vantage point a few yards away, Thorer could hear that Tyra had changed her voice to one low and soft.

"I killed him."

"You didn't just kill him." Tyra grabbed her husband's hand and thrust the flowers into his face. She raised her voice again until all the men still tending to the beached ship could hear her. "You shoved a reed of angelica down his throat and forced a serpent into his gullet! You watched as the snake ate him from the inside out!"

There was a cheer from the few men atop the *Ormrinn Langi*.

"Shut up!" Thorer hissed up to his men, who looked confused before going back to their tasks.

"This is the fate of all those who would defy Christianity and King Olaf Tryggvason!" Tyra finished.

"I know what you are doing, Tyra." Olaf took the angelica from Tyra.

"I am doing nothing but reminding you of your duty to me and to God," Tyra countered. "Accept this deal, use my lands to spread the Word of Christ, and we can deal with Jarl Eirikr. The jarls will support you fully if there is to be peace in their lands. There will be no one left to oppose you." She stood back and quietly awaited Olaf's answer.

The king looked intently at the flowers in his hand, then threw them into the river. He turned and strode back up the beach, his face hardened. "Thorer!"

His captain fell into step beside him, already mentally prepared for what he was about to hear.

"Put out a call. All my jarls are to come here within one month. Tell them to bring their finest men and ships."

"You are prepared to accept Sweyn's offer?"

"I intend to prepare for war."

Thorer struggled to match his master's pace.

"If this is real, then we have nothing to fear, but, if it is a trap, we will be a force to be reckoned with. I will make them pay with blood and steel." With that, Olaf strode off towards his hall.

Thorer watched him disappear before turning to stare at the waters of the Nid and the smiling Tyra who stood before them.

Chapter Twenty-Seven

The spray of the ocean felt good against his burnt skin. He stood there, on the prow of the ship, leaning into the spindrift. Letting it cool him. The sun had set some time ago and the sky above was lit with the shining light of a thousand stars. It was a new moon and he liked the darkness it brought. It meant he could clearly see the Bifröst bridge, the band of stars that curved above, their blue and red lights leading the way to Himinbjörg. He wondered if Heimdal was looking down upon him now, as he was looking up.

Arinbjorn had readily agreed to take the night watch; it might cost him some sleep, but he enjoyed the alone time. It had been a hard few weeks aboard Teitr's ship, the *Morgin-Skin*, *Morning Light*, and he coveted these brief few hours when he was not being shouted at by Teitr. The old trader had not been lying when he said it would be a hard journey. Three weeks they had been at sea, and Arinbjorn had had to learn quickly the requirements of sailing a ship like the *Morgin-Skin*.

Sigvaldi had been a great help. His father was a fisherman, and he still remembered many of the basic tasks: how to tie the ropes, how to tack, what "leeward" meant. Arinbjorn knew none of this and stuck to his old friend keenly during the day, taking direction as best he could. Teitr had wanted to throw him overboard at one point. Arinbjorn was sure he had tied the rigging down exactly as he had seen Sigvaldi do it, but, after a particularly strong gale, the sail tore free and whipped about the deck. It had cost them precious time and Teitr's face had turned purple from all the shouting.

In the end, Arinbjorn was told he could be a watchman. There was little chance of him screwing that up, Teitr had said, and he was told to stand at the prow of the ship and shout if he saw anything. Arinbjorn was just happy to be out of the way. It was days like that, when he had spent most of it failing, that he wondered what on earth convinced him he could complete his task. How could he avenge Skjalti if he couldn't even tie a knot properly?

Arinbjorn looked back across the deck and saw most of the sailors were sleeping peacefully, with only the skeleton crew to man the stations. Sigvaldi, in contrast to Arinbjorn, had impressed Teitr and was given the chance to pilot the ship during the evenings. He looked across at Arinbjorn from the steering oar at the stern and waved. Arinbjorn waved back half-heartedly and returned his gaze to the black horizon. He tried to focus on the sound of the waves beating against the hull, and the gentle creaking noise of the wooden ship as it strained against the sea. Tomorrow morning, they would arrive in Nidaross.

*

Arinbjorn pulled his cloak tighter about himself and held fast to the ship. The grey mist that surrounded the *Morgin-Skin* had come on quickly, and it unnerved him. It reminded him of the snowstorms that would blanket the land during the winter, but this seemed to stretch on forever. For a moment, he wondered whether he had died at sea and was now passing through Hel's chilled domain. He stood at the prow of the ship, still tasked with watchman duty, and cast his gaze across the river. The air was thick, and what light was coming through from the sun seemed diffuse and dull. He could see no more than a few yards ahead, and the whole world seemed still. He cocked his ears to see if he could hear anything coming: the sound of crashing waves upon rocks, the grunts of men rowing a *skeid* towards them, or even the sound of the gulls flying about them. Nothing.

The waters were calm. They lapped gently at the ship as it glided upstream and the only other sounds were the creaks and moans of the ship itself, the sails flapping listlessly. Arinbjorn did not know how Teitr did it, but somehow the old trader was successfully navigating them through the fjord. Looking back down the ship, Arinbjorn could see him at the tiller, his one dark eye narrowed as he stared ahead. He angrily gestured for Arinbjorn to keep looking forward.

They had spotted land late last night, the first time in three weeks, and Arinbjorn had looked upon the black cliffs of obsidian rock in awe. As they approached the mouth of the fjord, the sun had begun to crest the horizon, framing the behemoth cliffs with a dull red glow. He had seen nothing like it before; their sheer verticality loomed over him, casting deep shadows in the early morning light. He was so busy looking up, he did not notice the fog until it was practically upon them. It rolled down the river from the east and plunged them into an icy soup. Arinbjorn had been amazed how quickly the waters calmed, going from raging sea to relatively flat river almost instantly, as if they had passed an invisible threshold.

The *knarr* was not designed with rowing benches and relied upon its sails for travel; thankfully, Teitr kept long oars for moments such as these and he had them distributed immediately. Twelve men, Sigvaldi included, tentatively paddled the ship upstream. Teitr instructed everyone to be quiet so that they could hear better, but he need not have bothered. To a man, they were silent, each holding his breath as they stalked their way through the fog.

Arinbjorn did not know how long they had been in the mist now. According to Sigvaldi, Nidaross was a couple of hours upstream, but it felt like they had been travelling for that long already. In the endless white, Arinbjorn found his mind drifting back to Freya, their last encounter playing on his mind while he thumbed the defensive rune that hung about his neck. He had to go back and tell her what he really felt. Once this was all over, and Skjalti had been avenged, he would return to Iceland with no more plans to depart. He understood her need for a dependable husband, especially after all she had been through to build the life she had. He wondered if she understood him, too? Or whether she would greet his return as she had before.

A sudden increase in the sound of water crashing against rock brought Arinbjorn back to the present. He looked desperately about, thinking the sound came from starboard. There, not a few yards ahead, a sheer wall began to emerge from the fog. He shouted out his surprise and gestured wildly to the right. Teitr immediately went hard on the tiller and the ship began to turn towards port. The rowers on the right-hand side pulled up their oars and used them to brace against the oncoming rock.

They barely made it. The black rock of the cliff face came within inches of their vessel as they eased away. Two of the sailors snapped their oars as they desperately pushed out against the stone. Still, make it they did, and the group let out a collective sigh of relief.

"Well done, Arinbjorn!" Teitr shouted. "But maybe a bit more warning next time." For a moment, the old trader, with his thin grey beard and one eye, looked like Odin himself piloting the ship. He gave Arinbjorn a yellowed grin and gestured for him to look ahead. Arinbjorn blinked away the vision and returned his gaze to the fore.

There was only one other near miss as he attempted to navigate them through the fog. An outcrop of shattered rocks lay submerged near the cliff face, but thankfully the mist had thinned and Arinbjorn spotted it in plenty of time. Then, as abruptly as it came, the curtain of mist vanished and the *Morgin-Skin* emerged into pale afternoon light. Arinbjorn took a deep, welcome breath of crisp air, and the crew let out a satisfied cheer. Black clouds still hung in the sky, but his vision was no longer hindered; he could now see the breadth and majesty of the great river they were travelling upon. To the north, the cliff faces continued to bend and weave about the waters, splitting off into tributaries and lesser rivers. The south bank, however, had become a green and vibrant peninsular that jutted out from the land, and upon it was the largest settlement Arinbjorn had ever seen.

There were dozens of longhouses with green turf roofs, countless stone halls, and fields of cultivated land that stretched out far from the town. The waters leading up to the yellow sands were filled with ships. Some were small trading vessels like theirs, or fishing skiffs that bobbed in the shallows. The ones that caught Arinbjorn's attention, however, were the large vessels that lay beached before the town proper. They were bulbous and bloated, with huge ornate sails and rows of oars. Their hulls were decked with circular shields, and each prow seemed to have an intricate wood carving, the most magnificent of which was a hooked dragon, its fanged maw stretched wide as if to consume all before it.

"The *Ormrinn Langi*." Teitr's cracked voice made Arinbjorn jump. The captain had left the till and come down to join him, leaving a beaming Sigvaldi at the helm. "It's Olaf Tryggvason's personal warship."

"So that means—"

"We have arrived at Nidaross." Teitr placed a gnarled hand upon Arinbjorn's shoulder. "This will be where I leave you. Are you sure you want to stay?"

"I don't think you want me on your ship any more than I want to be on it, old man," Arinbjorn stated with a small grin.

"Perhaps not, but your Norwegian friend is useful." Teitr's attempt at a wink came out as an awkward blink. The captain's smile faded, however, as he looked across the water.

A *skeid* was rapidly approaching.

"All stop!" Teitr shouted, his old and worn voice still managing to make Arinbjorn wince with the strength of it.

The crew leapt to the command of their captain, and Arinbjorn could sense the sudden rise in tension.

"What's wrong?" Arinbjorn looked at the rapidly approaching *skeid*. It was a warship all right—not as large as the *Ormrinn Langi*, thank the gods, but intimidating nonetheless. As its rowers powered it through the water, the sound of drums bore down upon them.

"I do not know," Teitr said as he returned to the tiller. He relieved Sigvaldi, who then ran up to Arinbjorn.

"Well, we are here." Sigvaldi only had eyes for the town of Nidaross. He barely observed the warship that approached them, yet he was gripping tightly to his sheathed sax knife.

Arinbjorn did not have time to ask his friend what he was thinking, as the *skeid* came to a stop aside their port.

A tall man, with a mane of dark hair and a black beard, appeared over the shields that lined the edge of the warship. He was not as old as Teitr, that much was clear, but he had a hard, angular face that was heavily weathered. He looked down upon the *Morgin-Skin*. "What is your business here in Nidaross?"

Arinbjorn thought that Teitr had the most cracked voice he had heard, but this man sounded like lightning striking rock. His words boomed over the deck.

"We are traders, carrying goods for your king," Teitr replied, standing at the tiller, back straight and staring evenly up at the *skeid* captain. He spoke calmly and opened his arms wide to present his men. "We have no weapons."

"Your accent—Icelander?"

Teitr frowned at this. "Yes. Teitr, chieftain of Iceland. I have traded many times here before——" But he barely had time to finish his sentence.

As soon as he heard confirmation, the opposing captain gave a quick nod to his men. A dozen heavily armed archers appeared at the side of the *skeid*, arrows nocked. Every man on the *Morgin-Skin* put up their hands and began to shout in protest. Arinbjorn stood there dumbly until Sigvaldi nudged him, then he too raised his hands.

"What is the meaning of this?" Teitr shouted.

Warriors from the *skeid* began to jump into the water and swim over to the *Morgin-Skin*, all the while their comrades above kept their arrows upon the terrified sailors.

"No Iceland heathen is to be free in Norway—so is the decree of the king," the *skeid* captain replied. "You and your vessel are now the property of Olaf Tryggvason."

*

Arinbjorn vomited. He couldn't help it. The scent of blood and shit that permeated the cell as he was thrown in with the others was too much to bear. It was hot and cloying, and it choked him to breathe it in. He retched and heaved and coated the floor with acidic bile.

He felt a gentle hand on his shoulder. "Easy. Easy, Ari." It was Sigvaldi. "Let it out."

Arinbjorn brushed aside his friend's hand; he didn't want to be touched while he vomited. He dropped to his knees and fell back against the wall of the cell. He lay his check against the stone and found it cooling. The retching continued until his stomach ached. He lay there for a moment, quietly crying. This was not what was supposed to happen.

They had been boarded and escorted into the town of Nidaross. There, the crew had been split up; only Icelanders were to be taken.

Any awe or excitement Arinbjorn had felt at the grand scale of the settlement was lost as he and the remaining crew of the *Morgin-Skin* were paraded through the streets. The people looked upon them with a mixture of pity and disdain, and he was spat upon a few times. He had tried to look to Teitr for support, but the trader was in as much shock as he was. He had protested with the captain of the other vessel and had almost lost his remaining eye. He was left with a bloodied wound upon his forehead and was dragged through the streets with his crew, looking stunned.

At first, Arinbjorn had thought they were to be taken to the king. Their route through the town had led them up and away from the now-beached *Morgin-Skin*. He saw what he thought must be the king's hall: a two-tiered, steepled building made of wood that sat upon the hill overlooking Nidaross. It had intricately carved pillars, and the stone steps leading up to the front door were heavily guarded. They neared this building, but at the last minute they made a sharp turn and were led down a narrow dirt path between two longhouses.

Then he saw their true destination: a long, decrepit stone hut that lay behind the king's hall. The stench was overbearing, and even before they went inside Arinbjorn had to suppress a gag.

"Do not worry—you will find other Icelanders in here," the black-bearded captain was saying.

They were marched inside and Arinbjorn saw the reason for the foul smell. This was an old pigsty in which three large rudimentary iron cells had been set up. The floor was lined with rotten straw, and in the far corner there was a wooden chopping block, stained with blood. A candle burned low on a solitary table, its yellow flame flickering, and it cast its light over the poor people inside the cells.

There were at least a dozen of them, and some looked worse than others. In the cell on the far right, several figures clutched at severed limbs and stared forlornly at the new arrivals.

"Teitr?" a voice Arinbjorn did not recognize called out from the middle cell. A tall white-haired man emerged from the shadows and gripped the bars. "Is that you?"

"Gizurr?" The shock and confusion upon Teitr's face was palpable as they were herded into the final cell. "What in the name of Hel are you doing here?"

Now that the name was spoken, Arinbjorn remembered seeing Gizurr at Thangbrander's church. He was the one who seemed sullen and quiet during the Mass, taking no pleasure in the priest's angry rhetoric. The white-haired chieftain looked to be healthy, albeit dirty, and he spoke with quiet relief at the sight of his fellow Icelanders. Arinbjorn guessed that he must have been thrown in here recently, as the maimed men in the back cell looked ragged by comparison.

"By God, it *is* you," Gizurr responded. He reached out through the bars and clasped Teitr's hand. "You should not have come here, my friend."

"Since when did it become a crime to be an Icelander here?" Teitr asked as he shook the other chieftain's hand.

"Since Thangbrander failed in his mission, it would seem." Gizurr spat on the floor after mentioning the priest's name. "Now, all Icelanders here are Olaf's prisoners."

Arinbjorn's stomach seemed to drop, and his chest tightened upon hearing Gizurr's words. He could not help but stare at the men who lay maimed and broken in the far cell. They looked back with gaunt, hollow faces. Their eyes were listless and clouded, those that had them, and one man lay awfully still on the floor. Arinbjorn looked down at his own hands and wondered if that would be his fate too. It was then that he started vomiting, the thick cloying air getting the better of him.

"Is that Arinbjorn Thorleiksson that I see?" Gizurr cast a questioning gaze to Teitr.

"Indeed. He booked passage on my vessel," Teitr explained, while Arinbjorn finished being sick. "Along with his friend, Sigvaldi."

"Ah, yes, we spoke before. Do you remember?"

"I do, chieftain. And I appreciated your council," Arinbjorn said humbly.

"Teitr I can understand, but what has brought you out here to this fate?"

Arinbjorn managed to regain his composure and Sigvaldi helped pull him to his feet. After a moment of swaying, he wiped himself down and turned to address Gizurr directly. He knew the chieftain was a Christian, but right now they were all Icelanders.

"We came here to find Thangbrander," Arinbjorn said, looking carefully for Gizurr's reaction, to see whether he would have to lie about his intentions.

Gizurr flinched at the name and then cast his gaze to the floor. He held on to the iron bars, his knuckles whitening. "I understand." He looked up again. "You would be avenged upon him for his crimes."

"He committed no crimes!" This earnest shout came from a man with dark red hair. He was younger, around Arinbjorn's age, but Arinbjorn did not recognize him.

"Shut up, Hjalti," Gizurr admonished. He pushed the younger man back. "I apologize for my son-in-law. He is a firm believer in the priest."

"Yet you are not?" Arinbjorn eyed him quizzically.

"Contrary to what you would believe, not all Christians decry the Icelandic way of life. I believe in the law, our law, and I only ever fought for equal rights in the eyes of that law." Gizurr looked weary then, and he released his grip on the bars. "In fact, I came here with Hjalti to seek the assistance of King Olaf in the changing of that law."

"How is that working out for you?" Teitr asked. The old trader gave a thin smile. "I told you it was foolish to join them, old friend."

"It would appear Olaf no longer recognizes friend or foe when it comes to Icelanders," Gizurr agreed. "We were imprisoned the moment we arrived. And we have yet to see the king."

"You must accept his offer." They all jumped at the voice that emanated from the far cell. It was quiet, barely above a whisper, and came through shallow, ragged breaths.

Arinbjorn squinted in the low light and made out a thin, wrought figure pressed up against the cell bars. At first, he thought he was an old man; his hair was thin and greasy, and he looked like he had been branded multiple times—red welts covered his exposed arms. But when he looked up at them with glassy blue eyes, Arinbjorn realized this tortured figure was actually around his and Sigvaldi's age, and it made him want to be sick again.

"What offer?" Sigvaldi asked.

There was a long pause as the poor creature summoned his strength. It clearly hurt him to breathe. "You must convert if you are to leave here." He pushed his arm through the bars and Arinbjorn saw that his hand was missing at the wrist. Its bloodied stump was covered in flies. "Or else you will end up like us."

Arinbjorn managed to keep the urge to retch down, and instead faced Gizurr. "Is this your god's work?" he asked.

The chieftain shook his head. "Olaf is not God," he retorted. "But he is the agent of our Lord. I think he has it very wrong. If I could only see him, I could show him how to bring the

Word of God to our people without violence." He paced his cell, agitated.

"Do you really believe you can convince him?" The harsh, broken voice of the black-bearded captain cut through their discussion. He stood on the other side of the cells, flanked by two guards, and looked at Gizurr with interest.

"Yes. Yes, I do. God would not want this." The white-haired chieftain approached the cell door and stared evenly into the captain's face. "Who are you?"

"I am Thorer, captain of the *Ormrinn Langi* and the king's guard."

"You are a man of God, Thorer? Do *you* agree with this?" He gestured to the broken bodies of the men in the adjacent cell.

Thorer looked into the blackness of the cell with the mutilated prisoners. He stared for a long time and the whole pigsty was silent. Eventually, he returned his gaze to Gizurr. "No."

"Then please bring me before the king. I promise you, I can stop this." Gizurr was pleading openly now.

Arinbjorn looked between the two men, then back towards Sigvaldi, who was frozen taught. It was then that he realized what he must do.

"I wish to convert." Arinbjorn strode up to the cell door and reached out to the captain, who backed away. "We all do." A chorus of confused mutterings passed between those behind him, but he did not turn to address it. "Let us convert and we will help stop this madness."

Thorer looked at him, his face unreadable.

"Very well. Come with me."

Chapter Twenty-Eight

She threaded the weft between the warp, her fingers dextrously weaving the two lines of wool as she made her way along the loom. The square wooden frame towered over her and she sat on her stool, working from left to right, creating a thick, tight pattern that she hoped would make a warm and comfortable replacement set of bedding. Normally, Freya liked weaving. It was hard, monotonous work, but there was a certain relaxing quality to it she could not place. Her fingers could seize up and her back would ache after hours of sitting on the small wooden stool, but her mind was free to wander as she methodically worked.

Today, however, she was struggling. Several threads had been weak, fraying and disintegrating only after she had made it halfway through a new line. She had reset the loom multiple times, and the heddle stick she used to create shed in the warp threads had snapped. She stared at the splintered piece of wood forlornly for a moment before tossing the two broken parts to the floor. Leaning her forehead against the vertically falling warp, she closed her eyes and tried to focus. She simply could not cast aside her thoughts. They tumbled through her head like a waterfall crashing and burrowing into rock.

She could not believe how foolish she had been in heading to Bera's hovel. She had hoped the young witch would have supplies of goat's beard or hazelwort, and, if Bera suspected their use, she trusted that the witch could be discreet. Arinbjorn being there, however, had thrown her off her course. Seeing him topless and talking with Bera had caused a spike of anger. She knew she had no right to be, but she was upset nonetheless, and she realized then the mistake she had made in avoiding him all those months.

What she would do to go back and reach out to him when he had returned from the ice cave. Would he still be here now, had

she acted differently? Her cheeks felt wet, and she used the hem
of her sleeve to wipe away the tears that were forming.

No. He would still have left.

She'd told herself this every day since she parted from him
on the plains, the hoof falls of Aki resounding in her ears.
Arinbjorn could not give up the hunt for Thangbrander and
his allies; the Christians had simply taken too much from him.
He could never offer her the life she wanted with him. Yet, she
carried the thought of him with her always.

Freya stood from the loom and made her way over to the
hearth fire, where she began stirring the stew she had been
slowly cooking over the flames. It was a mutton stew, blended
with onion, garlic, leek, and turnip; steam from the bubbling
water rose into the air, carrying with it the scents of thyme,
rosemary, and nettle. She had been lucky, in a way; Njall had
found one of their wayward sheep, but it had died. Rather than
waste it, he had brought it back for food. But mutton was tough,
and the stew had several hours left before the meat would be as
soft as she liked it.

The sheep concerned her, though. Njall refused to tell her
how it had died. He came back from his search with Tongu-
Oddr shortly after Freya returned from the beach market.
When she questioned him about what had happened, the pair
of them shared a look, and Njall simply took it to the chopping
block outside and skinned the poor animal before she could get
a good look at it. But she was sure she had seen a wound upon
its neck. She could not help wondering if Njall's caginess had
something to do with the burning effigy.

Ever since she had found Njall outside their hall, staring into
the offensive flames, her husband had been quiet and fidgety.
He rarely sat still, and he often would patrol the farmlands and
the hall if he had nothing else to do. When they lay in bed at
night, she could feel that he was awake, staring at the ceiling.

For her part, she kept a wary eye on any journeyman,
farmer or thrall who was passing over their lands to get to
his own. The sight of a traveller passing by was a positive

one, under normal circumstances; managing the farm was an isolating experience and the arrival of new people to interact with was usually welcome. Ever since her encounter with Hallr, however, she had been suspicious of everyone she knew. She felt surrounded by her neighbours and she found herself ducking out of the way if she spotted people while outside the hall.

Given those circumstances, she was not surprised that Njall kept quiet. Still, the wound on the sheep's neck seemed all too clean and neat for an accident. She tried to shake away the thought but found she could not escape the image of its cold, glassy eyes staring listlessly out at her.

Her stomach had stopped rumbling. Scowling, she quit stirring and dropped the ladle in the pot, splashing stew into the fire. She was not hungry, after all.

The heavy creak of wood and a gust of wind signalled that someone had entered the hall. Looking up, she saw Njall approaching. He was dressed only in a light tunic and trousers as it was a warm day outside. He gave her a sad smile.

"You look like you need to lie your head under water, my love." Njall knelt down and stoked the fire, watching it burn for a moment, clearly waiting for Freya to reply.

"I have much on my mind," she said at last. She went over to the broken heddle stick she had tossed to the floor. Picking it up, she brought it over to the fire and dropped it in.

"You broke your loom." Njall looked sorrowful, and Freya had to reach over and raise his chin.

"It is a fucking loom. Nothing to worry about." She smiled at him. "I will ask one of the thralls to make me a new heddle stick."

Njall nodded, but did not return her smile. Taking her outstretched hand in his, he kissed her knuckle, his lips cool against her skin. He held her there a moment before releasing her.

"It looks like you have made a fine meal with the old ewe." He leant over the pot and took a deep breath in.

"Did you really come in here to talk about my cooking, husband?" Freya moved behind Njall, reached her arms around his waist, and held him. They stayed that way for a while, just listening to the fire pop and spit.

"I heard you had a run-in with Hallr at the market," Njall said at last.

Freya tensed, but did not let go. "Yes. But how did you know?"

"I sent Failend out to his hall to trade for some supplies. Hallr himself took her aside."

Freya frowned. Ever since the attack on Conall and Fergus, Failend had requested tasks that took her away from the farm, saying that she could not bear to be reminded of their loss. Freya understood and often sent her on longer journeys. Still, Hallr's hall was right by the coast and not the first place Freya would have sent Failend to trade. "Why would you send her to Hallr? We hardly know him."

"I know. But I am not sure I can trust the people I *do* know, of late."

"The fire—"

"Could have been set by anyone. But the Christians have enough on their plate." Njall squeezed her hand, the tell-tale signal that she should release him. She did so and they both stood, Njall turning to face her. "I have heard that Hallr made us an offer, through you. What was it?"

Freya thought back to her encounter with the Christian chieftain. She did not trust his intentions and did not believe the Christians would be any more forgiving towards Njall were they not so in need of his support.

"He said nothing of value, husband."

She went to move away, but Njall reached out and grabbed her upper arm. His grip was gentle but firm, and it rooted her to the spot.

"Njall!"

"Please, Freya. Tell me what was said."

She could see now, in the wide bloodshot eyes of her husband, the fear that had been gnawing at him since the burning. His hair looked more grey than usual, and the creases in his face seemed deeper. He had aged a lot in a few months.

"Let go of me, Njall." She tried to project as much force and strength as she could into her words.

Njall blinked, and his eyes softened. He looked at his arm holding Freya and released her. For a moment, he just stared at his hand. "I am sorry," he said at last.

"You need to tell me what is going on; I know you are keeping things from me," Freya replied. She took the opportunity to put some space between her and Njall and moved back around the hearth fire. She looked around at their hall: its low earthen roof where she hung herbs to dry; the sleeping area behind its low partition wall where the two of them lay together at night, barely touching; the hearth fire, where she seemed to spend so much of her time, laden with the soapstone and iron pots that rattled in the wind every time someone opened the door. It was a small, humble home, but it was hers, and she had already given up someone to ensure she would not lose it. "After everything that has happened between us, you must know that we are in this together."

Njall sat down upon a stool and ran his hands through his hair. He was trembling. "Ever since the burning, I have been noticing small things. Sheep going missing. Crops being dug up. Small glances from our neighbours." He looked up at her then, his eyes wide. His voice dropped to a whisper. "They are all around us."

"Why are they doing this?" Freya did not understand why their neighbours were tormenting them so. If they truly knew of Njall's leanings, they would have simply killed him by now.

"They are trying to scare me." He gave a weak laugh. "It is working."

Freya looked at her husband then, the man who had taken her as a bride to hide his true desires, the man who had denied her a normal life, and she felt pity. He may have married her under false pretences, but she had chosen to adapt to this life and make it her own. Any threat to him was a threat to her.

"Hallr was offering sanctuary," she said at last.

"Why would the Christians offer me sanctuary? They are no more accepting of…" He trailed off.

Freya was glad; she didn't need to hear it. "I suspect he wants our support at the Althing."

Njall frowned. "The one at the end of summer? Of course… the Christians have been pushing for a change in the law."

"And they will need as many people supporting them as possible, if they are to convince the chieftains to vote in their favour."

"Gellir is our chieftain; do you really believe he is one to be swayed?" Njall asked bitterly. He used the poker to hack at the fire, and the flames roared.

"What do the Christians want?" Freya knew about the struggle to push for representation at the Althing, but did not know what their ultimate intent was.

"They want a separate set of laws to govern the rights of Christians within Iceland." Njall let out a bark of hysterical laughter. "They are truly foolish to believe they'll get that!"

"They would sunder our entire country to get their way?" Freya was incredulous, the sheer audacity was almost admirable.

"Priest Thangbrander gave them delusions and stoked their fear. They would do anything to protect themselves." He quietened and his shoulders sagged.

Freya looked down upon him and took in a slow, deep breath. She loved the scent of the woodsmoke and nettle-filled air; it calmed her and focused her mind. Njall might not have been the husband she wanted, but he was still her husband. Now Arinbjorn had rejected her and gone off on his foolish journey, there was nothing left in her life except this farm and this man. She was resolved that none would take away the world she had built here.

"Until these attacks upon are farm are settled, we have to consider all our options," she said at last, pulling out a leather cord necklace she wore about her neck. It had a series of small glass beads threaded along it, but it was the obsidian carving of Thor's hammer she was interested in. She thumbed it thoughtfully. Would the gods object? "Even throwing in our lot with the Christians."

"Are you suggesting we accept Hallr's offer?" Njall's confusion was apparent, his face contorted in an almost amusing display. "*You* kept his offer from *me*."

"That was before I understood the depth of the problem we face. Do you believe Odin or Thor would want us to give up and accept the loss of our home? They are warriors, Njall. We need to be too."

Njall rose from his stool and strode across to her. She held out her necklace to him and he tentatively held it with her. His fingers tightened around hers.

"I cannot abandon my gods just to live, Freya." Njall's voice wavered, but she could sense his conviction. "They do not reward disloyalty."

"Is it disloyalty if it is but a trick?" Freya was getting frustrated now. Could Njall not see the way out of this? "Do you remember how Thor got his hammer back from the giant Thrymr?"

Njall looked utterly confused for a moment, before slowly recounting the story: "He disguised himself as the goddess Freya and married Thrymr, with Loki as his bridesmaid. Together, they tricked the giants into giving back Mjölnir."

"And then the two of them killed them all," Freya finished, a hard smile passing across her face. "We must be like Thor and Loki. We will 'accept' Hallr's offer of sanctuary and welcome their god into our hearts." She felt Njall tense in her grip, but she held fast to him, not letting him pull away. "I suspect whoever is doing this will strike out at the Althing. That would be the most public time to accuse you. We need the Christians' protection for then."

"If it is only our support at the Althing Hallr craves..." Njall mused.

"And you do not believe it will work, anyway."

"Then what is the harm?" He still seemed unsure to Freya.

She smiled up at him. "We are on our own in this world, husband. You are an honourable man; you rode to the glacier and helped fight against those who would harm our way of life. You fought for the very people who would now harm us, and you would be used by the Christians to further their own ends. We must carve our own path and use those who would use us."

"So, we go to the Althing with the protection of the Christians. Use it to root out our enemy?"

"The Christians and chiefs can argue about the gods." She released his hands then and held out the Mjölnir necklace; Njall took it. "We need to stop these attacks upon us."

"After all that I have done, the mistakes I have made, you would still help me?"

Freya paused then, looking into Njall's face. He had failed her before, but he was here now and the key to preserving the life she had built. Her hand instinctively went to her stomach; there was also so much more at stake now.

"We are in this together."

Njall nodded and pocketed the Mjölnir pendant. "Then we will be as Thor and deceive our enemies." He kissed her gently on the forehead and made his way to the exit. "I will send Failend to give Hallr our response."

He disappeared outside, his exit letting in golden rays of sunlight that lit up the interior for one brief moment before the door closed behind him. Freya let out a breath she had not realized she was holding. Change was upon them, she knew, and this constant battle between the gods could not last forever. The Althing would be where their fate was decided; someone had to win, she just had to make sure she was on the right side.

Chapter Twenty-Nine

Arinbjorn, Sigvaldi, and the other new arrivals from Iceland were brought into Olaf's great hall. Despite himself, Arinbjorn could not help but be awed by the construct. It was the biggest building he had ever seen. The ceiling stretched out above him, and it wasn't made of soil. Instead, countless wooden arches propped up a second tier that towered overhead. The walls, floor, and pillars were all ornately carved with imagery he did not recognize, and the stone floor was warm thanks to the braziers that lit the entire interior. The room was long and wide, and currently sparsely populated. Long tables were stacked up on either side, leaving only a slightly raised dais at the far end of the hall, before the hearth fire. There, sitting on two high seats, were a man and a woman. The man was not too old, his hair was still mostly golden save for a few greying hairs, and he looked upon the ragged group being brought in with mild interest. The woman was much younger, also blonde, and clearly beautiful. Arinbjorn did not relax upon seeing her, however. Something about the rigid way she sat, or the manner in which her long fingers played with the beaded necklace she wore, made him uncomfortable.

The group was brought to a stop a polite distance away from the raised dais. Arinbjorn looked about and noticed the flagstones seemed to be a darker shade where they were standing; for a moment, he could have sworn he saw blood. There was silence as the Icelanders and the two in the high seats observed each other.

"Kneel," Captain Thorer hissed from behind. He prodded Gizurr in the back with the hilt of his sword and the chieftain gracefully went to one knee. The others followed suit.

The man on the dais stood. He was wearing a dark red tunic hemmed in gold, and his fingers were laden with rings.

"You kneel before King Olaf Tryggvason, jarl of Nidaross, ruler of Norway, and champion in the name of our Lord, Jesus Christ," Thorer said, his harsh voice filling the entire hall.

For some reason, Arinbjorn was suddenly overcome with an urge to laugh—a hysterical, panicked laughter. He managed to resist by balling his fists and dragging them along the floor to make them bleed.

"I thought I had made it clear that no Icelander was to be free in my domain until Christianity was accepted by your people," Olaf said. He passed his gaze over them all, waiting for a reply.

"My king, we did not know of the ban. We set out before word reached Iceland," Teitr said. The trader looked frailer than Arinbjorn had ever seen before. He leant heavily upon Sigvaldi as he knelt, his one eye fixed to the ground.

"Why then did you come?" Olaf began pacing before them.

"I came to trade, my king. Nothing more," Teitr said, his voice quavering.

"And to deliver me and my companion here," Arinbjorn interjected.

The group all turned to look at him, eyes wide with surprise. Sigvaldi had gone almost purple. Arinbjorn ignored them and also tried to ignore the icy cloud forming in his chest. He stared into the eyes of the king and resisted the urge to stand up and flee.

Olaf arched an eyebrow and looked down upon Arinbjorn, "Oh?"

This was his chance. If he did not take it, he may never find his quarry.

"We came here to find Priest Thangbrander," Arinbjorn stated. He noticed Gizurr give him a long, studious look, but the chieftain said nothing.

"Really, now, were you one of his flock?" Olaf walked over and lowered himself until he was resting on his heels and eye to eye with Arinbjorn. He folded his hands before him.

Arinbjorn tried to look to Sigvaldi for support, but Olaf grabbed his face, his fingers taught and sinewy, and held it firmly within his hand.

"Do not look to them. Your king is speaking to you."

Arinbjorn stared into Olaf's eyes. They were dark blue, and they reminded Arinbjorn of the northern seas during a storm.

"I am sorry, my king. We did attend some of Thangbrander's Masses in Iceland."

"Were you baptized?"

Arinbjorn was suddenly aware of all the men who had been hidden within the recesses of the hall. They emerged from the shadows, coated in chain mail, their hands resting on their swords.

"The priest left Iceland before he could bless us." Arinbjorn struggled to remember what little he paid attention to in the one Mass he had attended. "We came here so he could induct us into the halls of St Peter!" He almost shouted out the last bit in relief.

Olaf must have mistaken this for zeal, for he gave a genuine smile that softened his face. "You braved the waters of the ocean, among heathens, just so you could be one with Christ?" Olaf laughed and looked up at Thorer. "This is the kind of man we need more of." He rose from the floor and returned to his seat. "What of the rest of you?" He gestured to Gizurr.

"My king, if I may, I am Gizurr the White, chieftain of Iceland and friend to Thangbrander. I and my son-in-law, Hjalti, came here to seek your council and to finish what the good priest started."

"Thangbrander believed you sheep fuckers could not be converted," the woman in the high seat said. Her voice was melodious, but her words cut into Arinbjorn. "What reason do we have to doubt him?"

Olaf reached over and squeezed his wife's hand. "Tyra is correct. I have been failed before. What solutions do you bring?"

"With respect, my king, Thangbrander did not know how to appeal to an Icelander's heart. We are a proud people, who have lived centuries fighting for freedom against those that would control us." Gizurr looked calmly into the eyes of the king. He knelt with his hands on his lap, palms facing upward, his voice sure.

"You believe his methods were too harsh?" Olaf sneered. "What rights does a pagan have in the eyes of the Lord?"

"You sent him there to bring the Word of God to my people. Instead, he brought pain and death to many—including those who would follow Him."

Arinbjorn looked to Gizurr then, eyes wide. Did the chieftain believe in the priest's crimes?

Gizurr did not look back; his gaze was fixed upon the king. "That turned many against him, and by association the message he brought. He was a blunt instrument, poorly wielded."

All turned in shock to Gizurr, sure that he had just brought about their deaths. Even Thorer looked stunned. The air was still, as no one dared to breathe.

Olaf leant forward to speak, but he was cut off by Tyra's giggle, which filled the great hall and made Arinbjorn shudder.

"He is right, husband," she said, laughing.

Olaf looked at his wife for a long moment, his fingers flexing against the armrests of his chair, before turning to face Gizurr once again. "Perhaps you are right, chieftain. What would you suggest?"

"Release the Icelanders here. Send them home, if you must." Gizurr's voice was strong now, and with each sentence he seemed to grow bigger. Arinbjorn understood why he had been made chieftain. He had a quiet power.

"And allow the heathenism to go unpunished?"

"Send me back with a priest. One who speaks the Word of God, without resorting to fear or violence. I will bring our case to the Althing itself. I already know that the Christians in Iceland intend to make a case to amend the laws and give themselves equal rights. I believe, with your help, I can persuade the other chieftains to grant that request."

"What good are your rights to me? I want to stamp out heathenism, not live next to it."

"You cannot convert people to a life of persecution," Gizurr said evenly.

"And if they do not fear retribution from their fellows," Tyra interjected, "then the Word of God can flow unheeded, husband." She reached across and squeezed Olaf's arm. He returned the sentiment by squeezing her hand.

"Then all you have to do is wait," Gizurr finished.

Olaf was silent for a long time. The flames in the hall crackled and popped, and the wooden walls seemed to creak and moan. The Icelanders tried not to look at each other, but Arinbjorn could feel Sigvaldi's gaze upon him. He knew he had a lot of explaining to do to his poor friend who he had dragged all this way.

"You speak the truth," Olaf said at last. "A rare thing indeed." He looked to Thorer. "Release them and their countrymen."

The captain gave a swift nod, a small smile spreading across his face.

"Rise."

The Icelanders slowly got to the feet. Teitr swayed slightly, but Sigvaldi caught him.

"I will grant you your request. Thormothr!"

A small, timid-looking man with rat-like features tottered out of the shadows. He was probably Arinbjorn's age, but he lacked any hair on the top of his head; instead, a ring of brown ringlets dangled around the sides. He wore the same type of robes Thangbrander had worn when giving his sermons.

"Yes, my king," Thormothr said. His voice was squeaky.

"You are to leave immediately with Chieftain Gizurr, here."

Gizurr smiled at the young cleric and gave a small nod.

"Take the Word of God to Iceland and succeed where Thangbrander failed."

Olaf and Tyra stood then, hands held, and began to leave the chamber.

"My king!" Arinbjorn shouted.

Olaf turned to face him.

The other Icelanders all took a step away from Arinbjorn. All except Sigvaldi.

"What more do you ask of me?"

"We came here to be baptized by Priest Thangbrander and…to join you." Arinbjorn looked to Sigvaldi and ushered him forward so they both stood together.

"What are you doing?" Sigvaldi hissed.

"Can you direct me to the priest so that we may fulfil our vow?" Arinbjorn had to swallow the bile that rose up at the back of his throat.

Olaf let out a laugh—a deep, booming laugh that was as overwhelming as Tyra's was cutting.

"Gizurr, you are now the leading Christian in Iceland," Olaf stated. "Would you vouch for these two?"

Arinbjorn turned to look at Gizurr. The chieftain was staring at him, blue eyes focused and arms crossed. Arinbjorn had not seen this coming; Gizurr knew their real reason for coming here and, if he revealed it now, he knew they would die there and then. The chieftain looked up to the ceiling. Arinbjorn followed his gaze but could not see what he was staring at, if anything. Perhaps he was simply trying to see his god.

"I have seen these men in Mass many times," Gizurr said at last. "Thangbrander and the man he serves deserve to have these men at their backs."

Olaf smiled, seemingly pleased. He opened his arms wide.

"Then I welcome you to my service! You will find I am generous to my men, especially those proven to have a strong faith. Thorer, take these two to Priest Thangbrander, then get them inducted into my fleet; we must set sail soon." With that, the king and his wife left the hall, disappearing into a small alcove off the side, his laughter echoing after him.

Arinbjorn mouthed a thank you to Gizurr, but the old chieftain did not acknowledge it. He simply turned and walked out of the hall with his men. That left Teitr and his sailors with Arinbjorn and Sigvaldi.

"We will escort you to your ship; it is the least we can do for your help," Sigvaldi said to the one-eyed trader as they filed out of the hall.

Teitr let out a weak laugh. "Thank you, but I require no more from you." He fixed his one good eye on Arinbjorn and lowered his voice: "I believe you and Gizurr saved our lives tonight. You are no sailor, but you have your wits."

"What will you do now?" Arinbjorn asked.

"I will not outstay my welcome. I will trade what I can and leave within a few days. I doubt I shall ever return here."

They emerged into the warm summer evening and looked upon the golden sky. They all breathed deep.

"Thank you. For everything," Arinbjorn said.

"I hope you find what you are looking for." Teitr reached out and shook their hands. He then began his slow walk through the courtyard, his men at his side.

Arinbjorn and Sigvaldi stood on the stone steps and looked down upon Nidaross for a few moments, taking in the sights and sounds of the great town. Finally, Thorer joined them. It was time for their meeting with Thangbrander.

*

Arinbjorn stared at the head. Its grey, pallid skin had gone slack, giving the impression of a mask hung loosely over a skull. The hair, more grey than black now, was dry and brittle thanks to its exposure to the salt air off the Nid. It hung loosely over the face, obscuring the look of dumb surprise that was permanently etched into the features. The eyes had glassed over, but seemed to stare at Arinbjorn no matter where he stood to look at the skewered head. A fly landed on the left eyeball, and he half expected it to blink. Instead, the fly crawled down the face, buzzing about the red meat that dangled from the severed neck. There was no doubt, Priest Thangbrander was dead.

Arinbjorn balled his fists, feeling his nails bite into his skin, and kicked out at the spear. It swayed briefly and Thangbrander's head lolled about listlessly. Arinbjorn looked at Sigvaldi, who was standing next to him. His normally trim beard was getting dishevelled, and he ran his hand through it nervously as he looked at the rows of other heads impaled on spears in the sand. There were half a dozen faces bobbing about in the wind, and Arinbjorn recognized the head of the one-armed man from the cell. It was still fresh, the blood running down the spear.

"Now you have seen the price of disobeying your new king, I suggest you learn to serve him well." The sound of Thorer's loud and raspy voice made Arinbjorn jump. He turned to stare into the haggard face of his new captain.

"What happened?" Arinbjorn gestured to the priest, unable to hide his despair.

Thorer came to stand beside him and gripped his shoulder, squeezing it as if for reassurance. "You knew the priest well?" he asked.

Sigvaldi stopped staring at the other heads and gave Arinbjorn a quick look, a small shake of the head.

"Something like that," Arinbjorn said simply. "He was the reason I came out here."

Thorer nodded, as if in understanding. "It is a shame, what happened to the priest; he made quite the impact over in Iceland." Thorer looked up at Thangbrander, and Arinbjorn was almost sure he saw a scowl.

"What did he do wrong?" Sigvaldi had grown tired of looking at the impaled faces.

"He failed in his mission." It was all Thorer would say on the matter.

Arinbjorn looked to Sigvaldi, who had kept mostly silent since their encounter with the king, and tried to reach out to his friend. Sigvaldi brushed him off and cast his gaze over the amassed ships that littered the Nid and the hundreds of men practising drills by the water's edge, then he walked off down the beach. He had every right to be angry, Arinbjorn thought.

Here they were, stranded far from home, here to kill a man who was already dead, and they were now in the service of the most powerful warlord in all the north. Loki must be playing tricks on him. What had he done to anger the trickster god?

He pulled out the sword-stave pendant that sat about his neck. He ran his thumb over it and remembered the words Bera had spoken. That he would not be cut down by his enemy so long as he wore this. It was old magic, the magic of the *gods*. He hoped it would protect him, wherever he was going.

Chapter Thirty

Freya could not sleep. Her back ached and she felt bloated. For the past few weeks, she had struggled to lie down as her throat was bitter and bile-filled; she found herself coughing frequently throughout the night. Not that Njall noticed. He had always fallen asleep quickly, and his snores seemed to bore into her skull. In the end, it was just too much for her. She rolled off the bed and padded to the crate where she stored their linens; she got dressed—not bothering to be quiet, as Njall did not stir—grabbed a sax knife and made her way outside.

It was still light. The red sun was half obscured by the horizon, but it would stay that way for many hours yet, and the sky above had turned a dark purple. It was quiet on the farm at this hour, the animals and thralls slept deeply, and she took the time to listen to the wind rustling through the mountain grass. It had been a while since she had done this; ever since the deaths of Conall and Fergus, she had not been able to bring herself to walk around at night. Even knowing Kormac was dead was not enough.

The thoughts of her attacker made her feel queasy and her stomach tightened. She fought the urge to run back inside and instead walked over to the edge of the hill that sloped down towards the ash trees where the two thralls were killed. It had been months since they died, and the trees looked utterly different from the gnarled and claw-like copse that had scared her then. The green leaves had returned, and the seeds that dropped from the branches spiralled about in the breeze. The constant sunset bathed the copse in a golden light and for a moment she forgot what had happened there.

The snap of a twig from behind made her whirl about. She reached for her sax knife and held it out before her. She eased when she saw Failend emerge from the thralls' sleeping hut. The young thrall's auburn hair was a tangled mess, and she wore her clothes loosely, as though she had thrown them on. She trudged out to meet Freya.

"Failend, what are you doing up?" Freya lowered the sax knife.

The thrall came to a stop before her, and only then did Freya realize she was holding something. She had bound a collection of herbs and flowers together. In the twilight, Freya could make out the white petals of *holtasóley* mixed with the purple leaves of *blóðberg*.

"They were Conall's favourite flowers..." Failend's voice was low, and her brown eyes were cast down towards the ground. "I wanted to bring them to his grave.

Freya felt the tears forming but did not stop them, letting them trickle down her face. She reached out to Failend and squeezed her arm. "May I join you?"

Failend looked startled but did not object; she just nodded, and the two of them began their slow descent down into the valley. It was strange walking about at night; Freya half expected her foot to crunch into deep snow, but instead the grass and lichen that lined the floor absorbed the sounds of their passing. Ravens, confused by the endless light, cawed from their nests. Their chorus intensified as Freya and Failend crossed the threshold into the forest. The canopy was thick and blocked out most of the light. The floor was littered with the seeds that had dropped from their parents; they were dry and brittle, snapping under the women's feet as they walked deeper into the copse. Eventually, they found the small pile of burnt logs that marked the funeral pyre of Conall and Fergus; grass and lichen had begun to take hold and the ash had long since blown away. As they approached, Freya spotted several bundles of old dead flowers.

"How long have you been coming here?"

"Once a month since they died." Failend walked up to the old flowers and knelt before them. She tossed them aside and placed the new bunch in their stead.

Freya stood back and remained quiet.

"Are you really going to join the Christians?" Failend asked, her voice low.

"They have offered us sanctuary," Freya replied. She went over to her thrall, her friend, and placed a hand upon her shoulder.

Failend flinched. Slowly, the thrall turned to look up at Freya. Tears streamed down her face, but it was set in a dark grimace, the freckled skin creased into a frown.

"I was the one sent to Hallr's hall; I have seen what his sanctuary is worth," she spat. "He has surrounded himself with weak thralls, poor freedmen, and lowly farmers. His priest is fled and Gizurr the White is gone. He needs men of good standing on his side."

"The Christians are the only ones willing to protect us," Freya insisted.

"A Christian killed *them*." She gestured to the old pyre, her voice cracking. "And attacked *you*. Do you so easily forget this?"

"Easy, Failend," Freya replied, seeing that Failend was clearly in distress. "I have forgotten nothing."

Failend brushed Freya's hand aside. Standing, she wiped off the seeds and twigs that clung to her knees. "You would forgive all insults to protect your buggerer of a husband." She had whispered it, almost as if saying it to herself, but Freya heard it.

Shock quickly turned to anger, but she tried to keep her voice measured. "Be mindful of what you say, Failend," Freya said through clenched teeth. "And to whom you say it."

"You would not have me speak of how your husband likes to be fucked?" Failend barked out a cold, emotionless laugh that was smothered by the close air inside the copse. "There is no one left in Iceland who does not know." She fixed Freya with a wide, manic grin.

The realization hit Freya hard. Her stomach seemed to fall away from her and the strength in her legs failed. She reached out to a tree for support, managing to find a purchase before she collapsed to the floor. She looked over to Failend, who was stalking around the pyre; her gaze did not leave Freya now.

"You," Freya said, her voice barely above a whisper. "You are the one who has been going around telling everyone."

"I have had you sending me far and wide since the attack." Failend smiled. "I thought you would be *grateful*."

"Grateful!" Freya shouted. "You have brought death upon my husband!" She let go of the tree and began to make her way over to the traitorous thrall. "What have I to be grateful for?"

She staggered towards Failend, her hands contorting into claws. Right then, she wanted to choke the life out of her.

Failend looked on, indifferent. "Njall is to be accused at the Althing. If you do not side with the Christians, he will have no one to protect him." She stopped circling the cold pyre as Freya reached her. "You would be free to pursue other men."

Freya slapped her. A cold, sharp smack across the cheek. Failend raised a hand to her slowly reddening face, which contorted into a snarl.

Freya instinctively reached down for her sax knife. "Bitch," she hissed. "Do not speak of your masters that way."

"He is no master of mine," Failend countered. "He stopped being that when he couldn't protect his own people!"

Freya had been ready to strike again, but those last words cut into her. Now she was close, she could see tears flowed freely down Failend's face. The thrall made no moves to defend herself. Instead, she simply stood there, chest heaving and fists balled at her side.

The two of them stared at each other for a long time before Freya finally spoke: "He could not have known Kormac would be so bold." The excuse felt weak, even to her.

Failend scoffed. "You forget, I was there when Kormac first came at you with his vile lechery. I was there when you begged Njall to stay and he went off again with Tongu-Oddr!" Her shout filled the forest around them and the ravens fluttered about in shock. She bent down into the dried and burnt logs and pulled out a piece of blackened and warped metal. It looked like a buckle. Failend squeezed it tight. "We are only here because of your friend, Arinbjorn. He seems to be the only one willing to avenge these deaths."

The mention of Arinbjorn was a step too far.

"You know nothing of the sacrifices I have made to keep this farm together. To keep you *safe*," Freya shouted.

"Safe?" Failend seemed incredulous. "We will never be safe under the protection of your so-called husband. He is too weak." She gestured to the pyre. "Look what he wrought. How can you still defend him?"

Freya looked down into the ashen, moss-covered logs, and for a moment she thought she could see the shapes of Conall and Fergus lying atop them once more. The knot in her stomach twisted further. They had been part of her life only a short while, but they had been a positive, happy influence in an otherwise difficult situation. To this day, she was convinced they would stride into the hall, singing the song which she could never remember, and mock each other as they worked. She missed them keenly. She understood Failend's loss, but that did not give her the right to bring harm to Njall.

"Tomorrow we begin our ride to the Althing," Freya said coolly. "I do not care who you have spoken to; I will ensure my family is kept safe."

"I know when you get there you will cower before Hallr." Failend began to move away. "And you will be forced to give up everything you believe in."

Freya reached out and grasped her arm. "You leave when I say you can leave." She squeezed as tightly as she could.

Failend's face was as a feral dog as she pried herself free from the grip. She pushed Freya to the ground, making her fall hard and twist her ankle painfully.

Freya let out a small cry.

"You are not so strong, after all," Failend said. "Perhaps you do deserve the company of the Christians." She strode out of the forest, not once looking back.

"You cannot leave! You belong to me!" Freya cursed herself for her stupidity. She had been so focused on her own distress, she had missed Failend's, and now the thrall had jeopardized everything. She lay there in the twilight copse and wept freely.

*

The journey to the Althing would take a couple of days and it required an early start. The Law Rock was located in the Thingvellir valley, and while they could make the journey on horseback in a single day, Njall had decided they would take the time to join up with the various caravans of farmers travelling from all over Iceland for the event. Freya had attempted to dissuade him of this, given the circumstances, but he argued that appearances needed to be upheld. He got up early and ordered the thralls to prepare their horses.

Freya watched from the door as Njall and Aesgir readied the horses. They packed heavy, and the poor stocky horses were laden with satchels containing tents, clothes, and food to last several days. Aki looked miserable as Njall tightened the straps on the horse's saddle, so Freya grabbed an apple and took it over to her mount. She ran her fingers through the black mane, scratching him just the way he liked, and fed him the apple. The sound of his teeth biting into fruit always made her smile.

"He is ready, my love," Njall said, moving around and finishing up the straps. "We can leave soon."

Freya merely nodded and continued to stroke Aki, while Njall went inside to collect the last of his gear. It was a bright, clear day, and the sun beat down upon her. She pulled her kerchief over her hair and down over her eyes to give her some shade. Looking about the farm and the lands beyond it, she tried to see if Failend could be spotted anywhere. She had not seen the thrall since she had returned home from their encounter in the copse the night before, and she had yet to tell Njall about it.

Freya had crawled back into bed late, but she still slept poorly. She managed to get up before Njall to try to find the wayward thrall, but there was no trace of her. Aesgir, the younger boy who so often got sent off to herd sheep, said he had not seen her since the evening before. A cursory inspection of Failend's sleeping cot revealed that it had not been slept in. She did not own many things, but it looked like some of her clothes were missing too. She was gone.

As Njall emerged from their hall, Freya went to mount Aki. It was getting harder to move about with the extra weight she was slowly putting on, and her ankle still ached from her encounter with Failend, but she managed to drag herself up unceremoniously. Njall jumped into the saddle of his own horse and looked about the farm. He called out for the thralls to gather and waited as Aesgir and the two newer men he had purchased to replace Conall and Fergus fell into place. Njall waited a moment longer, confusion etched into his face.

"Where is Failend?" he said at last.

The thralls looked at each other and shrugged their shoulders.

Njall turned to face Freya, his face creased deep with worry lines. "She must have been taken from us."

"I have released Failend from our service," Freya said, after a moment's pause. "She is gone."

"What?" Shock turned to confusion. "Why would you do this?" Njall seemed hurt, but also angry—a thrall was an expensive commodity.

"She was of no further use to us, husband." She gripped tightly to the reins and began to trot away from the farm.

Njall shouted out his orders to the thralls who were to keep the farm running in their absence, then he rode to catch up with her.

Side by side, they made their way down into the valley outside their home before setting out west across the grassy plains towards Thingvellir. The low, undulating hills were filled with shrubs, beautiful flowering plants that peppered the green sea with bright whites and purples, and moss-covered stones. Once they were a long way from their hall, and there was nothing but the gentle sound of hoofs upon the soft earth to fill the silence between them, Njall spoke again.

"What was all that about?" he asked. He was looking ahead, and Freya could see his hands were white as they gripped his reins. Anger was not something she was used to seeing in Njall, but it did not scare her.

"I spoke with Failend last night while you slept." Freya tried to remain calm. The encounter still rattled her, but she needed to be strong now. "She harbours ill will towards you."

"What?" Njall's look of confusion would have been amusing were it not contorted into a grimace.

"She blames you for the death of Conall and Fergus. She was close to them."

Whatever fire there had been in Njall was immediately extinguished. He relaxed his grip on the reins and his shoulders went slack. He closed his eyes and let out a low curse. "Fuck."

"She is the one who has been going around spreading the rumours about you," Freya continued. "We fought. She left."

"We have every right to have her killed," Njall said. "Why didn't you wake me?"

"Because she is right, Njall." Freya brought Aki to an abrupt stop, and Njall was forced to turn his mount around so they could talk face to face. "You failed us and people we loved died."

"She has been causing us terror for months!" Njall shouted. "Our very lives are in the balance because of her."

"Yes," Freya replied evenly. "I do not agree with what she has done, forcing us on to the path we are taking. But I was in no position to harm her." She looked down at her stomach.

"Is she pleased she has pushed us into the arms of the Christians?" Anger had returned to Njall, and for the first time Freya saw him as a physical presence. He seemed to broaden, his chest swelling and his arms steadying. A calm fell over him, and he stared at her with cold eyes. So this was the hunter in her husband.

"She did not expect that we would seek sanctuary with those who wounded us. She sees my decision as a betrayal."

"You should not have let her go." Njall sighed. He pulled on the reins and guided his horse back on to the path.

Ahead of them, moving down a hill to the north, Freya could see the beginnings of a caravan winding its way into the plains proper. It must have included dozens of people riding and walking.

Njall observed them too. "They must be coming from the northern farthing."

"Did you want to join them?" Freya asked as she spurred on Aki. She had to trot quickly to catch up with her husband, who seemed to be striding ahead in his anger.

"Yes. We must move quickly to discover who our friends will be at the Althing." He gave her a sidelong glance. "Do you really believe the Christians won't win the backing of the chieftains?"

"I honestly do not know."

They continued on in silence for a while, listening to the birds nestling in the shrubs and the wind rustling the mountain grass. Freya looked up into the deep blue sky and, for a moment, she thought she might fall into it.

"I guess we have little choice now," Njall stated.

"Whatever happens, whatever has gone before, I am on your side," Freya replied. She pulled up close to Njall and reached across to hold his hand. "I always will be."

Njall held her hand in his and squeezed it gently. With that, they continued their journey west to the Althing and to the fate of all Iceland.

Chapter Thirty-One

The sun had passed its zenith, causing the waters to glimmer in gold and red hues, and the salty air whipped at Olaf's face. He stood on the prow of the *Ormrinn Langi*, observing his fleet of longships and *karves* as they cut through the waters, golden wakes curtaining out behind them. After four weeks of travel, they were almost to Wendland, and now they found themselves in the Øresund Strait. This channel marked the most dangerous part of the journey, and he knew it was imperative they made it through before nightfall. Lands to the north and south of the pass belonged to Sweyn, and two shorelines progressively narrowed, making it hard for his fleet to manoeuvre. It was the perfect place for a trap.

He shook his head. Now was not the time for such worry; he had a duty to perform, one he rather enjoyed. He turned around and looked down the length of the ship. The rowing benches were full and the sails had caught the wind. The sailors moved their oars in rhythm to the drumbeat and their voices filled the air with song. Thorer stood at his side and, before him, kneeling at his feet, were the two latest additions to his crew: Arinbjorn Thorleiksson and Sigvaldi Magnusson.

"When you first came to me, you told me that you came in search of Priest Thangbrander," Olaf began, "pledging yourself to my service in return for seeing the priest. Do you still stand by that oath?"

"Yes," they said in unison.

Olaf had to stifle a laugh. Arinbjorn had two trails of dried blood under his nose—Thorer had obviously taken his training seriously—but the young farmer looked up at him stoically. Olaf was impressed; Thangbrander had clearly been wrong about Icelanders.

"Thorer has taken a liking to you. It was his idea to bring you aboard this vessel, my flagship, as a sign that Icelanders would be received into our bosom once more." He turned to look at Thorer, who gave the king a thin smile. "He was right. It is time you received what you came out here for." He reached into his leather pouch.

The two Icelanders seemed to tense and they shot questioning looks to Thorer, who remained stoic.

Olaf smiled; they must have thought he had forgotten. He pulled out two pieces of cord with simple wooden crosses as pendants. "It is time to induct you into the way of Christ."

Arinbjorn and Sigvaldi visibly relaxed.

Smiling, Olaf called for silence from the crew before hanging the necklaces around their necks. He observed them looking at their crosses with interest. "We have no priest here, but I had Thormothr consecrate this water." He produced a waterskin and untied the drawstring. He held it there a moment. "Who are you, that has come to seek out Christ our Lord?"

A quiet look passed between the two of them, the sound of waves beating against the hull filling the silence. A seagull flew overhead, its shadow sweeping across the pair of them. Olaf looked up and saw dozens of them circling the ship. He was reminded of his encounter with Burislav. The gulls had circled then, too.

"Arinbjorn, Son of Thorleikr."

"Sigvaldi, Son of Magnus."

Their names brought the king back to the moment and he shook off the cold feeling that had crept over him. "What do you seek?" he asked. He stepped forward and dipped his fingers into the holy water.

"Baptism," they replied.

Olaf reached out and marked the sign of the cross on each of their foreheads. "The Christian community welcomes you with great joy. In its name, I claim you for Christ our Saviour, by the sign of His cross."

He expected to see smiles across their faces, but they appeared more stunned than celebratory.

"You may rise."

The pair stood slowly, their feet unsteady on the rocking ship. They bowed slightly and thanked him.

He had performed many baptisms in his time, and witnessed many more, but he had never seen the newly baptized look like deer caught before a hunter's bow, as these two did now. He had to remind himself that they were but simple farmers; being part of this campaign must be overwhelming. They would almost certainly die if they got into a battle, but he reassured himself that he had at least guaranteed their place in heaven. It was as good a reward as he could bestow.

He waved them away and they scuttled off to join the rowing benches. He watched them resume their positions with curiosity. Once they were back in place, he returned his attention to his captain, who had been silent throughout.

"Are you sure about those two, Thorer?" Olaf asked.

"They crossed the seas just to find their priest. It is the kind of dedication we need." The broken-voiced captain ran his hand through his black hair. "Thank you for welcoming them on this ship."

"I know you found my orders for the Icelanders distasteful, Thorer," Olaf said.

His captain looked at him in surprise, his weather-worn face creasing in worry.

"Yet you did your duty regardless; I welcome them on board as a thank you."

Thorer bowed. He gestured to the lands about them. "We must discuss your plan for Wendland."

Olaf turned to face the prow of the ship and looked out across the waters. He took in a deep breath, letting the sea spray cool him. Once they had passed through the Øresund Strait, they would enter the Baltic Sea. Wendland, and Tyra's lands, lay there. He still had grave reservations about Sweyn and Burislav's missive of peace, but, as he gazed upon his amassed fleet, he found he was not afraid of battle. The white sails of the *skeids* caught the light of the sun and, to Olaf's eye, it looked like a golden fire was sailing across the waters. A holy armada that bore the cross to all who stood before it.

"When will we cross into the Baltic?" Olaf asked.

Thorer had clearly anticipated this, as he had already pulled out a parchment map. He took a moment to study it, casting his gaze over the low hills and rocky shores to the north-east. "At our current pace, we will make it past Svolder by nightfall. The Baltic lies shortly thereafter." Thorer rolled up the map. "Are you sure you want to be in those waters at night? I would suggest we make camp and leave with the dawn on our side."

"If they attack us while we are beached, we will be sitting ducks," Olaf replied.

"You are expecting an attack." It was a statement, not a question.

"Indeed, old friend, as are you. I fear our enemies lie just beyond, and I would meet them head on."

"My king, may I speak freely?" Thorer's question came out pained. He was leaning against the prow, his knuckles white as he gripped the wood.

"Of course. I have always welcomed your council."

Thorer took a deep breath. "We should turn back, use this fleet to take what lands you can from Sweyn. If he truly awaits us with ill intent, why meet him at all? We could be raiding the lands about us while he is assembled elsewhere."

"I do not fear Sweyn and Burislav, and nor should you," Olaf replied. "We have God on our side."

"Does God truly want Tyra's lands?" Thorer's voice was strained and he began to pace the deck.

"He wants me to bring the Word to all the world," Olaf answered. "Wendland is where we begin."

"I have followed you into hell, my king, and I will do so again. But I have to warn you, I think this is a *mistake*." The desperation was palpable, and it had begun to irritate Olaf.

"Your opinion is noted, Thorer." The king hardened his words; he'd had enough of explaining himself. "Go now to your new charges, see if you cannot get them battle ready, if you are so concerned." He turned from his captain and waited for the tell-tale sound of footsteps moving away across the deck.

Olaf stayed at the prow and tried to dismiss Thorer's concerns. As the day dragged on, the wind began to die down and the rowers were forced to increase their pace. Their choruses and songs filled the air as they fought their way through the water with their oars. He kept his gaze on the horizon, searching for any sign of an ambush, but, as the hours passed by, he saw nothing.

Thorer worried too much. The size of Olaf's fleet was substantial, and they had the right of God on their side. He had been ambushed, mutinied, shipwrecked, and gutted, yet he had survived it all by the grace of God. What was Sweyn when matched against that? God would see them through any hardship, be it storm or battle, and all would cower before His might. Olaf did not have a child to kill to prove his point this time, but he had no doubt the message from the last example still stuck with his crew. Einar's head had joined Thangbrander's on the beaches of Nidaross, for all to see what happened to those who failed him. If it came to it, he knew they would all fight for their God.

*

Arinbjorn swung his axe and parried the descending blow, the sword missing his gut by mere inches. He had no time to rest, his attacker was already on the counter-swing. Rather than attempt to block, he dropped to his knees and rolled underneath the arcing blade. He popped up behind his opponent and swung back at the exposed neck. His adversary spun about and he hit steel instead, their blades locked. He struggled to get back to his feet and, with one thrust, he was pushed off balance. Falling hard on to his back, he looked up into the eyes of his attacker, whose sword was held at his throat. Thorer was disappointed.

"Did you think you were being clever, rolling behind me?" Thorer chastised. "Never fall to the ground; you lose movement and flexibility and are all too easily struck from above." He hit Arinbjorn about the head with the pommel of his sword by way of explanation.

Pain, white and hot, shot through Arinbjorn's temple and he let out a cry. He lay there on the wet deck, salt water soaking his tunic, and felt the listing of the *Ormrinn Langi* as it passed through the Øresund channel. He waited a moment for the pain to subside and reached for the rune charm about his neck. Instead, he found the cross put there by Olaf; he had forgotten he had hidden his rune in his satchel for fear it would be recognized.

"You are going to get yourself killed if you fight like that," Thorer was saying. "Come on, on your feet."

The captain reached down, and Arinbjorn reluctantly took his hand. He got back up and took the time to compose himself, trying to ignore the laughter of the other recruits.

"Oh, could you do any better?" Thorer pushed Arinbjorn back into line before moving on to one of the other sailors that lined the deck with him.

He hated these sessions with Thorer, but they were necessary. Arinbjorn was no warrior, his encounter with Kormac had taught him that, and these men were all fighters. If he wanted to live, he needed training, and he was willing to take all that he could from these Christians.

Shortly after showing them Thangbrander's head, Thorer had conscripted them into the service of the *Ormrinn Langi*. They had arrived just in time to join Olaf's campaign to Wendland, a place neither Sigvaldi nor Arinbjorn had even heard of, and it was to be their honour as Icelanders to join his vessel. In the weeks since they'd set out from Nidaross, Thorer had spent much of his free time sparring with the younger recruits. Some were Icelanders like Arinbjorn, others Norwegian or foreign stock. All were better fighters than him.

The first night had been the hardest. They were placed in a housecarl barracks, a simple longhouse filled with dozens of cots, and left alone to consider their circumstances. It was only then that Sigvaldi had finally spoken after the encounter in Olaf's hall. Arinbjorn had caught him trying to sneak off in the night.

"What are you doing?" Arinbjorn had whispered, desperately trying not to wake the other housecarls that lay dormant in their cots.

"I am leaving, Ari." Sigvaldi did not slow down as he slipped out of the barracks and ducked between the shadows of the buildings.

"You cannot leave now!" Arinbjorn had to run to keep up with his friend. The beach was a little way down the hill, and Sigvaldi was not hesitating as he headed towards Teitr's ship.

"Thangbrander is dead, Ari," Sigvaldi hissed. "There is no reason to stay anymore."

Arinbjorn ran in front of him and had to physically push him back. "Sig, *listen*."

Sigvaldi pushed back, forcefully. "No. *You* listen. I have followed you from the very beginning." His voiced was laced with anger. "I supported you on each step of your journey without any word of complaint, but your mission is over, Ari. The priest is dead. We are avenged."

"I am not avenged. Not while Olaf still harms Icelanders— did you not hear Einar?"

"Since when did this concern you?" Sigvaldi scoffed. "You never cared about the greater politics."

"Ever since I heard Gizurr. He is going back there as we speak, with another priest from Olaf. The Christians are riled up because of what Thangbrander did *on Olaf's orders*. Their crimes will just keep happening so long as this king offers up more men for the cause."

"Gizurr is a man of honour, and the only reason your stupid plan worked. Do you not think he will stand by his word of no violence?"

"It is not Gizurr I do not trust; it is his master. Olaf butchered those people, *our* people, in the name of his god. What makes you think he won't do it again?" Arinbjorn was pleading now, freely letting his desperation show. They stood there then, in the darkened streets of Nidaross, their breathing the only sound in the night. "If you leave now, it will cast suspicion upon me; I will never get close to the king."

Sigvaldi let out a low curse. "Fuck," he whispered. He kicked out impotently at the ground. "Fuck. Fuck. Fuck. You are going to get us both killed. What do you think you can possibly do against Olaf? Look at the size of his fleet!" Sigvaldi gestured to the ships that were amassing in the waters of the Nid behind them.

"We do not need to go through his fleet, just get close to him," Arinbjorn explained. "We are already assigned to the *Ormrinn Langi*. We need only wait for the right moment to strike."

"How did you manage to get us on the king's ship?"

"I persuaded Thorer that it would go some way to repairing the damaged relations between our two peoples if Icelanders and Norwegians joined forces to defend the king."

"He believed you?" Sigvaldi asked. Before Arinbjorn could reply, he grew frustrated again and began to pace back and forth. "It is suicide, Ari. He rides to *war*."

"I know, Sig," Arinbjorn said quietly. "I cannot do this without you."

Sigvaldi was silent a long time. He stared up into the night sky. It was cloudy and the stars were only partially visible.

"Your stupid ploy has doomed us into Olaf's service. He means to make us *Christian*," Sigvaldi said at last. "You will have to take the cross to get close to him."

"I will say whatever I need to; Odin would understand."

"You would lie about your gods to get your way?" There was genuine horror in his voice. "Are you mad?"

"If we do not, so many more people could die."

Sigvaldi took in a deep breath, letting it out slowly and giving Arinbjorn a long, hard look. Arinbjorn could see the hurt and fear in his eyes. It broke his heart to push his friend like this, but there was no other way. He knew it.

"Then we had better head back to the barracks," Sigvaldi said, resignedly.

That night, Arinbjorn had lay awake, staring at the ceiling, listening to see if Sigvaldi would attempt to leave again. He never did.

"Are you finished gawking?" Thorer barked.

Arinbjorn blinked as he came back to the moment, only to see that the captain had finished punishing the others and had returned his attention to him. He was lunging at him with his sword. Arinbjorn quickly bashed it away with his long axe.

"Your enemy won't wait for you to regain your footing; they will bury their blade in your skull while you stand there dumbly!"

Arinbjorn countered with a thrust of his own to the gut, trying to wind the deep-voiced captain, before using the butt of the axe to strike his temple. Thorer easily knocked each blow aside, and Arinbjorn was left overextended. Thorer reached out and grabbed Arinbjorn by the scruff of his tunic. Dragging him in close, he headbutted him. Arinbjorn felt his nose rupture and hot blood spurted out.

"Clumsy," Thorer stated. "Predictable. Childish."

Arinbjorn cradled his face. Looking down, he saw snot mingle with blood and his head felt dizzy. He dropped to his knees, faint. "You broke my nose!"

"Your enemy would have killed you!" Thorer took a small cloth from a leather satchel on the deck and tossed it to Arinbjorn. "Here, clean yourself up."

Arinbjorn gingerly wiped his mouth and nose. It must have been the third time this week that Thorer had given him a nosebleed. Wincing, he crawled over to the edge of the nearest rowing pit and came face to face with a laughing recruit, who pushed him back into close quarters with Thorer. Laughter rang out from behind him; he turned to see Sigvaldi standing further up the ship. Unlike Arinbjorn and Thorer, who wore chain mail, his friend had opted to wear lighter leather armour. He had taken to the bow and arrow as his weapon of choice, training each day, and he held fast to the bow he had been given.

"Let us see if your training fares any better, Sig!" Thorer shouted.

Sigvaldi composed himself and gave the gruff captain a nod. Leaning over the starboard side, he lined up a shot, taking care to pull firmly back on the bowstring. He released and the arrow embedded itself in some driftwood bobbing in the waters. Sigvaldi let out a cheer.

"I don't know what you are celebrating," Thorer admonished. "My mother could hit a piece of still wood."

Several of the men about them burst out laughing.

Sigvaldi stopped cheering, but the smirk stayed upon his face. "Apologies, captain."

"I have wasted enough time with you all, today," Thorer said, his face hardening. "Get out of my sight."

The recruits dispersed wearily, many cradling fresh wounds. Arinbjorn got back to his feet and swayed unsteadily. Sigvaldi stowed his bow over his shoulder and went to join him, offering him his hand. Arinbjorn gladly took it and he leant on his friend until his vision stopped swimming.

"Wait, captain," Arinbjorn said. He had wanted to ask Thorer something ever since he had committed to his course of action. He was as close to Olaf as he was ever likely to get, but he could not bring himself to strike until he knew for *sure* that Olaf had instructed Thangbrander to kill. "May I ask a question?"

"Only if you make it quick." Thorer picked up the sack of axes and blades he had brought down to test them with and flung it over his shoulder, he began descending the stairs below deck.

"Why are *you* training the recruits?"

"There are countless housecarls who would be better placed to," Sigvaldi added.

Thorer stopped walking. Sigvaldi and Arinbjorn came to a halt behind him, looking down on him and the darkened hold below. He seemed to be staring at a spot on the deck, just a little way up the ship. Arinbjorn could see nothing there except the stain of old blood. "To make up for my crimes against your kin. The least I can do is keep any more Icelanders from dying."

"Do you not agree with Olaf's mission?" Arinbjorn asked. He whispered this, hoping the singing of the rowers and beat of the war drums would hide his question.

Thorer suddenly dropped the sack of weapons, which fell to the floor with a metallic thud. He strode up the stairs to Arinbjorn, his face mere inches away.

"I believe in everything our king does," Thorer hissed, the smell of fish on his hot breath. His black eyes were wide, and Arinbjorn took a step back.

"Just not in the way he does it," Sigvaldi offered.

Thorer went to reply, but the response died on his lips. Instead, he turned to look out across the sea at the amassed fleet that followed in the wake of the *Ormrinn Langi*.

"Did Olaf know what Thangbrander was doing in Iceland? What his methods were?" Arinbjorn pressed.

"I do not know," Thorer replied. "You were of Thangbrander's flock—you tell me."

"Skjalti, the *Christian* farmer that was murdered, was my kin," Arinbjorn said. "He had children."

"Children..." Thorer turned to stare at that spot on the deck again. The captain seemed pained.

"We have a right to know, captain. They were our Christian brethren," Sigvaldi implored.

"I said I do not know!" Thorer's cry rang out across the deck and several crew turned in their direction. He quietened. "But I suspect...yes."

There was silence between them then, as the words reverberated inside Arinbjorn's skull. There it was: the confirmation he needed. Arinbjorn looked up at the king, whose back was turned as he kept an eye ahead of the ship.

What would he do now?

His thoughts were stopped by a horn ringing out across the fleet. It was joined by another, and another, until the whole sea seemed to be filled with the sound of them. Arinbjorn was pushed aside as Thorer ran past him to look over the prow. Confused, Arinbjorn and Sigvaldi joined him. They scoured the waters, trying to see what was causing the alarm. Then, coming in from behind them, Arinbjorn saw it. A fleet of sails had appeared on the horizon. They were surrounded.

Chapter Thirty-Two

The sun rose over the Law Rock, bathing the triangular and jutting stone shelf in a pale yellow light. It rose several yards off the ground, giving the men upon it uninterrupted views of the Thingvellir plains before them. A sheer cliff face of jagged obsidian stood behind them; forty feet high, it marked the end of the plateau that dropped into the valley proper, and it reflected the morning light down on to the gathered chieftains. To Freya, and all those on the ground looking up, the thirty-six men on the rock seemed to be bathed in golden fire. Perhaps that was the point. Freya had always been fascinated by that rock face; it looked as though some great axe had hewn jagged square boulders and laid them atop each other to create a wall that surrounded the valley of Thingvellir. Perhaps the giants had built this place.

She felt an elbow in her side as an older man barged past her. He was carrying a woven basket full of dyed cloth and he was trying to get as close to the Law Rock as he could, shouting about his wares. She wanted to curse him but thought better of it; she had enough enemies here today. Looking about the crowd, she sought out her husband. Njall had been summoned to the Law Rock and they both knew what that meant: he was to be put on trial. He had gone on ahead to try to find supporters to stand by his side. Looking into the sea of faces, Freya saw hundreds of people from all over Iceland, but no Njall.

The Althing was nominally about the chieftains. They gathered here from all four farthings, brought together to arbitrate on law cases that had not been settled in their local courts. Only the most complicated or most bloody cases tended to make it to the Althing for judgement. Often, a blood feud made it impossible to placate the opposing sides with wergeld; most cases ended with outlawry, of one kind or another, and

whole families could be undone by a ruling. As such, it was a
tense time for the chieftains and the claimants.

There appeared to be a case taking place right at that
moment. Two groups of men had stationed themselves either
side of the Law Rock, with the assembled chieftains in the
middle, looking down. There was a lot of shouting from both
sides, and Thorgeir, the lawspeaker, was trying to arbitrate the
proceedings. Freya did not care about this case, she recognized
none of the participants, and it appeared none of the gathered
crowd were that interested either. Where *was* her husband? It
was almost time to meet Hallr.

Freya began to thread her way through the throng.
Hundreds of tents lined the grassy plains before the Law Rock,
and the smoke from dozens of fires rose into the clear sky.
Passing through the crowd, the air hummed with the sound of
a thousand people talking, trading, and sharing news. It was
overwhelming. She breathed deep of the scent of roasted meats,
herbaceous stews, and the sweet dry smell of woodsmoke. It
made her head swim and she found herself smiling despite
herself. These people, whether they had come here to see
their claims and grievances addressed or just to share in the
celebration that was community, were Icelanders. Her people.
Today, there was only one question on everyone's mind, one she
heard on the lips of many as she slipped through the crowds:
"What are we going to do about the Christians?"

It was the thought on her mind, too, as she made her way
over to their encampment. It had proven far larger than she
was expecting. Freya and Njall had made a discreet trip to the
Christian camp a few days ago, thinking that it would be a small
enclave. Instead, they found people of all kinds had declared
themselves followers of the new faith: farmers, traders, thralls.
Freya lost count of the sheer variety. Dozens of tents and
hundreds of people had created an island of Christianity off to
the west of the main gathering. The sheer scale of it awed her
and she wondered whether the Christians *did* have a chance,
after all. If they gave Hallr the support he needed, even to

save Njall's life, could Hallr secure the changes to the law he so desperately craved?

No, she reassured herself. Hallr and his followers were still outnumbered. She only had to stop and witness the groups of men patrolling the perimeter of the Christian camp, abusing any that attempted to enter or leave, to remind herself of the scale of their opposition. The Christians complained, of course, but they still only had two of the thirty-eight chieftains on their side: Gizurr the White and Hallr. Hallr appeared to be running the Christian enclave, but Gizurr was nowhere to be found. Without the chieftains to protect them, they could do nothing.

Thankfully, she managed to avoid a patrolling group of heckling men. They appeared to have found some poor thrall to abuse. Grimacing, she ignored the thrall's shouts for help as he was beaten by the farmers, his pained cries disappearing into the mud into which he was crushed. She pulled her kerchief lower to hide her face and headed straight to where Hallr had set up his tent. He had not joined the other chieftains yet; instead, he was spending most of his days handing out food and preaching to his followers. Freya was impressed by the quantity of food that Hallr had brought with him; he seemed to have emptied his entire estate and had used several horse trains to transport it all. Many fires burned in the centre of his encampment, and multiple pots of stew lay bubbling over them. Hallr stood handing out plates of food to those who came to listen to him. Freya did not know where he got all his supplies from; some people suspected he was getting support from Norway, as the trade ships always brought him wares. It would explain how he was managing to live so well, even for a chieftain. She had to give him credit; most of the newly converted Christians never ate as well as they did while attending Mass with Hallr. He was popular here.

She made her way over to the rotund chieftain. He stood over a fire pit, ladling out the food to a queue of a people. About him, his thralls and housecarls busied themselves with the preparation of vegetables, or cleaning. It was quite the operation.

He gave her a flushed smile. "Freya! I am so glad you came!" He handed his ladle to a thrall and instructed them to continue. He moved about the fire and came to meet her, wiping his brow and hands on his tunic. "Can I interest you in some stew?"

Freya shook her head. "No, thank you. Have you seen my husband? He was summoned to the Law Rock."

Hallr looked up at the sun. "Of course, the lesser cases will start after noon. I am afraid he has not been this way."

Freya felt the knot in her stomach tighten. If Njall had not been here, then he must have been waylaid. A wave of nausea passed over her. She resisted it.

"Will you stand by your promise?" she asked, struggling to hide the edge in her voice.

Since their arrival, she and her husband had found that the rumours spread by Failend had indeed spread far and wide. The thrall's words had even managed to make it to the northern farthing. The only people who had not heard of his charge were travelling far from the east. As a result, Njall and Freya had been subject to abuse the moment they were recognized. Njall had spent the majority of his time hiding in their tent for fear of being attacked. Had someone got to him?

"Do you know who will lead the charge against your husband?" Hallr asked.

"Chieftain Gellir." That had been the most damning revelation: Njall's own tithe lord would be the one who led the criminal proceedings against him.

Hallr let out a long, dramatic sigh. "Gellir will be difficult to dissuade. He is as a hammer to an anvil." He fixed her with a grin. "But, if you and Njall come out in support of our case, I promise you will have our protection."

Freya had to unclench her hands; she had balled them tightly and her nails dug into her palms. "You will keep my family safe?"

Hallr arched an eyebrow and gave a pointed look to her stomach. "A *family*?"

Freya instinctively pulled her cloak about her and simply stared at him.

"No. No. This is *good* news," Hallr said with a smile. "*Very* good news. We must—"

A horn blew out from the Law Rock, signalling that the case just heard had been dismissed. Everyone turned to watch as one of the groups of men was escorted away, while the other group shook hands in celebration. The lawspeaker called out, and his words were relayed back through the crowds.

"The next case to be heard will be the trial of Njall Bjarnisson!"

Even from this distance, Freya could make out her husband. He was being dragged on to the Law Rock by several men. She looked on in horror; he was all alone. He had found no one to support him.

"Hallr…" she began, her panic rising.

"Come. We must move quickly."

They ran.

*

"You have been brought here, Njall Bjarnisson, to answer for the crime of buggery," Gellir was saying.

The red-headed chieftain reminded Freya of the fire giant Surtr, standing as he did before Njall, his hair almost aflame in the light of the sun. He paced before the other chieftains, who stood in a semicircle about them, and addressed his accusation to both Njall and Thorgeir, the lawspeaker. Freya and Hallr were already late, most of the formal introductions had passed, but they could make it in time for the defence.

As they approached the Law Rock, they found their way barred by a ring of armed men.

"Gellir's men," Hallr hissed. "He never did like to play fair."

One of the larger men, a hulking brute Freya recognized as Saemund, one of Gellir's thralls, stepped forward. "No one may enter," he said. He looked down upon Freya, a broad grin upon his round face. He was bald, with a red, braided beard that came down to Freya's level. Her teeth clenched as she fought the urge to pull down on it. If she wanted her and Njall to survive this, she had to let Hallr take the lead.

"Do you know who I am?" Hallr was saying. He was trying to put as much force as he could into the statement, but he was wheezing heavily from the run.

"You're a Christian," came the reply from one of the other men behind Saemund.

Gellir's thralls jeered and brayed in support, with one leaning forward to spit. Freya watched the thick black mucous arc into the ground at Hallr's feet.

"You are Hallr Thorsteinsson." Saemund put out a hand to his men, silencing them.

"*Chieftain* Hallr. I have every right to be at this trial."

"The trial has already begun. None may pass." He gave a wide smile and Freya wanted to punch him in his yellowed teeth.

"Njall is my husband," Freya shouted over the head of Saemund, trying to get the attention of the chieftains. "I am here to stand as his witness!"

She looked past Saemund and up at her husband. He was on his knees, flanked by two of Gellir's men. His long, speckled hair seemed slick with grime and it hung low over his face. He gripped his sides and Freya thought she could see a dark stain on his tunic.

"Husband!" Freya continued to shout. "Husband, I am here!"

Njall turned to look down upon her, and Freya realized he was covered in dirt and blood. His left eye was swollen black and he bled from a head wound. Despite all that, he smiled as he caught sight of her. A bright smile that lit up his one good eye. She let out a breath she had not realized she was holding and reached out towards him. Saemund cut across and blocked her. Scowling, she returned her attention to the chieftain.

Gellir was busy addressing the lawspeaker, listing Njall's crimes. He ignored the growing confrontation at the base of the Law Rock and continued with his accusations.

"Do you have anything to say in your defence, Njall?" Gellir asked.

"All you have is hearsay, Gellir," Njall shouted. His voice was defiant but weak, his words laced with coughs. "Lies spread by those who would see me ruined."

"Indeed, Gellir," Thorgeir interjected. "Do you have any proof or witnesses?"

A crowd was beginning to form at the base of the Law Rock now, people interested in seeing how this trial would play out, hemming Freya and Hallr in against the thralls. Saemund's men had to reform their line to better encircle the trial and ensure no one got through. If enough people gathered, Freya might be able to slip past.

"Your perversion has cost valuable lives, Njall," Gellir was saying. "I have witnesses to that effect, lawspeaker."

Freya's attention snapped back to the trial.

"Then bring them forth," Thorgeir commanded.

Freya felt her legs go leaden and her whole body seemed to numb. She knew who was about to be brought out to testify against her husband. Her numbness turned to anger as she saw the figure ascend the Law Rock, passing through unhindered by Saemund's men and taking position at Gellir's side. Cold grey eyes, set in a freckled face and framed with auburn hair, looked down upon Njall and Freya.

It was Failend.

Chapter Thirty-Three

The moment he saw the fleet on the horizon, Olaf knew he was betrayed. He recognized the Wendland king's dragon crest on some of the ships, but the majority bore the mark of Sweyn, the Danish king. He was not entirely sure, but he thought he also spotted ships bearing the mark of Olaf the Swede, King of Sweden and son to Sigrid the Haughty, Sweyn's queen. Their combined forces had amassed at the end of the Øresund, blocking off Olaf's exit into the Baltic Sea. He could not outmanoeuvre them in this channel, and the sheer scale of the attacking fleet unnerved even him. It was not, however, until he saw the majority of his fleet sail on ahead, then slowly come about, that he realized the full scale of the trap.

The jarls had betrayed him. He stood on the prow of the *Ormrinn Langi* and watched as his fleet abandoned him. One by one, they defied his signals and went off ahead to join Sweyn and his allies. Olaf briefly wondered what the Danish bastard must have offered them: perhaps they would be vassals in his new state or had been offered protection from Eirikr's raids. It did not matter. In the end, only eleven of his ships stayed by his side—eleven, out of a combined force of seventy-one. Olaf knew he could not fight Sweyn, Burislav, and his own fleet. There must have been almost two hundred *skeids* arranged against him now, and he could not outmanoeuvre them in this channel. The Øresund was just too narrow a pass. Still, there was a way he could render their numbers meaningless.

"My king! What should we do?" Thorer rushed to his side the moment the horns blared out across the water, his one true ally and friend, the one who had warned him about Tyra's folly, the one who had told him to turn back.

Olaf had to hope that God had plans for him; he did not want to lose his friend because of his pride. "Bring the fleet in close and lash the ships together," he replied. "We cannot run, but we do not have to fight on their terms. Form ranks around the perimeter and prepare for boarders."

Thorer acknowledged and began barking orders to the men, who leapt to their tasks. The crew was tried and tested, and they knew their roles. All except two.

Olaf looked down into the rowing pits and saw the two Icelanders staring up at him. They seemed oblivious to the chaos around them.

"Did you not hear your captain?" Olaf screeched. "Bind the hulls together!"

It seemed to break their stupor and they ran off to assist their crewmen.

Perhaps it had been a mistake to bring them along, after all. Olaf did not have the time to be dealing with terrified farmers.

The rest of the crew, however, did not allow their fear to impede them. Thorer instructed the ships into a tight defensive pattern: five ships up front, five behind, with the *Ormrinn Langi* secured in the middle. He brought them as close as he could and had the crews bind the hulls together. In moments, the eleven remaining ships became a floating fortress, with three concentric circles of men forming defensive perimeters out from the *Ormrinn Langi*.

It was a good plan, Olaf reassured himself; by binding his fleet together, he had removed the advantage of numbers from Sweyn. Now they would have to slow down and fight a pitched battle, and Olaf's forces could overwhelm any ships that docked against them.

They survived the first few volleys of arrows easily enough. The sky blackened as hundreds of feathered bolts blotted out the dying sun, iron clouds raining death upon his men. Their shields protected most, but a few were too slow to react, the arrows burrowing into their skulls. That was when the pitch-covered flame arrows descended upon them, igniting their sails and spreading raw flame across the deck. Sweyn had begun targeting Olaf's ships instead.

Thorer proved, once again, to be an adept commander. Every time a fire started on a ship, he rallied the men on adjacent vessels to put it out. This left the crew of the burning ship to focus upon defending their borders. Then Sweyn began to send across boarding parties. Olaf watched as the enemy *skeids* circled about his small, bound fleet, trying to keep them guessing as to which ship they would attempt to board. In the end, the first wave consisted of three ships pulling up on the portside flank.

Olaf led a contingent of men from the *Ormrinn Langi* and charged the enemy head on. He fought his way through the throng, the sword gifted to him from Jarl Sigurd proving just as effective as before. He sliced, thrusted, and parried his way to the front line. The men he brought with him fought valiantly, but he saw a number of them fall to the arrows and pikes of the Danes. He narrowly missed being skewered himself. A spear was thrown past him and embedded itself in the throat of the man behind him, pinning him to the mast.

Olaf reached back and pulled the spear free, ignoring the gurgles and bubbling blood pouring forth from the sailor it had struck, and threw it back at the boarders. He saw it arc high above and land in the chest of the *skeid* captain, who had been busy gouging out the eyes of a man with his thumbs. Olaf let out a cheer and his men followed suit; they had taken some casualties, but nowhere near as many as the Danes. If they could keep this up, they may well outlast the assault.

Horns blared out across the battle and Olaf turned to see five smaller vessels approaching the starboard. Sweyn was targeting his right flank. Olaf rallied his men and charged back across the floating ships, leaving the dead and dying sailors to moan and cry in the hot afternoon sun.

*

As the crewmen assembled about them, rushing to enact Thorer's orders, Arinbjorn and Sigvaldi had stood rooted to the spot. Stunned, they remained in the rowing pit, staring up at Olaf, their target. The moment to strike him had been lost and now battle was upon them. Arinbjorn felt that all too familiar feeling descend upon him: the tightening of the chest, the sensation of a black, icy cloud gripping his heart. He reached for his rune charm about his neck and instead found the cross hung there by Olaf. Panicking, he tore it off and looked desperately in his leather pouch to find the charm.

"Did you not hear your captain?" Olaf's words cut through Arinbjorn's fugue. "Bind the hulls together!"

"Come on, Ari!" Sigvaldi shouted, grabbing him by the arm and leading him away from the pits and Olaf. "We have to get out of here!"

They headed for the stern of the vessel and looked about in horror. Thorer was at the tiller, shouting for the crews to bind the ships together. Behind the *Ormrinn Langi*, four of Olaf's *skeids* were coming into position and blocking off Arinbjorn and Sigvaldi's escape route.

"You two!" Thorer's haggard voice rose above the chorus of shouting coming from the crew. "Come here and help me!" He was pulling hard on a rope tied to a *skeid* off the starboard bow, bringing it in closer.

Arinbjorn reluctantly ran over to give a hand, and Sigvaldi followed suit. They heaved on the rope until the two hulls struck each other, causing Arinbjorn to stumble as the deck listed violently. Thorer rapidly lashed the rope to the deck and secured the *skeid*.

"What now?" Sigvaldi shouted.

"Grab a weapon and shield and get over there!" Thorer grabbed them and shoved them towards a ring of men who were taking up position on the port side.

Arinbjorn did not have time to object. He held up his axe and grabbed one of the circular shields that lined the hull. Falling into line next to the others, he tried to hold the shield high. Sigvaldi grabbed a longbow and stood behind him with the archers. They were in the inner ring, protecting the *Ormrinn*

Langi itself, but they could see the outer two lines of defence forming about them on the other *skeids*.

The chaos of the first few moments had passed, and now all they could do was wait and watch as the enemy ships began to bear down upon them. The black-hulled ships circled about and began to probe the outer defences.

"What are we going to do?" Sigvaldi hissed from behind. "We cannot strike at Olaf now—it's chaos!"

"Fight until we see an opening, then jump overboard." Arinbjorn knew it was desperate, but he had no other ideas.

"Into the sea, are you mad?" The waters looked rough. They beat at the hulls of the combined fleet and the waves rose high.

"We can swim to the northern shore." He pointed to the low hills behind them. "We can make it."

"Ari—" Sigvaldi was cut off by a horn blast coming from the outer ships on the port side. They looked over just in time to raise their shields as a hail of arrows fell about them.

A bolt pierced Arinbjorn's shield and he felt it dig into his left wrist. He cried out, but kept the shield up as more arrows fell. The man next to him was not so swift; a bolt penetrated his eye and he stumbled in shock before collapsing to the floor. Arinbjorn looked down at him, eyes wide.

Thorer was shouting something, but Arinbjorn could not hear him over the high-pitched ringing that had started in his ears. The world seemed to go mute as he stared down at the spasming sailor on the deck. He retched, looking about in shock as the forces of the king valiantly defended this floating fort.

The rigging that bound the *Ormrinn Langi* to the rest of the fleet vibrated violently, and the ship bucked against the hulls of its protectors. It gave Olaf a tight defensive line and forced the attacking fleet into a funnel. Their numbers meant nothing now.

Olaf could *win* this, Arinbjorn realised. He had to make sure he didn't.

*

Swinging his sword about him, he parried the offending blow and drove his blade through the open mouth of his attacker. Grabbing the man by his hair, he pushed the steel through his skull, not stopping until his hilt hit teeth. The attacker's scream died in a gurgle of blood, and Olaf cast the traitor aside. He paid no attention to where the body fell, just letting it lie on the deck with the others.

He blinked rapidly; his eyes stung in the thick, acrid smoke that permeated the air, and it was difficult to breathe. The *Ormrinn Langi* was on fire. Arrows of flaming pitch had embedded themselves in the hull, and the sails had been the first to ignite. Now, the setting sun cast muted red light through the smoke and ash, but it was still difficult to see. Wiping his brow, he tried to make out his crew in the chaos about him. Most of the men had formed two lines to port and starboard, archers up front and pikes behind. Their screams and cries were almost deafening as they repelled the boarding parties. To Olaf, it was a vision of hell itself.

A throaty, broken shout cried out from the rear of the ship. It was Thorer. The captain was fighting off three men over by the tiller. They had managed to climb up the back of the *Ormrinn Langi* and they were striking down upon the king's friend. Thorer was bleeding profusely from a head wound, his face contorted into a blood-red mask of pain and rage.

Olaf watched as the captain buried an axe in one man's head, but was caught off guard by another, a spear driven into his side. The king cried out in shock, his words dying in the melee about him. He had to get to Thorer. Stumbling, the deck slick with blood and viscera, he clambered over the bodies of fallen men and made his way to the tiller.

How had it come to this? Olaf would repel an enemy assault, but, before he could recover, Sweyn would have his forces circle about and dock at the opposite side. His men fought with all of their might and, despite Sweyn's best efforts, they held the line. Still, hundreds of Sweyn's men had poured into the outer ships, piling over the bodies of the slain. The wall of dead only further buttressed Olaf's defences.

But he was exhausted. The attackers never seemed to end. He had been struck several times, but his chain-mail armour had rebuffed most blows. The armour weighed him down though, and fatigue was setting in. His muscles ached, feeling tired and overwrought, and his bones felt more and more brittle after each strike. Each ragged breath burned his throat as black smoke filled the air. At some point, they had lost control of the fires and they had spread throughout his fleet. This is now how he found himself, struggling across the deck of the *Ormrinn Langi*, coughing up blood and ash. He climbed over the bodies that littered the deck, striking out at anyone who got too close. He only had eyes for Thorer.

The black-bearded captain had dropped to one knee, the spear still stuck in his side. Swinging wildly, he cut the arm off the man wielding the spear, but in so doing he tumbled to the ground. Olaf watched as more and more men climbed up and over the stern, their blades descending upon the lone captain. Thorer's cries joined his own.

"Olaf Tryggvason!" It was a voice he did not recognize in the shouting and screaming taking place about him.

The king turned, expecting to see the forces of Sweyn upon him. Instead, he saw the Icelander, Arinbjorn, climbing over a wall of dead bodies. He was battered and bloodied, and his left arm hung limp at his side.

Arinbjorn fell down at Olaf's feet, clearly exhausted, and looked up him. He held out a piece of severed rope. "I would have words with you."

*

"There are too many of them!" Sigvaldi cried, blindly firing his arrows into the attacking horde.

Arinbjorn attempted to defend him, hacking wildly at any who came near, trying not to slip on the entrails and bodies that coated the floor. He could no longer tell who was friend and who was foe, and his panic was giving way to exhaustion.

He swung his axe at a man who climbed over the stern, managing to embed it in his skull. The man looked at him stupidly for a moment and Arinbjorn suppressed a retch. He attempted to wrench his axe free, but ended up bringing the body of the man down on to the deck. He stumbled backwards into the blade of a man behind him, a slash cutting deep into his left arm.

"Ari, duck!" Sigvaldi shouted. He pulled an arrow from his quiver and drove it into the man behind Arinbjorn.

Arinbjorn did not so much duck as fall to the floor. He landed in the hot sticky blood that pooled from the slain. Crying out in pain, he looked down at his arm and saw a deep wound in his bicep. It was rapidly going numb.

"Sig…" It was all Arinbjorn could say.

Sigvaldi tore a piece of cloth from his tunic, dropped down to Arinbjorn's side and tried to staunch the bleeding. For a moment, the battle about them seemed to rage in the distance, the men fighting and dying were muted and far away.

Arinbjorn looked about at the flame-covered ships, the piles of dead bodies, and then back into the eyes of his friend.

"Ari, come on." Sigvaldi began to drag him towards the edge of the deck. "It's time to jump."

"No, Sig," Arinbjorn said, and he pushed his friend away. He looked down at his left arm; it was completely numb now and could feel nothing. "I can't swim like this."

"Then I will carry you." Sigvaldi began to pull at him again, tears streaming down his ash- and blood-covered face.

Arinbjorn reached out and cupped his friend's cheek. "No, Sig." An odd sense of calm had come over him. His fear and terror seemed to pass as the inevitability of the moment became clear. He looked into Sigvaldi's eyes and smiled. "You go."

"No!" Sigvaldi's cry was part shout and part wail. "I am not leaving you here!"

"You have to." Using his good arm, Arinbjorn reached into his pouch and pulled out the rune charm from Bera. He laughed inwardly; he never did have a chance to put it back on. "Take this, it will protect you."

Sigvaldi tried to refuse, but Arinbjorn forced it into his hand.

"I can't leave you." Sigvaldi was openly crying now.

"I need you to live for me, Sig." He reached across for his axe that had fallen by his side. "And for Freya. I could have had her had I not let this foolish quest for vengeance drive me here. She was your friend too. She should not lose the both of us."

"Ari—"

Arinbjorn raised his good hand to cut him off. "I should have left with you when we found Thangbrander's head." He let out a small laugh. Then he fixed Sigvaldi with a level stare. "Go."

"What are you going to do?"

"I am going to end this." He looked over his shoulder towards the tethered ropes that bound the *Ormrinn Langi* to its sentry ships.

"I can help." Sigvaldi pulled Arinbjorn to his feet.

Arinbjorn leant into his friend and the two embraced each other. He could feel their chests rise and fall and he fancied he could hear his beating heart. He could never have got this far without Sigvaldi, and his friend had given him everything without question. It was time Arinbjorn returned the favour.

Pulling back, he took one last look into Sigvaldi's green eyes and smiled. "I know."

Arinbjorn pushed Sigvaldi back and over the edge of the ship. Eyes wide, he tumbled overboard and fell into the waters below. Arinbjorn watched his friend flail about in the water, shouting and crying out in anger and hurt. He hoped Bera's rune charm would protect him.

He had to act fast; Olaf had formed a tight defensive line with all these ships bound together. But, if he could sever them, the king's defences would crumble. He turned towards the nearest rope and began hacking.

Chapter Thirty-Four

"**H**e abandoned us!"

Failend's words echoed over the rapt audience, the wind seeming to carry them across the plains. She stood there, head bowed and hands clasped before her, deferential to the chieftains arrayed about the Law Rock. Her grey eyes never left Freya's.

Freya looked up at her thrall, impotent in the face of Saemund's men, fists balled tightly at her sides.

"Hallr," she whispered, "we have to get up there."

"Do not worry," Hallr whispered back. Then, with a force of voice Freya had never heard before from the rotund chieftain, Hallr addressed Saemund: "We are passing by you…whether you like it or not."

Saemund grinned stupidly as Hallr stood aside, grabbing Freya as he did so. Saemund's eyes widened in shock as he looked over her shoulder. Confused, Freya turned around to see hundreds of people cutting a swathe through the crowd. Men, women, children, old and young, they all pushed their way through the gathered throng, crying out and shouting. She looked on, wide eyed; the entire Christian camp had emptied. Freya's eyes caught the glint of steel and she realized many of them were armed: axes, knives, hammers all glimmered in the sunlight. It was an army.

The first line of men came to a halt behind Hallr.

"A Christian never stands alone," he said. "We are God's people."

Saemund and his men drew their swords; they were outnumbered, but they did not yield. Up on the Law Rock, Failend stopped her long accusation and the chieftains paused to look down upon the stand-off.

"What is the meaning of this?" Thorgeir, the lawspeaker, shouted.

"I wish to take my place on the council, lawspeaker," Hallr replied. "This thrall denies me!"

"The session had already begun," Gellir said, his voice rising in pitch. "Njall has no party to defend him."

"We were waylaid," Hallr retorted. "We would take his side."

"You Christians have no rights here." This came from Chieftain Runolfr. His squat, balding head leered over the Law Rock and down upon the amassed Christians.

"Then perhaps that should be settled first!"

Both sides turned in the direction of the shout. There, riding in from the south, was Gizurr. Silence descended upon the crowd as he and a retinue of men slowly advanced through the throng.

Freya looked about the collective; what in the nine realms was *happening*? Her chest had tightened and her heart beat so hard it felt like it wanted to break out.

"Chieftain Gizurr!" The shock on Thorgeir's lips was heard by all. "What is the meaning of this?"

"Christian law has yet to be decided here, Thorgeir!" Gizurr shouted. "Until then, your trial has no standing." The white-haired chieftain arrived at the base of the Law Rock and dismounted.

Freya did not know the men with him, but she did recognize the strange clothing worn by a young bald man who travelled in the retinue. They were vestments, the same kind that Thangbrander had worn. Gizurr had returned with a priest.

Gizurr and his men strode up to Hallr and the two embraced. The thralls surrounding the Law Rock tensed. They looked to each other and Saemund for guidance, but made no move. For their part, the Christians revelled in their leader's return, but kept their weapons out.

"You are returned!" Hallr was beaming. "When?"

"My ship arrived last night. I came as fast as I could." Gizurr turned to look at Freya. "Who are you?"

Freya stood there dumbly for a moment, her mind blank.

"Freya Hoskuldsdottir," Hallr interjected for her. "Her husband is the one on trial."

"And he is Christian?" Gizurr asked.

At this, Hallr turned to face Freya, his face expectant.

Freya knew what she had to do. "We are Christian!" she shouted, taking the time to pass her gaze over each chieftain above her. Then she shouted it again with more force into the silent crowd behind her. Her words carried on the wind and filled the air throughout the assembly. "Njall and I, we are Christian. As such, we demand to be judged by Christian law!" She looked up into the scowling face of Failend and smiled thinly.

The crowd behind them erupted into a mixture of cheers and angry cries. Freya ignored them all and kept her gaze focused on Failend.

"What was his crime?" Gizurr placed his hand on her shoulder and drew her attention back to him.

"My husband has been accused of buggery." Freya managed to say the words without biting her tongue. "And preferring the company of men."

Gizurr was silent for a moment. His pale blue eyes seemed to bore into her, but she held his gaze. "Is it true?" he asked.

"Freya is *pregnant*, Gizurr." Hallr gestured to Freya's bump. She tried to hide her revulsion as they studied her.

"You will testify that your child is his?" Gizurr probed.

Freya took one last look up at her beaten and broken husband, his one good eye wide in desperation, and nodded her consent.

"Then he will be protected." Gizurr strode up to Saemund, unsheathed his axe, and lay the blade upon the thrall's chest. "Let us pass or die."

Saemund looked up to Gellir, his face contorted in panic.

"Let them pass," Gellir spat.

The thralls parted, and Freya, Gizurr, and Hallr ascended to the Law Rock. Freya immediately rushed over to Njall and they embraced. He winced in pain but held fast to her. For a long moment, she forgot about everybody else; all she wanted to do was take her husband and leap off the rock.

"Njall is a Christian!" Gizurr was shouting. His deep bass voice reverberated throughout the assembly. "Before he can be tried, we must settle on the laws for Christians." Silence passed over the entire Althing and his words seemed to carry across the plains.

"You have permitted us to try your kind before," Runolfr retorted. "You stood by as your own son-in-law was banished!"

"Indeed, Chieftain Runolfr. Because I have respect for Icelandic law above all else." Gizurr's reply was met with a cheer from the crowd amassed below. He tempered his voice and stared evenly at the squat chieftain. "But the Althing is a time to decide *new* laws."

"What is it that you propose, Gizurr?" Thorgeir asked. The lawspeaker's gaze seemed to flit between the heavily armed Christians and the thralls defending the Law Rock.

Freya followed his gaze and noticed that other members of the crowd had begun to unsheathe their sax knives. Children were being pulled back and out of the way by frantic mothers. The crowd was ready for violence.

"Come, husband," she whispered, beginning to coax Njall back off the Law Rock and away from the restless crowd before it.

They only managed to make it to the edge before Gellir called out behind them, "You stay until this is decided." He motioned for two of his thralls to break from their position and flank them. They were brought back to the centre of the Law Rock and held there.

"We must decide on a new set of laws to govern the Christian way of life," Gizurr said. He did not stop Gellir's men from their actions but took up position next to Freya and Njall. "One that can exist side by side with the old laws."

"You would see it that your people were above our laws?" Runolfr spat. "How is that respectful?"

People began to holler their support from the crowd below and the two sides began to advance on each other, separated only by the unwitting thralls who guarded the Law Rock. Freya watched as Saemund and his men were hemmed in on two fronts.

"Do you not listen, Runolfr, or are you just wilfully ignorant?" Hallr interjected. "We propose only that Christians judge Christians."

"This cannot be allowed!" Failend shouted, her demure demeanour vanishing, to be replaced with a snarling, contorted, and purple face.

Thorgeir raised his hands to silence her outburst and she dropped silent.

"That is not the way of things," Thorgeir said evenly to Gizurr.

"You do not understand, my fellow chieftains. I did not come here today to plead your assistance. I came here to tell you what *will* happen. If we do not come to terms this day, all of Iceland will be sundered." Gizurr spoke proudly and a cheer rose up from the Christians in response. They successfully managed to push Saemund and his men into the pagans on the other side.

The chieftains shouted out for it to stop, but it was too late. The Christians overwhelmed the thralls, who disappeared underneath the crowd, shouting and crying out for support.

"Look what is happening!" Freya screamed to the chieftains. "Can't you see they are going to kill each other!" She could not believe that they could just stand there and let their people butcher each other.

Gizurr ignored her. "There are too many of us to ignore, Thorgeir." He spoke calmly, as though the chaos below was not happening.

"You have to stop them!" Runolfr was shouting. "They will listen to you." The rest of the chieftains backed further and further up the Law Rock as the mob of Christians pushed closer. There were cries now, shouts of pain and anger as people struck at one another.

"They will listen only to a law that respects them," Gizurr replied evenly.

"Are two sets of laws not a sundering?" Thorgeir shouted so that his words could be heard over the throng. "Are not two peoples living side by side, but apart, not a sundering?"

"Indeed. But, if you will not recognize them within your law, why should they recognize you?" Hallr replied.

Freya looked desperately around at the gathered chieftains. Gizurr stood there stoically, staring down his peers while the crowds below fought each other. Violence was always a possibility at an Althing, but families feuding was one thing— this schism threatened to tear the entire country apart.

"Enough!" Thorgeir shouted. "Enough!" The lawspeaker's words reverberated about the Law Rock and down into the plains before it. He kept shouting until the two sides could hear him.

Gizurr, seemingly sensing a change, joined him, calling out to the Christians. Slowly, gradually, the heat of the fight left the crowd. Gellir's thralls, battered and bloodied, carved their way up out of the melee and began to push back against both sides, reforming the line.

"This cannot be the way of things!" Thorgeir continued. "We are brothers! Did our ancestors not flee Norway and Denmark to be free of *this*?" He gestured at the bloodied faces in the crowd. "Do you remember how they fought each other? How the peoples of those lands could not bear peace?"

The Christians passed looks among themselves, muttering. Freya could not tell if they agreed.

"Look to them now. They send gifts to each other and friendship exists between them!"

Freya noticed an odd look upon Gizurr's face then. The chieftain had clearly opted to let Thorgeir speak and, throughout the confrontation, he had looked calm and resolute. At the mention of Norway and Denmark being allies, however, a red flush seemed to take him. He hung his head low for a moment, only looking up again when the colour had passed. Freya looked about to see if anyone else had noticed, but they only had eyes for Thorgeir.

"We must not let those who wish to oppose each other prevail." Thorgeir gave pointed looks to Runolfr and Gizurr. "Let us arbitrate between them, so that both sides have their way in something."

There was a long silence then, punctuated only by the cries of the Icelandic terns that circled above. Freya glanced at her husband, who looked as stunned as she felt. Then a deep rumble emanated from below in the crowd. A low, harsh sound that began to thrum and fill the air. It took Freya a moment to realize they were clapping. Everyone was *clapping*.

Thorgeir turned away from the crowd to face the other chieftains gathered about the Law Rock. "We must all have the same law and the same religion. If we tear apart the law, we tear apart the peace."

The chieftains looked at each other.

"What are you saying, Thorgeir?" Runolfr asked, his voice quiet.

Thorgeir was silent for a long time, his brow furrowed. He fidgeted with his clasped hands. He took a long, sweeping look of the assembly before him and pulled out a necklace charm from his tunic. Freya recognized it to be the symbol of Thor.

"We cannot permit our lands to be riven in two by the gods. We must forge a new law, where our faith and theirs are considered equal." He looked pointedly at Njall, and the chieftains broke out into frantic debate.

Gizurr and Hallr moved into the collective, and Freya could hear them arguing. It was all just ringing in her ears. She looked across at Njall, his good eye wide in shock.

"What have we done?" Freya whispered.

Chapter Thirty-Five

"I would have words with you."

The Icelander stared up at him, blue eyes shining out of a mask of blood. Using his axe, Arinbjorn slowly climbed to his feet, swaying a little as he secured his footing, and stood before Olaf. He threw the bloodied rope at his feet. A low creaking sound began to reverberate throughout the ship, the sound of wood splintering and shattering as the hulls of his fleet smashed against the *Ormrinn Langi*. He watched in horror as the outer ships began to drift away, caught in the Øresund current, taking many of his men with them.

"What have you done?" Olaf screamed. He ran towards the nearest mooring post and desperately grabbed at the rapidly unravelling rope. It slid through his bloodied grasp, tearing at his flesh, and he watched as the *skeid* closest to the *Ormrinn* pulled away, only to be replaced with one of Sweyn's. His defensive line had disintegrated.

That was when the axe struck him from behind. Olaf looked down in shock; the blade had managed to break through the chain mail and lodge itself in his left shoulder. Crying out, he dropped to the deck and looked behind him. The Icelander was pulling back to attempt a second strike. Olaf rolled out of the way and deflected the blow. Shock turned to anger as he got back to his feet.

Another betrayer in the ranks, was that what this was? Had the Icelanders been sent to his court by Sweyn? That was it. That is why the fleet had left him. The filthy farmers must have infiltrated his ranks as revenge and now this Icelander had sabotaged his fleet's defences. Olaf felt rage bubble up inside him as he focused all of his hatred on to the Icelander before him.

The pair circled each other, ignoring the battle for the *Ormrinn Langi* about them. Arinbjorn was slow, clearly heavily wounded, and his attacks were clumsy. He swung out at Olaf with his one good arm, attempting to bury his axe in Olaf's head. Olaf was quicker and more skilled, but the blow to his left shoulder had made him weak. He managed to parry the downward strike, but had to leap back from the backswing.

"Why?" Olaf shouted as he dived forward, trying to drive his blade into Arinbjorn's chest.

Rather than parry, the Icelander leapt aside, dropping to the deck and rolling away. Olaf's strike instead hit the starboard rail and he had to wrench the blade free, giving Arinbjorn time to get to his feet.

"You killed Skjalti!" Arinbjorn began pushing dead bodies before him, forcing Olaf to climb over them. The hate and anger in the Icelander were palpable.

"Who the fuck is Skjalti?"

"He's the man you had Thangbrander kill!"

"Thangbrander? All this is about that stupid priest?" He brought his blade around and managed to cut diagonally down Arinbjorn's chest. It wasn't deep, but it severed the chain mail and blood oozed out.

The Icelander gave a cry and stumbled backwards, swinging his axe blindly. "He was family and you killed him for your fucking conversion!"

Oh. It all made sense, now. This was Thangbrander's plot to rile up the natives. Kill a Christian to create a sense of prejudice and force them to act. Olaf had not liked the idea of killing one of the converted, but he had authorized it on the condition that the murdered would be made a martyr. The greater good had demanded a sacrifice. It had worked too, by all accounts. If he was right, Gizurr and his new priest would be pleading his case to an assembly ready for change. If he could survive this battle, he would be returning to a Norway newly reunited in faith with its Icelandic colony. Then he could use those pig-headed farmers to strike back against Sweyn. Yes, that would be a suitable revenge. He would have them sent out on conversion raids deep into the heart of the Dane's territories.

All he had to do was survive. He looked about; the Icelander had shattered his defences and Danes were beginning to board in droves. His men were holding their own for the time being, but he knew they could not last now the line was broken. He had to abandon the ship. But not before dealing with the traitor.

Arinbjorn was clearly getting tired. His movements were becoming sluggish and he had begun to retreat from close quarters, attempting to put distance between them. He had fallen back towards the starboard prow, his parries listless as the strength in his good arm failed him.

Olaf looked down and realized he was standing on the same spot where he had killed Afli, all those months ago. He smiled; it was a sign from God.

"Do you know what is happening right now, Icelander?" Olaf taunted. He brought his sword about in a wide arc, batting away Arinbjorn's axe and grazing his opponent's cheek. "As we speak, my agents are telling the people of your assembly how unjust your system is. How you have allowed your hatred of Christians to sever your world in two."

Shouting out in anger, Arinbjorn launched himself forward. Olaf easily sidestepped the attack and sliced deeply into the Icelander's back as he passed.

"They are hearing all about your cruelty towards Christians. How you murder them in their sleep. For the simple crime of believing in my God."

Olaf ducked, avoiding a high swing of Arinbjorn's axe. He pressed the attack, parrying blows and slowly hemming in his opponent against the starboard guard rail.

"My people are angry, Icelander, and they will be ready to shed blood." With that, he brought his sword down in a sweeping arc and cut deep into Arinbjorn's shoulder. Blood poured out of the wound and coated the decking. Arinbjorn cried out and tumbled back.

"If they have any hope of stopping violence, your chieftains will have no choice but to adopt Christianity—and, by extension, my rule. And, when I am done with you, when your body is naught but meat for the crows, I am going to escape here and form a new army of your brethren. Your friends, your family will join me in my holy war and, with each new death, you will lose more and more of your people, until there is no one left to mourn you!"

Grinning through the pain that coursed through his shoulder, he advanced on the Icelander. It was time to end this.

*

"You're too late, Icelander," Olaf taunted.

Arinbjorn cried out in rage and pain, but found he could not advance upon the king. His strength had left him. He found himself laughing; he had got a good strike on the king's shoulder, but Olaf still wielded his sword with a grace and precision that Arinbjorn found hard to counter. How arrogant he had been to assume he, a farmer, could defeat the King of Norway in combat. He swatted at the blade strikes with his axe, parrying the blows. He could not help but feel that Olaf was toying with him.

Arinbjorn fell further and further back, until he hit the side of the *Ormrinn Langi*. He looked about, trying to keep his eye on the king. To his right, a boarding party of Danes had breached the prow; to his left, the tiller was overrun. At least the king was trapped too.

He was exhausted. Wheezing and coughing, he swung wide at the advancing king and watched in horror as Olaf moved into the blow, clearly expecting it, parrying the blade and knocking it far out of Arinbjorn's hands. He watched it fly away from him, clattering to the decking by a pile of bodies. Olaf continued to move through the strike and brought his sword down low.

He drove it through Arinbjorn's gut.

Arinbjorn felt every inch of steel worm its way into his stomach and out through his back. Blood pooled in his throat. He began to retch.

Olaf stepped up close, driving the blade as deep as he could. His words were practically a whisper: "Your people *will* turn towards the light of Christianity. The seeds are already sown."

Arinbjorn looked down at the sword in his gut, stunned. The cries and shouts that filled his ears seemed oddly muted; he watched as the last of Olaf's men fought back against the tide of Danes swarming across the decks. The inferno raged about them, a storm of fire and ash that had consumed the rest of Olaf's fleet. Bodies, mutilated and broken, lay piled upon the deck. This is what Olaf wrought. This is what he wanted to do to his people. To turn them from farmers to carrion for his battles. Arinbjorn could not allow it.

Glancing overboard, he looked into the black waters of the Øresund as they bubbled and frothed below, blood and fire spreading across the surface. He then looked back into the wild eyes of the king, and down at the heavy chain-mail armour he wore.

He smiled.

"Maybe..." He coughed. "But you will *never* see it."

Arinbjorn reached forward, ignoring the hot tearing pain in his gut, and wrapped his arms around Olaf. The king shouted and struggled, but Arinbjorn held fast, bracing himself, and pushed off the decking with all of his strength, heaving the two of them up and over the rail.

Olaf screamed.

Darkness, cold and deep, swallowed them both as they crashed into the waters below. Olaf fought to escape Arinbjorn's grasp, but the Icelander held fast to the king. Putting all that remained of his strength into his grip, he threaded his fingers into the chain mail and brought them both deeper into the blackness. Arinbjorn looked up and watched as the light from the battle dimmed, the shadows of the vessels passing above blocking out the sun.

He felt a burning pressure in his lungs as they fought desperately to breathe in. Arinbjorn held on as long as he could, but the pressure was crushing. He looked to Olaf. Even in the dim light he could see the look of horror etched into the king's face. He retched and clawed, his fingers desperately pawing at Arinbjorn's flesh. Wide eyes begged for freedom. Arinbjorn did not let go. Then, with one last terrified look, Olaf screamed a silent scream and then went suddenly still.

After a moment, Arinbjorn released his grip and the two slowly parted. He watched as the body of the king sunk into the black depths. After he had seen the pale, shocked face fade away, Arinbjorn stopped fighting and allowed the water to fill his lungs. His body screamed in defiance, but his mind was oddly calm. He had done what he came out here to do. Skjalti was avenged.

Epilogue

The winter sun hung low on the horizon, its pale light reflecting off the fresh snow that blanketed the plains. Freya looked out across the valley, watching as the wind whipped up the white ice devils that danced and twirled across the hills. A caw caught her attention and she looked up to see two ravens arc above the longhouse and fly off towards the ash-tree copse. She watched them disappear into the gnarled and twisted branches and suppressed a shudder. Behind her, the thralls were busy feeding the livestock; the squeals of the swine and squawks of the chickens filled the air. She ignored them and began to walk around the hall, keeping her eye on the horizon, watching the departing figure of Sigvaldi.

Once she was sure he was gone, Freya looked down to his parting gift: a rune stone, carved into lignite. The one Bera had given to Arinbjorn. She ran her finger over the stave.

Sigvaldi had returned a few days ago, arriving on a trade ship for the last market of the season. The weather had begun to turn and no more trade ships would come this year. He had immediately made his way to Njall's farm and told them both the news of Arinbjorn's death. Sigvaldi had tried to reassure her that he had died fighting Olaf, and that the monster who had harmed their people was no more, but it did not help. She had wept for days.

Sigvaldi himself had been distraught. He seemed older to Freya, his usually trim beard and hair had grown long and his face was littered with new scars. His flight from the battle had clearly taken its toll. In return for his kindness in passing on the news, Njall had offered him a place to stay, and he had informed Sigvaldi of all that he had missed. The chieftains had decided that, if there was to be peace, then Christianity would be accepted in law. The debate still raged as to what form it should take. Some chieftains reasoned that it would be easier to have pagans convert to the new faith, but still allow them to observe the old ones in private, than to force the Christians to abandon their God. Runolfr and Gellir balked at the notion, of course, but Thorgeir's argument that a splitting of the law would break the people seemed to be winning out.

Thorgeir, Gizurr, and Hallr were hailed as champions of peace; everyone, Christians and pagans alike, would once again be brothers under the law. Njall's trial was permitted to continue, but, thanks to the support of Hallr and Gizurr, he was found not guilty of his crimes. The only requirement was that Njall had to sever all ties with Tongu-Oddr.

The sound of a soft wail brought Freya back into the moment. She looked about and saw Njall emerge from the farmhouse. He was carrying a small bundle of heavily swaddled mewling.

"Time for a feeding, I think," he said as he approached.

Freya smiled and took her son, giving her husband a kiss on the cheek. He winced as his face was still tender, but gave her a weak smile before some squawking from the hens drew his attention away. He left her fussing over her son until he stopped crying, running her fingers softly over his eyebrows and cooing. The babe wriggled contently, bright eyes staring up at his mother.

Looking down, she plucked the cord necklace she was wearing out of her dress and held it there a moment. She ran her fingers over the wooden cross, feeling the rough-hewn wood splinter beneath her touch. She compared it to the rune stone in her hand. With a smile, she placed the rune stone in her baby's swaddling and patted it tight.

"A gift," she said quietly, "from your father."

THE END

A Note on Pronunciation and Anglicization

The pronunciation of Old Norse-Icelandic can be predicated either on reconstructed or modern Icelandic. In the English-speaking world, the usual practice is to adopt the modern Icelandic pronunciation.

Please see below for a vowel pronunciation guide:

á as in English *n**ow***
a (1) as in French *m**al***
(2) as in English *n**ow***
(3) as in English *m**y***
é as in English *y**e**s*
e (1) as in English *l**e**t*
(2) as in English *b**ay***
í as in English *e**a**t*
i (1) as in English *p**i**t*
(2) as in English *e**a**t*
ó as in American *r**oa**m*
o (1) as in English *l**aw***
(2) as in English *b**oy***
ú as in French *b**ou**che*
u (1) a sound between the vowels in French *p**u*** and *p**eu***
(2) as in the French *B**ou**che*
(3) as in French *h**ui**le*
ý as in English *e**a**t*
y as in English *p**i**t*
æ as in English *m**y***
œ the same sound as above
ø as in French *p**eu**r*
ǫ (1) as in *French p**eu**r*
(2) as in French *œ**il*
au as in French *œ**il*

ei as in English *b**ay***
ey the same sound as above

The following is the pronunciation guide for consonants. Note that double consonants are longer than their single variants. They are roughly equivalent to their English counterparts, barring one or two exceptions:

b as in English *b*uy
d as in English *d*ay
f as in English *f*ar
h as in English *h*ave
j as in English *y*ear
k as in English *c*all
l as in English *l*eaf
m as in English ho*m*e
p as in English ha*pp*y
r rolled, as in Scottish English
s as in English thi*s*
t as in English *b*oat
v as in English *w*in
þ as in English *th*in
ð as in English *th*is
x two sounds, as in Scots lo*chs*
z two sounds, as in English bi*ts*[1]

Throughout the novel, Old Norse-Icelandic names have been anglicized for ease of accessibility by an English-speaking reader. Thus, Óláfr becomes Olaf and Þangbrandr becomes Thangbrander. Where Icelandic place names, landmarks or period-specific terminology have been used within the novel, their Old Norse-Icelandic spelling has been kept.

---

1   Michael Barnes, *A New Introduction to Old Norse* (London: Viking Society for Northern Research, 2004), pp. 14–17.

Authors Note

Saxo Grammaticus, the thirteenth century Danish chronicler, when writing his prologue to the *Gesta Danorum* (History of Denmark) took the time to specifically cite Icelandic narrators as reliable sources for his great work. He expounded the opinion that Icelanders, while materially poor, were intellectually gifted and had a peculiar penchant for the collection and dissemination of history:

> They regard it as a real pleasure to discover and commemorate the achievements of every nation; in their judgement it is as elevating to discourse on the prowess of others as to display their own. Thus I have scrutinised their store of historical treasures and composed a considerable part of this present work by copying their narratives, not scorning, where I recognised such skill in ancient lore, to take these men as witnesses.

Perhaps Saxo is referring to the oral practitioners of skaldic verse, or skalds, who by this point had ingratiated themselves in courts across Scandinavia as chroniclers and authorities on history. That a distinguished and learned Latin scholar did not see it beneath himself to utilise these pre-literate sources indicates the respect he held for the medieval Icelander's authenticity and dedication to craft. It is a respect that I found myself emulating in the writing of this novel.

Faith of their Fathers, while manifestly fiction, is heavily predicated upon the historiographies of the medieval Icelandic saga authors. It is primarily influenced by the *konungasögur,* sagas which recount the lives of the early medieval kings of Norway, and the *Íslendinga sögur* (Sagas of Icelanders or Family Sagas) which concern themselves with events in Iceland from the beginning of the Norse settlement in the 870s until around 1030.

I was especially informed by *Íslendingabók* and *Kristni Saga*. They provided the bulk of information on the *Kristnitaka*, or Christianisation, of Iceland. Composed by Ari Þorgilsson, "the Learned", *Íslendingabók* is the oldest extant historiographical account of the conversion. For information about Norway during this time, I was informed by my reading of *Heimskringla*: a collection of *konungasögur* that relates to Swedish and Norwegian Kings up to 1177. These, along with the Latin texts: *Historia Norwegie* and Theodoricus Monachus' *Historia de antiquitate regum Norwagiensium*, and Old Norse accounts entitled *Ágrip af Nóregskonungasǫgum* and *Óláfs saga Tryggvasonar en Mesta*, were the font from which I drew my inspiration.

I have, of course, taken certain liberties over the course of fictionalising the account: merging certain historical figures, omitting others entirely and playing around with the order of recorded events. I hope the historians amongst my readership will forgive me this indiscretion in service to the wider narrative. I console myself with the notion that even historiographies are only half-truths, each told from a certain perspective with biases inherent in the telling. I hope, if nothing else, that this novel might encourage those who found its subject matter interesting to go off and read the sagas themselves and to learn more about Iceland's fascinating history. And, if I am *really* lucky, you may just enjoy my stories too.

Samuel M. Sargeant
Cardiff 2023

Acknowledgements

According to the Prose Edda, arguably composed by Snorri Sturluson in the 13th century, the Old Norse dwarves were made from the blood and limbs of the slain giant, Ymir. Born as maggots, they were moulded by the gods into new forms and granted human intelligence. The creation of this novel is not unlike that. My lowly initial writings would not be on the page before you today without the benefit of those willing to help it rise above its initial conception. First and foremost, I want to thank my two PhD supervisors: Dr Tyler Keevil and Professor Carl Phelpstead. The novel began during my time as a PhD candidate at Cardiff University and it was an honour to work with such respected and accomplished scholars within their respective fields. I am a better writer and researcher thanks to their tireless insights, questions, and support.

Second, I must thank Archna Sharma of Neem Tree Press who read my initial manuscript and wanted to take a chance on it. Archna and her brilliant team, Alison Savage, Amy Jade Choi, and Cecilia Bennet are the reason why there is a copy of this book in your hands at all. They shepherded my novel from manuscript to publication, bringing in the talented front cover designer, Andy Barr, and wonderful editor, Penelope Price. I am so very grateful for all their efforts over this long process.

I must also thank my mother and father who have both been incredibly supportive, and patient, regarding my writing ambitions. They encouraged a love of reading, learning and writing that continues to this day. Finally, I would like to thank Leila Habbal for her tireless love, support, and reassurances these many years. Leila is the reason I returned to writing and any and all successes can be directly attributed to her faithful encouragement. *Sine Que Non*, Leila.

Samuel M. Sargeant